D1157047

"I'm safe in your arms. But you have never been safe in mine."

—Lily

PRAISE FOR SYLVIA DAY

"A dangerous and sultry novel about lies, secrets, and the line between love and obsession. The perfect first entry of a two-book series, *So Close* drew me in and kept me reading, desperate to know what happened next. Domestic suspense at its sexiest."
—Samantha Downing, *USA Today* bestselling author

"Will have you furiously flipping pages."
—*Glamour*

"You know you're in for a good book when other authors—and I mean LOTS of other authors—recommend it."
—*USA Today*

"Brilliantly blends danger and desire."
—*Booklist*

"Dark passions and darker secrets."
—*Shelf Awareness*

"This bold, erotic tale of passion and revenge features a cast of colorful characters and a complex and intriguing plot."
—*Library Journal*

"A page-turner!"
—*Access Hollywood Live*

"Exhilarating adventure."
—*Publishers Weekly*

OTHER BOOKS BY SYLVIA DAY

Urban Fantasy

THE MARKED SERIES

Eve of Darkness

Eve of Destruction

Eve of Chaos

Marked

Single Titles

In the Flesh

Pride and Pleasure

Seven Years to Sin

The Stranger I Married

Omnibus

Afterburn/Aftershock

Carnal Thirst

Love Affairs

Scandalous Liaisons

Spellbound

Novellas

THE SHADOW STALKERS MINISERIES

Razor's Edge

Taking the Heat

Blood & Roses

On Fire

All Revved Up

Butterfly in Frost

"Hard to Breathe" in *Premiere*

"Mischief and the Marquess" in *The Arrangement*

SYLVIA DAY

TOO FAR

A BLACKLIST NOVEL

First published in the United States by Rōnin House, an imprint of Sylvia Day LLC.

TOO FAR. Copyright © 2023 by Sylvia Day, LLC. All rights reserved. Printed in the United States of America. For information, address Sylvia Day LLC, 5130 S. Fort Apache Rd., Ste. #215-447, Las Vegas, NV 89148.

www.sylviaday.com
www.roninhousebooks.com

Library of Congress Control Number: 2023914817

ISBN 978-1-62650-007-5 (hardcover)
ISBN 978-1-62650-006-8 (e-book)
ISBN 978-1-62650-008-2 (paperback)
ISBN 978-1-62650-010-5 (large print)
ISBN 978-1-49152-674-3 (Audio CD)
ISBN 978-1-49152-675-0 (MP3 Audio)

Cover concept and design by Croco Designs
Woman © Dmitry Lobanov, Skyline © deberarr, all Adobe Stock. Scorpion © 4x6, iStock Photo. Interior Chapter Graphics © Raman Maisei, Adobe Stock. Lilies photo in the black & white mode with shadow © Katlyn, Dreamstime.

First Printing: October 2023

1

LILY

I'VE KILLED EVERYONE AND EVERYTHING I EVER CARED ABOUT TO protect my obsession with you, Kane. Still, watching you leave – even for a regular workday, like today – is the hardest thing I've ever had to do.

You hesitate. As if you read my mind and feel what I feel.

"I don't like leaving you," you tell me when we reach the front door.

Your satchel waits on the sleek African blackwood console in the small entrance foyer. Two guards stand sentry in the elevator vestibule on the other side of the double doors. Considering the levels of security in place, it would be nearly impossible for an intruder to make it up to the penthouse.

I know the truth – you're not keeping people out but securing me inside.

"Don't they say absence makes the heart grow fonder?" I smile, even as something greedy for you claws at my throat.

"I've had enough absence," you say, your jaw taut. There's a flare of anger in your dark eyes, your rage a tangible heat. You keep it banked most of the time, but I know it's there. What I don't know is whether it's our separation that enrages you – or my return.

We've been apart several years, which is longer than we have been together, and you might never forgive me for that. But what you should hate me for is meeting me in the first place.

1

My craving for you was too powerful, and I'm a selfish woman.

"If I were any fonder of you, *Setareh*," you murmur, your gaze hot on my face, "you'd suffocate."

I don't think you know how true that statement is. Your drive and ambition, your charisma and intelligence . . . You are ablaze. That inner fire seared my soul, and together, the flames consumed everyone around us.

Stepping closer, I press my body to yours, my arms sliding around your lean waist. Your torso is hard and warm. You've always been the fire to my ice, and I melt into you, my slight curves aligning with your rigid planes. With a deep sigh, you embrace me, curving your taller body protectively. I'm safe in your arms. But you have never been safe in mine.

"I'll be right here, waiting for you," I promise because I know you need to hear it. You're smart enough not to believe everything I say if you believe anything at all. Still, you know I love you beyond all reason. That has been the only thing we have between us and the only thing we truly need.

In a distant corner of my mind, I picture a different scene. The two of us by a front door, about to rush out to different destinations as we start our day. Our lips meet in haste, laughing joyfully because the world is ours, and we have nothing to fear. We're wildly in love, with none of this angst. There is no fear that this parting will be our last.

Your lips press to the crown of my head. "I hope you're planning that honeymoon. As soon as ECRA+ launches, we're getting out of here."

"How does snow sound?" I suggest. "Heaps of it. A remote chalet with nothing around for miles. No way in or out aside from a snowplow. A massive fireplace with a pile of furs in front of it. And a steaming hot tub on the deck."

"Perfect." You pull back and kiss the tip of my nose. "I'll keep you warm."

There's no questioning that. Your craving for me is nearly as intense as mine for you.

Tilting my head back, I study your face. It's divine how gorgeous you are. The square jaw, the blade of a nose, the cheekbones so high there are hollows beneath them. It's a face to make angels sing, with lips so full and sensual they tempt a woman to sin. And those eyes, nearly black, with lashes so thick they'd make you pretty if you weren't so thoroughly masculine.

I wish that it was only your looks and potent virility that had drawn me to you. Lust rages hot and then burns itself out. Initially, I told myself that's what would happen between us, but I never believed it. From the moment we met, you saw me. Your keen, avid gaze pierced through layers of identities to see into my soul. And where others would find fear, you found love.

Lowering your head, you take my mouth in a deep, lush kiss. There is passion and fury, desire and longing. We made love with the sunrise, and I still feel the imprint of your hands and mouth on my skin, yet your kiss conveys such hunger I know you're not appeased.

Will it ever go away, the sense of borrowing time?

You're breathless when you pull away to press your forehead to mine. "This is torture."

You push me away abruptly and grab your satchel, yanking open the front door as if you don't leave now, you won't go at all. The latch nearly clicks shut before you thrust it open again and find me in the very spot you left me in. "I love you."

My lips curve and my hand covers my aching heart. "I know."

In the silence of your departure, I release my breath, and my shoulders sag. We're used to being alone, but now . . . sorrow fills me.

The penthouse is briefly quiet and still. It feels as if it lies dormant when you're away, resting until you return with your wildfire intensity and energy. The tiles beneath my bare feet are warm, radiantly heated, yet I imagine they retain your warmth like a rock in the sun.

I'm isolated in my grief, with blood on my hands.

The tower in which we live sways in the wind with a mournful groan. The sound is a familiar and oddly comforting elegy.

Now that I've killed Valon Laska and told you the worst of my secrets, I want to throw off the false identity I adopted to enter your life. Lily Rebecca Yates could finally find her resting place at the bottom of the Atlantic. You know I'm not her, that perfect woman who was kind and selfless with no skeletons in her closet.

But you want me anyway.

Still, everyone else in our life believes you're married to Lily. They can never know that Lily was a lie.

So, I suppose I'm not really isolated at all. The woman whose life and husband I've stolen shadows me, haunting her doppelganger every minute of every hour of every day.

2

LILY

May 1, 1999

MOST PEOPLE BELIEVE THEY WOULD RECOGNIZE DEATH, THE ubiquitous Grim Reaper berobed and armed with a scythe. But she never hid her charms that way. Her shroud was a waterfall of gleaming obsidian hair, she displayed her body for temptation, and her bloodred smile was her blade. I knew because she was my mother.

I prepared for her arrival with meticulous care over my appearance, just as she'd drilled into me. I lined my upper lashes with a quick, practiced flick of my wrist that winged up into a cat's eye. It was the same motion I had made earlier that day before heading to school, but I scrubbed my face clean and started over. My makeup – armor, as my mother called it – had to be fresh and perfect.

When I was ready, I turned my attention to the apartment. I hurried to push open the window sashes. She preferred fresh air. I'd rather keep the windows closed when I was alone. It felt safer without the frenetic noise of the Brooklyn traffic below. With the sashes down, the sounds of the city were a muted thrum, like the rushing of blood around the haven of a womb. My mother didn't live with me anymore, but she protected and provided for me, and the studio apartment I lived in felt like the safest place in the world. I often remembered her in the space so vividly it was as if she was always with me.

Creedence Clearwater Revival sang about looking out their back door via the turntable next to the television. My mother liked music from a different era and found current music lacking. Aside from Prince, whom she said was an exceptionally talented musician, she was unimpressed with contemporary artists. The air smelled like vanilla and cherry blossoms, courtesy of the candle burning on the shawl-draped coffee table. My mother liked spaces to smell good and specifically feminine. Musk and sandalwood were too masculine.

She hated men. I didn't know why. I never asked because our time together was so short and infrequent, and I didn't want it marred by unpleasantness. I wondered about it, though. Especially because men loved her; they'd do anything for her. Bankrupt themselves, break up their families and ruin their lives. Inherently weak, she told me often. Suitable only for flattery and insemination.

But she was never without one, although they didn't last long. She had a new man every time I saw her. Derek. Reynaldo. Pierre. Jeremy. Tomas. Han. And so many other names I've forgotten. I didn't focus on them when she talked. It was more interesting to see how animated – or not – she was when describing them.

Finishing my makeup, I looked myself over with a critical eye. Was my hair perfectly straight, without a single wave or bump? Was my lipstick precisely lined and more of a smear than a coating?

You're such a beautiful girl, my sophomore science teacher had told me the year before. *You don't have to wear any makeup at all.*

I mentioned that to my mother when she asked me how school was going. Her smile tightened at the corners. *I think I'll need to chat with Ms. Bustamante,* she said.

I knew the very day that meeting took place, even though neither mentioned it before or after. I knew because Ms. Bustamante no longer invited me to work with her after class, which I'd looked forward to because it spared me an extra hour or two of being home alone, and when she looked at me, there was fear in her eyes.

You're upset, my mother said when she visited the next time. *You miss her paying attention to you, even though that attention would have softened you and made you easy to mold into her image of what you should be. We're not weak like that, Araceli. We know who we are, and no one can change us. Get rid of anyone who tries.*

She was the only person who'd ever called me Araceli, the name she chose for me. She never gave it away to anyone else and taught me not to. I saw it as a fun game. If I liked a name, I could have it until I switched schools and took on another I liked better.

We don't live in boxes, she told me. *We're not trapped into being one thing all the time for the rest of our lives. We're free, you and me. We can do whatever we want.*

I loved her so much. I never forgot how lucky I was to be her daughter.

Hearing the key slide into the lock, I spun around quickly, tossing my long hair into disarray. I hastily combed my fingers through the mussed strands, panicking that she would find fault in me. It was excitement I felt, not nervousness. While my classmates struggled with their confidence and insecurities about their bodies, I knew that although I didn't look exactly like my mother, I was close enough to be beautiful. She could never make anything that wasn't.

"Hello, darling." Her voice was a siren's song.

For a heartbeat, I drank in the sight of her. I took in the towering heels with their thin ankle straps, the sleek one-shoulder black dress that hugged her lean body, the inky hair that shined . . . Then I devoured that face. Like an angel's. So perfect. Symmetrical in every way. Pale skin like fine porcelain served as a canvas for dark brows, emerald eyes rimmed in black liner and crimson lips.

I ran to her, throwing myself against her the way waves crashed into the shore. Her musical laugh filled my ears as she caught me close, and the scent of roses mixed with citrus saturated my senses.

Her heart beating beneath my ear was the most beloved sound. I was still growing taller, so I had to hunch a little to fit into the place I liked most. She was warm; her embrace was tight. A part of me always hungered for her, and I clutched her tightly, trying to fill that emptiness.

"It hasn't been that long," she said into my hair, and I didn't contradict her, although it had been weeks. As I grew older, her absences grew, too.

In middle school, they'd stretch as long as a week. Once I began high school, they extended to nearly a month. She called every few days, soothing my need for her with the sound of her voice. She made sure I had enough money to stock the kitchen, and every few months, we went shopping – vintage, always – for fun and necessity as the seasons changed and my legs lengthened.

It's crucial to dress timelessly, not trendily, she admonished. *And better to wear designer than secondhand mass-produced garbage.*

"*Comment vas-tu, chérie?*" she asked, testing me. I was taking Spanish in school; it was more practical. But I studied French at home and also Italian because knowing what people said about you was essential, especially when they thought you couldn't understand.

"*Merveilleux, maintenant que tu es à la maison!*" I squeezed her tighter because it was true – it was wonderful to have her home again. But she released me, reaching behind her to grip my forearms and pull my arms away.

"Let me see you."

It was hard to step back because it's always hard to let go of what you want more than anything, but I managed, tilting my head just a little so she could examine me.

Her fingers brushed a stray hair from my cheek, then traced the line of my brows. I tweezed them meticulously, keeping them full when I shaped them to resemble hers.

"You are perfection," she murmured with a proud smile. "Sixteen today . . . how have the years flown by so quickly? When you leave this little nest soon, the world won't know what hit it."

Panic fluttered in my belly like a butterfly's wings. More and more often, she spoke of me being out in the world. When would I see her then?

"Will I go with you?" I asked, despite knowing that wasn't in her plans.

You're with me always, she used to say. *I created and nurtured you inside me, nestled right below my heart.*

Her green eyes sparkled with laughter. "Maybe when you're older. You're too young yet to live in my world."

It felt like a knife to the heart that we lived in different worlds.

Then I reminded myself how lucky I was. My friends had ordinary mothers; mine was extraordinary. I loved that she was different. She danced when she felt like it, said what she pleased, and forced the world to accommodate her. My classmates threw parties when their parents were out for the night, but I kept my sanctuary private. To bring anyone home with me would feel like sharing her, and I had so little of her as it was.

"I thought I'd make stir-fry!" I said excitedly. "Or I can make a strawberry and chicken salad. If we use the strawberries in the salad, we can have peach shortcake for dessert."

"Absolutely not. You are not cooking your birthday meal. We're going out."

"Oh . . . we don't have to do that." And I didn't want to. I preferred for us to be alone for the few hours she'd be with me. Maybe she would tell me what she'd been up to since I saw her last.

"I said no, Araceli." She gave me a look that quelled further protest, so I stewed and fidgeted restlessly, too much emotion pent up inside. "Cooking for yourself is self-care. Cooking for someone else is sacrifice, and sacrifice is stupidity."

I exhaled in a rush, deflated. All my dreams of sitting on the floor cushions and eating at the coffee table withered into dust. We used to dine that way, in different apartments across the five boroughs.

"Don't look so disappointed, my love." She leaned down and touched her nose to mine. "It's your birthday! Sixteen years ago today, you nearly killed me, and only a handful of people could say that – if they were still alive to talk about it. You must be waited on, feted, and adored, my glorious child. You need to get used to being the center of attention and know how to exploit it because you are meant to have it all. Everything."

She pulled me into her arms again and held me tightly, if far too briefly. When she released me, her hand cupped my cheek. "Now, go put on that lovely Dior we found."

I hurried to do as she said because I didn't want to be away from her too long. I couldn't escape the fear that she might be called away at any moment and leave.

When I ran out of the closet with my heels in hand, I saw her closing the locked drawer of the end table we'd found in an estate sale years before. I didn't know what she kept in there because she always took the key with her, and I would never pry. Plus, I felt her eyes on me all the time. I don't know if she actually surveilled me, but it felt like it, and therefore I acted like it.

We were out all night, bouncing around town. We ate too much filet mignon at Peter Luger, and I only briefly questioned – in my mind – how we could pay for it. My mother laughed when I blew out the candle on my dessert. *Much more fun now that you're older!* she said. Her gift was a necklace, the pendant a diamond-encrusted heart with an enameled lily inside it. *You're blooming, too,*

Araceli! We went dancing in a jazz bar that smelled of whisky and cigars. We played pool, and my mother hustled a group of drunk men. The sun was lighting the horizon when we made it home. My mother told me to sleep and told me not to worry about school because she would call in an excuse. *No rigid social order for you today!*

It was one in the afternoon when I finally woke up on the sofa. The crushing weight of solitude descended as awareness returned. She was gone. I knew it before I looked at my bed, which she'd taken because it used to be hers. The tears were hot and heavy as they fell until the hair at my temples was wet with them.

It was three before I noticed that a tiny skeleton key protruded from the locked drawer of the end table. I stared at it for a long time before trying to ignore it, but it called to me as I showered and then fixed the meal I'd hoped to prepare for her the night before. As I sat cross-legged on the floor, my gaze kept returning to it. My mother wasn't a woman who made mistakes like that. *Never leave a trail,* she always said.

Did she leave it on purpose? Why?

It was nine o'clock before I couldn't resist any longer. As I leaned over slowly, I felt her gaze on me, sharp as a dagger. "Call me if you don't want me to look," I said aloud, feeling like it was some sort of test. But the phone – with a number she changed every few months – didn't ring.

The key turned with difficulty as if the lock needed lubricant. We'd restored the rest of the piece together with a deep cleaning and wood oil. Inhaling sharply, I yanked the drawer open.

An old cookie tin sat filled with tie clips, mismatched cufflinks, watches and rings – large rings, bands too big for our slender fingers. Frowning, I rifled through them, the metal ringing like discordant bells. I'd never noticed that she collected such things before. On all our trips to resale shops, I'd never caught her perusing the glass cases, and since I was always watching her, it seemed impossible that I would have missed any hobby of hers.

The gold and silver were initially cool but grew warm with my touch. As my palms began to sweat, condensation marred the shiny metal. Using the hem of my shirt, I polished off the evidence of my curiosity, briefly considering putting on gloves and polishing them all so I'd leave no fingerprints behind to betray me.

Ensemble pour toujours, Pierre – Sophia

I stared at the inscription in the band until my fingers began to shake, and I could no longer read through my trembling. *Together forever.* A wedding ring. Belonging to a man with the same name as one my mother dated. A coincidence. Strange but plausible.

A knot formed in my gut and tightened like a snake coiling.

Trophies.

I reached the conclusion too swiftly as if I'd shaken a box of loose puzzle pieces into a completed picture instantly. Had turning sixteen somehow sharpened my senses?

But she'd wanted me to know, hadn't she? Hadn't she tossed out clues for years? As closely as I wanted her to see me, did she also wish to be seen?

Bile rose into my throat, and I swallowed it down, but it surged in a rush I could barely hold back until I reached the toilet. The heaving was violent, covering my body in an icy sweat. It was endless, a soul-deep purge.

Sinking onto the cool penny tile, I leaned back against the bathroom wall, my thoughts both tumbling and frozen in place. It seemed like I couldn't make sense of what I saw and simultaneously like I'd discovered the answer to a long-standing question.

I don't know how long I sat there. It was dark outside when I returned to the living room and carefully restored the contents of the tin, returning it to the drawer. I locked it but left the key as I'd found it. I lit the candle on the table and pushed up the sashes, wanting to feel as if my mother were home with me again.

But it made me too afraid.

So, I closed the windows, blew out the flame and sat in the dark with my knees hugged to my chest.

"It has been
the desperate
attempt to
escape from
torturing memories,
from a sense of
insupportable
loneliness and a
dread of some
strange impending
doom."

—Edgar Allen Poe

3

WITTE

Now

RAINDROPS GLISTEN ON MANHATTAN'S GLASS-SHEATHED TOWERS AS I set the day's paper atop the gilded tray that sits on the ottoman in the master suite sitting room. The walls are encased in foxed mirror tiles that present me with my unavoidable reflection fogged and bespeckled in the way of old silent films. Some would say my career as a majordomo is equally archaic, but they don't know that my present vocation is as dangerous as the covert livelihood I left behind years ago. The man I work for has a family so cutthroat they're like a writhing bed of snakes with no regard for whose tail they're biting.

On any other day, I would leave the way I came, my task complete. Today, I continue crossing the room until I come to a halt before a clear mirror hanging against the reflective wall, anchoring a mirrored console beneath it. Like everything in my life, the mirror isn't what it seems. The black velvet ribbons that appear to hang it are an illusion. When I press my thumb against a disguised fingerprint pad, the mirror slides silently upward, exposing a safe.

Inside is an impressive array of jewels – necklaces, rings, bracelets and more, curated by Mr Black as gifts for his wife. I refer to her as Mrs Black. Others call her Lily, but that's only one of her many aliases.

We don't know her real name, age or history. She has fabricated dozens of identities that we've unearthed through exhaustive investigation spanning all the years she was believed to be deceased. She has acknowledged an authentic connection to only two people: her late mother and her mother's lover – Stephanie and Valon Laska.

Lily claims not to know her mother's true identity – Stephanie Laska is one of many aliases – and she's confessed to matricide to escape a smothering influence that threatened all she holds dear. The lover, Valon Laska, was a criminal hunted by state and federal law enforcement agencies. He was killed yesterday by an assassin who very closely resembles my employer's wife.

No doubt the woman who's moved into the penthouse – and my employer's bed – is dangerous.

We found her crossing the street in Midtown, a woman with Lily's incomparable face who is now accepted as the one and only Mrs Black. How and why she was presumed dead for so long is a puzzle we're still attempting to piece together. But Mr Black has accepted her without question as the wife we'd believed to have been lost at sea several years ago. To his mind, he's been reunited with his great love, and he is committed to facing any threat to keep her at his side.

To my left is the slightly ajar door to her wardrobe, which serves as a passageway to her bedroom. Behind me, a twin door leads to Mr Black's wardrobe and bedroom, but I know he's with her, in her bedroom, as he has been all night. It's because they are together that I risk searching the safe. As obsessed as he is, she is equally captivated by him. He is the perfect distraction, and I must take advantage of that fact before my employer departs for the day and frees her to be more aware of my actions.

I spent hours last night studying the police surveillance photographs of the woman suspected of killing Laska. The perpetrator's resemblance to Mrs Black is uncanny, which makes the subtle differences more apparent. She's a tall woman and slender as a reed, with the kind of figure coveted by fashion designers because every garment is shown to best advantage on such graceful lines. With skin as pale as moonlight and shoulder-length hair that is a true deep black, Lily's loveliness is bold and matchless.

The woman in the photographs is equally tall, with hair that falls to her hips. I don't recognize the dress and would if it came from the wardrobe of the lady I know. Some of the angles of the face aren't quite right, but it's undeniable that women in Lily's echelon of beauty are exceedingly rare. It's an impossibility that an unrelated individual nearly identical in appearance could exist.

My gaze rakes over the rows of glittering jewels, searching. I feel a spurt of adrenaline when I don't find the items I seek. I've entertained a million questions since Mrs Black reappeared, and now I have more.

Lily's laughter, a throaty contrast to her startlingly girlish voice, drifts to my ears. I crouch, searching for a telltale sparkle that might betray a chain or earring in the thick carpet pile. I know it's improbable, but I can't leave any stone unturned. I stand empty-handed, refold the drawers into the cavity in the wall and close the safe.

The jewellery is missing; there is no doubt.

I turn away and exit the sitting room through the master wardrobe, but I pause mid-step when the sound of their voices draws closer, and I surmise that they've entered the room after me. I risk lingering, feigning the act of straightening Mr Black's hanging suits so I can eavesdrop. His wife's proximity sends a current of energy across the space between us, and the hairs on my nape lift. Hers is the type of dynamism that pervades. The memory of her suffused the penthouse before she ever stepped foot into it. Once she took up residence, the home came alive around her. So, too, did Mr Black.

"Is there anything on your calendar in the next few weeks that would pre-empt inviting your family to dinner?" Lily's voice is distinctive. High-pitched with husky warmth. One doesn't expect her to talk that way when you look at her, yet once she speaks, you cannot imagine her sounding any other way. I cannot place an accent in her voice. She offers no clues about who she might be beneath the exquisite guise she so effortlessly wears.

Every opportunity I've afforded her to reveal something – anything – about herself has been passed over. She never discusses her past, even fleetingly. During the years when she was believed to be deceased, her acquaintances spoke of her as a woman deeply interested in others. Now that I've become acquainted with her, I know she encourages people to talk about themselves, so there's little room for her to do likewise.

"I'm at your disposal, *Setareh*." My employer only ever addresses his wife using that nickname. A name that means *fate* and *destiny*. Romantic, yes, and telling. Since he doesn't know her real name, it allows for truth between them instead of a lie. "Always."

The warmth in Mr Black's voice is something I'm still becoming accustomed to. Lily has been back only months, but in the most fundamental ways, she always has been here. My employer is the stranger, a man wholly transformed by her return.

After years of watching him suffer while deeply grieving his beloved wife, I'm elated to see him happy at last. I want to believe Lily's love for Mr Black is genuine, but she's capable of adopting myriad personalities and traits that are pure fabrication.

The abrupt intrusion of an additional voice reveals that they've powered on the sitting room television. The local cable provider always defaults to channel one, which offers twenty-four-hour repetitive coverage of recent news. Then the sound is muted, and I hear the rustling of the newspaper.

I risk peering around the doorjamb and find a scene of luxuriant domesticity – Lily sits on the sapphire sofa in a slaughterous red silk kimono and my employer lounges beside her in black silk trousers and matching dressing gown. Her legs are curled beside her, and she has a notebook and pen in hand, her glossy hair obscuring her face as she writes. He sits close beside her, reading the news. On the television screen above the fireplace, Valon Laska stares at viewers from one of his many mug shots.

I find I can't move, arrested by the sight of all three of them together. I wait vainly for Lily to look up, to see the man she claimed was not a father figure but who looked after her well-being. A man she claimed would kill her husband because that is what her mother would have wanted him to do.

"Setareh . . ." Mr Black turns his head slowly to look at her as if it's an effort to stop reading. That's the first clue to his deceit because there is nothing he would rather look at than his wife.

Holding the newspaper out to her, he sighs heavily. I can't see his face, but her frown of concern is insightful. She takes the paper but keeps her gaze on him. "What is it?"

"Laska," he says gruffly. "He was assassinated yesterday."

Lily visibly stiffens. A perfectly arched brow lifts as she turns her attention to reading quickly, her gaze darting over the words. His arm drapes over her shoulder and pulls her close. It's a gesture of comfort for the death of a man who would have killed him, as Laska had killed countless others.

"I'd say someone did the world a favour," she says finally with a tremor in her voice.

There is no emotion in her words, but her trembling fingers rattle the newsprint.

Mr Black rests his head against hers and tosses the unfolded paper back onto the ottoman. "I understand how you feel is complicated."

"It's not complicated." She glances at the television, but the reporter has moved on to another story, and she's left unaware of the previous segment. "It's a relief. You're safe."

"So are you, and that's all that matters."

I step back into the wardrobe and wait a few moments, curious to see if he'll elaborate on what he knows. When their conversation returns to dinner plans, I leave silently, my perspective altered again.

My employer knew yesterday what had transpired – I told him myself. That he should inform his wife of the murder this way, second-hand with feigned surprise . . . ?

The press knows very little of what I know about Laska's assassination. Especially that the woman responsible for stabbing Valon Laska was photographed and her presence witnessed first-hand by undercover policemen who had Laska under surveillance. I've built a network of individuals who can assist me with nearly any task in service to numerous employers and for various reasons. Mr Black knows much of what I know about the murder but didn't share those details with his wife.

What is he hiding from her? That the woman who killed Laska is her very likeness? Or that his resources and knowledge are far-reaching?

He's deeply in love with his wife, but does he not trust her? Or is he trying to protect her?

Lily's extraordinary beauty is the least deadly of her weapons.

Releasing my breath in a slow, controlled exhalation, I register how astonished I am by Mr Black's performance. If I didn't know otherwise, I would believe he was learning about Laska's murder for the first time.

They sit there together, husband and wife. Passionate lovers and professed soulmates who share everything but honesty.

Abruptly, I have an epiphany. I've underestimated the man I taught to sit and eat properly, to dress well, and to comport himself with authority and elan. His stepfather had lacked the grace and maturity to raise another man's child. And his mother had written him off, choosing to focus on nurturing his half-siblings.

Though Kane Black would have become a success with or without me; I won't take credit for his intelligence, ambition or natural magnetism. He knew he required mentoring, sought it out and is therefore directly responsible for the man he moulded himself into.

Somewhere along the way, however, our professional distance closed and eventually disappeared altogether. He's the closest thing to a son I will ever have, and that has made him a blind spot. But now I see.

He's as dangerous as his wife.

4

AMY

"ARE YOU FUCKING *KIDDING* ME?" I STARE AT MY BEDROOM TELEVISION with my mouth open, watching as Pat Kiernan on NY1 shares the high points of Valon Laska's murder. "No way."

Am I cursed? Someone can't have my luck by accident. I wouldn't be surprised if Aliyah, my witch of a mother-in-law, has an altar somewhere in her house with a voodoo doll of me stuck with pins or some other shit.

Things were going too well, so I should have been prepared for it all to go to hell. When I needed a new client, a former one picked up his phone and called me. I'm actively working on Laska's account, revitalizing the social media channels for a restaurant that's one of his legitimate businesses. Did I know the guy was a criminal? Of course, everyone did. But he never asked me to do anything illegal, never negotiated my price down, always paid his invoices immediately and sent me at least a dozen referrals. He was the perfect client.

When he called a couple of weeks back, I was ecstatic. His repeat business would help me reinvigorate my company and take it back from the Armands. Now . . . ?

Amusement bubbles up from somewhere inside me, and I double over laughing. It's seriously too funny. I sink to the floor, tears leaking from my eyes because I can't stop giggling.

Nobody tells you hitting rock bottom can be hysterical, but that would depend on your perspective. In my case, finding out I've been sleeping with my brother-in-law sure as fuck changed my viewpoint entirely.

"I've climbed to the top before," I tell myself breathlessly, swiping at my eyes. "I can do it again." And this time, no one's knocking me down.

Over the years, I've forgotten that I'm at my best when facing the worst. I've forgotten a lot of things, including who the fuck I am and what the hell I want. All I know is that I'm sick of myself, and I'm done with just suffering through it.

Sobriety changes your perspective, too.

Something's not right . . .

Rising to my feet, I turn away from the news and return to the bathroom to finish getting ready for work. I can control my career. I can succeed. And winning can build on itself if you play your cards right. So, I'll start there and work outward to the rest of my life.

I've been trying to focus on one thing at a time. I have to; otherwise, I wouldn't just feel like I'm going insane, I'd jump right off the fucking deep end. I've been confronted with one too many horrors in recent days.

I've mentally dissected the disastrous series of events that brought me into the Armand family a million times over the past few days of soberness. It was during my first business lunch with Valon Laska years ago that I originally spotted – and was spotted by – Kane. Within hours we were screwing like the world was going to end. In the days after, I couldn't stop thinking about him, but he ghosted me. That should have been the end, but I resorted to waiting for him outside the Crossfire building, where his company – Baharan Pharmaceuticals – is located, to stage a chance meeting.

When he spun through the revolving doors and exited onto the street, I felt something I might have misunderstood as exhilaration. Kane is so tall and perfectly muscular. His suits fit like they were sewn onto his luscious body. He moves in a way that tells you he's an athlete, with strength and elegance that hints at stamina and virility. I didn't notice Darius walking next to him until we were introduced. And while I was making polite conversation with his brother to appease and impress, Kane slipped into the waiting Range Rover at the curb, and Witte drove him away.

It was crushing to be passed over to another guy like that. I thought I could make him regret it, so I took Darius home and screwed his brains out. But did

Kane care? Not even a little bit. And now I have to wonder . . . Did I really do it because of Kane or because I needed to feel desired after being so thoroughly rejected? And for a while, it didn't matter why I ended up with Darius because we were deliriously happy. It wasn't until much later that I learned about Kane's obsession with his dead wife, Lily.

Kane fucked me because I look like her, and that's his fetish. How sick is that? That should've turned me all the way off where he's concerned. It sure as shit bothered the hell out of me. That was the turning point when I started dealing with anxiety and hyper-focusing on Kane.

But *why?* And why didn't I question turning into a headache? I knew something was off, that I wasn't feeling like myself. My perfect marriage with my ideal husband didn't feel safe anymore. Everything and everyone felt . . . sinister.

My therapist told me I've got daddy abandonment issues that skew how I process things, but did I work on them? No. I just kept wanting some acknowledgment from Kane that I wasn't disposable while putting up barriers against Darius.

And drinking myself into oblivion. Can't forget that part.

I've also been told I have all the baggage children of alcoholics get saddled with – impulsiveness, overreacting, feeling like a victim, being judgmental, people pleasing, paranoia and a gazillion other bullshit labels they slap on people to charge exorbitant fees for therapy sessions.

I eye myself in the bathroom mirror. The similarities Kane saw between Lily and me have been methodically enhanced. My nearly waist-length hair has been darkened to match her color precisely. The deep purple silk of the bra cupping my small breasts is a dramatic change from the golden neutrals I used to wear.

My closet was once modeled after my mother-in-law's – an utterly neutral palette. So was my bedroom. Both have now taken on some of the gothic luxury of Lily and the penthouse. But the studio apartment I had before I married Darius had been decorated in a cheerful mix of pastels.

When did I start hating myself so much that I wanted to be any woman but me?

Who am I? I don't fucking know anymore.

"You're not dressed," Darius says as he enters my bathroom in a charcoal gray suit with a tie that matches the brilliant blue of his eyes. He stands behind me, and our gazes connect in our reflection. Only Darius, Ramin and their sister

Rosana have those beautiful irises. Kane's are as black as coal. "But that's how I like you," he murmurs, lowering his head to kiss my shoulder.

Closing my eyes, I breathe in the scent of his cologne and search inside me for the joy I used to feel whenever he focused on me. When did we grow apart? Why did I let it happen? Because my parents gave me a master class in self-destructive behavior? Or am I not to blame? It takes two people to have a solid marriage.

Darius is gorgeous and fit, the very definition of tall, dark, and handsome, although he's not as tall as Kane. His desire for me runs hot despite whatever relief his assistant provides him. Not long ago, the feel of his suit against my bare skin would've incited instant lust, but there's only fury in me now that I know he's betrayed me.

My eyes slit open as anger heats my blood. "When did you start fucking your assistant?"

He stiffens and grows utterly still. His chest expands on a deep breath against my back, and his gaze meets mine in the mirror. His jaw is taut. "Say that again."

"Were you always a cheater?" My voice is clipped and cold. "Or am I lacking in some way?"

Straightening, he spins me around by the shoulders. "Let me get this straight. You think I'm fucking *Alice*?"

"Are you denying it?"

"Are you crazy? No, I'm not screwing my assistant." He scowls at me, and when I don't say anything, his gaze narrows into dangerous slits. "I know you're wasted drunk a lot, but I thought you knew how often I fuck *you* – my wife. I don't have the time or the energy to stick it to someone else."

His fury has bite and reads as affronted, not defensive.

"How come I can never reach you on Friday afternoons?" I challenge.

His brows lift. "I have a standing meeting with my mother. I work, you know, Amy. That's how I provide for you and give you whatever you want."

"I didn't come into this marriage with nothing, Darius!" I snap back. "I was very successful if you'll remember."

"Of course I remember! I fell in love with that successful woman and wanted to build a life with her."

My head jerks back, and my breath whistles through my teeth like I've taken a blow. For all intents, I have. "It's hard for me to feel like that woman when your mother has bulldozed me and undermined my authority."

"I understand that, and I'm working on it. You know that."

I hate that tone that says he's humoring me when it comes to his mother. As if I imagine how she talks to and treats me. "She's the one who let it slip that you've been cheating."

He stiffens again. For a moment, he's speechless. "What?"

"You heard me." I want to cross my arms because I feel too exposed in my underwear, which is ridiculous. No one in my life has seen me naked more than Darius. I stare at him, unsure of the truth. I think I know this man I married because I love him.

But I've read through the merger agreement that made my social media management company, Social Creamery, a subsidiary of Baharan, a rapidly growing pharmaceutical corporation. I know Darius is too intelligent to have missed the exit clause and other revelatory information I found. And barring legalese comprehension, a simple conversation with Ramin, who drew up the contract, would have been all it took for him to know our options. Darius must have known about the clause but denies it.

"Amy." He grips my arms. "Be very sure about an accusation like that."

"I know who your mother is, Darius. You're the one who has no clue."

Why did Ramin help me with the contract? Why does he insist he's been telling me about the exit clause for over a year? Why do none of the Armands tell the same story? I know Aliyah and Darius are unreliable. Ramin could be, too. He's fucked his brother's wife, so he isn't exactly trustworthy.

I swallow a rush of bile. I can't think about my other brother-in-law. Every time I do, a screaming wail of alarm deafens my thoughts and makes me violently nauseous.

"Amy . . ."

"If you want me to believe you, you have to believe me," I tell him flatly.

"Hey." His hands slide up to my shoulders and into my hair. His handsome features soften the instant before he pulls me into his arms. "Of course I believe you," he soothes. "It's you and me against the world. That's what we promised each other."

I lean into him, the feel of his hard body so familiar. I reach again for memories of how we used to be, but how I feel is divorced from what I recall. Yet another disconnect that makes me feel like I'm someone else.

Something's not right . . .

I take a deep breath and say, "I'm sorry I haven't been . . . me. I never thought of myself as someone who needs a career for validation, but maybe I am." I tilt my head back to look up at him. I don't have to try hard to look scared and vulnerable because that's what I am, even if I'm determined to move forward. "I can't believe I didn't work out some sort of exit clause or a back door in case the merger with Baharan didn't work out. Such a stupid mistake. I can't stop kicking myself over it."

"Babe. No. You can't blame yourself for that." He presses his lips to my forehead. "I've struggled with that, too. You relied on me to advise you, and I didn't even think of it because we're family, and working together for the rest of our lives was our commitment to each other."

Does he really not know? Is that possible? "Maybe a lawyer could review the contract and devise a way we haven't considered."

"You don't think I've tried that already?" he murmurs against my skin. "When did you stop trusting me? You know you're everything to me."

His hands stroke up and down my bare back, heating my skin, but my rage is so icy that goosebumps spread in a wave. I begin to tremble, fighting the urge to push, hit and scrape my nails down his face so everyone can see that I'm prepared to claw my way out of this lying, treacherous family.

"Let's go out tonight," he suggests. "We haven't had a date night in forever, and we need one. We've been so focused on work lately that we've lost sight of what's important."

I exhale slowly, carefully. It's not the time to make waves. They've got me in a corner with that goddamn contract, just like they wanted. "That's a good idea. I'd like that."

"I'll make the reservations right now." He kisses me again. "How long before we can leave?"

"Not long," I tell him sweetly, smoothing his lapels. "I'll be ready before you know it."

He smiles. "I'll be in the living room."

My husband leaves with his elegant, long-legged stride. The moment he's out of sight, my smile drops. Malice slides through my veins with the heat of fine liquor. Anger is empowering, and I embrace it.

I think Aliyah encouraged Darius to marry me. I've always thought it was she who suggested bringing Social Creamery into Baharan. My mother-in-law is cunning. She might have realized the fledgling Baharan needed direct access to the consumer. The cost of hiring reps to incentivize doctors is prohibitive. It's much cheaper to create a web portal through which prescribers seeking easy money can consult with patients online and ship the medicine through the mail. But that required luring the consumer to the portal, which is my specialty.

I walked into the Armands' trap with a smile, thinking they would become the family I'd always wanted. I left my alcoholic, mentally deranged parents behind long ago – to our mutual relief. They never wanted a child, and I was always treated like a freeloader.

Aliyah got her hands on my company through the merger. She's run it into the ground, but I'm sure that's by design. Now that I know her, I understand she would never want a hand in a business that helps other companies succeed. Everyone on the planet is in competition with her. She wanted expertise and total control, and she got it.

And Darius. He whittled me down until I was hanging out in our condo alone, my only real friends the colorful decanters on the bar cart, my house cleaned and meals prepped by a housekeeper I can't communicate with because we speak different languages, and my sole purpose to serve as a vessel for my husband's lust. I've never been anything to anyone aside from a pretty package to fuck. I don't have feelings or a mind.

Aren't they going to be surprised when they realize I've actually got a brain and a talent for petty revenge? Aliyah's really good at that, too, but she's tiptoeing around her kids. I've got nothing standing in my way except myself.

I open the bottom drawer of my vanity and pull out the pint of vodka I keep wrapped in my shower cap. My mouth waters as I stare at it, my fingers caressing the cool glass. I want to unscrew the cap and take a big gulp, knowing how good it will feel when it hits my belly. I've done a commendable job of weaning myself off, but that's not what holds me back now.

I don't trust ingesting anything in the condo anymore, not after the other night at Ramin's. I can do many terrible things, but cheating isn't one of them.

Monogamy and fidelity are two core values for me. I would never break from those tenets, even blackout drunk.

Something's goddamn wrong!

I need to set up the surveillance cameras I bought ages ago and hide them well. Initially, I planned to monitor what happened on the occasions I black out, but now I want to watch everyone else. My housekeeper, visitors and even my husband – the man who just lied to my face so convincingly it's hard to disbelieve him, even knowing the merger contract as well as I do now.

My losses of memory and unaccountable behavior aren't courtesy of alcohol. I remember standing in Ramin's condo and feeling like a passenger in someone else's body . . . someone else's life. I thought then that they must be warping my mind somehow, and the more I go over the past few years, the more I'm certain I am either being drugged or gaslit or both, and until I stop drinking, I can't rule out anything.

Before I change my mind, I unscrew the cap and pour what's left in the bottle down the drain. The smell is both repulsive and enticing. The fumes seem to flood my senses, running down the center of my body in a violent shiver. I rinse out the bottle and put it back. I'll have to remember to throw it out when I can access the trash without being seen. My fucking home but I've always felt like a guest here.

Straightening, I catch myself in the mirror again. I roll my shoulders back and lift my chin. The green of my eyes is darker than Lily's, more like emerald, less like jade. When I first saw the photograph of her hanging on Kane's wall, I thought youth and an orgasmic glow gave her a slight edge over me. Then I met her in person and realized that edge is razor sharp. She's a honed blade that gleams in a way that conveys wealth and classiness.

I'm working on polishing my rough edges. I've narrowed Lily's advantage. I was a pale imitation before, but soon I'll be able to hold my own.

Heading into the bedroom, I see my phone screen brightly lit with Clarice's picture. I answer the call, greeting her with a cheery, "How's my favorite account manager doing this morning?"

Clarice was my first hire at Social Creamery, and she's somehow survived working under Aliyah. She's a four-foot-eleven dynamo, and I'm taking her with me when I leave the family empire in shambles.

"Oh my God, Amy, have you seen the news this morning about Valon Laska?"

"Oh, yeah. The timing sucks. We haven't even invoiced him yet."

She huffs a startled laugh. "The guy's dead, and you're sorry you didn't bill him?"

"He was a piece of shit." I head into my closet. "A stain on humanity. No one will miss him except me, and if I only miss his money, that's better than nothing."

"That's a fair point. What are you going to do?"

Surveying my options, I'm more conflicted and unsure than ever. I want Lily's bohemian sensuality and Aliyah's rich elegance. I want their confidence because mine has taken a beating. I also want to see the woman I was before I stepped into the Armand funhouse. How sick is it that I'm envious of my former self?

Before I second-guess myself, I grab a giraffe print DVF wrap dress I bought after I signed my first client. I also grab a cream-colored blazer inspired by Aliyah, then gold hoops, a waist-length necklace, and some studded heels that add Lily's flair. I can learn from them without *being* them. I don't even like either of the bitches. "Laska reminded me that it'll be easier to recapture former clients who know what we can do than to convince new clients to take a chance on a company that looks like it died."

"What's your plan? We're still working on revising the ECRA+ creative before the launch."

I put my phone on speaker and start dressing. "Social media, of course. We didn't reactivate our channels for nothing. We'll run a special. Half-off a refresh for former clients. Since they're all following us, they'll see it, but let's reach out to them, too."

"Amy . . . I wonder if we have the staff to run specials, although the idea is great. Not to mention, Aliyah won't like it. At all."

"I'll deal with Aliyah. She needs a reminder that I still contractually control the decisions for my company. As for staff, we've got the three new hires, and I'll focus on the rest of the applicants today. We're spoiled for choice since we offer remote work and excellent benefits."

"Yes, the benefits package was an upside to merging with Baharan."

"And I'm going to take advantage of it while I can. The Armands certainly owe me that and a lot more." I secure one of my gold hoops. "I'm going to hang up now. Darius is waiting. I'll see you at the office."

We end the call, and I quickly look in one of the full-length mirrors as I pass it. For a moment, I see Lily Black, dangerously sexy and powerful.

But I also see me. I remember splurging on the dress as a celebration of my success.

The thrill I feel is pure fucking adrenaline.

5

ALIYAH

I DREAD FACING KANE – MY SWEET, STRONG, LITTLE BOY – AS I PULL INTO the carport space reserved for my neighbor's apartment and put the car in park. When I reach for the ignition key, my hand shakes so severely I pull it back, wrapping my arms around my waist. The trembling comes from deep inside me, from a place of horror and soul-wrenching pain.

Tears burn my eyes and course like fire down my face. Everything hurts, every millimeter of skin, every orifice. Whenever I think I've been demeaned and humiliated enough, I discover there's no end to the depths of Alex Gallagher's depravedness. I lost control of my bladder when I first saw him today, but that didn't repulse him. He only laughed as if my degradation was the most amusing thing in the world.

Nothing I do stops the nightmare I'm subjected to. I've shaved my head, so there's no longer any hair to rip out by the roots. I wear no makeup or deodorant or perfume. I don't shave any part of my body. I'm repulsive to myself, but he never fails to become erect.

I suck in a breath that rattles my lungs, fighting the urge to sob with no care for who might hear me. But I can't fall apart. The neighbor watching Kane has to go to work soon and needs her car returned now. I'm so grateful for her. I've learned to cover the driver's seat with towels, so I don't stain her upholstery, but that was a lesson learned the hard way. She forgave me the first time I came home with blood on her seat. I see the pity in her eyes when she looks at me. I don't know where she thinks I go when Alex calls or what I do, and I don't want to know.

I don't even want to be alive.

But I have Kane. He's a victim, too. He's only a child who wants his father. And his mother, but I'm not that woman any longer. He cried when I shaved my long, dark hair off. He watches me sadly when I struggle to sit without wincing.

I hate that we live in a rough neighborhood with dangerous things on the ground, like hypodermic needles, used condoms, broken bottles and spent shell casings. I shove a chair under the front door at night and have towels hanging from the damaged blinds to keep prying eyes out. We sleep on a single mattress on the floor and appreciate that basic cable is one of the few amenities.

Wiping my face with both hands, I pull myself together. Weakness is a luxury I can't afford. I turn off the ignition and hold the keys tightly in my fist, so I don't drop them. I shove open the door but getting out is infinitely more challenging. My legs shake so badly, I fear they won't hold me, and the pain throbbing between my legs is excruciating. I end up supporting most of my weight with my arms on the steering wheel, my lips trembling as I feel the sticky wetness between my legs that isn't courtesy of a menstrual period.

I haven't had a period in months. While at first I was terrified that my birth control pills had failed and I'd been impregnated by my rapist, I realized stress and malnutrition were to blame. But Kane is healthy. That's all that matters.

Supporting myself by holding onto the door frame, I reach gingerly down for the bloody towel I was sitting on. I lean against the side of the car as I fold it in a way that disguises the stain and wrap it around my waist to hide the matching stain on my sweatpants. Once I step out from under the carport roof, Kane will see me. He's constantly checking through the window when I'm gone.

He's barely five years old, but he's whip smart. He knows I'm less and less of myself every time I leave and return. I hope he's young enough to forget this time in our lives, because it won't be this way much longer. Every chemical patent I claw back from Alex is an insurance policy that will reap rewards once I find the right person to help me monetize them.

I stood side by side with Kane's father, Paul, while we built Baharan. He may have sucked the lifeblood out of the company, but the remaining pieces have value, and I will get my due and my son will get his inheritance. I won't allow him to grow up in poverty, undereducated and surrounded by corroding influences. I may have nothing to barter but my body, but I will get what my son and I deserve. Even if it kills me, and it just might.

I lock the door and shove it shut with what little strength I have left. I'm vibrating inside and crumbling. I breathe through my mouth in a vain effort to avoid smelling Alex's sweat on my skin. Stepping into the evening light, I tilt my head back and find Kane's sweet face peering from the second floor. I pull a smile from somewhere and lift my hand in a wave. He lights up so brightly he's like the sun to me and then disappears. He'll open the door and wait for me on the landing. I'll pretend that every step isn't agonizing and that I'm not holding on to the railing with everything I have.

I'll do it for him, my reason for living. The one perfectly pure thing in my life that I made with love and hope for a future that has now been burned to ashes.

6

ALIYAH

I WAKE TO THE DISCOVERY THAT MY HEART IS POUNDING, AND I'M drenched in a hot, sticky sweat. The urge to leap up and run is powerful but for a moment, I'm paralyzed. Fear and disgust roil in my stomach until I think I might vomit.

I wrench myself onto my back, gasping for air. I smell cologne with the inrush of vital oxygen, and my familiarity with the scent is unexpectedly soothing. I struggle to comprehend where I am and why, my mind cowering from memories I've long ago locked away.

I seize on the understanding that someone is in the bathroom. It was the sputtering of the showerhead as the water turned on that pulled me from the nightmare.

Throwing the comforter off, I sit upright and slide my legs to hang off the side of the bed. The cool air chills the perspiration on my skin as I note the dress slacks and shirt tossed on the bench at the foot of my bed. I force the fog of troubled dreams to clear my mind.

I'm home. *I'm safe.* Stress unlocked the memories of Alex Gallagher that I avoid revisiting, but that time was a lifetime ago.

Glancing at my bedside clock, I realize it's early morning. I haven't had a man spend the night since I moved into my condo. I prefer to fuck men in places less personal, where I won't be reminded of them after the fact.

I consider whether the circumstances suggest I'm weak or strong. I needed comfort and reassurance, but those were provided by a security expert who just happens to have a penis. That I ended up having that penis inside me most of the night is both a bonus and a way to keep him committed to doing a good job.

I move to stand and find my legs aren't quite steady. "Damn it."

The abrupt silence in the bathroom warns me that Baharan's security chief will appear soon. In the void left by the absence of spraying water, the sounds of the city outside press in. Like blood flowing through arteries, the ceaseless flow of traffic is a steady thrum.

I steel myself, expecting discomfort at having my privacy intruded upon, but instead I feel relief when Rogelio strides into view unabashedly naked.

It's been a long time since I leaned on anyone. I hadn't realized how exhausting it is to rely solely on myself. But really, I'm the only one I can trust not to screw me over.

I watch Rogelio's reflection in the full-length mirror propped against the wall opposite the bed. His body is lean. His movements as he dresses are both relaxed and powerful. He keeps his dark hair cut high and tight, almost militarily precise, which makes him look even younger than he is. I take in the view of us together. I've preserved my looks well, and while I don't look like I'm in my twenties like he does, I don't look old enough to be his mother, either.

He looks over at me as he buttons his slacks. "It's going to be fine," he says. He has a way of being deeply reassuring when he chooses. His poise is one of his best traits.

Studying him, I note how he's changed since I brought him into my confidence. I started fucking him because he looked at me with defiance and more than a bit of scorn. His manner with me was overtly sexual and straddled the line of disrespect. I've rarely failed to rise to that sort of bluntly masculine challenge to my femininity. I'm not prey. Once, but never again.

Now, his velvety brown eyes have lost that edge of derision. I'd hate him if he looked at me with pity, but he simply looks at me as if he's recognized my humanity. Women in power are often stripped of emotions and compassion.

I may have had a sea change in how I regard him, but he's had one, too.

Turning at the waist, I face him. "If the police show up at Baharan because of

Alex Gallagher, I don't want a scene. I'll be damned if I'm walked out in handcuffs in front of everyone."

"I won't let that happen." He shrugs into his dress shirt, his chest and abs rippling with muscle.

Before last night, I thought of Rogelio as an average lover. With energy and virility to spare but lacking stamina and consideration. Now I wonder if he just didn't like me much until hours ago, when he was a different lover, tender and attentive to my pleasure when I was most vulnerable.

"And with every hour that passes," he goes on, "that becomes less likely."

Time has twisted in the two days since Alex crossed my path again. It seems like forever ago. And like only moments have passed.

"I asked him how much his penis is worth." I hate the quiver in my voice. I don't even remember stabbing Alex in the groin with a broken wine glass stem. Still, in that moment of madness, I thought quickly and appealed to his immense avarice, which might have staved off consequences I couldn't live with. I should be celebrating that.

Rogelio looks at me with raised brows. "Impressive. And scary."

"I can't go to jail." My hands fist in my lap. "I had to remind him that he prefers direct torture. And money."

Rogelio's jaw tightens. "He's not in control here, Aliyah. He'll have other victims. A rapist is incapable of controlling his urges. I'll find them and –"

"I don't want anyone to know about this!" I snap, alarmed by the thought. I never wanted anyone to learn about what my former husband's partner in Baharan had subjected me to nearly thirty years ago. All to reclaim the chemical patents Paul was directly responsible for. By licensing the patents, I could keep food on the table and a roof over Kane's head until I could remarry. Alex made me pay for the patents like a whore.

The company failed because of Paul's embezzlement. One could say Alex didn't owe me anything. But then he didn't act out of altruism, and I paid with my soul.

Now, I've surely maimed – if not castrated – him, and it will cost me dearly to prevent him from pressing assault charges. I'm sure the restaurant's CCTV caught the incident, so the only case I could make is temporary insanity. That would require detailing exactly how he affected my mental well-being, and he'll argue that I agreed to his demands. Given that, a jury would be unlikely to find that I was under extreme duress.

Some will think I could've gone to a women's shelter until I got on my feet or turned to a girlfriend for help. *There are alternatives to selling your body*, they'll think. But they don't know me or what condition I was in after learning that my beloved husband stole everything and abandoned his family for another woman. In my way, I contributed to Baharan as much as Paul did, and I'd be damned if I would accept not having anything to show for all my hard work.

"No one needs to know about it," Rogelio assures me. "Real soon, he's going to forget you ever existed. And he's going to put as much distance between you as possible."

"You don't know how he is."

"You don't know how *I* am," he retorts, grabbing his wallet from the nightstand and sliding it into his pocket.

I let that sink in, along with his body language. My fury is like fire, but Rogelio's is like ice, and I can feel the chill across the room. I tell myself not to read more into it than there is. His anger may not be on my behalf but just on principle. I don't care either way. If he's emotionally invested in removing Alex as a threat, that benefits me regardless of his rationale. "If you tell anyone about this, I'll ruin you."

His full lips are tilted in a smirk as he walks toward the door. "There's the Aliyah I know."

I feel the effect of that careless smile in the pit of my belly and resent it. "I'm not a charity case, Rogelio. I haven't forgotten that Lily knows confidential information even Kane isn't privy to, which tells me your failproof security system isn't so flawless after all. You probably think if you help me, I'll be grateful enough to overlook your mistakes."

Rogelio stops midstride and turns to face me. His boyishly handsome face is hard. "*You* called *me*, Aliyah. Remember? You ordered me to come over. You could've told me about Gallagher without going into the history – which is none of my business, so I wouldn't have asked – but you laid it all out for me. Then you wanted to fuck. Fine by me. I've said it before: You're a hot lay. Then I ended up staying the night. If you feel a little too exposed now, own it. Don't try to put me in whatever place you think I should be."

"That's the most egotistical –"

"Shut up," he snaps. "As for my system, it is flawless. But it's not the only thing keeping your secrets, is it? When it comes to leaking information, it's not a program you should be questioning – it's your confidants."

My lips purse. Darius is the only person who knows about the proposed new Seattle research facility – and my investment in a construction company to build it. As Baharan's CLO and family attorney, Ramin looked over the legalities of my stake, but he doesn't have context. "How and why would my son share confidential information with his brother's wife? A woman we hardly know. No, she found out some other way."

I want to call her an imposter, a fraud, a mystery woman whose motives aren't yet known and can't be trusted. But I won't share any more of the family's dirty laundry with Rogelio. What he knows already is dangerous enough.

"I can prove my system didn't fail. Can you say the same?" He turns his back to me. "I've got to go."

"Stop." I stand, hating that I'm suddenly so conscious of my nudity. I tilt my chin up defiantly. I reclaimed my sexuality, and nothing is going to take it from me again.

He eyes me with brows raised, holding my gaze. I try to gather my thoughts. There's so much on the line and anxiety vibrates through me. I'd always imagined I would be righteous and wrathful if I ever crossed paths with my rapist again. Instead, the fear was so great I can still feel the echoes of it.

Who am I?

A fighter. A survivor. Still, just the thought of Alex is like a million ants crawling around my vitals.

Rogelio's smirk comes back. I hate it. It echoes the dismissiveness I'm used to from him. What the hell do I want? Which version of him would put me at ease?

"Listen," he begins. "Don't overthink last night. I'm just a good guy doing a nice thing for someone I know." The smirk turns into a grin, and I feel that punch in the gut again. "Now, I'm going to get ready for work, where I've suddenly got an active investigation to oversee."

He leaves my bedroom, and I follow him. I watch as he crosses the living room, his dark figure conspicuous in my all-white decor.

"Good guys don't cheat on their wives," I call after him.

Rogelio keeps walking, pausing only when his hand is on the knob of my front door. He's the guy I've known and have occasionally been fucking for years, but he's also not. "If you ever bothered to check my file, you'd know I'm not married."

My breath catches. He wears a wedding band on his ring finger and has often mentioned a wife. "You lied?"

His powerful shoulder lifts in a careless shrug, reminding me how it feels to lay under that muscular body and feel it moving against mine. "Unavailability keeps things clean."

His disclosure changes the dynamic yet again. As a woman whose cheating husband ruined her life, I have no respect for unfaithful men. A man with commitment phobia, however, is a challenge.

The door is closing behind him when I say, "Thank you, Rogelio."

"Think nothing of it," he tosses back without pausing.

Ramin would've been the safer choice to call. My youngest son values family in a way my other boys don't. But I won't have my kids feeling horror and pity when they look at me. I am the core of my family, and nothing can shake or loosen my position.

I can always fire Rogelio, but I'll keep my children close for the rest of their lives.

7

LILY

Watching you leave is excruciating. But you can never know that or why.

You hesitate. As if you read my mind and know the clock's ticking is marking the moments until I have to leave, too. Permanently.

"I'll be back late," you remind me when we reach the front door. "The bachelor party is tonight."

Your backpack waits on the console table in the small entrance foyer of the beach house. It's a commitment for you to commute to Fordham from Greenwich, but you make it for me because I won't risk the two of us being seen together in public, especially not around the city. Not because I'm ashamed of you – my shame is mine alone – but because I'm afraid.

My mother is out there, and she can never know about you. As scared as I was when I emptied her bank accounts, I'm more terrified about your safety. My mother was proud of me for taking the money; it proved my evolution into her likeness was complete. But that pride will be shattered if she learns about you, the man who lures me like a moth to the flame.

"Stay in the city," I tell you, "if it gets too late and you're too drunk."

Pulling me into your arms, you nestle my body against yours with easy familiarity. You know exactly how our bodies fit together, how best to tuck my curves against your muscular torso. My blood heats, even as I still tingle from the sex we had less than an hour ago.

"I'm not sleeping away from you," you say with a finality that tells me you'll crawl back to me if necessary. You reach down to cup my buttocks in both hands, tugging me upward to press the ridge of your erection between the V of my legs. You nuzzle against my neck. "God, the way you smell makes me so hard."

"Kane." I am instantly languid and lustful, aching for you. But I arch back in your embrace, resisting that pull.

Your dark eyes are hot on my upturned face as if I'm drenched in sunshine. I love how you make me feel like you've pulled me out of the shadows and into the light.

My hands smooth your T-shirt over the hard muscles of your chest.

"I'm more than happy to get there late," you murmur, your voice deep and heavy with growing arousal. "The guys know how to get the party started without me."

Shaking my head, I force myself to pull away from you and step back. To be safe, I enter the kitchen and put the island between us. It's hard to break our connection. So hard it hurts. And I hate that. I need to be miles away from you, but even separating by inches is painful.

"You need to go," I insist. Ryan is your best friend. "You planned this party and arranged everything. You need to make sure it all runs smoothly."

You growl low in the back of your throat, your hands clenching at your sides, fighting the gnawing hunger you feel for me. For us, lust is an intoxicating blend of desire, rage and violence. Not that either of us would ever hurt the other, but we're both fighting losing battles and resent it.

I've tried to make you hate me. I have done the worst I could think of, and it still wasn't enough. But you still feel that anger, and I still feel it, too, whenever you hold me down and make love to me with such ferocity, I scream from the pleasure of it.

"I've never told you I'm sorry about what happened with Ryan," I say with deep sincerity. "I know that hurt you. But please, don't let it – me – affect your friendship with him."

You'd walked in on Ryan fucking me. It's what I wanted to happen, what I'd arranged to happen. Hoping if you saw me that way, your disgust would overtake your lust, and I would become a mere footnote in your past, a small part of a stupid time when you coveted your best friend's girlfriend but got over it.

"You wanted to hurt me," you say tightly. "I know that. And I'm with you despite

that, and I'm Ryan's best man anyway. I'd have no problem telling him you're mine now, but you won't let me, so I keep my mouth shut."

"It's better this way."

You prowl toward me, rounding the island. When you reach me, you take both of my hands and link our fingers together. "It's less messy this way," you correct. "Until you decide I'm worth sticking around for."

"Kane, that's not true!"

But I know why you said it. And why you believe it. You've been left behind or pushed out too often by those you love best. To think there is some test you have to pass to be worthy of me is heartbreaking. I'm the one who is unworthy and always will be.

"It's okay," you assure me. "I know you'll get there. And I'll be waiting for you." You smile as if your subtle declaration of love didn't just shatter me.

I can't reply; my throat is too tight.

"I understand the laws of nature, Setareh. The most beautiful things are often the deadliest." Your mouth curves into your heart-stopping grin. "I see that in you. I know and accept it. I will live with it as long as you let me. And if I die in your arms, I'll consider that a fine, grand death."

Ah . . . I can't catch my breath. At this moment – this precise instant I will never forget as the turning point – it becomes too late for me.

I fall in love with you. Irrevocably.

You see me as I am and still accept me as the other half of a single soul.

I never even dreamed of a love like this. Never hoped or wished for it. Even dreaded it because I knew it would end with someone in a grave. But now, somehow, I hold that precious gift in my hands. An unexpected treasure worth dying for.

Worth killing for.

Bending, you press your mouth to mine in a sweet, soft kiss. "Now, let's try this again. I'll be late getting home, but I'll be back. Got it?"

I nod. You shimmer in my vision within a wash of tears, but I don't let them fall.

"Ryan will have an epic send-off to bachelorhood," you go on. "I'll take good care of him. And when I get home, I'll take extra special care of you. You might want to take a nap. Got that?"

"I can't wait," I whisper. I even smile.

You head to the foyer with your long-legged stride. Grabbing your backpack, you open the front door and pause, looking over your shoulder at me. "And in case you missed it, I love you."

My hand covers my aching heart. "I know."

The door shuts, and I release my breath in a rush. I stand there for a long time, long enough that the slant of sunlight moves to the other side of the room.

I love you. It's still astonishing to realize that. I would kill to protect you, Kane. From my history. From me.

You won't be dying in my arms, my love.

I will kill first, then I will die first.

And set you free.

8

LILY

THE FRONT DOOR SHUTS BEHIND YOU AS YOU LEAVE FOR YET ANOTHER workday, and I take a moment to process the loss of you. That's what it feels like to me every morning and I nurture that grief, savoring it until the pain is acute. It's not enough in the way of penance for what I've done to you, but I suffer what I can.

Eventually, I turn away and find Witte nearby.

"Such drama," I tease, knowing how we must appear to onlookers – desperate to stay together beyond all reason.

"Such love," he says with kind eyes.

Those blue eyes can be hard and are always sharp with intelligence. When they look at you, they sometimes betray pride and concern of a personal nature. Have you ever wondered or guessed at the role I played in Witte's hiring?

I smile at him with genuine warmth. Witte is supremely elegant in every way. Though he always wears the black three-piece suits reserved for majordomos, they are of such quality and so expertly tailored as to command respect. He is exceptionally handsome and notably fit. To me – and possibly others with the knowledge to judge such things – it's obvious he's been trained in self-defense to an elite level. He's light on his feet but powerful, and moves with swift precision, sharply observant at every moment. When he accompanies you into the city, he wears a sidearm. He and I sense in each other competing predators yet recognize that we're guarding the same man.

He doesn't return my smile. "Mr. Ryan Landon is in the lobby. He'd like to see you."

There's a spurt of anxiety that jars me for an instant because my guard is down. Your best friend – and my former lover – is a complication I was hoping to avoid for a while.

I recover with my next breath and nod. "Please show him into the living room while I dress. Coffee would be great."

"Of course." Witte pivots neatly and walks away.

I drift down the long hallway to my bedroom. Somewhere, the maids – Lacy and Bea – are working, but I have yet to hear them. When I enter my room, I find it already cleaned, the bed stripped and remade. Clear, precise rows in the rug betray a vacuum, but I've never heard the sounds of vacuuming disturb the quiet. The penthouse only ever shows its best face.

Moving into my closet, I study my choices, focusing on Lily's wardrobe. It's heartbreaking to see how you've kept all her things, yet more painful to wear them. I can smell you here, even though only a few of your belongings mingle with mine and Lily's. You've left your essence behind as you passed through our connecting bedrooms, making my heart flutter.

"*Rogelio called.*"

I turn at the sound of Lacy's voice. The pretty redhead wears a gray maid's uniform and twirls a feather duster by its leather cord. Even the dangerously astute Witte hasn't seen the accomplished killer lurking behind her blue eyes.

"He had to spend the night with Aliyah." Her softly pink lips twist in a grimace. "The man's committed, I'll give him that. She's such a soul-sucking bitch, I'm surprised he's not a mummy this morning."

My sigh is loud and long. Rogelio owes me nothing, never has, while I've used his talents to achieve my aims. That our goals were sometimes aligned doesn't absolve me of blame. "He should walk away. You should, too. I was surprised when I found out you'd shown up with Bea this morning."

"We all talked about the exit strategy. For, like, five minutes." She gives a slight shrug. "Until we're one hundred percent sure you're safe, we'll be sticking around."

"I can take care of myself."

She shakes her head as if I can't. "Aliyah's in big trouble."

"Big trouble how?"

"He was in a hurry when he called. Says he'll fill us in later."

"Okay." I return to my choices and select a burgundy velvet slip dress trimmed in black lace. A black cardigan will finish it off, keeping it casual and modest. It's also an outfit I wore while dating Ryan. "Landon is here."

"For you?"

"Yes."

She whistles. "You got this?"

"It was only a matter of time. I would've preferred to set the stage for our reunion, but sometimes the universe forces our hand."

"I'll be nearby. Say the word, and I'll have Tovah call and give you an out."

"What word?" I inquire.

"You tell me."

"Perrier."

"Okay. Wear something that shows your tattoo." She leaves me, and I admit that I'll have to be the one to cut ties with the crew I've built – they'll never leave me of their own accord.

I change quickly and by the time I exit my closet, Lacy has moved on to another room. Following her suggestion, I selected a black sleeveless sweater dress that skims my ankles. With a bateau neckline in the front and a plunging back, it has two faces – like its wearer.

I walk slowly but with purpose to the living room. In the mirrored hallway, Lily is reflected beside me. My unfortunate bob is now nearly to my shoulder blades, which allows me to look similar to how I looked then – at least from the front – while still exposing my back. Large diamond studs glitter in my ears, and my necklace has a pendant, an open heart encrusted in black diamonds.

Lily is now a second skin that no longer fits. It's a guise that fits so tightly, I sometimes feel like I can't breathe. Yet it's a familiar and known identity, even if I resent it. For now, it's easier to be her once again than to admit the truth: I don't know who I am when I'm not pretending to be someone else.

Who am I? Will you love the woman I truly am once I figure that out?

Pausing on the living room threshold, I find Ryan Landon standing with one of the framed photographs of you and me in his hand. Though he's a few inches shorter than you, Ryan is still slightly over six feet tall. He doesn't have the athlete's body you do, but he's hale, his broad shoulders nicely filling out his blue business suit jacket. His wavy hair is a rich sable brown, neatly groomed. When he turns around, I know his eyes will be the color of amber, set within an undeniably attractive face. He returns the photograph to its place and picks up another.

When you're home, my love, you fill the space perfectly, but the vastness diminishes Ryan in size. The living room is my second favorite area after our sitting room. It's sunken, with two steps leading to a conversation area filled with velvet sofas draped in furs. Ebony tables are topped with sterling silver disks, reminding me of moons reflected on a tranquil pond. Although sunlight pours in from the many large windows with expansive views, the room never loses the feeling of being lushly dark and secretive.

Ryan senses me and turns abruptly. I examine his face with curiosity, watching as his attractive features betray deep shock, disbelief, then joy.

I know you're not Lily because the Coast Guard recovered her body. Aliyah's viciously voiced words ring through my memory. She has no one to compare me to, as I've only recently entered her life. But Ryan knew me before and can note the differences.

"Ryan. It's good to see you." I take the steps down to him, holding my hands out in welcome while maintaining an arm's length distance between us.

"My God." He doesn't move until I'm close, then his body jolts visibly as if snapping out of a daze. He takes my hands in his. "How . . . ?"

I squeeze his cold fingers and gesture for him to take a seat. I take one of the armchairs and flash my back at him before I sit. I hear his breath catch at the sight of my tattoo.

He settles by the sofa arm nearest me, sitting on the edge so that his knees are angled toward mine. His gaze darts all over me with astonished fascination. I can't help but think of you and how different your reaction was to my return. It took you months to rein in your fury, but your acceptance was never in doubt.

"I'm sorry," he says finally. "I'm being rude. I just can't get over it. When did you . . . ? How . . . ? I just –"

I laugh. "You're rarely speechless."

He smiles bemusedly, despite himself. "You look great."

"Thank you. Maybe death becomes me."

"God, that's a terrible joke."

Witte rolls a cart laden with a coffee service into view. Our gazes meet briefly – his conveys a question, while mine conveys assurance. So far, I think I'm in control.

"How's your wife?" I ask. "Angela, isn't it?"

His brows twitch as if debating between a frown and surprise. "She's good. Great, actually." He exhales and straightens as he gathers himself. "How's Kane?"

"Managing, I would say. Starting to accept the miracle of it. And the happiness." I settle back in the chair and curl my legs up, conveying my ease with being in the penthouse.

He nods, and I can see the wheels of his mind start to turn again. I wonder how much he knows. As much as Aliyah? Would you share with your best friend? I can't imagine it. We guard our love so fiercely from others.

"How are you, Ryan?"

"Never been better. LanCorp is doing great. I've made some good decisions and taken some risks that paid off. Angela is very supportive and a partner in every way." He pauses for a beat. "She restored my faith in relationships."

"That's wonderful. I'm very happy for you." I smile my gratitude as Witte hands me freshly poured coffee from a French press. I know he wishes to eavesdrop. How people can overlook such an obviously powerful presence says more about him than them. Witte is a wolf who knows very well how to wear sheep's clothing, just as I do.

"How are *you?*" His gaze moves over me again and narrows. "Did Kane do that to you?"

"Do what?"

"The bruises."

Looking down, I search for what he sees. I find the twin shadow rings, one on each arm. For a moment, I remember you as you were earlier when we made love. You pinned my arms down as you rode me hard, forcing pleasure into my body until sanity slipped away. "Yes. It's somewhat of a honeymoon period for us. We can get carried away."

"Why are there guards at the door?"

I keep my face studiously impassive, even as I realize that might create more problems than we need. We certainly have plenty. "Why does anyone guard anything? To protect what's important."

"Protect you from what?"

49

"Maybe I'm protecting Kane," I tease, trying to lighten his glower, then I shift gears and grow serious. "My mind is a sieve, apparently. It feels like I've just woken from a nap, but years have passed. The world has moved on without me."

"Aliyah said you have amnesia . . . ?"

"The doctors say I have amnesia," I correct. My shrug is more of a self-hug to portray vulnerability. "Aliyah is embellishing with whatever comes to mind because I'm a threat."

His brow arches in silent inquiry that seems like a dare. A challenge to tell the truth or a really exemplary lie. "In what way?"

"She didn't know Kane rebuilt Baharan with the proceeds from my estate."

His stare is unblinking until Witte hands him a cup of coffee. Since Witte didn't ask how he takes it, I assume Ryan has been around enough for his preferences to be known. I hope he's been a good friend to you and you've both put aside your earlier relationships with me when I was Lily.

He takes a sip. "Thank you, Witte," he says absently.

"You're welcome. Would you care for anything else?"

"No, thank you." He continues to give me that penetrating stare until Witte retreats to the cart. "I find it hard to believe she didn't know."

"Yes, well, that makes two of us. Apparently, he didn't tell anyone." Since the majordomo lingers, I draw him in. "You didn't know either, Witte, did you?"

His head tilts in a slight nod. "I didn't, no."

Ryan's raised brow lowers into a frown.

I go on. "Kane also holds his company shares in our joint LLC."

"So, you're a shareholder," he murmurs. "No, I don't suppose she would like that at all. How do you feel about it?"

"Proud. Kane has accomplished everything he intended. Spectacularly."

"Of course." He manages a slight, humorless smile. "But I was referring to controlling part of Baharan."

"I have zero interest in it," I say flatly.

"It's successful and about to be more so."

"I wouldn't expect anything else with Kane at the helm." My lips curve against the lip of my mug. "But I obviously didn't marry him for his money since he didn't have any then."

"I'm not sure much is obvious at this point." He finally settles back into the sofa, his gaze briefly returning to the photos of you and me. "You haven't reached out to anyone we know."

"The doctor has advised me to limit my stress, which is believed to have triggered the amnesia."

"It's stressful being with friends?"

"Waking up is stressful, Ryan. Looking in the mirror and seeing a different face than the one in my mind is stressful. And this little reunion we're having now isn't exactly restful. You're vacillating between challenging me and concern."

"I'm sorry," he says. "You meant a lot to me for a while. I had to come to see you when I heard you were back."

"When Kane isn't here."

"He didn't tell me you were back," he retorts as if that explains his behavior.

"He probably didn't realize he was obligated to – his mistake. You'll have to forgive him. He's finding it a struggle even to leave for work because he's afraid his wife will vanish again." Steel threads through my voice. "Doubt me all you like but tread carefully with Kane. He's been through enough."

"Why would I doubt you?"

"That's a good question. You know me, Ryan. You've had six years to change, but I'm the same, trapped in time. For all intents and purposes, my marriage is still in its infancy and burdened by grief. I have months, if not years, of psychotherapy and analysis ahead of me. And my mother-in-law is trying to take advantage of my situation to protect her interests. I won't apologize for not picking up the phone to face endless, repetitive questions from old friends on top of everything else."

"I didn't mean to upset you."

"What did you mean, Ryan? What is it you came by to see or figure out?"

He takes a deep breath, his gaze roaming. "Kane said you weren't together long before you . . . went missing."

"We weren't. He didn't approach me until you got engaged. The timeline might seem rushed, but Kane is a good man who would never take advantage of a friend's circumstances."

"What about you?"

I want to tell him I would absolutely take advantage of anyone's circumstances; it's how I've gotten by my whole life. But Lily would never say something like that, and for now, I still have to act the part.

"No," I reply simply. "I was halfway out the door when Kane showed up with the news that you'd gotten engaged and said he couldn't live another second without me. I'd already moved out of the city after graduation and was leaving the beach house, too. Most of the furniture was covered, and it was my last night. I had a plane ticket to London the next day."

"And he won you over so fast you married him weeks later?"

"I'm not going to say there was never an attraction, only that we didn't act on it. Consideration for you kept us at a distance. Frankly, you should appreciate that. What does it matter anyway? You've never been better."

"It doesn't matter. I love my wife. You and I ended up with the people meant for us." He stares into his black coffee like he'll find something there. "Kane grieved like he was married a lifetime."

I exhale the vibrant pain his words evoke. "That's his nature. He's fiercely loyal. To you. To me. Even to his family. Losing a loved one is always terrible, but in the honeymoon stage, when everything seems perfect, and there's so much to look forward to, it would be exceptionally tough."

He nods pensively. "I'm sorry I dropped in without warning. I was on my way to work and couldn't resist, knowing you were here."

I uncurl and stand. "Please call Kane and let him know you came over."

"I will." He gains his feet as Witte comes to collect our mugs. "When you feel up to it, I'd love to have you and Kane over for dinner. You'll like Angela. Everyone does."

"Thank you for the offer. I'll look forward to taking you up on it."

Ryan fidgets for a moment. He briefly extends his hand, then changes his mind, pulling me in for a quick hug. "I'm glad you're back. Glad for Kane and you. For everyone." He tosses his hands up and gives me a rueful smile. "I can't figure out what to say or how to say it."

I smile. "That was perfectly fine."

When he moves toward the front door, I turn my back to him and walk to the windows, looking at the city outside.

I've distracted him, but he'll return after the shock of seeing me again has worn off. And he won't be so easily deflected then.

9

WITTE

As I escort Mr Landon to the door, he pauses and turns back. Lily stands on the other side of the vast space, facing away from us, her back a sleek column of pale skin with a magnificent tattoo. A dazzlingly coloured phoenix stretches its wings across her shoulder blades, its tail curling down to disappear inside the daring dress.

"What's your impression of her?" he asks me quietly.

"Mrs Black is a woman who is both extremely fragile and uniquely strong, and I would say she's very much in love with her husband."

He gives a short, harsh laugh. "No need to warn me off, Witte."

We step into the lift vestibule, and he eyes the two guards. "Is she free to come and go?"

"Of course."

When he doesn't press the call button for the lift, I understand there is more on his mind.

Shaking his head, he looks back at the closed front doors. "I can't put my finger on it, but there's something . . . off. But how? I mean, look at her. She's exactly as I remember. The hair is shorter, but the feel of her . . . the scent . . . that voice."

"The eyes, perhaps?" I will never forget how Mr Black looked and spoke when his wife regained consciousness. *She looks like Lily. Has her voice. Her skin. Her scent. But there's something about her eyes . . . Don't you see it?*

He stills. "Yes. Yes, you're right. It's the eyes. They're very . . . hard. Calculating."

"We must consider that while she can't seem to remember the past several years, her mind hasn't forgotten. With luck, she'll be able to tell us in time, and we'll better understand the forces that shaped her during her absence."

"Yeah, maybe." Lips pursed in thought, Landon turns and pushes the call button. Then he shoves his hands in his pockets and rocks back on his heels. When the lift doors open, he starts to enter, then pauses. He looks at me and I see his concern. And inner conflict.

"Is there something else?" I ask.

"I've always been available if he's needed me. Now . . . maybe he doesn't feel like he can reach out about Lily, but of course he can. Maybe you could remind him of that if it comes up."

I incline my head in acknowledgement.

"Have a good day, Witte."

"You as well."

Once the car has started its descent, I re-enter the penthouse. Lily hasn't moved. She glances over her shoulder at me.

"He knows about me," she says flatly, her eyes displaying the hardness Landon described. "Or, more aptly, he realizes he doesn't know me."

I don't reply or give any outward reaction. Sometimes, silence is the greater inquisitor.

She faces me directly, moving with sleek fluidity. The physical therapist who worked with her marvelled at how quickly she regained her mobility and strength. It's her body's natural state to be physically fit. I've seen her react with swift precision, without the delay that comes from thinking something through rather than acting on instinct.

"Aliyah knows I've changed identities multiple times," she explains, "and so does Ryan. I'm more concerned that he didn't mention it than I would've been if he had."

My brows lift. That she would choose this moment to be forthright takes me aback. And that she's so perceptive. "How would she have learned that information?"

"How did Kane?" she retorts. "She'd have no reason to investigate my background while I was presumed dead, and there's hardly been time for her to rectify that since. So, she's learned what he knows, and you'll have to figure out how she could. She threatened me when we met for coffee the other day. She wants me to leave him. I haven't mentioned it to Kane yet."

"Do you suspect he already knows?"

Her lips curve in a shadow of a smile. "Are you asking if I think Kane discussed it with her? My mother did tell me to always anticipate the improbable."

"You don't believe he would."

"I doubt everything, Witte, but not his love. He wants me to suffer, and he wants me never to suffer. There's so much rage inside him because of the pain I've caused. What is that if not love?" She flashes a grin. "Aliyah doesn't know what love is. If she ever viewed him as a blessing, it was long ago. In her mind, their mutual dedication to Baharan puts them at odds. He's become an impediment."

I step down into the living room. "An impediment to what?"

"Her ambition. Her need for control. Does she hold his father's actions against him? Does she see Paul in Kane? She'd make a fascinating study, really, but that's irrelevant. She's profiting from his grief, and we must ensure she doesn't cause any damage."

I suspect Lily was always astute at assessing others. Ryan Landon was correct that there's calculation when she interacts. That she also majored in psychology at Columbia University would only have honed that natural talent. "She can't intimidate you."

"She doesn't have what it takes to scare me off, and Kane doesn't need to know about her attempts, so you won't tell him." Her tone brooks no argument. "Focus on how she can impact him professionally. I'll deal with her personally."

"You prefer handling such things yourself."

She gives an elegant shrug. "When I'm working alone, I know who to trust."

"Are you trusting me now?"

"To look out for Kane's best interests, yes."

I sigh, perceiving a new, wary woman beneath the brittle reply. Too often, inner strength comes from necessity, not nurturing. "I'm here to assist you in whatever way you require."

"Focus on Kane." Her eyes close, and her shoulders relax on a slow exhalation of breath as if she's willed away any emotion that could influence her. "Please."

"What do you think Mrs Armand will do with the information that could be harmful?" I ask, although the answer I genuinely need is how harmful the information is.

Her eyes open, and that brilliantly green stare pins me. "I hold my secrets like lovers. She's a pressure cooker, and she's let off some steam by talking to Ryan. Who's next? Ramin or Darius? – if they don't already know. What will they do with the information? How would shareholders feel if the majority stockholder was a liability in any way?"

It's deeply unfortunate that Mr Black's family is the most concerning threat to his well-being.

She sighs. "Whether Ryan was the first to know or not, he won't be the last."

10

AMY

I SIT AT MY DESK, INHALING AND EXHALING SLOWLY AND DEEPLY. I'VE always hated the essential oil diffuser Aliyah has in her office, but now I'm tempted to steal it while she's at lunch. It usually never bothers me to smell food odors coming out of the employee breakroom, but someone is eating something fucking rancid today.

"Hey." Clarice darkens my doorway with her tiny frame. She's leaned hard into her retro style today in a lipstick-red dress with a frilly petticoat and a cap-sleeved bodice. She'd look almost childlike if not for her curves. "I'm heading out to lunch. Want to join me?"

I shake my head and swallow bile. "No, thanks."

She walks up to my desk. "Are you okay? You're looking a little green."

I can't tell her what I suspect – that I'm going through withdrawal. Not from alcohol but from whatever drug I've been exposed to. Making that accusation aloud would only make me sound crazy, which is what my mother-in-law wants.

But is Darius conspiring with Aliyah? The fact that he lied to me about the contract makes me suspect everything he says and does. And while I'm really fucking pissed off about that, I'm deeply hurt, too. When did my marriage go completely off the rails? Did I sabotage it? God knows I had a perfect how-to lesson in dysfunctional relationships from my parents.

In any case, I've spent the past week carefully pushing food around on my dinner plate and pretending to eat. If I had any doubts that I'm being drugged, they're gone now. I haven't felt this nauseous since I was a child.

"Might be food poisoning," I tell her and pat myself on the back for being both honest and opaque. Somewhere along the line, I lost my ability to be subtle, but it's returning. *I'm* coming back.

"Or maybe you partied last night?" She waggles her brows and grins.

I grit my teeth. "I fucking wish, but no. I'm doing that detox, remember?"

Her face immediately wipes clean of all expression. "That's right. I was just teasing. Want me to bring you something back? Ginger ale, maybe? Some Saltines?"

"Yeah, sure. That'd be great."

"No problem." She gives me a last questioning look, then leaves.

I collapse into my chair, then straighten when the tilting makes my stomach turn. I know what withdrawal looks and feels like. Every once in a while, my parents would decide to stop drinking. Sometimes they lasted a few months sober, but the dreariness of life with each other always drove them back to the bottle. The chaos of fighting and fucking like maniacs was more enticing than harsh reality.

That's why I weaned myself off the bottle by limiting the hours I could drink, then by decreasing the proof of alcohol I chose as my poison. Liquor became wine, and then wine became beer. I had the shakes, the sweats, and nausea in manageable degrees. But this . . . this is something else. I know because I drank a shot of vodka to take the edge off, and it only made me puke my fucking guts out.

Is that scientific? No. And I need proof to defend myself. And all for what? A company Aliyah has starved to the bone. I mean, how crazy is that?

Exhaling heavily, I look around my tiny office. When Social Creamery was independent, my office was easily four times larger. My first office at Baharan had been larger, too, but Aliyah gave it to someone else. Now, I have a child-size desk with a single drawer. My sofa has been reduced to a loveseat. And my bookcases have been replaced with open shelving.

"How's your day going so far?"

I return my attention to the doorway and find Ramin lounging nonchalantly against the jamb. My chest constricts, and my pulse quickens. He's a handsome man, more boyish than Kane and Darius. Shorter and stockier. The three brothers could be nesting dolls, with Kane swallowing his younger siblings.

Ramin's wearing dark gray slacks and a dress shirt of the same color. His tie is burgundy, and his jacket is probably hanging on the back of his chair. He wears his hair slightly longer than Kane and Darius, emphasizing those bright blue eyes that are an Armand trait. His smile is a lopsided grin, both charming and cocky. He is Baharan's CLO, and I understand he's a great attorney, but he struggles with being overshadowed by his siblings. That's given him an inferiority complex, which leads him to speak and act rashly when he's not on solid footing.

The entire family is a hot fucking mess.

"Well, you know . . ." I shrug, and then the smell of his cologne wafts to me. My stomach heaves. I swallow, trying to stem the tide, but there's no stopping it. Shoving my chair back, I fall to my knees and grab the trash can.

The next few moments pass in a blur of vomiting. I'm vaguely aware of Ramin gathering my hair and stroking my back. Finally, the heaving stops, and I rest my head against the spindly leg of my mirrored desk. I don't have the energy to fight Ramin when he pulls me into his lap and holds me. His chest is hard beneath my cheek, his torso a warm and supportive wall of muscle.

Why did I sleep with him before I married Darius? Stupid question. I know why. I couldn't believe my relationship with Darius was so perfect. I couldn't help but try to sabotage it. I couldn't silence the voice that told me I was delusional to think a man as handsome and accomplished as Darius would ever fall in love and want to spend his life with me.

Ramin could have been a friend, an ally. Now, I avoid him as politely as possible because just looking at him smothers me in guilt. That's why I know I'd never fuck him again if I were in my right mind.

"If Darius walks in," I murmur weakly, noting the closed door, "he's going to be pissed."

There is a sea of cubicles just feet away, filled with staff and Kane himself, who thinks it looks better if he forgoes an office to work alongside peons. I used to have a direct line of sight to him when I had my former office. Now I just look at a bunch of miserable people who know every keystroke and phone call is recorded for security purposes.

"I don't care," he dismisses. "Do you feel better now?"

"I feel like burrowing into bed and sleeping for ten years." Maybe I'd be lucky, like Lily, and wake up to find Darius running Baharan and my home turned into the penthouse. If he clung to me the way Kane clung to Lily's memory, I'd forgive him anything.

"Have you been drinking?" Ramin asks.

"Fuck you." I try to pull away, but his embrace tightens. "Why is everyone asking me that? I'm sick, not drunk."

His chest expands with a deep breath. "Maybe you're pregnant."

I'm stunned, then a sharp laugh escapes me. "That'd be a neat trick."

"It's not outside the realm of possibility." Ramin runs his fingers through my hair.

I try pushing away from him again, and when he resists, I tell him, "The smell of vomit is going to make me sick again."

When he releases me, I scramble unsteadily to my feet. I use my desk as support as I skirt it. Grabbing the trash can, Ramin ties off the bag and places it within another bag he finds stored in the bottom. Then he lines the can again, shooting me a wry smile over his shoulder. "In case you need it."

"Oh, go away." I sink into the sofa and press my palm to my forehead. It doesn't feel feverish, but then I know I'm not sick. My body is purging whatever has been used to make me crazy. I can suffer through this and will because every day I gain more clarity.

Ramin settles into my desk chair and leans back. "Food poisoning? Stomach bug?"

"What do you care?"

"I think it's obvious I care a lot," he retorts, his gaze hard with growing anger.

"Sure. Whatever."

"Answer the damn question!" he demands, his body jerking upright.

"What does it matter?"

"If you're pregnant, I have a right to know."

"God." I close my eyes and let my head fall against the icy blue velvet cushion. "You don't have a right to anything involving my uterus or any other part of me."

"I've never suited up with you."

That pronouncement hits me like a punch to the gut. Here I am, thinking my life can't get worse. "I have an IUD, Ramin. And a horny husband."

"Why are you such a bitch when I'm not actively fucking you?"

Lifting my head, I look at him with narrowed eyes. "I realize it's news to you, and I've admittedly acted to the contrary, but I hate cheaters. I hate myself for cheating. Monogamy is important to me."

"You never wanted the marriage, Amy, which is a mitigating factor." Ramin holds my gaze with those incredible blue eyes, his square jaw taut.

"Seriously?" I shake my head. "I was desperate to marry Darius. There's nothing I wanted more."

"Bullshit. Brides-to-be don't seduce their future brother-in-law if they love their groom."

"They do if they're fucked up in the head. I've got enough baggage to fill a warehouse."

"Or maybe you secretly knew you should've been marrying me."

My mouth falls open.

"Don't look so shocked, Amy. You know how I feel about you."

"No, actually, I don't. No –" I hold up my hand. "Don't say anything. We need to stay in our lanes, Ramin. You don't want to be the guy who fucks over his brother."

"Why not? What has he ever done for me?"

I stare at him. "How would I know? But we don't do good things just to get something out of it. We do the right thing because we're good people."

"You really aren't feeling like yourself."

"What's that supposed to mean?"

"Forget it. I was trying to be funny. Listen . . . you feel something for me, too. You're just afraid to admit it. Darius isn't what you need. He's never been what you need. Why do you think I included that clause?"

"I can't deal with this right now," I say, primarily to myself, because I'm beginning to feel ill again.

"We're going to deal with it because I'm tired of this shit." He shoves back from my desk and stands, turning to look out the window with his hands on his hips. It's a good view of him, showing off his tightly muscled backside. He could have any woman. It's beyond fucked up that he's fixated on me.

"If you'd left me alone after that first time," he goes on, warming up, "we wouldn't be here now. I was committed to letting you go when you went through with the ceremony. But then you showed up on my doorstep."

"Ramin . . . It had to be obvious that I wasn't acting like I usually do. I mean, come on . . . Behaving like Dr. Jekyll and Mr. Hyde isn't normal!" Massaging my temples with my fingers, I try to stave off a building headache.

He spins to face me. "What are you saying?"

I purse my lips, holding back the truth. The Armands squabble amongst themselves, but outside threats are dealt with by a united front. I can't trust that Ramin will believe me or protect me. "My drinking has gotten out of hand."

"Yeah . . . we've all noticed that. You're not happy with Darius and –"

"I was!" I snap. "I don't know when that changed or why, but I wanted a happy marriage."

"I *love* you, Amy!"

My mouth hangs open for a long, terrible minute. "Are you kidding me right now? That's not even remotely funny."

But he doesn't flash his cocky smile or laugh. Reality warps into a sick and twisted freakshow as his face mottles with fury.

"That's all you have to say when I tell you I fucking *love* you?!"

"Keep your voice down! For fuck's sake, I don't need another scene at work."

His scowl is so fierce it reminds me of Kane. "*That's* what you're worried about? What about *me*?"

My God. The irony. It takes everything I have not to dissolve into hysterical laughter. *Again.* I've been borderline hysterical for days now. What are the odds I would delude myself into thinking Kane was endgame, while Ramin was thinking the same thing about me? We're both totally perverse, wanting things we not only can't have but aren't even remotely what we need or would be good for us.

I change the subject quickly. "Explain that other clause, Ramin. The one that gives control of Social Creamery to Darius if I'm unfit to run it."

That caveat would've comforted me when I signed the agreement and as recently as three days ago. Now, it's motive to gaslight me.

Confusion clouds his gaze. "You didn't have a clear hierarchy of power in your company. It was important to establish someone to look after your best interests if you were incapacitated."

"So, you're saying you did me a favor?"

His arms cross defensively, his biceps straining. "There had to be some structure."

I snort. "Okay."

"What's going on, Amy?"

My gaze narrows. "I can't tell you."

"Who else would care as much as I do?" he argues.

"I don't trust any of you." I swallow rising bile and stare at where the bar cart once was. Unusually, the thought of alcohol makes my stomach roil, so I look away, my gaze darting over the objects displayed on the open shelving.

I pause on the framed photograph of Darius and me. It's a professional shot, with me seated and dressed in a cream Chanel business suit and Darius standing behind my chair in a black suit with matching blue shirt and tie. It's a power couple look, and I've considered it a portent of things to come for so long now.

"What are you referring to?" Ramin rounds my desk. "Lawyers? Men?"

"Armands."

His gaze narrows dangerously. "I will not be judged on my brothers' behavior. I'm not like them."

There's a cold glint in his sky-blue eyes. Abruptly, my perception of him changes, and I feel a frisson of genuine fear. Yes, he's smaller than Darius and Kane, but much bigger than me. And he's showing a side of himself I haven't seen before.

The perspiration misting my skin is abruptly chilling.

I take a deep, slow breath and exhale just as slowly. My mind races. "If I hire you as my attorney, there's privilege, right? You can't tell anyone what I tell you?"

"Amy . . ." His eyes close, and he scrubs a hand over his face. "I wouldn't tell anyone anything you told me in confidence. Not because I'm a lawyer, but because you're the woman I love."

He says the words with such finality my fear deepens. If he's convinced that he loves me, I have another serious problem. "Even if it has to do with your family?"

"You're my family, too," he says, his features softening. "And not because you're married to Darius but because you're the woman I hope will soon be married to me."

"Jesus, Ramin." My pulse flutters with panic. What a total fucking train wreck. Is it any wonder I'm being driven mad when I'm surrounded by crazy people? How did I not see from the beginning that the Armands are all lunatics?

He sits on the edge of my desk. "What do you want to tell me?"

I need someone on my side. If it's an attorney with insider knowledge, that has to be good, right? Or does that create a conflict of interest . . . ? My brain hurts just trying to untangle all of it. "I'm being drugged to look crazy, so that clause will kick in, and I'll lose control of my company."

He stares at me for a long minute, then blinks.

"At some point, your mother must have become aware of the exit clause, or maybe she always knew it was there. Knowing I could leave with Social Creamery, she decided to weaponize the incapacity clause." I start to stand, but I stay put when the room spins a little. "Darius has been telling me that he's working on a way to get Social Creamery back. He's been acting like it's hard and a lot of work, so it's taking time. Either he's in on it with your mother, or my housekeeper, Griselda, is working with her. Your mother is the one who found her for us, after all, since I'm apparently not capable of taking care of Darius by myself. Aliyah's not around me enough to be directly responsible."

"Amy . . ." Ramin takes a slow, deep breath like he's gathering himself. "He may not be familiar with the contract. Or maybe he suspects you're preparing to leave him and is trying to buy more time to work things out. You can't –"

"Don't tell me what I know. He's lied to my face about the exit clause. So has your mother."

"Okay. Tell me what you know."

"I lose track of time. Darius and your mother tell me I'm wrong about what I remember. Things at home go missing. Decorations are moved around – paintings, knickknacks."

He rubs the back of his neck. "Amy, you drink – a lot."

My gaze narrows. "I just said as much, didn't I? But having a buzz doesn't mean my memory is worthless."

I want to tell him that a decent guy would've called me a cab if I showed up on his doorstep while obviously not sober. But I'm afraid to antagonize him.

"What you're accusing Darius of is criminal," he says in a slow and cautious tone. Quietly condescending. The Armands are experts at wielding that tone to punishing effect.

"And?"

"And while I know he's not the guy for you, he would never set out to deliberately harm you."

That shouldn't make me feel better, and I know I'm fucked up for letting it. I don't want to believe my husband could do anything horrible to me, but maybe he would if he thought it would keep us together. Still . . . "If he loved me, he'd get us out of here."

"Do you love him?" he queries sharply.

I've asked myself that question a million times over the past few days. My mind has been so crowded and confused for so long now that I'm unsure how I feel about anything. All I know now is that Ramin's feelings are involved in unexpected and unwelcome ways, and I'm to blame for that, even if I'm not ultimately responsible. "It's hard to love anyone when I don't love myself at the moment."

He looks surprised, then sympathetic. "All you have to do is walk out," he says softly. "I'll make sure the paperwork goes through quickly. You can stay with me, or we can take it slow."

I stare at him in horror. His stubborn refusal to grasp what I'm telling him borders on deranged. I can't begin to understand it because he has memories of me that I don't have, and I'm afraid to be blunter because he's already not handling the situation well.

"Remind me" – I clear my dry throat because I'm rasping – "what the prenup gives me if I just walk out."

Ramin's pursed lips answer the question before he speaks. "Without a child, not a lot. But I can take care of you."

"I'm sick of being taken care of!" My hands fist with frustration.

"When was the last time you saw your therapist?"

I bristle. "You wanna talk about *me* being crazy?! That's rich."

"Don't freak out. You've told me you suspect my mother – and possibly my brother – are trying to claim you're unstable and you're hoping to fight the prenup. It would be wise to preemptively corroborate your sanity with a regular therapy schedule."

"Oh." I study him, looking for any sign that he's manipulating me. "Yeah, that's a good point. It hasn't been that long. I've just been busy getting back to work."

The truth is I don't remember how long it's been. Days blended into weeks. How long have I been deteriorating? When was the last time I felt happy and safe, and sane?

Why didn't I question *anything*?

Ramin stares down at the floor, nodding, lost in his thoughts. I hope he's starting to register what I've been saying. Silence grows, then stretches. I close my eyes and focus on breathing, willing away the pervasive sickness exacerbated by increasing disquiet.

The door opens abruptly, and I jolt, my eyes opening to find Darius standing with one hand on the knob and a thunderous expression on his handsome face.

"Why is the door closed?" he snaps, glaring at his brother. His nose twitches. "And why does it smell like vomit in here?"

Panicked that Ramin might say something he shouldn't, I blurt out the first thing that comes to mind. "I think I might have morning sickness."

My husband visibly freezes, staring with shock, and then he transforms. His frown morphs into the faintest smile of wonder.

Will he keep drugging me if he thinks I'm carrying his child?

I return his smile as he joins me on the loveseat. He wraps me in his arms as if I'm precious and breakable. He's talking about tests and doctors with growing excitement, and for a moment, I'm caught up in his enthusiasm.

Then I catch sight of Ramin's hard, flat gaze and feel dread.

11

ALIYAH

May 1, 1999

I TURNED ONTO THE RESIDENTIAL STREET LINED WITH IMPOSINGLY large homes and anticipated reaching my own. It was the home of my dreams. It was a twist of fate that the life I lived inside it was a nightmare.

As always, I briefly indulged in the fantasy of my first husband, Paul, imagining he was waiting for our daughter, Rosana, and me to return from daycare pickup. He was playing with our three boys on the large front lawn, waving at the neighbors as they drove by, his handsome face lit with joy. I felt that same joy for an instant before I squashed the stupid daydream like a bug under my heel. Then I fantasized stomping on the accelerator instead, my SUV bouncing up the driveway and onto the grass before smashing into him and sending him flying over the roof.

It infuriated me that the thought didn't bring pleasure, only pain. Thinking of Paul always made me terribly sad. After everything I'd suffered, why did I still miss that faithless, worthless bastard? Was it because he'd left me before I realized our love was a lie? Was it the lack of a slow, painful death to our relationship? Is that what made it so hard to accept that he'd deserted me so easily?

I took a deep breath as I pulled into my curving driveway, slowing as I waited for the garage door to open. That was the point where I pretended being Mrs. Armand was the life I'd always wanted, that Lucas, the husband inside my dream home, was a better father than Paul had been, and our marriage stronger and more passionate. The relief I felt at seeing the empty spot where his Jaguar was usually parked contradicted my fabricated reality.

"We're home, Rosie!" I called out with feigned cheer, putting the car into park and turning off the engine.

"Home! Home!" she called back, with genuine excitement that mocked my pretense.

Sometimes, during holidays or vacations, I watched my four children and thought they'd never really know me. I did everything possible to make sure of that. Yes, it was lonely faking contentment, but that was the price to be paid to keep their childhood insulated from ugliness.

And besides . . . that's what I did, didn't I? Pay and pay and pay some more. But I was keeping tabs. Eventually, others would pay me for everything they took with no regard.

Releasing the car seat harness, I freed my daughter from the backseat. She extended her arms to me, and I pulled her close as I straightened, her tiny body so dear and beloved. She was the best thing to come of my second marriage, the purest and easiest. Boys were harder. At least my boys were. Especially Kane.

I kicked the door shut with my foot, careful not to mar the glossy surface. The sleek silver M-Class was more than just transportation; I was clawing back everything that had been taken from me.

I'd lost my previous Mercedes when Paul bankrupted us by embezzling from our company. Marrying Lucas Armand and giving him three children was the price to recoup my losses, which was nothing compared to what Paul's partner, Alex Gallagher, had demanded in exchange for the chemical patents Paul had been instrumental in obtaining. Alex had left scars on my soul and my mind. He'd made me aware of just how depraved men could be.

"Kane!" Rosana cried excitedly, her legs kicking. "Kane!"

"Yes, yes." I adjusted my grip as she bounced on my hip. Darius, Ramin, Rosana – they all adored their older brother, who was really more of a father to them than Lucas.

It was annoying now, but initially, I had appreciated Lucas's focus on appearances. He wanted everything to look perfect. I'm the perfect wife with our three picture-perfect children in his ideal life. He preferred to disregard that I'd ever been married previously or had Kane. The perfect wife wouldn't have been married to someone else first.

I went along with it because it was important that anyone looking at me would see no trace of the woman who'd lost all of her possessions when her husband abandoned her. Lucas ensured that I looked better than ever. And he was the partner in his law firm who oversaw the chemical and materials group, responsible for industrial patents of all types. Because of him, I could monetize Paul's patents to build a nest egg for myself, which would come in handy once I outlasted the terms of the prenup agreement.

My heels clicked across the speckled epoxy flooring in the garage. It was spotless, boasting dark wood cabinets and neatly arranged tools on pegs. When the garage doors rolled up, our neighbors saw beauty, order, and – most crucially – wealth.

Entering the mudroom from the garage, we were greeted by Cotton, our beautiful white Labrador. He pranced with excitement, his tag wagging so hard his hindquarters rocked with it. I put Rosana down and watched her race the dog down the hardwood-lined hall as she shouted for Kane.

There were a dozen years between my eldest and youngest child, but Kane was as good with her as he was with his brothers. While Rosana kept my hands full, he took Darius to baseball practice and helped Ramin with his homework. How Kane managed to graduate from high school a year early while holding down a job and helping with the kids still amazed me. He truly is a credit to the way I reared him.

I once wished that Lucas would be more considerate of Kane, but I came to accept that Lucas was too mean-spirited to find room in his heart for another man's son. And really, he didn't show much love for his children. Thankfully, he became afflicted with erectile dysfunction and learned how humiliating it could be when he didn't leave me alone. After what I suffered at the hands of Alex Gallagher, providing sex I didn't want or enjoy was nothing less than traumatic.

"Mom." Darius hurried toward me, the wainscoting and geometric wallpaper in the hallway making him look smaller than he was. His blue eyes were red-rimmed, and his nose was pink. He, too, was growing up too fast.

I steeled myself to a semblance of calm. The tension in the house was so thick it made the hairs on my nape rise. Anger rose, tempered by fatigue. I was exhausted by all the concessions I had to continue making daily. I'd already sold my soul to create the illusion of stability for Kane and me.

"What is it, darling?" I asked, brushing his dark hair back from his brow, even though I already knew the answer.

"Dad's mad at Kane again," he sobbed, crushing himself against me, his arms tight around my thighs. "He hit him in the face, and Kane's bleeding."

Rage surged so swiftly and fiercely that I trembled with it. It was no longer tenable to keep Kane with me, even though his support and presence brought me joy. Holding on to him when he would be safer anywhere else was selfish.

"Shh . . ." Bending, I hugged Darius close. "Don't cry. I'll take care of Kane."

"Dad's mean! Kane was just helping Ramin with his homework. Dad said he was teaching him wrong on purpose."

My eyes squeezed shut, and my breath whistled out between clenched teeth. It disgusted me that Lucas was jealous of a child. Jealous because Kane resembled his father so much, and that resemblance made it impossible to ever blend into the ideal family image Lucas prized. Lucas also knew that he would never be loved by me the way I once loved Paul, despite my best efforts to disguise my distaste. If he'd been capable of even tolerating Kane, maybe things could've been different. As it was, I made him pay for every infraction against my son – countless little cuts and discomforts.

"It was just a misunderstanding," I lied. "Go to your room and play Zelda until I call you for dinner, okay?"

His little body tightened with anger and frustration. He loved Kane so much and worshipped him in that pure way known only to younger siblings. Then Darius nodded, stepped back and obeyed. That wasn't always a given. The boy was willful and reckless.

I watched him run away, then turn toward the stairs. I waited until his footsteps raced across the second floor and silence returned before I moved an inch.

Mothers aren't supposed to have a favorite child. I loved all four of mine, but Kane was exceptional. There were moments when he reminded me of Paul's betrayal, which was painful, but he also reminded me of the best of times. And he looked out for me, even when I told him it was my job to look after him. Of any man I knew, Kane was the one who was selfless when it came to me.

Brushing my hands over my dark hair, I glanced into the mirror on the wall and decided that when I was done with this time in my life, I would never see this sad, powerless woman again. I'd see another woman entirely; someone transformed in every way by authority and control.

I headed into the central part of the house.

Lucas was a coward. He didn't want to face me when I learned that he'd hit Kane – again. He believed I calmed down if he stayed away a few hours, revealing how little he knew me. He never even considered that the key scrape down the side of his Jaguar or the screw piercing the sidewall of his tire could be courtesy of me. He never even thought of me when time-sensitive messages somehow weren't on his home office answering machine. Nor did I come to mind when he suffered occasional bouts of violent diarrhea his doctor couldn't explain.

What had I done to myself by marrying him? Would Paul even recognize me now?

The entire situation was his fault. Remembering that alleviated my guilt about what I had to do. His abandonment put me in this position, and I couldn't change course without negatively impacting my children's lives. I wouldn't do that for any price.

I knew exactly where to find Kane. Unlike Lucas, he didn't hide. He sat with Rosana on his lap at the kitchen counter, the very heart of the house, his dark head bent over Ramin's as my youngest boy labored over schoolwork. Cotton lay at his feet, watching me. Ramin was bright, as all my children were, but he strove for perfection. He railed against any grade lower than one hundred percent, blaming himself for not studying harder. He also enjoyed Kane's attention and worked more than he needed to just to have it.

"Kane, darling," I said softly but firmly, steeling my heart.

It didn't help. My breath caught painfully in my chest when he turned, revealing a bruised eye beginning to swell. Tears burned, reminding me I could still cry and that there was always more suffering to experience.

He looked at me with his dark eyes, his gaze old and wise and devoid of any spark of childish joy. He'd been forced to mature too quickly to overcome my shortcomings and those of his father and stepfather. As devastatingly handsome as Paul, Kane would only grow further into his innate attractiveness until he became a hazard to any woman who fell in love with him. I'd been blind to Paul's flaws, and Kane would soon surpass him in handsomeness.

"I need to speak to you," I told him.

"I hate Daddy!" Ramin said defiantly, his pale blue eyes hot with fury. "He got the answer wrong and blamed Kane!"

"You don't hate your father," I corrected. "You're mad at him, and I understand why but saying so will only make things harder for all of us."

"I don't care!"

I shot him a quelling look, and his lips tightened into a scowl. His legs began to kick, his sneakers banging into the side of the dark walnut island. I didn't have the strength to fight him, too. "Kane."

"Yeah." He unfolded, rising to tower over me. His father, too, had been very tall. He set Rosana down on the barstool and ruffled her hair. "I'll be right back."

I led the way out of the kitchen and into the formal living room, listening to Cotton's claws clicking over the tile floor. The dog was never far from Kane, and when my son sat on the red chintz sofa, Cotton sat upright by his legs. I joined them, briefly looking out the large picture window at our lawn and the house across the street. When the residents of that home looked back at us, they saw what we wanted them to see. A reminder that appearances were always deceiving. The question at the forefront of my mind was whether I could deceive Kane.

"You should ice that," I told him. His right eye was darkening by the minute. He'd have a shiner for days.

"It won't go away," he replied, clearly referring to more than just his black eye.

"I know. That's why it's best if you move out," I said abruptly before I lost my courage.

One of Kane's dark brows arched, but he remained wholly composed. "I've been thinking the same thing about you."

I frowned. "You know I can't do that."

"Sure you can. And I can help. You know I can."

"That's not your responsibility."

"You're my responsibility," he said matter-of-factly, with a level of command he shouldn't have had at only seventeen years old.

"Damn it, Kane. You don't have to worry about me. It's time for you to start worrying about yourself."

"I hear how he talks to you, and you know he's not good with the kids."

"You're not in a position to comment on my marriage or how my children are raised."

"If not me, then who?" He shoved his hand through his hair. His strands were darker than his siblings', more jet than chocolate.

"Stop it!" I snapped. "This isn't a debate."

His jaw clenched. So did his fists. He had a temper, my boy. Reining it in would always be a challenge for him.

My own hands fisted tight, too. Because I wanted to explain why he needed to leave for his safety, but I knew he wouldn't leave his siblings or me for his own sake. I had to make him believe that leaving would benefit me.

"You think too hard," he said tightly. "And too long. You should've planned this speech a year ago and kept it in your pocket. What's it going to be? Leave because it's best for you, or leave because it's best for me?"

His insight was incisive and put me on the defensive. "Don't talk to me that way! I'm your mother, and you will show me the respect I deserve."

"You make that kinda hard when you stay with an asshole because he's rich."

"Don't sit there and judge me! You have it easy. You get what you want when you want it."

"What do I get besides punched?"

My hand went to my throat, my fingers finding a racing pulse. I didn't want to fight with my son or wound him in any way, but neither could I bear to be wounded. I hadn't yet healed myself. "You're a manager at work and make good money. You start at Fordham in the fall, and you've never needed a car – girls are lining up to drive you wherever you need to go. You don't need me anymore."

"So, I'm a burden."

"I didn't say that!" I took a deep breath, striving for composure. He was wily, my son. And contrary and argumentative. I knew he baited Lucas on purpose, which didn't make my husband's actions acceptable by any measure, but . . . dealing with an angry teenager was hard. "It's not in our best interests for you to remain in this household. Can't you feel the constant stress and strain? It's wearing me down, Kane. It's not good for you or the children."

"So, I'm the source of all your problems."

My gaze narrowed, and he held it momentarily, then bowed his head. At that moment, I saw the child he still was, and my heart broke. "There are things I need to finish here before I can leave. I'm not walking away with nothing. I've been left that way before, as you know. Never again. If you want to blame someone for our circumstances, blame your father. He's the one who put us in this situation."

A few more years. Once Darius turned eighteen, I could leave with all I'd earned.

"You know," Kane said quietly, "I blamed my dad until it got too exhausting to keep going. You can't let it go, though. You're prepared to put up with Lucas to even the score with a man who couldn't give a shit. And you're willing to kick your son out to keep your marriage going long enough to make it financially advantageous."

"You don't know what I've sacrificed to keep the peace this long!" I stood, unable to contain my agitation any longer. My arms crossed.

"Then tell me."

"Never!" I hissed. "If knowing it's been hard isn't enough for you, the details won't make a difference."

He looked at me with both brows raised, defiant and skeptical, a young man doubting a woman because he couldn't possibly relate or commiserate.

"I've got some money put away," I told him. "I could help you –"

"I can take care of myself. I've been doing it a long time now."

"That's not fair!"

"Neither is what you're doing now. I need Darius, Ramin and Rosana as much as they need me, but that's not a consideration, is it?" He stood and turned his back to me, walking away with his long-legged stride, the dog at his side. "Gimme a couple of hours, and I'll be out of here."

"You don't have to leave tonight!" I protested, my anxiety swelling. He'd been my anchor for so long, my motivation. Would I be stable now if I hadn't had him to care for?

Pausing, he turned to look at me. Cotton looked at me, too, with a judgment I resented. Kane waited patiently, stone-faced. I could feel the pull of his longing and hope. The urge to go to him and take him into my arms was nearly overwhelming. I swayed a little on my feet, fighting it. Sending mixed messages for my own sake would be wrong. He couldn't stay here; it wasn't safe. I couldn't leave.

With a heavy sigh, he finally gave up and left me, taking the stairs two at a time, silent where his brother had been loud.

He'd forgive me one day. As soon as Lucas was gone, he'd see how things would be moving forward, and this would all be behind us.

Reaching a hand out, I tried to break my fall as my knees gave out, and I sank onto the sofa.

Would I ever forgive myself?

12

ALIYAH

Now

I'LL BE THERE IN ABOUT 15 MINS.

My fingers tremble as I read Ryan's text on my phone.

I hurry to the mirror to check my lipstick and hair, anticipation thrumming through my veins. It bleeds away when I see the woman reflected at me. Even the ECRA+ cosmeceutical line can't hide the horrors revealed in the depths of my gaze. My past was carefully contained in a tightly sealed vault, but it's been breached by crossing paths with Alex Gallagher again, and I can no longer ignore it.

It's been a week since I attacked Alex, and I haven't heard a word from him or the police. I don't feel any relief at the silence, only a looming anxiety that increases in weight with every hour that passes. In quiet moments, I feel the chill of inevitability. Something vital inside me fiercely rejects any possibility of revisiting the memories of degradation and torment. Other recollections, however, refuse to be suppressed. I can't stop re-examining my life as if watching a movie that auto-plays repeatedly. It's driving me to madness.

I want to celebrate what I did to Alex Gallagher. I've allowed myself to recall how it felt to penetrate soft flesh with all the mighty force of hatred and how it felt to penetrate soft flesh with all the mighty force of hatred and vengeance. It's a luxury I relish. I close my eyes and sway to the music of his screams reverberating through my mind. It's infuriating that I could be considered a criminal and forced into exposing my private pain to explain the justice of my actions.

Fluffing my bleached hair, I mentally note to schedule time at the salon. And the spa. And with my plastic surgeon. I can't look haggard or haunted. Not at work and certainly not at the dinner Lily has planned for my family. That woman already thinks she has control. If I show any weakness, she'll lunge for my jugular. And Amy. I've never met her family – they likely disowned her as I long to – but they must have good genes because she remains lovely despite how hard she hits the bottle.

It's disturbing how physically alike the two women are. Assessing myself, I wonder what it is about me that my sons see in their wives. It's well documented that men marry women like their mothers. I try to picture how I would look if I wore my naturally dark hair because it can't be our personalities that connect us. Neither of my daughters-in-law has my fortitude or tenacity. Both rely too much on the appeal of their beauty and sexuality. Lily is cunning, I'll give her that, but her currency is that face of hers – and Kane's all-consuming obsession.

I turn away from the mirror, absently smoothing the cream sweater dress that hugs my curves. I use my sexuality, too, but to dominate, not surrender. It's a helpful distraction. When men are aroused, they rarely notice that they're being outwitted. They can't use the brains between their ears and legs simultaneously.

Of course, I probably destroyed Alex's second brain, leaving him hyper-focused on his hatred for Paul and me. He must think we've ruined him in every way possible. If only that were true. If only he were dead.

The agony of waiting for the other shoe to drop is suffocating, and I suck in a deep breath of air. I can't lose my edge now when I most need it.

My stiletto heels sink deeply into my office carpet's thick pad. The other offices have thin industrial pile, which would be much easier to walk on, but I need extravagant surroundings to convey wealth. Wealth is power. Having the largest executive office isn't enough because being a woman puts me at an immediate disadvantage. Colleagues and partners inevitably attempt to turn to Kane for direction and approval. I wanted us to appear as equals, with side-by-side connecting offices, but he refused to have an office altogether.

He has the luxury of appearing egalitarian because he's a tall, dark and extremely attractive *man*. Lowering himself looks like strength. I have to work twice as hard just to get my due.

I pause, debating whether to sit at my desk or settle in the seating area. Do I want to look like I'm hard at work – which I was – or create the effect of intimacy by sitting in one of the club chairs? They offer protection of a sort and room for only one. Unlike the long sofa in Alex Gallagher's office where he enjoyed raping me. I knew he would have stared at that sofa from his desk and relived those hours with great relish. I couldn't bear to have such a handy horizontal surface in my workspace.

So many innocent pleasures and conveniences are forever lost to me. Would a district attorney or jury ever grasp that?

Walking over to my desk, I pick up the phone receiver and tell my admin to wave Ryan in when he arrives. I'm holding out hope that he can help me with the problem of Lily. I have too much on my plate now: Alex, Lily, Amy's return to work after years of drinking herself into daily stupors, plus the hoped-for Seattle research facility I've been working on in secret. I resent having to put the latter aside for now – it's time-sensitive – but Lily's effect on Kane makes her a wild card. I need an ace in my back pocket if she influences my son to meddle with Baharan.

She knows too much about plans I've guarded with the utmost secrecy for me to assume she's only interested in spending Kane's money on indulgences.

I'm relieved when the knock finally comes on my door. "Come in."

Ryan steps into view and offers me a half-smile. I spend a split-second debating whether I should remain seated before rising to my feet. Power versus vulnerability is an age-old female stratagem.

But there is something about Ryan that is just so . . . easy. He's affable and handsome, a man comfortable in his skin, a trait that naturally puts others at ease. I try imagining him with Lily and find I can't do it. She's a viper, while his wife, Angela, is –

I pause mid-step, my thoughts tumbling. I think of Angela's long dark hair and lithe body. Not as close a resemblance to Lily as Amy bears but notable, nevertheless. A type, perhaps; most men have one. But still . . . Why didn't I see it before I approached Ryan with my concerns? How is it that neither he nor Kane ever mentioned that Ryan dated Lily first? Of course, Kane became infuriated if I even tried to broach the subject of his wife, and Ryan was immediately forthcoming when the topic was finally raised, but to find out only recently . . . ? Is there something to be read into the timing?

Of course, it could be argued that Ryan moved on from his breakup with Lily to marry someone else, something Kane couldn't do, but that doesn't mean Lily doesn't have a lingering hold over him.

At least the Lily he used to know, not the imposter.

It was either a terrible mistake turning to Ryan or a stroke of genius. Who knows? Maybe he'll be enraged and as invested as I am in exposing her.

Quietly, of course. We don't want any scandals. Our partner, Gideon Cross, won't stand for any negative press, and we need him to make ECRA+ a success.

My pulse races, and I feel momentarily dizzy. I'm lying across the knife edge of a panic attack at every waking moment. I've woken in the middle of the night, drenched in icy sweat. I can't take any more shocks or surprises.

"Hi," Ryan says, closing the door behind him.

My chin lifts as my shoulders roll back. "It's good to see you, Ryan. Thank you for coming over. I know how busy you are."

Ryan's company, LanCorp, is one of the bigger rivals to Gideon Cross's Cross Industries. I was so surprised when Kane told me he'd approached Cross to partner with. He knows Ryan and Cross's rivalry is a personal one. As untrustworthy as Kane's father Paul, Cross's father destroyed fortunes and lives in a notorious Ponzi scheme. The Landons lost everything in the aftermath, and Ryan resents the success Cross has attained since. I see now why Kane could be so careless with Ryan's friendship – Ryan once stood in the way of his being with Lily, which might yet be a sore point.

There is something about Ryan's slight smile that unnerves me. I can't put my finger on it, but there's something distant about his demeanor. He's looking past me as he gestures toward the seating area, acting as if he's hosting my visit rather than the reverse. Midtown is displayed to prime advantage through the adjacent glass walls of my corner office, but his attention should be on me.

My spine straightens, and with my jaw clenched, I choose my desk chair instead, forcing him to follow. I settle in and back, crossing my legs. I don't prompt him because silence will do the job for me.

"I saw Lily the other day," he begins, unbuttoning his jacket and adjusting his slacks to sit. When he meets my gaze, his face is somber. His wavy brown hair is slightly disarrayed, perhaps by a stiff breeze – or restless fingers.

My tongue wets dry lips. *The other day* . . . yet this is the first I learn of it. I don't know why, but I thought he would report back to me more quickly. "Is it her? The woman you dated?"

"Yes." His head tilts slightly. "And no. She's changed. But is that unexpected? I'm not the man I was when she and I were together."

"How do you explain the recovered body you helped identify as her?" I ask tightly because he's pensive, which I don't like. At all.

"I don't have an answer for that yet," he says mildly, crossing one ankle atop the opposite knee.

"Are you trying to find an answer?" It takes tremendous effort to keep my tone even. He's too relaxed. He lacks the urgency he displayed when I presented the information to him. His response is . . . surreal.

"No, because I know where the answer is – it's with Kane." Ryan's dark gaze holds mine. "He signed for the body's release and was responsible for it. If she was buried, the body could be exhumed for forensic examination."

"*If?*"

He shrugs. "He might've chosen cremation."

"You don't seem concerned either way," I snap.

"Maybe the body would help us identify who Lily is, but if our sole motive in investigating her is to protect Kane, that's not our place. He knows what you and I know. If he doesn't feel threatened, we have to trust his intuition. As next of kin, he almost certainly knows more than we do."

"Ryan . . ." I stare at him in dismay. "I can't believe I'm the only one who sees a problem here. Kane is incapable of seeing a threat because he's delusional. He's wanted his wife back all these years, and he doesn't care how that happened. He's not in his right mind, so to say he's responsible for his decisions does him no favors. It can't be coincidence that there were two women with the exact same tattoo, and one was fished out of the ocean while the other is sleeping with my son!"

"I can't explain that, or why she's taken on so many identities. I can only tell you that the woman I met the other day checks all the boxes. I believe she's the woman we knew before. Yes, there are differences – defenses, even – but this is the first time we've crossed paths since we ended our relationship, so some awkwardness isn't unexpected. As for whose body was fished out of the ocean . . . It's a mystery to us – although possibly not to Kane – and maybe that's best."

I'm speechless.

"That said," he goes on, "Kane's marriage may be none of my business, but Baharan is. Having an additional majority voice is something to keep an eye on. Which is why I'm going to petition to join the board."

It takes me a long minute to gather my scattered thoughts. I don't understand his reasoning at all. "Well, that's . . . that's great news."

"I'm glad you still think so."

For years, I've thought Ryan's business acumen would be a tremendous asset to Baharan. Still, I understood that LanCorp was his primary focus. "I'll begin talking to the others –"

"I've already spoken to everyone," he interjects. "You and Kane are left, and he and I are having lunch after this. I'll let him know then."

"Let him know," I repeat, astonished. Preemptive corporate maneuverings are never a good omen. "As if his agreement isn't necessary."

"Why would he object?" he shoots back. "Why would you? You've both asked me to take a seat before, so there was no reason to anticipate any resistance. Do you have an objection now?"

My breathing quickens along with my heartbeat. He's shifted from calm to calculating in the blink of an eye. Those who are easygoing are often underestimated. I've never made that mistake with Ryan before. LanCorp wouldn't be what it is if a fierce competitor wasn't hidden beneath his civility. I just never considered he'd have cause to conflict with me.

My brow lifts in silent query, meeting his challenge with one of my own. I don't know why it feels like Lily turned him against me somehow. What could she have said? Would she tell him about my ties in Seattle?

Or is this simply a ploy to get closer to her? Maybe he can't admit that urge. Perhaps keeping it professional is the only way he'll allow himself to pursue her. Or the only way he can, considering he's married.

With a push of my foot, I spin my chair around, taking in the expansive view he found so fascinating moments ago. His enmity for Gideon Cross is so well known; it's mentioned in every news piece that covers him. I thought the ECRA+ partnership with Cross Industries would sway him to join the board, but that wasn't a compelling enough reason, and he declined. That Lily's stake in Baharan matters more to Ryan than his infamous feud disturbs me greatly.

Maybe Ryan isn't so amenable to Kane taking Lily away from him now that he's seen her again for the first time since their breakup. Baharan is a way to hurt them both.

Damn it. Ryan's motives are now as murky as Lily's.

"No, of course, there's no objection," I assure him, dropping my foot to the floor to stop my revolution. "I'm literally spinning with delight."

The smile on his lips doesn't reach his eyes.

And I have another problem to add to the rest.

13

LILY

"*YOU'RE GLOWING.*"

I've always loved the sound of your voice. It mesmerizes me in the way of a snake charmer enthralled by the cobra. I know the strike will come, that piercing of fang into vulnerable flesh followed by the burning sting of poison. I know and still love . . .

The wind roars with the same fury I feel inside me, turmoil that whips my hair across my face and scatters my tears to fuse with the rain. The sea heaves beneath us, but you appear strong and graceful amidst the storm while my palms bleed from gripping the lines for balance.

"*I wish that glow came from personal triumph,*" *you go on,* "*but no. You're glowing because a man professed his love so you'd let him ejaculate inside you whenever he wants. I raised you for more.*"

"*You didn't raise me at all,*" *I argue, shivering violently as the windchill sinks into the marrow of my bones.*

In truth, I've been chilled for days. Ever since I realized you'd ordered a hit on the man I love. If not for Rogelio's overprotective surveillance, Kane would be dead now. I can't allow you to try again. Just watching my love go about his day, blissfully happy and unaware that you wanted to slit his throat in broad daylight, is too much for me to bear. I can't eat. Can't sleep. Fear is all I know.

"Be fair, Araceli. I led by example." Your smile is brilliant and beautiful, even though it doesn't spark warmth in your luminous gaze. It's those emerald eyes that reinforce the truth: you *will* kill him. The bloodlust and fury you feel spark a mad light in your pupils. You usually hide that insanity so well most don't see it. Even I've searched for it in the past and couldn't find it. But a vengeful jealousy seethes inside you now, so toxic it's cracked your perfect facade.

"Telling you how to survive is lazy parenting," you tell me. *"When a mother's done her job right, her children are self-sufficient. I showed you what it looks like to thrive as a woman in this world."*

My head shakes in denial. "You taught me to take, use and exploit. But I'm not like you. I don't enjoy hurting people."

Your laughter is like bells and echoes beautifully, like a call to worship. Even the raging wind adores it, swirling the musicality of your dark humor around me, amplifying it until it seems as if the storm itself laughs at me. *"You're hurting the man you profess to love. You know I won't let you waste yourself on him, but you're selfish. You want what you want, even if it means he's going to die."*

Words are weapons, and you always know how to use precisely the right ones.

Your dark hair flows in a streaming banner. Your silk cargo jumpsuit of flame red is pressed against your curves by the wind. You are a siren of the seas, pulling the very fabric of my world to the shore so it can be ripped to shreds.

"You have to steal happiness to have it, Araceli. The world won't give you joy – you have to take it."

"You believe that because you're twisted, but it's not true."

"I would never lie to you. You're the one lying to yourself. Romantic love is a myth. Only a mother's love is real. Only a mother makes sacrifices selflessly. Every other relationship is a negotiation of self-focused benefits and compromises to achieve them."

"He would do anything for me!" My words are ripped from my lips and strewed to the high winds. La Tempête is at her best on calm seas, and I wonder if the same could be said of me. I feel battered by living while you thrive with adversity. Only Kane has ever been a shelter for me, but you want me to see him as the eye of the hurricane, the most dangerous place I could be.

"Val would do anything for you," you correct. *"Not because he loves you or me but because he chooses to be responsible for you."*

"Valon Laska is a monster!" And so are you . . .

"He's a monster on a leash, and you're missing the point." The edges of your crimson smile grow sharp as blades. "Would Kane choose to be in love with you? Would he choose to betray his closest friend and throw away everything he's worked toward? My God, Araceli. What do you find attractive about that? He has no loyalty, no spine."

My thoughts are as turbulent as the savage ocean because you've twisted me into knots like you always do, weaving your truths with my reality. Yes, helpless fury eats at Kane; I feel it every time he touches me. He hates that he can't control how he feels about me, hates that he's acting in ways he regrets. And don't I feel the same? I've longed to walk away from him, but I can't. Or is it that I just don't want to?

"Don't you see?" You press the point, smelling the blood seeping from the wounds you've inflicted. "Love is a form of coercion, and you're valuing what a man does under duress rather than what he does by his own will."

I can't deny the truth of what you're saying. I have only one defense: "We're happy together."

And you will never comprehend that. You'll never help me choose a wedding dress or indulge in a mother-in-law dance with my groom or smile beside me in photos of my magical day. You were so proud of me for finding and siphoning the money you'd hidden away in numerous offshore accounts, but putting someone's happiness before my own? Death would be preferable in your mind.

"You're two people who've become so uninteresting you bore yourselves," she snaps. "He can't make you less lonely. He can't fill the void in you that comes from not liking yourself enough to be content alone. He's a shard of glass masquerading as a bandage, and that shard is needling deeper into your heart with every breath. He's a splinter, and you're trying to protect the thing that will cause you to bleed out."

It's the first time you've ever suggested experience with heartbreak, but I knew you'd suffered it at least once in your lifetime. Not heartbreak the way others experience it. You wanted someone once and couldn't have him. Was he my father? Is he dead now?

Did you kill him like you're threatening to kill Kane? Like I have to kill you?

"The snake
which cannot
shed its skin
must die."

—Friedrich Nietzsche

14

LILY

THE PENTHOUSE MISSES WITTE WHEN HE'S GONE, AMPLIFYING HIS absence until I feel it keenly. Not in the way I feel yours, my love, but it's a noticeable void, nevertheless.

Still, it's an opportunity for me to get together with Rogelio and the rest of the team: Tovah, our costumer; Salma, our makeup and hairstylist; and Lacy, the one who requisitions what we need. Their titles are misleading, as all of them are multihyphenates. What makes us work is that any of us can step into nearly any role as needed, from driving a getaway car to occasional minor larceny.

As I walk the mirrored halls to reach the front doors, I'm still unsettled by my recent and all-too-familiar nightmare. I shouldn't have indulged in a mid-morning nap, but I'm always tired lately, weighted by grief, guilt and regret. Still, I know better than to risk sleep when you're not beside me. You calm me and make me feel safe. My mother never understood how essential you are to my well-being.

Or maybe she knew and hated you for it.

As I move past the living room, I absorb the feel of our home. Should I tell you that I sense a heartbeat in the penthouse? It reverberates through me, matching rhythm with my pulse. Or perhaps it's a measure of time, like the ticking of a clock's second hand.

Is it counting down? If so, to what?

Witte has run out to pick up the ingredients he'll need for whatever he's decided to serve for dinner. He's become somewhat adventurous with his meal planning in recent days.

Lacy reaches the door before I do, opening it to reveal Rogelio. His face, somber as usual, brightens when he sees us. He hugs Lacy tightly as if they don't get together often, which I know they do. When he steps back, he looks at me and studies me thoroughly. His expression softens further.

"Come here," he says with his arms open.

I step into his embrace with a sigh. He's dressed for work at Baharan, and the feel of his suit material beneath my cheek is so familiar. So is his scent and the shape of his body. This is what family is, this feeling of welcome and care. I hope one day I can share these important people with you. They're the part of my past I'm proud of.

"You look exhausted, *querida*."

"Do I? I'll have to work on that." I keep my tone light and teasing because I don't want them to know I'm struggling. They worry enough about me as it is.

"They fuck like the world is ending," Lacy offers drily. "I'd be exhausted, too."

"Lacy!" My face heats, which makes them both laugh. Being separated from the family I built has been the hardest of all the changes I've made since you found me crossing the street in Midtown.

"You two head back to the sitting room," Lacy says. "Rogelio's already told me about Alex Gallagher, so I'll wait here for Tovah and Salma."

Frowning, I ask, "Who's Alex Gallagher?"

Rogelio takes my hand. "Come on. We should sit down before I start."

We walk back to the master suite, holding hands as siblings do when they're young. When I first realized Rogelio viewed me as a surrogate sister, I didn't know how to accept such affection. It means the world to me now, and I'm so grateful to have him in my life.

I sit on the deep-cushioned sapphire velvet sofa, curling my legs under me and draping my arm along the backrest. Rogelio shrugs out of his jacket and tosses it across the ottoman before taking the seat beside me. He offers me a crooked smile, then he starts talking.

The news is mixed. He's happy to tell me there was no evidence of a boat or any communication with my mother on either Val's phone or in his cloud storage. He says I can live happily ever after right here with my prince, atop the tower that stretches so high into the sky it sways and moans like a ship on swells.

Despite the sudden, consuming pain that assails me, I exhale with exaggerated relief and even manage a quick smile. The agony is so intense it briefly darkens my vision. It isn't right that I mourn my mother so profoundly while knowing who she was and what she did.

And that I'm the one who ended her life.

But I can't help it.

I glance sideways at Rogelio. He's one of the most intuitive people I've ever met, and he knows me so well. Can I hide my grief from him? It's a relief to find that he's not looking at me.

You would know how I feel, my love. You've always seen what's buried in the darkest heart of me.

Then Rogelio hits me with the news of your mother.

By the time he's done outlining Alex Gallagher's assaults on Aliyah and why she never publicly accused him of rape, I'm deeply unsettled. Limiting her to a caricature, a villain, was so much easier. Now I have the backstory to her behavior. It doesn't negate the hurtful things she's done, but what she suffered is something no one should suffer for any reason.

"We have to do something about Gallagher," Rogelio says.

"Do what?"

"Rogelio's right." Lacy interrupts as she enters the room with Salma and Tovah. "Guys like Gallagher don't change unless you castrate them."

"Aliyah already took care of that, so you'll have to be more imaginative."

They all look grim. And determined.

Salma's dressed in jeans and a knotted T-shirt emblazoned with the members of Mötley Crüe. Her thick dark hair frames a face that is artfully and flawlessly made up. Still, I see the young girl she was when I found her, before I started the transformation meant to be reparation for what my mother had taken from her.

Tovah's petite form is wrapped in a bright aqua dress. Her matching heels are precariously tall, but she's still shorter than the rest of us. What she lacks in stature, she makes up for in sheer energy. Like all of us, she's been broken, too. A child who lost her father to my mother's twisted sense of right and wrong.

"Not that Gallagher isn't a piece of shit," I say, "but he's none of our business."

"He's very much your business," Rogelio argued, "because he can impact Baharan if Aliyah runs into any trouble with the law."

"No, he can't. This is a private matter between Aliyah and him. We shouldn't even know about it," I scold. "And if you think I care more about what he could do to Baharan than what he did to Aliyah, you don't know me as well as I thought."

"That's not what I meant."

"I didn't think so," I say coolly. "You're being rash. You're focused on how you feel rather than what's best for all of us."

"And what is it you think I feel?"

"It doesn't matter what any of us feel about it, Rogelio. The safety of the people in this room should be our priority. Always."

"We know how to protect each other," Tovah interjects.

"You were the boss when we were hunting Laska," Rogelio retorts. "Now, we've all got a say."

My brows lift. "If you're going to do whatever you want, why mention it to me?"

"Because we need you!" he snaps.

"Let's calm down," Salma says, dropping onto one of the wings of the sofa. "Arguing will get us nowhere."

"Where do you want this to go?" I ask.

Rogelio shouldn't be sleeping with Aliyah. He was only supposed to covertly share the trackable passcodes to Baharan's security system. We had to know what she was doing and keep her out of any files or information where she could cause harm. I won't question Rogelio's methods or personal motives, but it's undeniably messy now that Aliyah's confided in him.

"I can't ignore this," he says firmly.

"None of us are ignoring it." Lacy stands behind Salma with her arms crossed. "This is exactly the sort of thing we've trained to handle."

"I'm feeling blindsided," I accuse. "We trained to eliminate Val, and he's gone. The job's over. Now, you've gotten together to decide we're going after strangers, like Alex Gallagher?"

"It's a justifiable takedown, and we've got the skills. Why waste what we've learned?" Lacy's pixie-like face and adorable freckles contrast jarringly with what she's saying.

"We're not wasting anything. We accomplished what we set out to, and we're done. You're supposed to travel the world now and fill up your memory book. And you, Rogelio, are supposed to meet a nice girl, start a family and stop fucking my mother-in-law!"

His dark gaze narrows. "I don't comment on your personal choices, so don't tread on mine. Or Lacy's. She'll go when she's ready. I'm not going anywhere. So, let's figure out what our family looks like without Laska in the picture."

"I was hoping it'd be normal. You know . . . holidays, celebrations and the like."

"This is normal for us, *querida*."

"So, my mother wins," I say flatly. "We stay sick and twisted and never break free."

"We break the cycle for others," Lacy says with a hard glint in her blue eyes.

"We can just live our lives." My gaze rakes over all of them. "Can't we?"

Rogelio gives me an arch look. "We're already vigilantes. Let's avenge someone else for a change."

"Listen." Lacy's glance takes in all of us. "You guys know I'm not a fan of Aliyah. But what happened to her makes my skin crawl, and knowing Rogelio, he hasn't told us the worst of it."

I push to my feet in a rush, too anxious to sit. Rounding the sofa, I stand in front of the windows.

"Hey," Tovah says behind me. "Don't shut us out."

"I'm not. I can't." I sigh heavily.

"Are you having a pity party?" Salma needles me.

"Maybe. And I won't apologize for it, so fuck off."

There's a heartbeat of silence, then they all laugh. The stiffness in my shoulders loosens a little. I inhale deeply and face them.

"We don't have to attack Gallagher physically." Rogelio shoots a warning look at Lacy that cuts off any protest. "We can do a lot of damage virtually. Wipe out his bank accounts, ruin his credit rating, rack up parking tickets –"

"We're not doing anything illegal. He's the criminal. Let's prove it and let the law deal with him."

"He deserves worse than a cage," Lacy counters.

"Karma's already been sharpening her claws on this guy," I remind her.

"She's right." Tovah nods her agreement, her chocolate curls bouncing against her back. "We don't need to punish him."

"We just need to make sure he gets the justice he deserves," Salma says.

Lacy deflates with a long exhalation. "Okay."

Rogelio gifts me with one of his lopsided smiles.

"I'm going along with this for *you*," I tell him grimly. "Because Aliyah's only going to be grateful for a second. Then she's going to remember that you're a threat."

"I know my days at Baharan are numbered, but that was the case regardless."

"It won't be enough to fire you, Rogelio. By proving that Alex Gallagher is guilty, we also insulate you. You'll have information that makes you too dangerous to attack."

His lips thin into a tight line. "I haven't lowered my guard, *querida*."

I think he believes that. But I don't.

15

WITTE

IT WAS SO GOOD TO SEE YOU TODAY, NICKY. I MISSED THE FEEL OF YOU inside me. Please come again soon. ;-)

With a swipe of my thumb, I close the messages on my mobile. But pushing aside thoughts of my lover isn't so simple.

I exhale in a rush. I can still smell Danica, recall the silk of her skin as she pressed her curves against my body, feel the clasp of her pussy around my cock.

Before this afternoon, I'd never visited Danica during a workday. Our time together has always been limited to my Saturday afternoon and Sundays off. But since Mrs Black's reappearance, our time together has become sporadic.

My assistance has been needed at all hours, every day. While my employer never asked me to forego my personal time, I made the adjustment because I want to be nearby.

During Mr and Mrs Black's recent brief holiday at their Greenwich house, I spent over a week with Danica. It's the longest stretch of time we've spent together, as I spend my four weeks of annual holiday with my daughter. Those uninterrupted days with my lover changed the dynamic of our relationship. Incompatibilities can be glossed over or hidden with infrequent dating. Now, we know it's possible to spend days together and still want more.

She's been the only woman I've dated for several years. With so little free time

She's been the only woman I've dated for several years. With so little free time to myself, I am not inclined to seek other relationships. Besides, Danica White is a singular woman, and it would be pointless to imagine another could compete with her.

It's decidedly out of character to have dropped in on her today. I fought the urge to call her, then gave in. While we are, de facto, monogamous – to my knowledge – we've never discussed exclusivity. I don't want to know if she's intimate with anyone else. Dangerously sentimental, I know.

For a brief spell, I wondered why a brilliantly intelligent, cultured, stunningly beautiful woman would share her time with someone more committed to his work and employer than anything else. It was Lily who made me understand and feel the echoes of heartbreak. I felt them again today when I arrived at Danica's condo and found her baking cookies in bare feet, worn jeans, and one of my dress shirts I left behind. Her glossy white hair was piled high in a messy bun, and my tightly knotted shirt supported her full breasts sans bra.

"Nicky!" She greeted me with a wide, delighted smile. And I hugged her so firmly her feet left the floor.

A deep voice interrupts my reverie. "Witte. Is everything all right?"

I sigh heavily. The sands in the hourglass are slipping at an ever-faster pace.

Turning to face Mr Black, I slide my mobile into my pocket. "Yes. Everything's fine. What do you need?"

He walks to where I stand near the living room. Since dinner, he's changed into black silk pyjama trousers and a matching dressing gown, and his dark hair is still damp from a shower. There's an ease to his movements that I've only noticed recently.

"Nothing now. But it's been a while since we enjoyed a drink in the library. Up for one tonight?"

I smile. "I'd like that very much."

We walk side by side, our steps in tandem.

"Has Mrs Black retired for the evening?"

"No, she's cleansing her crystals." He glances aside at me from his greater height, a broad smile on his face. With a shrug, he laughs. "It's a process. Sea salt, rose water, and I can't remember what else before she lines them up on a windowsill to soak up the full moon. It's been a ritual of hers as long as I've known her."

I return his smile and marvel at how much he's changed. He's a new man, one I don't know but hope to. "There are numerous crystals in the penthouse."

"Yes, she'll be busy."

When we enter the library, he moves straight to the bar trolley. The spire of the Empire State Building is framed by the window at one end of the long, narrow room. At the other end, Central Park is a black void in the heart of the brightly lit city. The walls on either side are lined with black bookcases filled with colourful volumes. Many of the books are Mrs Black's. She has always been here, living with us, even before she returned.

I turn on the fireplace with the remote control, then pause to study the photo above the mantel. It's a large photo of Lily's pale, slender back and her extraordinary tattoo. Since I've been in his employ, I haven't known Mr Black to photograph anything. No subject or moment was deemed worthy of preserving for the future during the years she was absent. But he captured his wife on film many times. I know where his camera is. I should remove it from storage so he can resume another aspect of his former life.

Carrying over two tumblers of fine single malt scotch, he hands one to me before settling into one of the wingback chairs flanking the fireplace. We've sat here together often, mostly in silence, ending the day with a nightcap and our private thoughts. He would often stare at the photo of his wife's elegant back. I'd think to myself how unhealthy it was to focus on her turned away from him like that, forever in the act of leaving him.

"Lily was right," he says. "Rogelio figured out how my mother got her hands on Rampart's report. She logged into my terminal the day we left for Greenwich. I called Giles Rampart today, and he confirmed she stopped by and questioned him."

I roll the liquor around in my mouth, then swallow. "A regrettable lapse on his part."

"I didn't beat him up over it. My mother has a way of getting what she wants. He told her that meddling would only screw things up, which obviously didn't deter her."

"I'm sorry." Perhaps he'll never know how much. It pains me that his family undermines him at every opportunity, despite everything he's done for them. Maybe they resent his emotional unavailability, but he was dead to everything while his wife was gone.

"So am I. But I brought my mother into Baharan because I knew she'd do everything she could to make it succeed. Can I blame her for acting exactly the way I hoped she would?"

"You can blame her for being selfish in a way that risks your happiness."

Mr Black takes a drink, his mouth working as he savours the fine scotch. He contemplates the fire, then looks up at the photo of his wife. "God, I was furious when I got off the phone. I don't care how much my mother wants to protect Baharan, that she wouldn't consider protecting my wife more important . . . I know it's been a long time since she cared for me, but the lack of simple human kindness just blows my mind."

I don't know what to say. I love him as much as I do my daughter, and he isn't mine. I don't understand how Aliyah can be so heartless towards her own blood.

He stares into the amber liquid in his glass. "And the fact that she turned to Ryan first instead of approaching me. To her credit, she didn't know about Lily and Ryan. She assumed he'd do what was best for me, which she expected would also be in her best interests."

It troubles me that such a talented, promising young man should be cursed with a family who can't love him. I don't know if that neglect has the power to hurt him anymore, but it's unpleasant, nevertheless. "And will he do what's best for you?"

"He's decided he wants a board seat."

The tower creaks in the evening wind, swaying imperceptibly, yet I could swear I feel it. "At your mother's request?"

"Not according to him."

"What would be the possible ramifications?"

He sighs. "I'm sure he'll be a tremendous asset, whatever his motivations are."

"Do you disagree with his decision?"

"Well, that's the thing, Witte." He looks at me. "I really don't care."

"About Mr Landon's motives?"

"Any of it."

A chill courses down my back. "You've dedicated tremendous time and energy to Baharan. The company is successful because of you."

"Do I want to fight over it? I don't know. Maybe I got what I needed out of it. I have this" – he gestures around at the penthouse – "and somehow convinced you to take a chance on me. And at the end of the day, I married that girl with the beach house in Greenwich and that's all I wanted. That's my biggest success."

I recall how Mr Black described their first meeting: *I never thought I'd meet anyone who lived like that, who had friends who could afford cars like that. It was like something out of a movie.* It was the turning point of his life when he revised all his plans and dreams. But that future he envisioned was never fully realized because shortly after their marriage, Lily was presumed dead. Mr Black inherited what she intended him to, but he always suspected there were additional assets he didn't know about. Which seems to have been confirmed in recent days as items have been ordered by and delivered to Mrs Black without using household monies. "What are you saying?"

"It's not necessary to battle my family to have what I want, so why bother?"

"Because of Mrs Black's war chest?" I use the same phrase he did last week when we became aware that his wife was making purchases with private funds.

"It certainly makes the decision easier to reach," he says cheerfully.

Holding my tumbler up, I eye the play of the flames through the liquid. I tell myself I shouldn't worry about Lily. She's competent and cunning. Still, she's also a woman whose presumed death in a boating accident remains a mystery. "Have you discussed your thoughts with Mrs Black?"

"A little. She tells me I should be happy, and if Baharan isn't what I need anymore, I should move on to something else."

"That's very supportive of her."

"It's unexpected," he admits, "considering how she pushed me into it before. But she's different now."

He runs his hand through his hair. He used to wear it shorter, but he's recently had me allow it more length when I trim it. It reminds me now of when we first met.

"Have you questioned her about her past?" I query.

"No. She'll tell me when she's ready."

"And when will that be?"

"When she feels safe enough to."

"Safe from what?" I press, frustrated at his inertia.

"Safe with me," he murmurs. Staring into the fire, he smiles.

16

AMY

I NEVER REALIZED SALTINE CRACKERS TURN INTO PASTE WHEN YOU chew them. Of course, I've never had many occasions to eat the damn things. Being sick to my stomach every morning has changed that. I now have boxes of Saltines on one of my shelves. What pisses me off the most, though, is not being able to have coffee. It still smells delicious, but if I try to have a cup, the urge to vomit is so intense I fear I'll snort puke out of my nose.

I am *not* having another fucking embarrassing scene at work. I relive the last one enough as it is, playing it over and over in my mind until I squirm with embarrassment. I wish I had punched Aliyah in her lying, treacherous face. Then some of the blood on her would've been her own, and I wouldn't keep kicking myself.

And damned if Ramin didn't freak me out with his pregnancy talk the other day. The possibility of being pregnant was so terrifying I ran off to Duane Reade to buy a test. It was negative, as I knew it would be, which left me even more confused. What's causing me to be nauseous all the time?

And Darius. He was so disappointed. He wants us to start trying for a baby and that tugs at my hopes and dreams in a way that's especially painful.

It infuriates me that I can't trust my husband. I feel so alone, without anyone to lean on aside from Ramin, who I want to avoid for the rest of my life. I wish he'd stop texting me.

I've gone back and forth, debating with myself about what I'm feeling and my husband's role in this fiasco, but there are no answers, only clues. Like the locked wooden box at the back of the pantry's bottom shelf. Why is it there? What's in it? If I had more than five minutes to search my house, I'd know more.

The knock at my open office door makes me jump. My heart pounds violently, and I curse the fact that I'm always on edge lately. "For fuck's sake!" I snap before I register who's standing on the threshold.

Kane.

He fills the doorway in a way his brothers can't, completely blocking the sea of cubicles behind him. I could imagine we were alone if I couldn't hear people talking and the incessant clicking of keyboard keys.

He's jacketless, revealing gray suspenders with bloodred stripes that match his tie. I've never had a high opinion of suspenders and figure they're stuffy pretentiousness that Witte pushed onto him, but there's no denying that Kane makes them look sexy as hell. I'm sure there are a dozen ways to use them to tie a woman up before fucking her, and he's probably tried them all.

But abruptly, he comes into focus in a way he hasn't before. Yes, he's very handsome, but Darius is more so. What he has that Darius lacks is confidence; Kane exudes it.

"Do you have a minute?" he asks.

"Of course." I watch as he steps into my office and closes the door. The room is instantly too small.

Now that he has Lily back, there's an ease to his movements and demeanor that is new. He's comfortable and relaxed. Happy.

I brace myself to feel the bitterness and rage I've become used to, but as he takes one of the two chairs in front of my desk, I'm just curious.

If he worries about whether the delicate chair will hold him, he doesn't show it. I have to hand it to Darius. He found just the right selection of minuscule furniture to fool the eye into seeing the office as larger than it is. But Kane's big frame breaks that illusion handily.

"I saw the updated ECRA+ concepts you sent," he begins. As tall as he is, he's supremely comfortable in his skin, even confined in a tight space. "They're very impressive, Amy. No comparison to what we've been using so far. Great work."

"Thank you." My mouth twists in a wry smile. "And thanks for not sounding surprised that I'm good at what I do."

"Amy . . ." He gives me a gently admonishing look like a big brother would. "I saw what you could do before our companies merged. Your suggestions for improving our Baharan channels are also very savvy. I look forward to seeing the consumer response to them."

"Aliyah hasn't approved them."

"Do you need her approval?" he queries, his mouth curved in an acerbic half-smile.

The question seems to cover many things – hell, my whole life. My work, my marriage, myself.

But I stick to business. "Contractually, no."

"Then don't wait for it. You know what you have to do."

Again, I feel like our conversation has hidden significance. I give an awkward shrug because I don't feel like I can or should get into how difficult Aliyah is for me to deal with or what I suspect she's up to. Despite the backbiting and infighting, the family defends itself against external dangers.

"I'll talk to her," he offers as if that's the easiest thing in the world. For him, it probably is. "Tell her you're moving ahead, and I agree that you should."

"I appreciate the support." Sliding my seat back, I cross my legs. My outfit today is an off-the-shoulder, long-sleeved dress of deep purple with a pleated skirt. The nude Rockstud heels on my feet were the only shoes I could pair with it, but the towering height is uncomfortable. I no longer care if I can be as tall as Lily. I just want shoes that don't make me dread standing.

Thinking of Kane's wife, I ask, "How's Lily?"

"Good." He smiles ruefully. "That's the quick answer. Every day gets a little easier. More settled. I'm very fortunate to have a second chance."

"Yes, you really are." I want second chances, too. I hope I get them.

"Listen, Amy . . . I owe you an apology." He exhales in a rush, and it seems like all his confidence deflates. He's not diminished in any way, but he's unexpectedly vulnerable.

I stare at him, unable to find words. He looks perfectly composed, but then I see his hands curl around the armrests until his knuckles turn white.

Swallowing hard, I find my throat is dry. I want to say something to fill the silence, but my brain won't cooperate.

"I know it's far behind us now," he continues, "and it might even be better not to say anything at this point, but you deserve to hear I'm sorry for how I was when we first met and over the past few years."

There's no denying the sincerity in his voice, and I can't help but respond to it. "Well . . . I appreciate that."

He holds my gaze with those fathomless dark eyes. "Being miserable isn't an excuse for being an asshole. You've been gracious when I wasn't worthy of it. Thank you."

My breath leaves me in a rush. For a moment, I wonder if I'm dreaming. Haven't I imagined this scenario a million times? In my head, I've worn a dozen different outfits and been in a dozen other rooms when I heard this apology from Kane. And in those fantasized meetings, I'm filled with triumph as I show him the album of photos on my phone with all the women he's banged. *Look how fucked up you are!* I tell him, laughing.

What the hell was wrong with me that I would think those things? It's like a maniac hijacked my thoughts.

Agitated, I push to my feet and turn away from him, wanting to hide my shame. I stand before the window and look out at the city's ribbons of black town cars and grungy yellow cabs. The sidewalks are clogged with people hurrying to get where they're going.

Somehow, I stopped going anywhere.

"Don't thank me, Kane," I say finally, my voice husky with unshed tears. Maybe it was easier to blame him than to examine myself and my failures. "I wasn't always feeling charitable."

He huffs a laugh. "No, I wouldn't think so."

"But I appreciate the apology." Facing him, I sigh heavily. A weight has been lifted that I shouldn't have been carrying to begin with. "I was confused at first, but I understood when I saw Lily's photo and heard her story. And now, it's all water under the bridge."

He flashes his teeth in a wide smile tinged with relief. For the first time since we met, I feel seen, and I realize how awful it would be if the lens through which he saw me was more intimate than as his brother's wife. I'm already going through that with Ramin, and it's terrible, creepy and so twisted. How could I have wanted that for so long? Why did I obsess about that one night with Kane when Darius satisfies my every need?

Rising, Kane faces me across my tiny desk. "I want to thank you again for being so receptive to Lily. It means a lot to her, I know, and to me."

My arms cross, and I nod slowly, revisiting my motives for reaching out to her. None of them were generous. The irony is that while I focused so tightly on looking like Lily, she and I have much more in common than our looks. I feel like she must: as if I've just awoken to a reality that isn't what I remember. Out of everyone I know, she may be the only one who could possibly understand what I'm feeling and vice versa.

"I'm looking forward to seeing her again when we come over for dinner next week," I tell him. "Maybe we'll plan something then. A spa day or something."

"Yeah, dinner. Fun times." He laughs, and I'm astonished by him. He really is a totally different man.

It shows me it might be possible to be happy amidst the Armands. Maybe. We haven't had a family gathering since Lily returned; before that was my wedding. I was too stupid then to register the tension as sharp as razor wire when the family gets together, and I was too engrossed with Lily.

Now, I'll be watching everyone like a fucking hawk. And learning.

17

ALIYAH

I'M STANDING OVER MY ASSISTANT'S DESK WHEN I SEE KANE STEP OUT of Amy's office. For a long moment, I just stare, registering that her door had been closed and that Kane looks . . . different. His hands are in his pockets, there's a spring in his step, and he's whistling. I blink rapidly to clear the vision of a younger version of my eldest child, but it remains.

He's changed his hair, reverting to the longer length he used to wear. And he's relaxed.

What the hell was he discussing with Amy? With the door closed, no less. Nothing good, that's certain. Those two have avoided even glancing at each other for years now.

Kane catches my eye and pivots smoothly.

I straighten, dig deep and find a smile. "Good morning."

"It's looking good so far," he says breezily, flashing a grin that makes my assistant's pupils turn into little hearts.

I'm not immune to the effect of that careless smile, either. His father's deft wielding of that charm helped build the first iteration of Baharan and lured me into marriage. I haven't seen a trace of Kane's charisma in many years and while part of me is delighted by it, I have other considerations beyond his happiness.

"Do you have a few minutes?" he asks.

"Of course." I gesture toward my executive suite graciously as if I'm not required to accommodate him. I could play a power game and ask Rachel to fit him into my schedule, but it's a game I can't win. Kane will do what he wants. If I want to know what that is, I have to be open to listening on his timetable.

He tilts his head, gesturing for me to lead the way and so I do, my jaw clenching. I don't like it when the members of my family act in ways I don't expect. The world is filled with unpleasant surprises; those closest to home should be open books.

I debate where to sit, then choose my desk. I'm already lowering into my chair when I realize Kane remains standing.

At every opportunity, my son makes it clear he wants to be in my presence as briefly as possible. It's a sharp, painful repudiation that gets my back up.

"What can I help you with?" I ask brusquely. I have other things I'd rather be doing as well.

"Amy's moving ahead with the revised social creative she proposed, for both Baharan and ECRA+, so you'll start seeing them rolling out."

I'm not sure what I expected him to say but that's not it. My brows lift. "Did she ask you to speak for her?"

"No." He stands there, still with his hands in his pockets, and offers nothing more.

"Isn't that why you were in her office? Does she feel like she needs reinforcement?"

"I don't know what she feels. I'm talking about her work, which is exciting."

"Fine. Let's talk about that. I think it's too playful. Pharmaceuticals are serious business."

It's not the strongest argument I could make but I resent having to present one at all. Brand identity has always been under my purview, without complaint – or compliments – from anyone. Now, because of Amy, Kane has an opinion?

His expression turns flat, almost bored. "It's redundant to point out the obvious."

"You've never had a problem with our messaging before. You want me to believe Amy didn't initiate this conversation? I know she can't face me directly."

"Being bullied is never pleasant for anyone."

"Oh . . . wow." It feels like I've taken a punch to the gut. I lean back heavily. "You're criticizing me for protecting everything we've built?"

"Failing to improve how we market ourselves doesn't benefit the company."

"You're making the mistake of looking at the picture from only one angle – Amy's. I used to think she was just a drunk. Now, I've begun to wonder if she's mentally unstable. She's been deteriorating for years but she's changed recently and alarmingly."

He crosses his arms, transforming from relaxed to militant. "So, we rule out good work product based solely on our personnel's private lives? That policy might negate advancements made by a number of our employees."

"Amy isn't an employee, she's *family*. She has our last name. You can't tell me you haven't noticed the change in her."

"*Your* last name," he corrects.

My gaze narrows. "Are you deliberately baiting me?"

"Maybe. But then, you've been trying to bait me into discussing Amy for weeks now and I'm not open to doing that."

"The problem is that you haven't been here to witness her episodes. She's on something. She vomits in the bathroom multiple times a day!"

He arches a brow. "How would you know that? And is this a backdoor way of criticizing me for working from home while my wife recovered from a coma?"

The urge to scream is nearly overwhelming.

"In any case," he continues smoothly, "what does this have to do with the quality of Amy's work?"

"Do you not care about any of us? Is Lily the only person worthy of your concern? You seem to forget she *abandoned* you, too."

"Don't bring my wife into this!" he snaps, unfolding his arms and expanding in a way that's intimidating.

"We have to discuss her at some point, Kane!"

"You want to have this conversation now? Okay."

I watch him take a seat in front of my desk and my heart skips. It's been so long since I was given his time and attention. Since the day he accused me of abandoning him for my own financial gain.

"You're the head of this family," I tell him, carefully modulating my voice to sound calm. "I do what I can, but you're the one everyone listens to. I need you to –"

"No one gives a shit what I think about anything." Kane bends forward with his elbows on his knees. "Except, possibly, Rosana."

"That's not true! Your brothers look up to you. They try to emulate you but can never win your approval."

"They don't have to win anything. If I didn't think they were good at their jobs, they wouldn't have them. I'd tell them that, but since they can't be in the same room with me without being assholes, I don't bother."

I push to my feet, propelled by frustration. "This is your family we're talking about! Being good or bad at anything should have no bearing on how you feel about them."

His gaze narrows. "Bullshit. You were the one who said it was distressing for them to see and hear from me. When I limited contact to cards and gifts on special occasions, those were returned. I don't know what explanation you gave, but when I finally saw them again, they hated my guts and that hasn't changed. Now, you want me to fix a problem you created?"

"That's not –" I stop when he stands abruptly.

"Fair? I felt the same way. But it is what it is. I've done what they allow me to do, which happens to be work-related, so I stay in my lane and I'm telling you now to stay in yours. Leave Amy alone. And my wife is not your concern and never will be." He moves toward the door with an unhurried but combative stride.

"Kane!"

He pauses but keeps his back to me for a long moment. Then he looks at me over his shoulder.

"Tell me . . . do you think I tried to make the best decisions I could for my family?"

He turns slowly to face me. "You probably thought you were doing the right thing."

That's something. To be fallible is to be forgivable.

"Then I'm going to ask you to give me the same benefit of the doubt now." I set my hands on my hips. "Yes, I've been open about my dislike for Amy, but I would have these concerns about *any* employee exhibiting the same signs. We have to be extra cautious. We're vulnerable right now."

His eyes have a merciless chill I swear I can feel. Goosebumps spread across my skin. He's thinking about Lily. I'm thinking about Alex Gallagher. Who the hell knows what Amy is thinking about, but she needs rehabilitation, not responsibility.

"We all have skeletons tucked away in closets we don't want anyone opening," I say quietly. "Amy needs help. She isn't well and I'm concerned."

He studies me with that sharp, shrewd gaze. "Have you discussed any of this with Darius?"

"Not yet. I could use some support." I strive for impassivity.

But something he sees in me softens his demeanor. "If this is one of those times when you believe you're making the best decision, I caution you to tread lightly. If there's anyone Darius holds dear, it's Amy. You may lose them both."

"I will take that risk because the risk Amy presents is greater. She's not in her right mind. She was working with a criminal, Kane! That Laska character they've been talking about on the news. Can you imagine what would have happened if our names and reputations were tied together publicly? We can't have gangsters as clients! It's a blessing that man was killed before Amy had him under contract. If Gideon Cross were ever to find out, he would end our collaboration and ruin us."

Obvious tension gripped Kane shortly after I started talking and I'm relieved he's starting to take me seriously. If I can't get him on my side, I've no hope of talking sense into his brother.

"Amy knew Valon Laska?" he asks sharply.

"Yes. Can you imagine? No sane person would ever want to be in that man's orbit, and it wasn't the first time she'd worked with him. Who knows if there are any of his associates tied to her, too. Think about it. What do we really know about her? We've never once met anyone from her family, not even at the wedding. She never goes to visit them, and they've never come to her. Darius says she hardly ever talks about her past and then, only vaguely."

"How did you find out about Laska?" he asks, his dark gaze brilliantly hard.

"It's my job to know what our employees are doing. In the bathroom and elsewhere."

Kane's dark brow wings up sardonically and I see knowledge in his eyes. Does he know that I've also discovered Lily's secret identities? Fear is like a block of ice in the pit of my belly, but I lift my chin. I don't care if he knows. Everyone in the family is working on their own agenda and operating in silos. That is what's making us vulnerable, and it has to stop.

"You should have led with the Laska information," he says as he turns away and walks toward the window, leaving me staring at his back.

"Forgive me for wanting to be trusted without having to explain myself."

He laughs softly and shoves his hands in his pockets. I see the echoes of his father in his towering height and wide shoulders, the effortless blend of elegance and power. In how many intrinsic ways is he a measure of the man who fathered him?

"Pull together everything you have on Amy in hard copy," he tells me in a deceptively lazy tone that doesn't fool me at all. He is at his most calm after his killer instinct has been roused. Baharan no longer rules my son since his wife's return, but the company remains a demanding mistress and he'll protect it, if only because he enjoys being cutthroat whenever he has the opportunity. He gets that from me.

"We're not taking rumors or conjecture to Darius," he finishes before turning away from the view of Midtown and moving to leave my office.

"I have proof."

"Once we've reviewed it together, we'll discuss next steps. Have a good day."

"You, too." I watch as he leaves. As soon as the door closes, I press my hand to my forehead and give a shaky sigh. He and I have accomplished so much together but I'm aware we could be damn near invincible if we were a true partnership. That we're not is one of the innumerable things Paul's desertion cost me.

"Aliyah, Ram Singh is on line one," Jennifer tells me via the speaker on my desk phone.

"Is he?" I say quietly in the tone that frightens grown men. I sink into my chair and pick up the receiver to answer her. "Thank you, Jennifer. I'll take the call."

The contractor in Seattle has been calling my cell for the past few days but I've got enough on my plate now and he can wait just like I'm waiting. It's Lily's fault that I haven't yet been able to move forward with the Seattle research facility because I have to focus on her and her hidden agenda – whatever that may be. And I'm wary of bringing it up now that Ryan has joined the board. I don't know his motives or whether he'll be an ally or an impediment.

I rub at my temples, trying to stave off a headache. I debate leaving Ram on hold until he hangs up. It's a chore to delete call records from the database.

My eyes close against the feeling that I'm completely overwhelmed. Not long ago, I had complete control over every facet of my life. When did I lose it?

Doesn't matter, I tell myself. I've never run from a problem and won't start now.

"Ram," I answer, my voice holding a marked chill. "I never gave you this number. You're only supposed to call me on my cellphone. I've made that very clear."

"We missed meeting with you last week," he says, his words accented with the flavor of India. "Can you make a trip out here soon?"

My fingernails tap a rapid staccato as I drum my fingers. "If I could, I would. I can't get away just yet. We have a new product launch coming up, and there is some family business that –"

"Yes, we know you're very busy," he interrupts. "The problem, Aliyah, is that we are not. We set aside time in our schedule to break ground and start building but –"

"It's going to take a bit more time. Not a lot but more."

"I can't keep crews sitting around."

"They're being paid, Ram. Don't act like they're not."

"And don't act like three-quarters pay isn't a burden," he counters.

My jaw clenches for a moment. "Nothing is stopping them from working elsewhere and making more than usual combined."

"I didn't call to argue with you."

"You shouldn't have called at all."

He sighs heavily. "I need to tell you that a bid we submitted for a new office complex was accepted, and we'll be starting work next week."

My back straightens. "Next *week*? And you're just telling me *now*?!"

"We'd hoped to tell you in person and show you our plans, but you didn't make it out here."

"Don't blame me! You had to know about this for some time and kept it from me. I'm not just a client, Ram – I'm an investor. I also have a mortgage on the land we're supposed to develop. It can't just sit there indefinitely while you work on other things!"

"That's exactly what it's been doing," he retorts. "As an investor, you should be excited about us being awarded this bid. It's not only lucrative, but it also has the potential to elevate us to one of the top contracting firms in the area."

"I'm the fucking COO of a pharmaceutical corporation, not a goddamn builder!" Enraged, I stand and slam the receiver into its cradle. My blood is hot and my thoughts wild. "The fucking *gall!*" I yell, fighting the urge to throw something.

Kane said it was too risky to expand now when we're on the cusp of releasing ECRA+. I disagreed, thinking ahead to the launch of the planned adjacent skincare line. Cross's wife Eva is a media gold mine; her every outfit and hairstyle change is reported ad nauseam. My darling Rosana is nearly as popular with a slightly younger demographic. With their combined clout, our joint venture will be wildly successful; I have no doubt. The initial launch may sell out, which will only drive demand, but we don't want actual supply issues that impede quick restocking. And we have to be prepared to innovate quickly.

I planned to ensure the future of Baharan. I can't be proven wrong. My reputation would never recover from a misstep of this size.

"Hi, Aliyah," Jennifer interjects again through my phone's speaker.

I growl. Forget trying to retain some decorum. If Ram wants to persist, he gets what he deserves. I snatch up the receiver. "No, I don't want to talk to Singh!"

There's a short beat, then Jennifer says carefully, "Alex Gallagher is on line two."

The shock of that name is a brutal blow because I'm still reeling.

"Aliyah?" she prompts. "Should I tell him you're busy?"

With great effort, I gather my scattered thoughts. "Is Rogelio in today?"

"Yes." She sounds relieved. "I saw him just a minute ago."

"Have him come to my office, then put the call through." I hang up and spin around restlessly, as if I'm searching for the specter of my past. Agitation has me vibrating, my heart fluttering in my chest in a way that makes it hard to catch my breath.

It seems like forever before the knock on my door. Before I can speak, Rogelio saunters in, as arrogant as always. The suits he wears to work diminish him, straitjacketing his dangerous aura until he becomes entirely unremarkable. It's a clever disguise that I didn't see through until recently.

He smirks. "Finally time to christen your office?"

"Be serious. Alex is on hold."

The security chief switches instantly into hyper-alertness. "Answer it," he orders, abruptly taking control of the situation. "And remember, his only weapon is your silence. If there's no secret to hide, he loses a lot of leverage, so act like you're not worried about the truth getting out."

"As if going to jail isn't a terrifying prospect."

"Not for you," he says grimly, "because that's not an achievable outcome for him."

His utter confidence bolsters me. I reach for the speaker button and activate it. My hand trembles but I'm anchored by my fury. Kane is still fresh in my mind and our estrangement is Alex's fault. My son needed me more than ever after his father left, but I was only a shadow of my former self, filled with self-loathing and a pervasive feeling of helplessness. I made the choices I did to reclaim what I could of Baharan and the company is meant to unite my children into a single, powerful force. I won't allow Alex to take any part of it. I've traded my soul for the company before and I'm perfectly willing to do so again.

"Hello, Alex." My voice is throatier than usual, which makes me sound perversely seductive. "How are you?"

"Remarkably intact," he rejoins, and I shudder because the hatred threading his voice is chilling. "Are you disappointed?"

Viciously so, but I don't say it. "Are you still in the hospital?"

"No, I'm home and ready to discuss what you owe me. I gotta say, Aliyah, it feels like a lot. You've put me through hell."

"What would you call what you put me through?"

"I'm not responsible for whatever guilt you may feel for betraying Paul."

My head jerks back in surprise. "Guilt . . . ? What are you –"

Rogelio straightens abruptly, gesturing for me to cease talking with a slash of his hand in front of his throat. "You're playing games, *cabrón*."

There's silence for a long, painful moment, then a soft query, "Who's with you, Aliyah? A lover? A lawyer? I'm guessing a lover who's too stupid to avoid antagonizing someone you owe a debt to."

"It doesn't matter who I am," Rogelio answers, "only what I know."

"You know what she's told you. Perhaps you'd like to watch what really happened instead. Baharan recorded everything then, just like now. You can never be too careful."

I feel the blood drain from my face as my vision narrows to a pinpoint. I'm suddenly hot enough to perspire. "You lie!"

In my mind, the repudiation is vehement, but my voice comes out as barely a whisper.

If Alex heard me, he ignores my accusation. "I'm not proud of what happened between us, but Paul's embezzlement and subsequent disappearance screwed us both up. I focused too much on trying to save Baharan, at the expense of my marriage, and Aliyah and I – both newly single – leaned on each other for support."

Rogelio mouths, *What a prick.*

"In trying to find our way through a very difficult time," Alex goes on, "we crossed a line. I would feel equally guilty if we'd been together only one time, but I'm ashamed to admit our affair went on for months. We –"

"*Affair?!*" My voice shakes as I tremble with rage. I expected him to argue that his rapes were consensual sex, even anticipated that cruel blow. Yet nothing could have prepared me to hear him say it aloud. "You disgust me!"

"I understand that being left by Paul was traumatizing," he continues, in a soothing tone that rings with insincerity, "and perhaps PTSD from that made it hard for you to accept the end of our . . . indiscretion. But you've tipped over into something very disturbing. You need help, Aliyah, and that's why I hope to avoid taking legal or criminal action."

"You'll need a miracle to sell that steaming pile of bullshit to anyone," Rogelio interjects with hard humor in his tone.

I realize I'm shaking my head violently, repulsed by the depths of Alex's depravity. Is he completely insane? Or purely evil? Is there any way he can make a case that I'm a former lover who can't take his rejection?

Infuriated, I set my hands on my desk and bend down to the speaker. "I'm not afraid of the truth, Alex," I lie. "But you should be."

"Is that a threat?"

"Only if you're threatened by the truth."

Rogelio hits the speaker button again, killing the call. I immediately deflate, my knees weakening.

He catches me by the elbow and directs me to my chair. "You handled that well."

"I'm not handling it at all!" I bite out crossly. "I should have killed him. I used to think about the letter opener on his desk and stabbing him in the neck with it.

I didn't have the balls to do it. Kane needed me and I –" I take a deep, shaky breath. "I was just as afraid of going to jail then as I am now."

Bending to set his hands on the armrests, Rogelio brackets me and meets me at eye level. "Stop worrying about that. This guy's too stupid to realize he's digging his own grave."

"I don't know what to do." It pains me to say that aloud.

"You need to track down the women who worked with him back when he was in charge. There's going to be a pattern of behavior, possibly even other victims he intimidated into silence."

I frown. "That was a lifetime ago. I wouldn't even know where to begin. And what is the liability in doing that? Can they come after present-day Baharan for damages?"

"You worry about all the wrong things, you know that? Do what I'm telling you." He straightens and starts toward the door, leaving with the same haste as my son.

My earlier meeting with Kane seems like it happened days ago instead of minutes. It feels almost as if I'm aging at an accelerated pace. I feel old and tired. My pulse is thready and my head light.

"Hey."

I glance toward the sound of Rogelio's voice and find him paused with his hand on the knob.

"You okay?" he asks, concern in his eyes.

"I survived Alex Gallagher before." My low-voiced reply is barely audible. "This time, he won't survive me."

18

LILY

I'VE ALWAYS LOVED THE OCEAN. ITS BEAUTY, THE WAY IT SHIMMERS WITH light. And its danger, how quickly it can shift to pull you into the abyss and never let go. I see my mother in those dark depths, and so many transformative moments in my life have happened either on the water or beside it.

It's been a couple of years since I left you, my love, and somehow, I was able to reconnect to the sea despite the trauma I associate with it: our separation and the loss of my mother.

At the moment, as I pace the cabin with long and restless strides, I am acutely aware of the gentle rocking of the water beneath the boat. My gaze is drawn to the view of the Mediterranean Sea and the massive, ostentatious yachts that dot its surface. Sunlight sparkles off gleaming railings and the rotors of helicopters skillfully landed on upper aft deck helipads. The superyacht we'd rented blended in, but we aren't in Monte Carlo to play. The gamble we're making is with a man's life, not casino tokens.

Being left behind to wait is never easy for me. The worrying is the worst. Rogelio told me I need to trust in my team's abilities.

"I trust all of you with my life," I'd argued. "But I never wanted any of you to take a life yourselves!"

"'Ours is not to reason why; ours is but to do and die.'"

I gave him a withering look. "Quoting Tennyson? Seriously?"

He winked. "We appreciate that you don't want us to have blood on our hands. But you trained us for this. Get out of our way."

"I've turned you all into heartless killers. That's just great."

Cupping my face in his hands, Rogelio held my gaze. "I wish you'd stop hating yourself. But don't worry, querida. *We love you enough to make up for it."*

He pressed a brotherly kiss to my forehead.

I snorted. But I couldn't argue his point that my doubts undermine the team's confidence. So, I feigned nonchalance until they were all on their way and now, I suffer silently in their absence.

No woman has the luxury of being powerless. Helplessness is a feeling and only you are responsible for how you feel.

My mother's voice echoes through my mind like a song played on repeat. For me, however, strength comes from action, and I'm locked into inaction, waiting for others to act – my crew, my friends who've become family and who hadn't been trained from birth to be lethal.

Did I teach them enough in the limited time I've had? Why did I agree to this? Could I have stopped them if I'd tried?

In any case, it's too late now. The moment Lacy identified Hyka as the man who'd orchestrated the brutal assault on her mother, we were left with no other options.

Coming to an abrupt halt, I glance at my open laptop and the casino's security feeds, which we'd hacked into a few days ago. On a split screen, I have four vantage points at once, allowing me to supervise while unable to assist.

In one view, Salma drips with fine jewels, her voluptuous figure cinched into a form-fitting, backless gown. She blows on the dice cupped in her hand and then tosses them onto the craps table with a flourish. The tall, thin man beside her never takes his eyes from her, not even when the other bystanders erupt in joyous cheers.

Rogelio is seated at the poker table behind her, maintaining a close eye as Salma works to keep Endri Hyka, the mark, distracted by her flamboyance and beauty. While Rogelio only looks over his shoulder when the raucous crowd warrants a peek, I know he's acutely aware of what's going on behind his back.

I can't take credit for his situational awareness. He'd been running with criminals when I found him, treading a fine line that would likely have seen him end up in prison. He'd delved into the underworld searching for his sister and it had been slowly swallowing him alive. I'd awarded him a grant to cover the expenses of a college degree and he couldn't separate the gift from me, deciding that I need his protection. Nothing I say or do convinces him to take the fresh start and run with it. And I'm weak, admittedly, having gone a lifetime without anyone to share my life with. To have him as a brother is too irresistible to deny.

Movement in the adjacent feed draws my attention to Tovah, who walks down a hotel hallway lined with room doors. She's staring down at her phone and a second later, my messenger app notifies me of an incoming message.

> The waiting never gets easier.

Her text turns my attention to the feed from Lacy's body cam. Through it, I see her hands rifling carefully through a drawer filled with clothing. She's already been through Hyka's in-room safe and luggage.

"You're doing great," I say aloud, my words transmitted into the earpieces worn by all four of them.

I'd argued against searching at all, wanting to limit Lacy's exposure even at the cost of losing some clue to Val's whereabouts. But Rogelio said we had to give Lacy something more than a gun.

"While this hit is personal, I think it's wise to tie it into the larger picture. The first kill is always the hardest, even if it's deserved. This gives her a chance to make it about more than her."

I agreed because he's right to have thought of it. To my shame, I always focus too much on the details and not enough on the human element. It makes me very good at executing plans and terrible at interpersonal relationships. Consideration for others isn't one of the traits my mother instilled in me. Thankfully, I have Rogelio, whose heart is big enough for both of us.

Love, for me, is always anguish.

I return my attention to the casino feed. Rogelio stands, drawing my gaze to him. When he turns to Salma and grips her biceps, I understand that Hyka has propositioned her. Salma leans into Rogelio, laughing as she presses a kiss to his cheek. They look like a longtime couple and Hyka's face betrays humiliation tinged with anger.

"I could go up with him if he hits on me," she'd originally offered. "That way Lacy has a second."

"No," I'd denied. "When they find him dead, they'll look at the last people with him. That's not going to be any of us. Lacy knows what to do."

"I've got this," Lacy confirmed, her lips thinned into a fine line of determination.

Watching the mark closely, I notify the others. "Rogelio and Salma are out, but Hyka hasn't left the floor yet."

Hyka watches Salma walk away with a chilling look on his face, then he shrugs it off with a roll of his shoulders and looks around aimlessly. I hold my breath as if that might hold back time.

The next few hours drag, and the sky turns an electric orange as the sun begins its dip beyond the horizon. Salma and Rogelio linger in the casino until dinner, then move into Le Salon Rose *to stay close by. Tovah retires to her room, waiting for my signal to resume her post in the hallway. Lacy waits in Hyka's darkening room. When he finally retires, it's all over in less than a minute.*

There's a flare of brightness as the room door opens and the light is switched on. I see his face for a moment and the spark of surprise before a hole appears in his forehead, followed by another in the breast of his suit jacket. His body drops to the floor and for a long, terrible moment, the camera remains focused on his wide-eyed corpse.

"Lacy," I prod gently, "you need to get out of there. The job's done."

With that, I alert everyone. I wait until her hand is on the doorknob and then I turn off the hallway cameras for exactly ten seconds. When I turn them back on, I expect to see an empty hallway, with Lacy safely moved into Tovah's room across the hall where she'll disguise herself before leaving out of the adjoining bedroom.

What I see instead is my mother.

She stands before Tovah's door, looking directly into the camera with a wide smile.

My blood runs cold.

I watch as she opens the door and disappears inside. Panic galvanizes me into a run. I reach the cabin door. Wrenching it open, I dash through it . . .

. . . and stumble to a halt on a rooftop.

I spin wildly, trying to gain my bearings. The moon is fat and bright, its light illuminating the city with a silvery glow. To my right is a water tower. On the buildings around me, I see more of the same.

New York. *How? Why?*

"Hey, you!"

I turn at the sound of Tovah's voice to find her running toward me with a bouncy, joyous stride.

She crashes into me, hugging me tightly. "I can't believe we did it!"

"Where's Lacy?!" I pull away. "What's happened?"

"I'm right here."

I turn straight into Lacy, who wraps her arms around me in a quick, tight embrace. I search her dear face, her eyes. "Are you okay?"

"Yeah, why wouldn't I be?" She grins. "Can you believe he got the job?! I swear he can do anything."

Frowning, I grasp that we're talking about Rogelio. I want to ask about Monte Carlo, but I realize I already know what happened. It's in the past. Everything went off without a hitch. And now Rogelio has been hired by Baharan.

"Are you okay?" she asks, her smile fading. "You seem out of it."

Rogelio steps up behind Tovah, followed immediately by Salma, who holds a bottle of champagne in one hand and a stack of Solo cups in the other. We've converged to celebrate our success, a gathering we can rarely pull off because of the risk.

I shake off my lingering confusion, Monte Carlo melts away as I focus on the moment. It's time to revel with my family.

The rooftop door opens behind me. I turn, concerned at being intruded upon while we're all together.

My mother stands in the open doorway, dressed in black with her lips a glossy red. She lifts a gun to eye level and in rapid succession kills the people who hold my heart.

19

LILY

I WAKE IN AN EXPLOSION OF HYSTERIA, JACKKNIFING UPWARD FROM THE bed with a loud gasp. My heart pounds in my chest and perspiration dampens my skin. The room is so dark, I can't see my hand in front of my face. I can only feel the lingering hold the nightmare has on me and listen to the sound of your deep, steady breathing. You inhale sharply and turn toward me, instinctively responding to my distress, but I can't bear to be touched now. Not with the sound of my mother's laughter so fresh in my mind and with the stink of fear clinging to my body.

Sliding silently from the bed, I grab my kimono from the side chair and head to my closet, knowing the exact stride and steps needed to make the journey without running into anything. One of countless lessons my mother taught me which would be irrelevant to people living normal lives.

I pass the racks of clothes that remind me of phantoms lined in rows, judging me. When I reach the sitting room, I'm no less haunted. In the murky mirrors that surround me, I see the ghost of my mother.

Will she haunt me forever? Now she's infecting authentic memories of my family, inserting herself into past events through my dreams. Terrorizing me by keeping her promise to take anything or anyone away from me who might make me vulnerable.

When will I stop fearing her? She can't hurt me or anyone I love ever again.

I sink onto the velvet couch and lift the damp hair from my nape, exposing my skin to the cool air. My stomach still churns; the fear and horror are more real to me than the penthouse.

Resting my head against the cushions, I close my eyes and absorb the disquiet that won't release me from its grip. I should be lying in your arms, nestled safely within the circle of your love. Being with you is a dream that's come true. But my mother still denies me peace in my sleep.

All these years, I've told myself that if I just eliminate the threats of my mother and Val, you and I would have nothing standing in our way. Now they're gone and I must acknowledge once and for all that they were merely excuses to avoid the truth: I'm not worthy of you and will hold you back.

Why did I never realize how much easier it is to play a role than to simply be myself? Is that why my mother chose to live her life as so many different women?

Opening my eyes, I stare up at the ceiling, which reflects the ambient light of the brightly lit city. It doesn't matter what my mother chose – *I* have to choose. To stay or go. To find myself or lose you.

I sense your presence before you give it away.

"*Setareh?*" The richness of your voice enfolds me. "Having trouble sleeping?"

I sigh, turning my head to watch you approach, yet another specter from my past. You're gloriously naked, your powerful physique rippling with muscle as you move toward me. The glow of the moon bathes you in soft, cool light. You look as if you could be made of marble, but you are fully human, flawed in ways you're too arrogant to hide.

You've never doubted my love, but I've failed to do the same for you. I've failed in so many ways.

Sitting up, I make room for you beside me. I don't want to be alone anymore or to turn away from you. I can't allow my mother's ghost to come between us.

"My name is Araceli," I confess, holding your dark, gleaming gaze.

Your stride doesn't falter but I feel your sudden alertness. Your attention has sharpened from sleepy concern to intense focus.

"Araceli," you repeat, testing it out. "Gorgeous, like you. What does it mean?"

"Altar of Heaven."

You sit beside me on the blue velvet, stretching your arm out to welcome me against you. I curl up, draping my legs over your knee and resting my cheek over your heart. Breathing you in, I hold the scent of you inside me.

Your lips move against the crown of my head. "I couldn't've picked a more perfect name for you."

"I don't know how you can say that when you've been through hell."

"Only without you. When we renew our vows, we'll use your real name."

"But I don't know my last name." I tug my kimono tighter around me. "And I'll always have to be Lily, but it doesn't matter."

"You don't have to be anything but my wife," you murmur, running your fingers through my hair.

Would you find it strange that it matters less if you love me than that you no longer love Lily?

Now that I've won you over, I should hate that false identity less. Who cares if she was everything wonderful and universally loved?

I care. Because she deserved you and I do not.

"I wish it were that easy," I say with a sigh of regret.

Nuzzling, you press a kiss to my forehead. "Thank you for telling me your name, Araceli."

I laugh without humor, even as tears sting my eyes. "I've never been called that name by anyone but my mother. You're the only other person I've ever shared it with."

And that feels defiant and rebellious. My mother's dead and can't hurt us anymore, but it feels as if I've betrayed her.

Your fingers stroke up and down my spine like a musician with an instrument. "I'm just happy to have your trust."

"You've always had it." Beneath my cheek, your chest is hard and heated. Our weeks together haven't dulled the surreal sensation of being in your arms.

When you long endlessly for something, it takes as long to believe it's finally yours.

"That's not quite true, is it?" Your tone is gentle, but your gaze is not.

"I can trust you and still keep things from you."

"And I can be patient. I've proven that."

Feelings of inadequacy tighten my throat and you let me keep my silence. The comfort of that reminds me why I'm drawn to you and always have been.

You make me feel like time is irrelevant. That there's no hurry to change, reveal or discard. That as long as we're together, the rest will come.

You and I alone, connected, is all I want forever and always, yet I cling to my silence. There are secrets and lies between us, but they have no power if we don't give them air. In another time and place, maybe we'd never speak at all. But here and now, that's not an option.

"What if I want to forget my past and never discuss it?" I ask quietly.

You hesitate a moment. Then, "Eventually, I'll need to know all of you. Every tiny piece. That's the only way I'll feel secure that you won't leave me again."

Your honesty mocks my dishonesty, and my remorse deepens. "Being with you is all I want, Kane."

"That hasn't been enough, has it? And I need something to be enough. Knowing that my love is truly unconditional is what will ensure you always come home to me."

I pull away and straighten so that we're facing each other. Staring at you, I understand that any lingering pretense that our separation was an accident has been dispelled. Abruptly, my heart sinks and dread weighs on my mood. You've suffered so much at my hands, wounds that were too similar to the ones inflicted on you by your parents. And you've steeled yourself for more, taken on that risk because you love me beyond any sense of self-preservation.

And what can I say? Yes, I've already told you that I killed my mother. But Val? The others?

"You said you wouldn't care what I did while we were apart."

"I lied." You reach for my hand and link our fingers together, turning your head to press your lips to my wedding ring. "I was too raw and vulnerable to be honest then. And I was dazzled by you, *Setareh*. I always have been. You're a bright, shining light in my life."

Turning your head, you stare out the window at the night sky. Your chiseled features are brought into sharp relief as clouds drift through the moonlight.

I'm dazzled by you, too, my love. Always.

"The truth is that shadows avoid the light," you go on, "and that's what I was before and without you – a shadow of a man. I realize now that it's the darkness in me that's drawn to the darkness in you."

I'm stunned by your words.

"I wonder if you've ever seen that side of me or if you just choose to ignore it.

I wonder if you'll still love me if I'm just as fucked up as you think you are." You look at me with eyes that are luminously black. "I take that risk and you will, too, because whatever you've done, whatever you'll do in the future . . . it doesn't matter how or why or who. I love every part of you, including what you think you're hiding from me."

I recall Aliyah's words: *I know you're not Lily because the Coast Guard recovered her body.*

My fingers tighten on yours. "Nothing good grows in darkness."

"You did. We both have. Our love did, in the beginning. And then we made our own light."

I think back on that far-too-brief time we enjoyed as newlyweds, separated from the world and perfectly content with only each other. Two people, used to being alone in the most fundamental ways, who found shared solitude.

The heat of your dark eyes softens to a slow burn. "I never would have aspired to this" – you gesture at the space around us – "if not for you."

I exhale in a rush. "I'm sorry."

"Araceli . . ." You pull me closer and hug me tightly. "I don't regret the work I put into Baharan, but I was reclaiming something from the past that I don't necessarily want to carry into the future. I'm not married to the penthouse or the company. I'm married to *you* and if you can't be yourself in this life I built, let's build a new one."

I wrap my arms tightly around your lean waist. "I'm not complaining, Kane. Being with you and making you happy is no sacrifice at all. I'm sorry if you thought that's what I meant."

"Listen . . . Building Baharan probably saved my sanity when you weren't here. But in reassessing what we have and what I want, I've been thinking about what I wanted before Baharan became the goal."

"I gave you that goal. You wanted to provide consulting services and I pushed you in a different direction."

"Stop. No one makes me do anything I don't want to." You massage my nape with firm yet absent-minded fingertips. "In hindsight, you and I are aligned in wanting to help others achieve their goals. Fundamentally, I think it's one of the affinities that led to us falling in love. Do I think we should focus on that together? That we'd both be happier if we did? Absolutely. But rebuilding Baharan was important for my mother, so I'm glad you inspired me to do it."

I press my cheek against you. "I've disliked your mother for how she treated you but that's unfair considering my mother's interference. Aliyah deserves my pity, and she has it."

I can no longer think about your mother without thinking of what Rogelio told me. My eyes squeeze shut against the images that want to fill my mind. My mother victimized Aliyah and thereby started a cycle of victimization. The trauma became generational, affecting you and your siblings. It's staggering and overwhelming to contemplate. And in working to reverse the damage, I've only managed to inflict more. I don't know how to live with that. By staying with you, I force you to live with it, too.

"I'm starting to view her differently, too," you tell me. "She wasn't always the way she is now. She changed after my dad left. I remember her laughing. All the time. My father's sense of humor just tickled her. I can still hear the sound of her laughter in my memories, but I can't tell you the last time I heard it aloud. Having lived through losing you, I understand how and why she's become someone I don't recognize anymore. Baharan gives her a piece of her life back and she should have it. It's time to move forward with you and a life that fits us both better."

My hand covers your heart, feeling its strong and steady beat. "I don't know who Araceli is, Kane. My formative years – when I should have found my identity – I had too many. I don't know what traits are mine and what are fabrication."

You touch my chin and tilt it up so you can look into my eyes. "They're all facets of you. You're a complex, fascinating woman. It'll take me a lifetime to discover everything that you are and that's all the challenge I need."

I contemplate the future you're suggesting and feel a soul-deep longing.

The man you've become suits the woman I am.

To be the man you once were, you need Lily.

20

WITTE

THE DAY IS OPPRESSIVELY HUMID, WITH THE KIND OF MOISTURE IN THE air that makes it hard to breathe and impossible to be comfortable. Beside me, in a florist's stall, an aproned worker spritzes water onto the drooping flowers. The vegetable vendor whose wares I'm perusing continuously mops sweat from his brow with a small towel. I've made some accommodations myself, having rolled up my shirtsleeves after leaving my jacket and tie in the Range Rover.

A few stalls down, Mrs Black is bent over a display of cheeses in refrigerated bins. While many visitors to the outdoor market look wilted, she manages to look cool and fresh. A wide-brimmed straw hat protects her pale skin from the unrelenting sun, while a sleeveless chambray shift dress hangs loosely from her slender frame. Backless and short-skirted, it manages to be casual, demure and alluring at once. It's not something I would have selected for her based on my knowledge of her tastes, but she's changed recently, in numerous ways.

She is often barefaced now, with only a subtly shaded gloss on her lips. She's taken to airdrying her hair, revealing soft waves. Today, she's wearing flat sandals with thin straps rather than any of the many pairs of heels that fill her wardrobe. Tovah is a frequent visitor, arriving with new clothes every few days.

The woman I knew so well in absentia is transforming into someone else entirely. The change began with the death of Valon Laska, which only deepens my suspicions. Yet the softening I see in her appearance and demeanour isn't absolute. As I watch, she glances around casually, offering a friendly smile when catching someone's eye. She appears perfectly at ease, but I recognize the signs of hypervigilance and note that she carries herself with defensive control. She is aware of everything and everyone around her, and she's searching the crowd.

Why hasn't she relaxed her guard? Is it too ingrained? Or is there something more to fear?

I accept the bagged carrot bunch from the vendor. "Thank you."

"There's saffron over there," Lily says as she joins me. "In pretty little jars."

I smile as I glance at her. She's wearing black-framed oversized sunglasses that hide much of her face. Freckles dance across the bridge of her nose. Mr Black likes to gently tap them with his fingertip when chiding her about something. He's been changing, too. He no longer brings work home with him, and his deep, throaty laughter often resonates through the penthouse.

"I make an excellent paella," I tell Mrs Black. "Or so my daughter says."

I can't see her eyes, but the smile she gives me is wide and delighted. "I love paella. How is your daughter, by the way? Good, I hope."

"Catherine is doing very well. She's planning our annual holiday together. Harbour Island this year. She wants to see the pink sand."

"Pink sand? That sounds amazing. You'll have to share pictures when you get back."

"Of course. She wants to bring her young man this time. I suppose it's serious." I shrug helplessly. "I can't keep her a child forever. But that's enough of that . . . Go back and get some of that saffron, and I'll catch up with you after I go back for the prawns – shrimp – we passed."

She worries her bottom lip between her teeth. "I don't want to throw off your meal plans."

"Please do. I love paella."

I'm gifted with a blindingly cheerful grin before she moves away. Again, she turns her head insouciantly from side to side, hunting.

Don't let her out of your sight, Mr Black ordered earlier, his mouth grim. He still fears her leaving, and I understand why. He bears the scars of grief, and his wife, despite being more at ease with us and within the penthouse, has a haunted look in her eyes when you catch her unawares. She fights inner demons, and without knowing what they are, we can't be sure of anything, let alone that she's told us all we should know or even been truthful about what she has elected to share.

All the information we've gathered, surmised or ascertained still leaves us understanding very little of who Lily Black is.

Regardless of my employer's concerns, I retrace my steps and leave his wife behind. She's not a prisoner, and I won't be her gaoler. Mr Black will need to face and conquer his fears because if Lily chooses to leave him, there's nothing anyone can do about it.

"Excuse me. Mr Witte?"

"Just Witte, please." I turn to the woman who's been shadowing us. She'd glanced at me repeatedly as she lingered a few stalls behind, but I couldn't acknowledge her with Mrs Black at my side. I don't have to search my memory for her name because it's memorable. "Ms Ferrari. Good to see you again."

"That's not true," she accuses with a glare. "You've been gatekeeping me from Kane. Does he know I've been trying to reach him, or does he just not care?"

Taking her cue, I speak with directness. "He knows and would like to speak with you." Painfully aware that Lily isn't too far away, I gesture in the opposite direction. "Would you mind walking with me?"

Her brows lift, and her gaze hardens, but she nods. Before we move on, I glance back at Mrs Black.

I pause. She's pulled down her sunglasses to stare into the crowd, ignoring the vendor speaking to her. Following her gaze, I try to spot what's arrested her attention so completely, but the crowd is unremarkable.

Then I see a flash of red and long, silky black hair. Like Lily, I'm suddenly paralysed.

The crimson hue is unmissable, especially on such a hot day when most have elected to dress in lighter, cooler colours. It's a shade of red meant to be seen and stop traffic. That it clings to a woman with the height and slenderness of a fashion model makes it especially eye-catching. I can't look away, frozen by a bone-deep chill of startling familiarity.

As shoppers ebb and flow around her, the woman appears and disappears. She's heading away from us, but there's no questioning that she looks like the woman photographed leaving Valon Laska's corpse in a restaurant lavatory – same dress, hair and figure.

"What are you looking at?" Ms Ferrari asks impatiently.

"My apologies." I glance at Lily again as I turn away, concerned that she remains motionless. With so much activity around her, she's like an off-key note in a playful tune, discordant and jarring.

"Witte?"

"Yes. I thought I saw someone I know. Let's go." But each footstep is a trial, my every instinct urging me to pursue and find answers.

"I don't see how it could be difficult for Kane to reach me when I've repeatedly left my number."

"You left it with me when he didn't wish to speak with you, so I didn't retain it." I speak more bluntly than I should, aggravated by her inconvenient timing and consumed by curiosity about what's transpiring behind me. "When you called his admin, you didn't leave your number."

I resist two urges: to glance backwards and to apologize for my employer's behaviour. It's also unpleasant to acknowledge the collateral damage that I facilitated. "I'm sorry. It gives me no pleasure to say these things."

"Yes, well . . . I suppose I should respect your honesty." The glance she gives me is narrowed with indictment.

When we reach the shellfish stall, I pull out my mobile to note her contact number and take the opportunity to really study her. There is a superficial resemblance to Lily, although the comparison isn't flattering to Erika Ferrari. That's not to suggest she isn't a beautiful woman. Her face is flawlessly made up. The dress she wears is an emerald that matches her eyes and suits her tan, and the material clings to her figure in a way that draws looks from bystanders. In espadrille heels with designer sunglasses perched atop her head, she presents an elegant picture – it's also a revealing one.

I'm already shaken by the woman in red, so the appearance of Ms Ferrari is doubly unnerving. My feelings of alarm intensify until my pulse accelerates.

I struggle with gathering my thoughts. "Give me your number, please, and I'll pass it on to him today."

"Why don't you give me his instead?" she retorts.

"I'm not at liberty to do that. However, I can give you mine."

"You know . . . I'm sure you're great at your job," she says snidely, "but you can't do everything for him."

"I'm doing what I can," I counter, "for both of you."

She glares at me for a long moment, then releases a frustrated sigh. Digging into her oversized shoulder bag, she withdraws her mobile, and we exchange numbers.

"This is obviously urgent," she tells me, dropping her phone back into her bag. "I wouldn't keep calling just for the hell of it."

"I understand."

"Who have you found, Witte?"

Lily's voice tenses my spine, yet it's also a relief to have her once again in my line of sight. Knowing she can care for herself doesn't make me less protective. I shift slightly to open space for her.

She extends a hand tipped in long crimson nails to Ms Ferrari. I note it trembles slightly.

I make the introductions.

"Wonderful to meet you," Lily says as they shake hands. She's warm and friendly. Seemingly perfectly at ease. I wish I could see her eyes, but she's resettled her sunglasses atop the bridge of her nose. Still, I can see a tightness around her lush mouth that betrays strain.

Ms Ferrari frowns when she hears Lily's name. "Yes, lovely. Are you related to Kane?"

"You could say that. I'm his wife."

"Uh . . . w-o-w. You don't say."

Lily doesn't react visibly, but when she speaks, her voice is gentler than before. Kinder. Because she's astute and has grasped the situation. "Kane and I were separated for a while."

Ms Ferrari gasps out a harsh laugh. "Separated? I was told you were *dead*."

"Well, that's not wrong. I can explain if you're open to listening."

"That's not your job. It's his." Shaking her head in denial of everything confronting her, Ms Ferrari's hand goes to her belly and rubs in circles. "God, I can't believe this. I'm sorry."

"So am I."

I wince inwardly and feel powerless.

"I have to go." Ms Ferrari backs away, her eyes big and dark. She pivots abruptly before I can say anything and pushes through the crowd.

Lily exhales in an audible rush, watching her leave. "Go after her, Witte," she says without looking at me. "Let her know he'll be in touch."

"Of course." But I hesitate, sensing her fragility. She was out of sorts when she first approached; now, she's clearly in crisis.

"Go on. I'll wait here. Try to calm her down if you can. She shouldn't be upset now."

Reaching for her hand, I give it a firm squeeze. I feel some of what she does, the distress and confusion. Leaving her is the last thing I want to do, yet also the most pressing. I set off quickly to catch Ms Ferrari before I lose her.

With my mobile still in hand, I speed-dial Mr Black.

"Witte. Did you two manage to run your errands without melting?" His tone is light and teasing, so distinctly different from how he spoke before Lily's return.

I speak without preamble. "We ran into Erika Ferrari."

There's silence. Then, "How's Lily?"

"That's another matter entirely. Kane . . ." I so rarely call him by his given name that I know he understands the gravity of what I'm about to tell him. "Ms Ferrari is pregnant."

21

AMY

"It's good to see you, Amy," Dr. Rochester says, smiling widely. "You look lovely."

"Thank you." I settle on the psychiatrist's pale gray couch, dropping my Louis Vuitton Neverfull on the seat beside me. "You look great, too."

Truthfully, she looks exactly the fucking same as she always does – like a female version of Mister Rogers. I don't know if she thinks the khaki skirt, white dress shirt, and cardigan combo is familiar and soothing or what. It's certainly dull.

In contrast, my emerald silk cigarette pants and black silk shell make for a striking and feminine outfit, especially when paired with layers of gold chains of varying lengths. Better yet, they're pieces I owned before I met Darius.

"How have things been lately?" the doctor asks, her hands folded in her lap. Her hair is a shade of blond that matches her skirt. It lacks lowlights and highlights, so she probably colors it herself. It looks dry and stiff, and washes out her skin, which makes her look slightly jaundiced. A little blush would help, and some mascara, but she's mostly barefaced. At least she wears lipstick and hoop earrings.

I'll have to remember to bring her some ECRA+ products next time. Maybe she'll use them.

"Good," I answer.

On the end tables are microphones that record every session. Dictation software turns the recordings into patient records. She might think her steady focus without note-taking breaks makes clients more comfortable, but there's nothing pleasant about inquisitions that pry out secrets. But if this is what I must do to prove my sanity, I'll show up daily. Aliyah isn't going to win this time.

"I've been super focused on work lately. Which isn't a complaint," I qualify quickly because I may need the shrink's help to break Social Creamery free of Baharan. "I love what I do."

"That's always a plus," she says with a vacuous smile. "Have you been getting along with your mother-in-law?"

"Eh . . . We haven't really crossed paths."

Her brows lift. "Do you no longer work in the same office space?"

"We do." I shrug. "Maybe we've just managed to avoid each other."

"Would you call that a truce?"

"No." I laugh. "Definitely not. I think she's busy plotting against me, as always. Now, Kane . . . I'd call that a truce."

"We'll touch back on your mother-in-law in a bit. Her name is Aliyah, isn't it?" She mimics my nod. "Kane is your brother-in-law."

"Yes."

"Who extended the white flag first?"

"He did." I look away, my eyes going to the framed degrees behind her desk, nestled between two bookcases with no books, only vases and family photos, including a few of an adorable little white dog.

Why don't Darius and I have a pet? It would be good for us to have one, I think. A cat, maybe. Where's the nearest animal shelter?

"Tell me about that."

Sighing at her interruption, I look at Dr. Rochester again. "He came into my office one day and apologized for ghosting me. He seemed sincere. And ashamed, actually. If you knew him, you'd know he's not the kind of guy who smooths things over just to keep the peace. He also admires the work I've been doing, which I don't want to say is validating, but it kinda is."

She scrutinizes me closely in a way that makes me want to squirm even though her vibe is friendly, and her smile looks more genuine than before. "I'm pleased to hear he's made amends, but more pleased about your calm reaction. You appear to have taken it in stride."

"Yeah, more or less."

"Before you'd entertained vengeful scenarios around his apologizing to you."

"Well . . ." Frowning, I look down at my hands in my lap. I'm playing with my wedding ring, spinning the eternity band around my finger. I still haven't fully reconciled the thoughts I used to have, the anger and desire for violence. "I've stopped drinking."

"Have you? Cold turkey?"

"Sort of. I weaned myself off booze over a few weeks and then just said to hell with it. The clearer my thoughts became, the less drinking seemed like something I wanted to do. I'm not even sure how I got started."

"A few weeks? You didn't mention it the last time I saw you."

"Well, that was a while ago, doc."

She frowns. "How long ago was it?"

"You're asking me? You're the one who records everything."

Her head tilts to one side like a confused dog. "I record things because my memory isn't the best. Remind me, please."

I rack my brain, resenting being put on the spot. It feels like a test. Like a *how-sober-are-you-really?* challenge, when she should be the one proving that she's actually doing something for all the money I pay her.

She waits patiently with that same irritating half-smile.

It doesn't seem that long ago when I was here last, but it was definitely before Lily returned. When I think back to springtime, it was before then, too. I frown, searching further back in my memories, before the holidays.

Agitated, my foot begins to tap. "I can't remember exactly when. There's been a lot going on in my life. The days all run together."

"Okay. How have you been coping on your own?"

"Coping?" I snort, then sit up super straight, grinning. "You know . . . pretty damn well under the circumstances."

"What circumstances?"

I lean back into the sofa and cross my legs. "I found out my husband has been lying to me. And I think Aliyah is trying to steal my company. Kane's on my side with that, though. He got over being an asshole just in time to offer some support. And my other brother-in-law, Ramin, has a weird fixation on me that makes me really uncomfortable. I keep finding little notes from him everywhere, like in my purse or my desk. I need to hook him up with someone. Maybe my friend Suzanne. She can handle him."

"There's a lot to unpack there."

"I may also need to have you testify on my behalf," I tell her in a rush.

Her brows raise. "Are you considering litigation? Or a divorce?"

"Not a divorce, no. I love my husband. And I don't want to go to court to fight for my company if I can help it, but I don't think Aliyah will give me a choice."

"Have you and Darius discussed his infidelity? Is the lying related to that?"

For a moment, I'm stunned that she knows about Darius fucking his assistant. When would I have told her about that? Aliyah dropped that bombshell on me during the holidays, so I had to have come in for a session since then. For fuck's sake! Am I literally losing my mind? Because that's what it feels like more often than not.

"I confronted him about it, yes. He denies it, and you know . . . I believe him. There's no way he faked his reaction. And since it was Aliyah who first told me, I shouldn't have believed it anyway." I rub my damp palms over my thighs. It's early evening, about the time every day when I feel like I imagine a hot flash must feel. Like heat is exuding from deep inside me and radiating outward. "I know he loves me."

"And how do you feel about the lying?"

"I'm pissed about it for sure. I hate being lied to. And I just couldn't wrap my head around it. Like, *why* lie to me? *It's you and me against the world*, he says, so why lie? I realized it's because of Aliyah. Because he's having a hard time approaching her about getting Social Creamery back and doesn't want me to think less of him because he can't."

"Do you think less of him?"

"Well . . ." I gesture helplessly with both hands. "Yes. I hate to say that, but I do. Kane stands up to her. Ramin does, too, to an extent. Rosana is gentler about it, but she's no pushover. I mean, I'm his wife. Fighting for me should give him balls, even if he wouldn't speak up in other circumstances."

"About her plotting against you?" She looks at me inquisitively.

"Partly. Not really." I exhale harshly. "I want to take my company back. It's not working out as part of Baharan."

"And Aliyah doesn't want you to do that? Why not?"

"She's not giving up control. She lives for that – ruling over everyone with an iron fist."

"That's what she said?"

I groan quietly in frustration. "She doesn't have to say it. It's just who she is."

Dr. Rochester leans back in her club chair and resettles how she crosses her hands over each other. "Have you discussed your thoughts with her?"

"I haven't, no."

"Why not?"

"Well, I thought Darius was working on it. He told me he was."

"But he wasn't, and you believe he's struggling with approaching his mother about it. Is it possible for you to open that discussion with her?"

What the fuck? So, now I'm to blame? Shaking my head, I glare at her. "Aliyah's the problem here, not me."

"Amy . . ." She resumes smiling kindly. It's an affectation that's ruined by her sharp, penetrating gaze. "I'm simply wondering if you've been communicating your thoughts and emotions to the people around you. I'm very happy to hear that you had an open conversation with your husband, resolving a vital issue in your marriage. It would be good for you to continue having those crucial talks with others."

"It's impossible to talk to Aliyah. She wants me to go away, period."

"I can't comment on her because she's not my patient, but you are, and you're a woman who has a complicated relationship with her parents. That affects all of your other personal connections."

"What relationship?" I scoff. "We're dead to each other."

"That's my point, more or less. As alcoholics, your parents weren't able to bond with you. You grew up in a cycle of being ignored and negatively reinforced. Aliyah is yet another parental figure whose relationship with you is fraught with conflict and disapproval. It must seem familiar to you and unpleasant. Familiar situations elicit familiar responses unless we course correct."

My hands have slowly fisted in my lap, my nails digging into the soft flesh of my palms. "So, I have to change. That's what you're saying. Then Aliyah will become Mother-in-law of the Year?"

"Again, I'm not concerned with Aliyah. I'm suggesting that changing how you approach her could empower you, even if the outcome remains the same.

You've said previously that she doesn't think you're good enough for her son. Perhaps approaching her calmly with a well-prepared argument will affect the result, maybe even adjust her opinion, and if it does neither of those things, you should still feel as if you've taken positive action and control."

Leaning forward, I set my elbows on my crossed legs. "Doc, the fact is some people are just awful, evil, terrible people. If you met her, you'd understand."

"Maybe you could ask her to join us."

I laugh. "She wouldn't come. But man, I wish she would. I'd love to get a professional's take on her."

The doctor surprises me by leaning forward and setting her hand over one of mine. "All we can do is try, Amy. Quitting drinking and communicating with your husband are big, bold steps in the right direction. Don't stop now."

There's something so sweet and caring in her voice. My eyes burn and then become blurred by tears. I blink them back and pull my hand out from under hers.

I can't show any hint of weakness. I need to have my shit together.

She pulls away and sits back. "Anything big coming up for you soon?"

My nose wrinkles. "Family dinner at Kane's."

"Who's invited?"

"Darius and me. Ramin and Rosana. Aliyah. Do you think that'd be a good time to set Ramin up with Suzanne?"

"Probably not. How's the family dynamic changed since Lily returned?"

"How much time have you got?" I shoot back.

When my hour is finally up, I hurry out, having scheduled a rideshare pickup on the drive over. I'm exhausted. Emotionally wiped.

When Darius asks me how it went over dinner, I tell him to ask me some other time. If I still drank, I'd congratulate myself with a martini for getting through therapy. Instead, I have a bowl of ice cream and go back for seconds.

It's not until I'm smoothing serum on my face before bed that I realize Dr. Josephine Rochester wasn't surprised when I mentioned Lily. And being aware of Darius's infidelity . . . ?

How does she know things about my life I haven't told her?

22

ALIYAH

"YOU'RE TOO QUIET," I TELL RAMIN, TAKING MY GAZE OFF THE RAPIDLY changing floor numbers to look at my youngest son. He lounges with his shoulder propped against the elevator wall, one hand in his pocket and the other holding his phone. He scrolls aimlessly with a bored expression on his handsome face.

"Talk to her, Rosie," he mutters to his sister.

Rosana glances at me and shrugs.

I yawn to pop my ears. Kane's penthouse views are unparalleled, but there's always a price to be paid for flying too close to the sun.

Looking at my children, I study Ramin especially. He's always been a brooder, the one most affected by Kane having left early for college. Tonight, my youngest boy seems especially pensive. There's petulance in the frown he wears, and I sense the weight of melancholia.

I haven't paid enough attention to him, I realize. Possibly ever. When he entered my life, I still worried most about Kane. Then Rosana came along, and I felt fear unlike anything I've ever felt. Protecting her and teaching her how to protect herself became a driving force. She's so lovely and sweet, a tempting target for the unscrupulous. I still worry. About all of them.

Ramin needs a partner.

The thought enters my mind abruptly, and I close my eyes against it.

Thankfully, the elevator comes to an imperceptible halt and the doors open, allowing us into the penthouse's entry vestibule. I open my eyes as Ramin straightens and tucks his phone away. He's dressed in black jeans and a black dress shirt left open at the collar with the sleeves rolled up to his elbows. He always looks handsome and polished in a rakish way. Women love to look at him, but he's single. And truthfully, I've preferred that to the alternative of another daughter-in-law I can't tolerate.

But delaying getting him hitched is a missed opportunity, really. I could find the right woman for him. If the choice is mine, I'll know I can live with it. I certainly can't leave it to him. My boys have the absolute worst taste in women.

Stepping out of the elevator first, I eye the two burly security guards in their requisite black suits. At least the suits are tailored. But why is there a need for clearly pricey professionals? What is Kane protecting himself from? Is there a known threat, or is my son just being cautious because the woman he's fucking is as trustworthy as a rat?

One of the two double doors open, and Witte stands there, looking delicious as always. I'd love to get my claws and teeth into all the majordomo's brutal muscle, which he tries to make civilized with custom suits. It's the nature of the beast for men to resent powerful, dominant women, which often leads to the hottest sexual encounters.

"Witte," I purr. "Always a pleasure to see you."

"Mom!" Rosana whispers furiously at my back, which widens my smile.

"I'm doing my job correctly, then," Witte replies with customary aplomb.

One day, my daughter will play power games with men and win. For now, she can watch and learn how it's done.

I pass my clutch to Witte as I step past him and into the main living area of the penthouse. A glint of light draws my eyes to a gilded frame I've never seen before, which holds a candid photo of Lily and Kane. There are several more scattered around, displaying intimate moments between them.

Who are they for? Kane or visitors? Are they meant to remind my son of how happy he is with her and allay any doubts that must pop up from time to time or to show guests that she's now vital to his life despite her long absence?

Shaking my head, I look away from the carefully presented scene of blissful matrimony. Ramin and Rosana can't resist, though. They step down into the living room to take a closer look.

"Lily is drop-dead gorgeous," my daughter says to her brother with a note of reverence.

I wish she would drop dead. Again.

The penthouse feels strange now. Not that it hasn't always had a peculiar energy to it, but now it's different. Smells different. Even looks different somehow.

"*Aliyah.*"

Wincing inwardly at the sound of "Lily's" voice, I school my face and turn around. My breath catches quickly at the sight of her. She looks so young and fresh-faced. It takes me a moment to understand why – minimal makeup, wavy hair, and flat sandals. She's wearing a sleeveless, tiered dress with lace trim and a black floral pattern. While the neckline plunges, it's hardly the attire of a seductress. If I didn't know better, I'd take her for the younger sister of the woman I had coffee with only a few weeks ago.

I greet her with an arched brow. "Hello, whatever-your-name-is."

While my voice is pitched low, so my children don't listen, Lily has no trouble hearing me.

"My name is Araceli," she tells me, extending both hands as if we're dear, old friends. "But, please, call me Lily."

Startled and wary, I catch her hands in my own. It's then I notice that the hard look she usually has in her gaze is absent. She looks doe-eyed and . . . compassionate.

I tug her toward me so we're only inches apart. "What game are you playing now?" I hiss.

"I don't have the energy to play games," she says in a low tone that hints at weariness. "You're worried about your son and your business. I would die to protect the one and couldn't give a shit about the other. Luckily, I can prove both of those things, and I've decided there's no good reason not to."

I study her closely, noting the shadows beneath her eyes that she's attempted to conceal. Her exceptional cheekbones are even more sculpted because she appears to have lost weight she could ill afford to lose. "Are you on drugs?"

"Ha!" Her lovely face brightens with laughter.

"Lily!" Rosana hurries toward us. She's dressed in a cap-sleeved catsuit in pale blue with white striping down the sides. It's a piece from her capsule collection for a fashion retailer that targets shoppers her age. There's a lengthy waitlist to buy it after the initial launch sold out in minutes online. Consumers imagine they'll look as good in it as she does.

Rosana and Lily hug, their dark heads coming together. While my son's wife is taller, Rosana is much curvier. They couldn't be less alike, yet I can see they're partial to each other. How and why is a mystery to me. They've spent less than an hour together in total since Lily's return.

Kane appears at the end of the hallway that leads to the master suite. He's a dark figure that emerges from the shadows with a confident, powerful stride. Wearing blue jeans that are clearly well worn and a black Fordham T-shirt, he looks youthful. When he joins us, he first wraps an arm around Lily's slender waist and pulls her close to kiss the top of her head. He's gentler than he has to be and more tender. Is it because she suddenly seems so fragile? Is he troubled because she might be ill?

I want her to go away, but only in a way that Kane can accept. If he's left in worse shape than before, it does me no favors.

"Mother," Kane says by way of greeting, without moving from Lily's side. The softness of his expression when he approached her is absent when he looks at me, and my chest grows tight. I can still see how he looked at me when he was a child, and I grieve for the affection he no longer feels.

Rosana surprises us all when she rushes forward and hugs her brother. For a moment, he looks wholly startled, but then he releases Lily to return his sister's embrace with both arms.

I have an epiphany. Is reconnecting Kane with us, his family, all it would take to eliminate Lily, the snake in our midst?

A scream builds inside me. Lately, I've been questioning everything: every decision I've made, every conclusion I've drawn.

For good reason, Baharan has been the holy grail at the end of my quest. It reunited us all as it was meant to, but it hasn't brought us together. Acknowledging that doesn't mean I made a mistake. It simply means the first phase is complete, and a second phase must begin. I *will* accomplish the rest of my aims.

I look at Ramin, who is staring at one of the framed photographs of Kane and Lily, which he's picked up and holds in his hands. I should've noticed his loneliness, but was it really an oversight? He's always been so cocky, never showing up at events with the same woman twice. I assumed he liked variety but then again . . . I have only to look at his brothers. They each settled on one woman early in their lives.

"Why are you looking at me like that?" Ramin queries, which reminds me I'm staring.

"You look very handsome tonight," I tell him.

I'm spending too much time in my head lately. I feel overwhelmed by Alex, the Seattle project that's dead in the water, Lily, Amy . . .

With a snort, Ramin returns the photo to its shelf and faces Lily as she descends the short steps to him. When she approaches with open arms, he looks at her quizzically for a moment. Then he shrugs and accepts the hug.

"Would you care for something to drink, Mrs. Armand?" Witte asks, stepping into view.

I see Rosana talking animatedly to Kane while Ramin converses with Lily, and I resent that Lily's invitation brought them all together. Especially here. There's a peculiar frenetic energy in the room. Maybe it's in the entire penthouse. I can't stand it.

"A gin martini," I order. "Filthy. Extra olives. And don't bring me one of those stemmed glasses. Grab a pint glass and fill it up."

His expression doesn't change at all. He simply tilts his head in acknowledgment and moves over to Ramin to serve him as well.

When Darius and Amy finally show up, they enter holding hands, and I'm halfway through my glorious drink. My middle son wears navy dress slacks and a white polo shirt. Amy's especially attractive in a green silk blouse, bouclé shorts, and heeled sandals. Like Lily, her style has changed in recent weeks. She hasn't dressed like me in a while, and I can't decide if I like that or not. It is certainly indicative of her altered state.

Lily offers them both hugs, and they reciprocate, although Darius's embrace is too short, and Amy's lasts too long. I also note that Amy greets Kane warmly, and he replies in kind, but she and Ramin won't look at each other. It's a complete reversal of how they all behaved before Lily dropped like a bomb into our lives.

Has the world gone utterly mad? I take another gulp of my martini and seethe with rising fury. Like Kane, Darius appears especially solicitous of his wife. I wonder if he's also concerned about her well-being. He has to have noticed that she's not in her right mind. Just yesterday, I walked past the breakroom and saw her standing there completely zoned out, staring at a framed motivational quote like a robot whose batteries had died mid-activity.

I wish Darius would approach me about her problems rather than the reverse. It would save me from looking like the villain. After all, I'm only doing what's best for my family and company. I've never shied away from drastic measures when it comes to either, and I won't now. Not with so much at stake.

Everyone settles together in the living room. The women naturally gravitate toward each other, three strangers who've become family. My boys, who once cared so deeply for each other, hardly speak and then, only about work. I roll my shoulders back, feeling the muscles relax as the gin and vermouth work their magic. The half dozen olives on a skewer are also delicious.

Witte approaches Lily and whispers to her. He used to notify Kane when dinner was ready. Now, Lily has become the mistress of the house. The smile she gives him is affectionate, and I understand that he's supporting her presence. I tolerated him when his duty was solely to take care of my son. Why would Kane need a wife if he has Witte? Maybe it's time to get rid of the butler, too.

When Witte moves to pass me, I thrust out my empty glass. "I'll take another."

"Of course."

"Let's move into the dining room," Lily announces, extending a painfully thin arm in that direction.

Where will she sit everyone at the table? Positioning is everything to a woman, and Lily knows this. She does nothing without calculation. In that regard, I see myself in her. She'll preside at the head, opposite Kane. Perhaps I'll take the space between Ramin and Rosana, and suggest Darius sit across from me. But if I do that, will Amy sit beside Kane? I don't want them getting along more than they are. The girl has to go, and I'm so, so close to making that a reality.

But Lily surprises me again. "Take the head of the table, Aliyah," she says as she stops at the seat beside Kane's. I search her face for subterfuge, but then Witte comes over and sets my new drink at my seat, and I no longer care. I'm meant to be at the head of the family. Why question her recognition of that?

The first course is an herb salad with a champagne shallot vinaigrette and freshly baked loaves of rosemary bread. It's all so delicious I want seconds, but I don't say so because Witte's arrogant enough as it is. The two maids – whatever their names are – assist him in the kitchen, and they're so deferential to him that it makes my eyes roll.

"This is really nice," Rosana says from her place beside Kane and next to Amy. "Getting together like this."

"I think so, too," Lily says.

"We should make a habit of this," I suggest. "Although . . . While I'm grateful my family is so connected, it does feel like it should've expanded with marriage. You didn't want to invite your family, *Lily*?" I ask, lifting my glass to my mouth.

Kane shoots me a warning look.

"My mother was my only family. And sadly, she passed."

"How did she die?"

"Mom!" Rosana admonishes, shooting me a horrified look.

"What, Rosana? Isn't that the purpose of this gathering – to get to know each other better?"

"She was murdered," Lily answers bluntly. "Shot while trying to help somebody she loved."

"Oh my God." Rosana stares at her. "I'm so sorry."

"So am I." Lily glances at Kane when he sets his hand over hers.

"What about grandparents?" I press her, leaning back as the maids collect the empty salad plates. "Aunts or uncles? Cousins? Siblings?"

Ramin sets his fork down and leans back as if settling in for a show.

"She's already told you it was just her and her mother," Kane shoots back, steel threading his words.

I debate pushing further, but a look in his eyes warns me off. I decide to circle back to her later.

Turning my attention to Amy, I notice she hasn't touched her glass of white wine. There's one pre-poured at each place setting – except for Lily's. "What about you, Amy? Why don't we plan on having your family join us next time?"

Darius gives me the same look Kane did but it's not as effective.

Amy responds as I expect, by staring at her now-empty placemat and taking a deep, slow breath. Then her head lifts. "I've spared you my parents this long. I'm not going to subject any of you to them now."

My brows lift. "Whatever do you mean, dear?"

"Knock it off," Ramin snaps.

I glance at him with wide eyes, surprised that he would be the one to come to her defense. "Why? It's not a burden for us to host Amy's family. I would love to know more about them."

"You don't want to know them," she mutters. "Trust me."

"Did you have a falling out? Were they worried about you? Did they not understand your choices?"

She glares at me. "Why do you assume it's my fault? Oh, I know. Everything's my fault, right?"

"No parent wants a rift with their child."

"Some parents don't want the child to begin with," she retorts.

"Well . . ." I lift my pint glass, which is somehow already half empty. "That explains a lot, doesn't it?"

"What the hell does that mean?!"

"Drop it already!" Darius bites out.

I look around the table. "I didn't mean to bring up any sore subjects. Of course, my family is your family since you don't have one and neither does Lily."

"You say that like this family is a *gift* instead of a total fucking shitshow. No offense to the rest of you." Amy leans back slightly as the main course is carried in two at a time. "Tell you what, Aliyah. I'll give you the last contact information I have for my parents, and you can knock yourself out. I suggest trying around one p.m. their time. They're usually some semblance of sober when they first wake up."

"See?" I say to everyone. "Suddenly, Amy's raging alcoholism has context. Some studies suggest alcoholism is a genetic disorder."

The red-headed maid leans around Amy's chair to set down her dinner plate and has the audacity to squeeze her shoulder as if offering comfort.

She'll have to go, too.

"Or maybe that's just how I survive you being a raging bitch," Amy says sweetly, finally picking up her glass. She chugs the wine down in nearly one swallow.

Ramin applauds.

"Don't be crass," I tell him.

"Don't bully my guests," Lily says, the hardness back in her gaze. "Please."

"I'm sorry if you think that's what I was doing."

Kane's fierce gaze meets mine. "That's who you are now," he growls. "But you weren't always like this. Since we're all getting acquainted, why don't you tell us how you came to be this way."

My foot taps beneath the table. I want to ask him about the body he identified as Lily's years ago, and where Lily's money came from, and who *Araceli* is. What kind of name is that anyway?

"I would love to hear this." Amy gestures for her glass to be refilled.

Now that I've got her going, if I can keep her drinking, maybe she'll reveal herself to the others. Something more potent than wine would help with that, but we're not in an environment I can control.

"I'm not nearly as interesting as you all are," I deflect, picking up my knife and fork. "Have you regained any of your memories, Lily? Anything at all?"

"Some." She feigns eating, cutting her food but never lifting it to her mouth. She pushed the amazing salad around her plate, too. Kane noticed, of course, because he's focused so completely on her. And he looks worried.

"Really?" I put a morsel of succulent lamb in a rich curry-based sauce in my mouth and nearly moan at how delicious it is. Witte is irritatingly pretentious, but the man can cook, I'll give him that. His martinis are superb, too. "Will you tell us about it?"

"No, I don't think I will." She looks up at Rosana. "How about you, Rosana? Kane tells me you have a dozen or more irons in the fire."

My daughter smiles. "I *am* swamped doing collabs, but they're fun. I'm kinda toying with the idea of starting a book club. I love reading and getting recommendations, but I haven't found a book club that fits me, so why not make my own. You know?"

"That sounds fun. What kind of books do you like to read?"

Rosana enthusiastically jumps into the topic, listing titles and authors I've never heard of.

I'm more focused on Witte, who's stepped behind Kane and whispers in his ear.

Amy's making quick work of her second glass of wine while Darius talks to her in a low, soothing voice. Ramin is eating like he hasn't had food in days. Of course, he's a bachelor, so who knows what he considers a meal when left to his own devices. He really should have someone look after him. I'm committed to finding her – whoever she might be.

"Excuse me." Kane pushes back from the table, drops his napkin by his plate and stands. He answers Lily's questioning glance with a look before bending down to kiss her.

There's something about his posture, though. It's not relaxed, as he usually is with Lily, and there's none of the command he displays while working. I can't place his mood now. It's like he's shuttered himself. Withdrawn.

I wait until he's disappeared around the corner to the living room before I push back from the table. It's a shame to leave such a decadently scrumptious meal to cool, but more important to know what's happening. Plus, with Witte occupied with dinner minutiae, I might have a chance to wander and look around.

As I gain my feet, I feel myself sway and catch the back of the chair for support. Damn it. I'm inebriated and embarrassed by it. Especially when I look at Amy and find her smirking. She raises her wine glass in a silent toast, her green eyes hazy. My glass is somehow empty again, but it will stay that way. I've had way too much as it is.

Turning away, I amble toward the bathroom, which is partway to the living room, the lights of which have been dimmed for a relaxed ambiance. I pause when I hear a voice I don't recognize. Someone has come to visit. Who would show up this late?

Perhaps Kane anticipated that getting the family together would prove to be an unmitigated disaster and planned for an excuse to leave early.

I take a deep breath, willing my mind to clear. I haven't been drunk in ages and hate how it feels. I steady myself with a hand against the wall, trying to walk slowly and carefully so that my heels don't click across the obsidian tiles.

A different voice speaks. Or is it the same, just clearer? Do we have multiple visitors? That can't be right. I tiptoe closer until I'm beside the bathroom. I turn the knob, opening the door for an excuse if I'm caught. The alcohol has started a buzzing in my ears, making it hard to grasp words out of the air. I teeter on my heels and slip my feet out of them, startled for a moment by the warmth of the floor as my sluggish brain tries to catch up.

A man in a dark suit steps into the hallway that circles the entire penthouse. One of the security guards, maybe? But then he puts his hands on his hips, pushing the edges of his jacket back. Something glints on his belt.

With a gasp, I duck into the pitch-black bathroom and push the door partially closed.

It's a badge. A cop. Detective. And there's more than one. His partner stepped into view beside him in a lighter plaid suit. Why on earth . . . ?

Alex. Alex talked to the police after all.

My hand goes to my mouth, stifling my terror. My heart pounds in my chest so hard it hurts. I want my phone. I want Rogelio. But I gave my clutch to Witte, and who knows where he put it.

I should've known Alex wouldn't bide his time. I've rejected all his calls, unwilling to give him the pleasure of recording more of his lies and building up more of his story. He wants money but destroying me is also on his agenda.

With my ear to the cracked door, I listen even though I can't hear what's being said. Are they going to interrupt our family evening even more than they already have? Worse . . . will they tell my children why they're here?

Are they telling Kane about what I did to Alex now? It would be a nightmare for my eldest child to know, but of all my children, he's the one I would choose to tell. Kane would take it better than the others, and he has Lily, who swears she loves him and will protect him. Maybe she will.

The voices move away, and I realize they're not going to the dining room but in the opposite direction to Kane's office. I risk stepping out, peering down the hallway until all three men turn the far corner. I almost trip, my legs are so wobbly. How did I let myself get falling-down drunk?

I can't talk to the police in this condition. My mouth is so dry I'm not sure I can talk at all. And I need my wits about me to refute a man as viciously cunning as Alex Gallagher. They'll want to believe him. Two male cops? They'll sympathize with him for how I attacked his manhood. I have to be at my best to survive this.

Grabbing my shoes, I run to the door. My sweaty feet slide on the glossy floor. I startle the guards when I rush into the vestibule. I have to leave my bag and phone behind. My family behind. Possibly my life behind if I can't save myself. I am *not* going to jail.

I stab viciously at the elevator call button.

My stomach roils. I dart into the elevator car as soon as it arrives and breathe a sigh of relief when it begins its descent. I don't know where I'm going or how I'll get there, but I'll find a way.

I always do.

23

LILY

I TRY TO FOCUS ON WHAT ROSANA IS SAYING, BUT MY MOTHER IS reflected in the window behind her. I see her everywhere, all the time. In my dreams, in every reflective surface. I've hardly left the penthouse, but when I have, I've seen her on the street, in cabs driving by, sitting in restaurant windows.

I've begged her to forgive me and screamed at her to leave me alone. I've cried tears that bleed from my soul and raged with anger that burns like acid. She haunts me. My grief and guilt eat at me. I grow thinner by the day. And you worry, my love. My crew worries. Witte hovers, always offering things to eat, but my stomach is knotted at all hours.

Why did you leave the table, my love? I need you. When you're with me, I'm reminded why I must stay sane. I have to stop hearing my mother's voice and laughter. I have to stop smelling her perfume.

But I still have to talk about her with you. Talk about Erika Ferrari, too. But you've asked me to give you time and I do, because you've been so patient with me. Returning that courtesy is the least I can do.

Glancing around the table, I see everyone sitting with their shoulders hunched and their lips tight. Rosana is gamely trying to keep the evening afloat. That's my job, but I can't focus on it. I should've called off dinner, and I'm not sure why I didn't.

That's not true. I chose not to cancel because I want normalcy. I want to believe I'm not going mad.

My gaze lingers on the empty chair at the end of the table. Your mother is a vicious, nasty drunk. Her relentless questioning was pure cruelty. I'm embarrassed for you and your siblings, and sorry for Amy. But I'm also aware that Aliyah's behavior isn't like her. She walked into the penthouse on the defensive, looking as chic and beautiful as always but radiating tension. I noted the fine line of worry between her brows.

I feel guilty about her, too. Her life was very different before my mother entered it.

"*Mrs. Black.*"

Tilting my head, I lean toward Witte, who bends down beside me.

"Mrs. Armand has left."

That jolts me into glancing aside at him.

He nods grimly.

I look back at everyone and wonder what to say.

"Also," he continues. "Detectives Yellen and Ambrose are in Mr. Black's office. They wish to speak with you."

My vision narrows to a fine point and then widens so suddenly the chandelier's light becomes blinding. The detectives are investigating the hit-and-run that brought me back into your life. It's a crime that I had no hand in, but there are many other crimes in my past that make every interaction with law enforcement a cause to be wary. I glance beyond Rosana to my mother in the window. We're on the ninety-sixth floor, but there she is, ephemeral and lovely. And she gives me a look I know well.

Pull yourself together, Araceli. Remember what I taught you.

"You'll have to excuse me, too, I'm afraid," I say to everyone, as I crumple my napkin and rise to my feet. "We have unexpected visitors. Kane and I will be back as soon as we can."

I wait until Witte's tucked my chair beneath the table to add, "Also, Aliyah's left. She didn't say anything, so maybe she'll be back."

"Let's hope not!" Amy chirps. She's no longer sober, either. "With any luck, she'll have the hangover from hell."

As I head toward your office, I gather myself. I used to see Lily in the

158

mirrored hallway, but now I only see my mother. As we walk side by side, she coaches me to pull my shoulders back, lift my chin, find my smile.

You've let yourself go, she chides. *You're a mess. You'll need to clean yourself up first.*

When she last said that to me in a dream, I laughed it off. *You can't stand that I'm finding myself,* I told her, *and separating myself from you.*

Now, I feel naked without my full makeup routine, but nothing can be done about it.

I knock on your office door and step inside when you call out. The two detectives sit in the chairs in front of your desk while you sit behind it. All three of you stand when I enter.

"Darling. Detectives." I shut the door. "What brings you by so late? Can I get you some coffee? Soda or water, perhaps?"

"We're good, thanks," Yellen answers. He wears the patterned suits. Tonight, it's a gray plaid. He's the *good* cop in their pairing. The one who handles the pleasantries. His hair is pure white and stylishly cut. "How are you feeling?"

"Better." That he doesn't answer my question about his visit is an answer all the same. I grow more wary. "Thank you for asking."

I sit on the russet velvet sofa and settle my dress around my legs. "Have you discovered who hit me?"

"We think so." Ambrose speaks now. He sticks to solid-color dark suits that are a size too big. He's the serious, all-business one. Tall and thin with a salt-and-pepper beard. "We took a chance with the traffic camera footage, showing it around to detectives from other precincts and departments, hoping the driver's face would jostle someone's memory."

He reaches into his pocket and pulls out his phone. After swiping a couple of times, he turns the screen toward me. "Recognize this guy?"

I look at the photo, a candid surveillance shot taken on the street, and shake my head. "No."

"I didn't think so." He sets his phone down on his knee. "The guy was a thug. He worked for a gangster named Valon Laska."

I can't hide my surprise. For Val to be even tangentially involved in hurting me is such an impossible notion; I can't entertain it. Still, I have to run with the pretense. "Valon Laska. That's the guy who was all over the news not long ago?"

"Same guy," Yellen says.

"Wow." I feel your gaze on me, hot like flame. "Well, we knew it was totally accidental. I was in the wrong place at the wrong time. Is the driver in custody now?"

"He's dead," he answers flatly. "His girlfriend says he was dragged out of their apartment at gunpoint the same day he tried to run you over."

My blood turns cold. "What do you mean, 'tried?' Why would he try to kill me?"

"That's the crazy thing – and let me just say, when you've been at this as long as we have, nothing's surprising anymore." Ambrose hasn't looked away from me. In fact, he's hardly blinked. "Laska was killed by a woman who looks a helluva lot like you. I mean, practically identical."

He lifts his phone again and shows me a picture of myself leaving the restaurant after killing Val.

"That's . . . oh my God. That's really uncanny." I lean in closer as if I have to examine the photo because inside my brain it feels like a bomb has detonated, scattering my thoughts in a million directions.

"Here." He holds his phone out to me. "Take a good look."

I do because I don't have a choice, but my eyes don't see anything but a blur. Val would never order a hit on me, and none of his men would dare to break ranks. Nothing the detectives are saying makes sense. "When you look closer, you can see she's older than me. But yes . . . at first glance, there's a startling likeness. Did you see this, Kane?"

"Yes. I'm not fooled by it. But then, I'd know you anywhere." There's something in your tone that jerks my gaze to you.

"Do you know who that woman is, Mrs. Black?" Ambrose queries.

"Uh . . . I'm sorry, Detective." I tear my attention away from you. "This is a bit of a shock. What did you just ask me?"

"Do you know who that is in the photo?"

"No. Do you?"

"That's Laska's wife," Yellen tells me. "Stephanie."

Handing the phone back, I shake my head to clear my racing thoughts. "What are you thinking? That he wanted to kill his wife but screwed up and she retaliated?"

"Possibly." This time, Ambrose puts his phone away. "Remind us why you have guards at your front door."

"Why not?" you interject smoothly. "I entertain a lot and guests are impressed by things like that."

The detective turns his shrewd stare on you. "You're not worried about anything in particular?"

"Aside from ruining my wife's carefully planned family dinner tonight? No."

Dressed as you are, you look like the Fordham student I first met, but there's little of that young man in your demeanor and voice. You've thrown up a wall and effectively ended any further cooperation on our part.

"We're sorry to have interrupted." Yellen stands and smiles. His amiability seems genuine, but he still has that flat, incisive cop's gaze. "As for the guards, it's not a bad thing to be too careful. Especially under the circumstances."

My brows lift. "What circumstances?"

"Those loyal to Laska will want to avenge him," Ambrose tells us as he pushes to his feet. "They've already mistaken you for Stephanie once. Warn your security and take them with you when you go out. But try to stay home if you can."

Yellen nods grimly.

You stand, too. "I'll make sure she's safe."

"We may have more questions for you," Ambrose says. "Let us know if you decide to leave town."

"You'll know where to find us," you rejoin.

I stand to walk them out, and you round your desk to drape your arm around me. Your fingers flex in a soft squeeze of reassurance.

You'll have questions, too, and I won't know how to answer them. I don't even understand. Why would someone affiliated with Val try to kill me? I looked into Val's eyes in his final minutes. He spoke to me. I would have known then if he wanted to kill me. And despite how careful you've been about protecting me – if he wanted me dead, that's what I'd be.

Would my mother have ordered the hit?

When would she have done that? Before she joined me on the boat that fateful day long ago? Did she suspect I would kill her, as I would kill anyone who threatened you? Did she think the only way to save me from you was to end my life?

She could do it if she thought it was best for me.

I think of her as she was that afternoon, resplendent in red. Had she knowingly taken the risk that her child would murder her? A final test. And if I couldn't pass it, was a failsafe already in place? Since then, my frequent travel and myriad identities would've made tracking me down nearly impossible.

Tears scald my eyes. My heart aches. Any remaining illusions I held dear about my mother have been shattered.

And because they were all I had left, my mourning deepens until it threatens to drown me.

24

WITTE

IT'S A CLOUDLESS SATURDAY MORNING, AND THE SKY IS THE COLOUR OF a robin's egg. Entering my employer's office after visiting his mother, I immediately sense his turmoil. Kane Black is a man given to strong passions. When his emotions are high, the space around him becomes charged with energy, a portend like the shadowing of the sun before a storm.

I imagine that was part of the initial attraction between him and Mrs Black. Considering how strongly he feels about her, he must have swept her up like a tornado. And compared to her life of shadowy covert actions and false identities, he must have been a breath of fresh air.

He stands at the window now, his arms crossed as he views the city. Dressed casually in light grey trousers and a black T-shirt, he has nevertheless been hard at work all morning, focused on his family – his wife, in particular.

"Witte," he says without turning around. "Was she home?"

"Yes. And she's quite hungover." His mother was feeling so poorly in fact, she didn't even bait me with a sexual overture as she usually does. But I don't tell him that.

"Well, she deserves it after last night." He returns to his desk and sinks elegantly into the chair. Sighing, he gestures for me to take a seat. Picking up his mobile, he makes a call on speaker, and I hear the ringing.

"Yes, Kane," his mother answers, her voice throatier than usual. "If you've called to berate me, I'll warn you I don't have the stomach for it now. You'll have to call back later."

His mouth curves in a rueful smile. "Do you remember when exactly Amy first worked with Valon Laska?"

There's silence for a moment, then a long sigh. "Four years or so ago."

"You said you have proof," he rejoins. "That would include dates."

"For heaven's sake . . . Hold on a minute, and I'll look it up. I don't see why this must be discussed now. I've got a killer headache."

"I appreciate you taking the time," he says without inflexion of any kind.

A few minutes pass in which we hear her breathing and typing on a keyboard. "Yes, I was right. April 2012. At least that's when the contract for her services is dated."

His brows raise. "Okay. Thank you very much."

"Kane, wait!" She clears her throat. "I'm sorry I left early last night. I wasn't feeling well. Did the rest of the evening go smoothly? Did you have any trouble with anything?"

"No, everything went well."

"Oh . . . That's good."

"I have to go. I hope you feel better soon. Goodbye." He ends the call and sits there, staring at the wall.

"What are you thinking?" I ask.

Mr Black blinks and, freed from his reverie, turns his attention to me. "I'm trying to piece together when Laska first intersected my life. What are the odds that his working with Amy had nothing to do with me?"

"We can't yet rule out coincidence," I say, "but I would place the probability very low. A gangster hiring a social media management company, even for a legitimate business, is unexpected and suspicious – all things considered."

"Exactly. I met Amy at around the same time. Right before or right after. I looked at the memory book she and Darius gave out as wedding favours, and it lists May 2012 as when they started dating, which was weeks after she and I were together."

"You saved the memory book." The statement comes out like a question because I'm startled. It's such a sentimental thing to keep, which betrays a deeper affection for his brother than I realized he felt.

My employer waves it off. "I'm going to take Lily to Greenwich for a while. I don't know how long. I'll just feel safer if she's out of the city for now."

"Are you worried the detectives are right about her being in danger?"

"I'm worried about everything," he says tightly. "Especially her. She's not well – I know you see that."

I nod. "She's not eating."

"And not sleeping well. She's still out cold after tossing and turning all night." He takes a deep breath and releases it in a rush. "She thinks her mother ordered the hit on her several years ago, when we married. Since my wife's been operating under multiple aliases and travelling the globe since then, her recent return to New York was possibly the first time she could be located. She's devastated by the thought of her mother making that choice."

"Understandable." My foot taps silently with my agitation. "Thus far, we've been told that Laska would do anything Lily's mother wanted. Why kill the man following her orders if that's true?"

"I don't know. We're cobbling together information, and it's not adding up."

"Do you think Lily's lying?"

He shrugs, and there's something weary about the movement. "It doesn't matter. I can't live without her."

There's such finality in his tone. *She's an addiction that's eating me alive*, he once said.

"It matters a great deal," I say gently.

Mr Black glances at the photo of his wife on his desk. "I've been disposable to everyone else I've loved, but my wife killed those dearest to her because she'll protect me at any cost. That's the most important truth. The rest will come in time."

He looks at me with his deep, dark eyes, and I see a reflection of Lily's recent suffering. They're bound, the two of them. If she's in torment, so is he.

Sighing, my employer leans back in his chair. "We both believe we're not good enough for the other. I don't care; I won't let that stop me. But she cares."

To be with someone I shouldn't be with is something I know all too well, and it renders me unable to comment.

"Anyway . . ." he continues. "She's starting to open up to me. I'm hoping that seclusion together will speed that along. We also need to discuss Erika Ferrari. It's time."

I don't envy him that discussion. "The beach house is ready for you, of course. I'll ensure security has thoroughly searched the house and grounds and that the team is settled into the guesthouse before you arrive. Would you like me to join you?"

"I may, but not yet. I'm hoping that if we're alone, she'll tell me more." His fingers drum atop his desktop blotter. "I've got to figure out if Laska approached Amy because of me and, if so, what he hoped to get out of it. What would be the point?"

"Your thoughts parallel mine."

"Lily has done everything possible to get away from these people. The toll it's taking on her . . ." His eyes burn with fury.

I share my impressions. "She seems to be suffering something very much like grief. Or guilt."

"Grief?" He scowls at me but doesn't refute my suggestion.

"She may need to see a doctor," I propose quietly. I don't want to frighten him unnecessarily, but it's always best to be prepared.

Mr Black laughs silently. "A shrink? Or a medical doctor?"

"Perhaps both."

"If that becomes necessary, we'll have someone come to her. I won't have her in environments I can't control." He looks at her photo again. "They're dead – Laska and her mother. How do I fight ghosts?"

"Let's deal with the living first." I release a deep breath.

For too long, I've been concerned that Mr Black might have had something to do with his wife's boating accident years ago. Why else would she run from him when we found her again? I clearly recall the terror on her face when he called out to her, and she saw him.

Further, as a working university student on an athletic scholarship, he was dazzled by her lifestyle and wealth to such a degree that it's still evident when he recalls the day they first met. Now, with context, I gather that her fear was *for* him, not *of* him. And I chastise myself for ever doubting him.

"You're right." He rolls his desk chair forward, ready to attack the problems we're facing. "It's highly likely that if Laska was focused on me, Lily wasn't far away. She was here for him, not me. I believe that's why we found her."

It still astonishes me how often our thoughts conjoin. "That would align. And I don't believe she's working alone."

"No. The timing was too precise when Laska was assassinated. In and out within minutes. There's no way for her to pull that off without someone inside cueing her."

I blink at him, shocked. "You know."

His mouth twists ruefully. "That my wife killed Valon Laska? I immediately thought of her when you told me the news. The photograph only confirmed it."

I'm still too gobsmacked to reply until he opens his desk drawer and withdraws the missing jewellery from the safe – jewellery photographed being worn by Lily when she assassinated Laska.

"I looked for those pieces recently," I confess.

"Did you? Nothing gets by you, Witte." He hands them to me. "Have them melted down. I don't know if the police will get around to dissecting what she was wearing, but it's best to be safe."

Looking down at the earrings, bangle bracelet and necklace, I'm reminded that Kane Black is not a man who is easily misled. "Do you think she wanted you to know?" I ask.

"Why else would she wear personal gifts from me while killing Laska, pieces I couldn't fail to recognize, instead of junk jewellery?" He shakes his head slightly. "It stands to reason that whoever is working with her is nearby, too."

"I've already begun deeper dives into your close associates."

He stands. "Of course you're on top of it."

I rise as well, sliding the jewellery into my pocket. "Can these pieces be traced to you?"

"No."

Many pieces in the safe are unique and so valuable they were paid for with bank wires. That Lily would select untraceable pieces must be by design. "Do you think your wife knew that, too?"

Mr Black smiles grimly. "I think she knows everything. I'm the one playing catch-up."

But I know that's not entirely true. He knows a great deal, more even than he's sharing with me. Of course, I have secrets, too.

As I leave his office, I pull out my mobile and make a call.

"Nicky, darling." Danica's voice is like a contented cat's purr, and my blood heats in response. "Are you on your way?"

I'll have to make vital decisions about her soon. Mr Black is contemplating drastic life changes.

"I'm running a bit behind, but I'll be there as soon as possible." Getting the security team in place in Greenwich will take time.

"I have a surprise for you," she teases. "It's very naughty. You're going to love it."

"I'll hurry," I say gruffly.

She's laughing as I end the call. I stand there for a long moment, knowing my future forks in two different directions, and I will have to choose which to travel very soon.

"Is everything all right, Witte?"

I collect myself and turn to face Mrs Black. Dark circles rim her eyes. Her customary silk kimono seems too large on her slender frame. There's no doubt she's anguished. Her husband thinks it's the past that haunts her. I wonder if it's something in the future she dreads.

"Always," I answer. "Can I get you some breakfast?"

"I'm not hungry yet, thank you."

I know she loves her husband. He believes that's the reason for her recent decline. He also believes she's chosen him above anything else. But is that true?

He talks of leaving Baharan and the penthouse, actions that might lead to a liquidation of his assets. Has Lily cunningly planted those seeds in his mind and nurtured them? Has she truly returned for him, or is she here for the money she stole from her mother and left behind? The question must be considered.

And it must be answered.

25

AMY

"Hey, girl." Suzanne, my closest friend, greets me warmly as she opens the door to her condo. "Long time no see."

She hugs me, enveloping me in the familiar scent of her perfume. Oliver, her beautiful black Labrador, shifts position to lean his side heavily into my thigh.

Standing in her tiny entry foyer that barely holds the three of us, I fight tears as I hug her back and reach down to scratch behind Ollie's ear. I used to have so many girlfriends and, over the years, steadily lost touch with all of them. It's Suzanne – the friend I cultivated solely as a stupid, useless dig at Aliyah – who's stuck with me as my life spiraled out of control. She's been good to me always, and I've never been as thoughtful in return. The worst part is I don't understand why I've been such a shitty friend.

Of course, there's not much that makes sense to me anymore.

"Yeah, it's really goddamn good to see your pretty face," I tell her in all honesty, embracing her tightly. "I've been trapped in the Armand looney bin and missed the hell out of you."

Pulling back, she gives me a thorough once-over. "You look fantastic."

"Thank you." I return the compliment and mean it. I used to resent her effortless beauty – the tight curls that frame her heart-shaped face, the full lips and the thickly lashed eyes. But most of all, I was jealous of her poise and regal confidence. I still envy her self-possession, but not in the greedy, hateful way I did before. "How's the book coming along?"

"I finally found my groove." She flashes a bright smile tinged with relief. "I'm still slower than I'd like to be, but I'm getting there."

"What's the story about?" I enter the living room in front of her, feeling more at ease in her bright yellow home with its colorful African art than I do in my place. Ollie keeps pace with me, his tail wagging and nose twitching as he shrewdly determines I've brought treats for both of them.

"Don't get me started." She floats to the couch in a gorgeous, embroidered silk caftan in shades of chocolate and sinks into the cushions gracefully.

My shame deepens. Suzanne is a popular romance author with several family-focused series that readers have followed for years. Set in small towns, sprawling ranches, and tight-knit coastal communities, her series have ardent fans, and she keeps them happy. "Is it a Dancer Family novel?"

She gives me a cat-with-cream smile. "It is."

"I hope it's Dane's book."

"Not yet. This one is DeAndre's. Dane's next, after I write another Bridget Bay book."

"Well, I can't wait." I've spent the past couple of weeks reading her novels, something I should have been doing all along, but I was too busy being a sloshed-off-my-ass bitch instead. Now, I'm a fan, too.

Joining her, I set my tote bag on the floor and pull out the pastry box I brought. Below it, my phone screen is lit up with a notification. I see Ramin's name and feel a now-familiar mild panic. He texts me more and more each day. I want to block him but he's family, even if he has crossed the line between uncomfortable and creepy.

I set the pale pink box down on the trunk Suzanne uses as a coffee table. "Good thing I brought some motivation fuel for you."

Ollie grins at me.

"Are those what I think they are?" Suzanne leans forward excitedly.

"They are." Breaking the tape seal, I open the top to reveal freshly baked madeleines partially dipped in chocolate. I hand her some napkins from the bakery.

"I've got something for you, too, Ollie." I reach for the peanut butter-flavored bully stick I picked up from a gourmet pet store and hold it out to him. He takes it joyfully and quickly trots over to his corner bed.

"How 'bout some coffee with Baileys?" Suzanne offers with a mischievous smile.

"Go for it, but not for me, thanks. I stopped drinking."

She pauses in the act of reaching into the box, studying me with wide eyes. "For real?"

I nod and rub my damp palms over my jeans. It's brutal living with not knowing how repellent I must have been when I can't remember. Watching Aliyah turn into a complete dumpster fire at dinner was humiliating for her and me. How many times have I acted like that? And how easy was it for me to fall back into old patterns by reaching for the wine?

Too goddamn easy.

"When did you quit?" She takes a bite of the tiny cake she holds pinched between two fingers, and pleasure washes over her lovely face.

"Weeks back. Cold turkey." I wrinkle my nose. "At least until Aliyah turned into Queen Bitch the other night when we had a family dinner at Kane's. She would not let up. I didn't think she could be more of a raging monster – typically, she's more subtle with her bullshit – but she leveled up that night."

"She always sounds like a nightmare. I don't know how you deal with it." She sighs. "That said – and I don't want to take away at all from the fact that you don't want to drink anymore – but having wine to cope with a bad situation isn't quite quitting cold turkey."

"I know. It was stupid. And I could totally see that's just what she wanted me to do, which killed me. She got this smug bitch-ass look on her face the moment I reached for my glass." My mouth twists wryly. "I woke up the next day feeling like crap and kicking myself. But you know what? I don't know how those drinks didn't make me fall off the wagon, but I haven't touched a drop of anything alcoholic since. I don't even want a drink. At all."

"That's called luck, girl. Just don't bank on it. If I can help in any way, just let me know."

"Thanks. I appreciate that." That's Suzanne. She keeps it real while also focusing on the good.

Still . . . it just doesn't make sense that I can pick up alcohol and put it back down while blacking out so often and completely that I was apparently fucking my brother-in-law without realizing it.

Am I a drunk or not? Or am I being drugged?

I'm still randomly nauseous midday, enough that I can't hold down my lunch. I figured out it happens after Clarice picks something up for me and puts it in the breakroom fridge until I'm ready for it. Aliyah can't get to me through my housekeeper anymore because I fired Griselda and hired a commercial service instead. And Darius and I have started picking up dinner on the way home. But at work . . . Yeah, my mother-in-law could absolutely tamper with my lunch if she wanted to. Sometimes, I even think I can taste something medicinal in my food.

Next up: a personal fridge in my office with a lock.

But really . . . Am I just hoping for an excuse that absolves me of all this fucking blame and guilt? I don't think that's it, not deep in my bones. I used to trust my instincts. Not anymore.

Suzanne swallows the last of her madeleine and sits back. "I'm really proud of you. Please, just stay away from the stuff if you want to quit. Don't take chances."

"I know, I know. My parents do that. They'll go months without a drink, then have 'just one,' which inevitably leads to drinking everything they can get their hands on."

"I'm sorry. That had to be rough on you."

"Don't be sorry. I'm the one who owes you an apology – dozens of apologies. Looking back, I'm disgusted with myself. I don't know how you've put up with me, but I'm grateful."

Setting her hand over mine, she offers a kind smile. "What are friends for? And it's not like it's a chore. You entertain the hell out of me. Brainstorming plotlines with you is the best! I love how crazy you get with it. All that over-the-top violence and revenge."

"Oh, yeah. I'm living that dream," I say wryly.

She laughs, and it's a full-bodied, unbridled sound. "I can't ever use any of it in my books, but it's fun going wild tossing out ideas. Gets the creative juices flowing."

I'm grinning like I think it's hilarious, too, but I can't remember ever doing that with her. Not even once. In fact, I've always tried to avoid talking about her books because I previously didn't give a shit about them or her or helping anyone with anything.

Deep inside me, an alarm begins to ring until it reverberates in my ears. I run my fingers under my bottom lashes to spread the tears I couldn't blink back.

Fortunately, Suzanne thinks they're tears of laughter.

She picks up another madeleine. "But back to your mother-in-law. You know you've got to tell that woman to fuck all the way off. She can't keep screwing with you."

"She does it so well, though," I say with sarcasm, drawing in a shaky breath to collect myself. I can't think about the gaps in my memory or I'll go batshit crazy. I have to focus on what I do know and try to make sense of that. "She lied to me about Darius having an affair. For months, she acted like she accidentally let it slip that he was fucking his assistant, but it was all lies. She just wants to break us up."

The horror on Suzanne's face legitimizes everything I've felt about Aliyah. All this time, I've been dealing with the bullying alone, without support from anyone. Except for Ramin at dinner the other night. I could've kissed him for stepping up for me, and that's really saying something considering how uncomfortable I feel around him.

It's actually fucking wonderful to have someone listen to what I'm saying about Aliyah without telling me I'm misunderstanding or just need to deal with it.

"God." She shakes her head. "I don't even know what to say about that. That's just evil. But girl, come on. You should've known better. Darius worships the ground you walk on."

I look out the window, so she doesn't see me on the verge of losing my composure. Thinking about Darius lately always makes me want to cry.

I'd finally gotten around to digging out the hidden cameras I bought ages ago. And buried in that same drawer was a pretty floral shoebox filled with love letters.

"I found these letters," I tell her, "that I used to write to Darius. I kept them along with the cards and notes he's given me over the years. I totally forgot I had them. How do I forget something like that? Worse, I forgot how I felt about him. Like seriously? How is that even possible? It was like reading a stranger's thoughts, but they were mine. People talk that way to each other in your books, not in real life."

"He still talks to you that way," she says gently.

"He does." I swallow past a lump in my throat. "And now I remember how happy I was to find him after dating so many assholes. He's thoughtful, affectionate, great in bed. He spoils me and doesn't want me worrying about anything."

Shaking my head and sighing, my remorse deepens. "I was reading about how excited I was for our wedding, so I'd know he was mine forever. I wonder if Aliyah just couldn't stand that I had a man like that after her husband ditched her . . . ? Or maybe she's just a twisted cunt, but she did a number on me with her lies, and now . . ."

I shrug, even though my heart is breaking all over again.

"Amy . . ." Suzanne takes my hand, which stops my relentless twisting of my wedding ring around my finger.

"Do I sound batshit crazy?! Like, who forgets they love their husband? Who forgets how they felt on their fucking wedding day? I feel like I'm going insane, and I can't." I yank my hand out from under hers and swipe furiously at the tears streaming down my face. "I can't lose my goddamn mind. That's what Aliyah wants."

"Amy! Calm down. You're not crazy." She cups my face in her hands. "I'm not a shrink or an AA sponsor, but I expect that getting sober comes with a lot of clear thinking. You've dealt with the stress of having Satan as your mother-in-law, but your man is a prince who adores you, so you'll get through this and come out stronger on the other side."

I grip her wrists and hold on tightly. "I want to believe that. But honestly, almost everything I believed up until now has turned out not to be true."

"Aliyah is screwing with you, but you've figured it out. You know who you are and who your husband is. You know your job, and you know who your friends are. Anything else is just noise."

"I want to confront her," I say aloud, having played with the thought for a few days. "I actually want to punch her in the face, but just telling her off would feel amazing."

Pulling back, Suzanne nods. "Do it. You need to put her in her place, which is way outside your marriage. She's got no business meddling in your life or your man's life."

I exhale a shaky breath and admit that I needed a pep talk before moving forward. A not-so-gentle shove toward doing what I have to do. "She's so vile, though. She makes me feel like a bug she's crushing under her shoe. I imagine I can handle her, but when we're face to face, I just want it to be over, not escalate."

She gives me a gimlet-eye. "You've got it in you to take care of her. Think of all those elaborate and devious plots you come up with. All those sharp comebacks and outrageous plot twists. Whatever she says, you can sting her much worse. You've been holding back, being respectful, but it's time to take the gloves off."

Looking over her shoulder, I appreciate how authentically *her* everything in her condo is. Suzanne knows who she is and is proud of every facet: her creativity, passion for living, and heritage. I used to be that way, too. Will I ever feel that way about myself again? Will I always live with shame now?

I need to tell Aliyah that I know what she's done to me, and I won't just deal with it anymore. The constant criticism. Trying to steal my company. The dishonesty that nearly derailed my marriage.

She tried to gaslight me about giving my office away. She filled my desk drawer with condoms – I know that was her. Has she also been systematically poisoning me? The sick glee on her face when I drank wine the other night was impossible to miss.

I'm not above calling the police. Let's see how she handles the situation once cops are involved.

26

ALIYAH

I ARRIVE AT DARIUS'S CONDO FIFTEEN MINUTES LATE. BEING PUNCTUAL is both a courtesy and a sign of respect, neither of which I owe Amy. It's bad enough I'll be late going into the office because of this little tête-à-tête, but she insisted.

We need to talk. And we're not doing it at work where you can make me look like a raging lunatic again!

Of course, revealing how crazy she is in front of witnesses is exactly what I want to happen and what I've been preparing for, but she's surprised me by being clever enough to dodge that.

In other circumstances, I would've have insisted on meeting in my office anyway but Kane's not at Baharan. He's working from home again, and he's the most crucial ally I could have. Ramin came to her defense at that dreadful family dinner, and Darius lives in a fantasy land where his wife is concerned. Without Kane around to observe, it's probably best not to embarrass the family in front of the employees again.

So, here I am. Being on her turf is not ideal, but I know Darius's condo nearly as well as my own. I've been inside it often enough to feel comfortable taking the upper hand here. And it's Amy, after all. She's probably drunk already. That seems to be the only way she can find the courage to take me on.

I ring the doorbell and tap my foot as I wait. It's not long before my daughter-in-law pulls the door open and extends one arm in exaggerated welcome.

"Decided not to work today?" I sweep past her and into the living room. "Must be nice to be lazy whenever you feel like it."

"I'll go in when you do," she shoots back. "Besides, I can work from home as well as Kane can."

"Oh, is it not worth showing up if he's not there?" I pull my phone out of my bag, turn on the recorder app, and set it on the coffee table. Maybe I should be more subtle about it, but what would be the point of recording a conversation muffled by the interior of my purse? "Should I remind you that you're married to one of my other sons?"

"That happens to be the truth," she says tightly, dropping into one of the armchairs as I take the sofa. "Usually, the things you say are bullshit."

I scowl. "What the hell are you talking about?"

"It's a long list, Aliyah. It's hard choosing where to begin."

"Pick something and get on with it. I don't have all day."

She glares at me. "How about the time you gave my office away and said I agreed to it?" She leans forward to speak into my phone. "I had no fucking idea at all! And FYI, I'm recording this conversation, too."

Studying her with raised brows, I note her polished presentation. She's been looking a lot better lately. More pulled together and more like the girl Darius initially brought home to meet me. I actually liked that young lady. At least as much as I could like any woman who wanted to take my son from me. She was intelligent, an entrepreneur, seemingly madly in love with Darius, who clearly adored her.

Then she married him, stopped working and started drinking. Belatedly, I realized she'd signed up for a free ride, and the picture she'd presented was a fraud. Is it any wonder that I want her gone?

Today Amy's dressed in a long-sleeve maxi dress of emerald with a magnolia pattern that starts with random floating petals on the bodice and ends with big, bold blooms along the hem. She looks bright-eyed and alert.

I lean back and cross my legs, draping one arm along the back of the cream sofa. The entire apartment resembles mine in both color palette and design. Amy hasn't made her mark on it at all. Well, except for the tea service of pale pink floral china she's put out on the coffee table. It's definitely not something Darius would buy.

I'm mildly impressed that my daughter-in-law can be so civilized. Although she's made the error of pouring the tea before I'm ready for it – if I ever will be. I'm not here to socialize. I note the steam rising from the tea in the dainty cups and acknowledge that she was preparing for my arrival in that respect, at least. She obviously didn't prepare what she wanted to discuss in any orderly way.

"You're sober today," I point out. "You probably weren't the day we discussed your office."

"You know, I probably wasn't," she agrees. "But drunk or sober, I'd never agree to give it up."

"So you say now." Knowing it will irritate her, I shrug, then smile inwardly when her jaw clenches.

"Darius also isn't cheating on me," she says tightly.

My lips purse. It's unfortunate that Amy's finally spoken up about that. I wonder when she brought it up and why Darius hasn't discussed it with me. Whatever. "I never said he was."

Her mouth falls open. "Do you even know how to tell the truth?"

I wag my finger at her. "I only implied that he was, and you ran with it. My sons are good boys. They know how to treat their women. I actually think they treat you and Lily too well, but . . ." I shrug again.

"You are the most atrocious woman I've ever met," she accuses.

"That's your view, Amy. I think a mother trying to protect her son from an alcoholic gold digger is a woman doing a good thing. You think it's terrible. That just means we're far apart in our values, not that you're right."

She leans forward, clutching the chair arms with white-knuckled force. "You want to make me a bad person. But I'm not."

"Seriously? I can't even make you go away."

Her laugh is grating. "Does painting me as the villain make it easier for you to steal my company out from under me? It's gotta be easier than admitting you're just a greedy, insecure bitch."

"Insecure? That's the best insult you can come up with?" I laugh. "Do you really think you can compete with me? That's hilarious."

"Fuck you."

My smile drops instantly. I will not sit around and be insulted by a drunk.

"I'm done here. I'm not going to listen to you complain. I know the real reason for your faulty memory and paranoia. It's called alcohol. And whatever else you might be addicted to."

"That's complete crap!"

I stand. "Coming here was a monumental waste of my time. Darius is the one who signed up to deal with your delusions, not me."

"Sit your ass back down!" she snaps, her cheeks flagged with angry color.

For a second, I see Lily. Then I blink, and it's only Amy. But still . . . I pause, feeling suddenly uneasy. "Excuse me?"

"You heard me. I'm not done with you, Aliyah. Not by a long shot." She stabs her finger at the couch in a silent order for me to resume my seat.

There's something wild about her eyes. I don't know why I didn't see it from the outset. She looks paler than usual. There are dark circles that she's attempted to hide with concealer. She hasn't lost the weight Lily has, but I see the same sort of . . . deterioration.

"You need help, Amy." My voice is softer now, my tone more conciliatory.

"I'm not fucking crazy!" she yells, her hands clenched at her sides as she rises from the chair. "Stop trying to gaslight me!"

There's pure rage in her voice now. And something else. Hatred, maybe.

I sit, moving slowly, cautious not to make any sudden moves. I don't take my eyes off Amy, but I want to grab my phone.

How colossally stupid and arrogant of me to agree to be alone with her.

She begins to pace back and forth in front of the television, her dark hair tangling around her arms as she pivots at each end of the coffee table. I start to tremble as fear builds. Unable to stop myself, I reach for my phone.

"Don't touch that!" Amy whips toward me. Her forehead is beaded with a fine sweat. "You don't get to edit this conversation by recording only what you want!"

I quickly pick up my cup and saucer. "I wasn't reaching for my phone."

"Liar! My God, you're fucking pathological." Eyes big and wide in her pale face, she resumes pacing.

"I am not trying to gaslight you, Amy," I say calmly while tea sloshes over the rim of my cup into the saucer because my hands are shaking. "I've done some things to you that weren't kind," I admit. "I'm not proud of them, but my intentions were good."

"Like your intention to steal Social Creamery from me?! Well, you can't have it. You'll never have it!"

I'm so startled for a moment that I can't form a thought. "What?"

Her pacing is frenzied now, enough that her dress twirling around her legs nearly trips her. "You heard me. It's my company and it's going to stay mine!"

"Do whatever you want with Social Creamery," I tell her. "I never wanted it. Darius was –"

"Shut up if you're just going to lie! You're not getting away with what you've done to me. You're going to pay."

I don't know what else to do other than attempt to appear composed, hoping that will slow the rapid escalation of her fury. Lifting the cup to my lips, I sip the cold tea I don't want and try to talk her down. "Is this about money, then? Are you in financial trouble? I can help you."

"That's why you filled my desk drawer with condoms? Because you were trying to help?"

It feels like anything I say could fully unhinge her. "I've apologized for that, Amy. And I meant it."

"That's not enough, Aliyah! An apology?" she scoffs. "That's not going to fix what you've done. Your power grab will cost you a lot more than a fucking *I'm sorry*!"

My mind spins as I try to understand what she's saying. But there's no way to make sense of insanity. She's completely off her rocker, and I'm trapped with her until Darius gets home, hours from now.

I seize on the thought of my son. "Let's call Darius," I suggest, trying not to sound too eager. "Let's get him here, and we'll figure out how to get you what you need."

"What I need," she snarls, "is for you to stop trying to steal Social Creamery from me!"

"I'm not! And if we get Darius here, he'll tell you I'm not."

"Will you tell him you've been slipping drugs into me for God-knows-how-long? Are you going to tell him how you've been making me look deranged so you can steal my company?"

"Drugs? What are you thinking? I would never. Not to anyone." The room tilts to one side, and perspiration blooms all over my body. She's a maniac. I can see the madness in her eyes now.

Amy points her finger at me. "I'm done feeling stupid! You've stolen chunks of time from me and made me do unforgivable things, but I won't accept the blame for your actions anymore! You're going down, Aliyah. All the way down."

My tongue feels thick and hot as I try to wet my dry lips. It's hard to gather my thoughts. My heart is pounding so hard that my chest hurts. The teacup rattles in the saucer as I set them down carefully, not trusting my sweaty grip. "I don't know what you're talking about. What are you saying?"

Returning to her seat, Amy leans toward me and looks at me with narrowed eyes. She suddenly seems more contained. "I'm keeping my husband and my company. Is that clear enough for you?"

I swallow hard, and the room shifts abruptly to tilt in the other direction. There's a medicinal taste in my mouth. "What . . . what have you done?" I ask her, but my words come out slow and slurred.

"I've had my blood drawn, and I've set up cameras."

"What?" I began to list from side to side. I look toward my nearly empty teacup and panic bubbles up from my belly until it threatens to choke me. "W-what's in that? What is t-that?"

"Tea, you psycho bitch."

"I'm going to be sick." I cover my mouth with my hand but can't stop it. I look at her, but she melts into a blur. Something is shoved into my lap – a bowl, maybe – and the jostling is too much.

I hunch over as my stomach heaves and vomit launches from my mouth. The room's spinning is like a merry-go-round. Everything around me is a haze of white and green that must be Amy's dress. Her perfume swirls around me and makes me puke again.

I hear her voice in the distance.

"You're . . . trying . . . to . . . kill . . . me," I gasp just before I throw up again. The fear I feel is overwhelming. It's worse than anything I've ever been subjected to, a sheer stark terror that makes my skin feel like it's crawling with ants.

I feel something sting my thigh, like a bee. My hand flails, trying to swat it away. The buzzing is so loud in my ears, it's all I can hear.

It's endless. The gut-wrenching pain, the interminable vomiting, the violent spinning. The whirling room of white narrows into a fine point and then winks out entirely.

27

ALIYAH

"Aliyah?"

I wake violently, my arms and legs flailing. A weighted object falls into my lap, and I push at it with my hands, feeling something cold and wet. I look around wildly. My head is pounding.

Amy kneels at my feet.

"Get away from me!" I yell, scrambling back on the sofa until my back hits the armrest. "Stay away, you crazy bitch!"

"Stop it!" she orders, rising to her feet and coming after me. "Calm down!"

I smack her away when she reaches for me and open my mouth to scream.

Her hand slaps over my lips. She bends into my face. "Aliyah! You have to calm down. I didn't do this to you."

The room is twirling again. I realize my eyes are rolling wildly as I struggle against sheer hysteria. My head feels like it's splitting in two.

"Listen to me!" she yells. "You've been poisoned. I didn't do it. It's what's been happening to me. I thought it was you. I thought it was you doing it."

Grabbing her wrists, I yank her hands from me so hard my nails gash her skin. "Get off me!"

"Ow! Goddamn bitch. Fuck! That hurts!"

I lurch to my feet, needing to feel less vulnerable. My legs wobble, but I manage to remain standing. "I don't know what you're talking about! You've lost your mind. You" – I look around – "you put something in the tea? *Why?*"

"Fucking listen to me. For once!" Amy's face is even paler than before; the green of her eyes looks nearly black. "Someone is drugging me! That's what I've been telling you. I need you to tell me the truth if that's even possible – did you do this? Did you make yourself sick to pin it on me?"

"Are you *demented*? No!"

A rush of emotions contorts her face for a moment. "Then the tea was meant for me."

Recoiling from her, I try to process what she's saying. My palm presses against my forehead. Hard. Again and again. But I can't stop the mad throbbing that feels like a creature trying to burrow through my skull. "Who would do that? Why would they do that?"

Her face scrunches, and she begins to sob. "I don't know. I don't know. I've been doing that" – she gestures toward a trash can by the couch – "for weeks. I can't remember. There's so much I can't remember. I've been seeing my therapist . . . telling her things. Whole sessions. I can't remember them. She says I did but I can't remember. And other things . . . They're not real. They didn't happen. I thought I was crazy . . ."

There's something on the floor – a washcloth. I remember the wet thing in my lap and think Amy must have had that on my face. Reaching down, I rub a sore spot on my thigh and recall a sting. Or do I? It's hard to remember how I ended up in Darius's condo in the first place. "Did you inject me with something?"

Amy nods and falls into the side chair as if her legs can't hold her, still sobbing like her heart has broken into pieces. "I had to get a prescription for the vomiting. I couldn't function. Ramin . . . It has to be Ramin. All his notes . . . the voicemails . . . But *why*?"

Ramin? She's delirious. My son would never drug anyone, especially not his brother's wife. None of it makes any sense. Why take care of me after making me sick in the first place . . . ? Is she bipolar? Schizophrenic?

Amy reaches into her pocket, and I back away, stumbling on my heels. I watch as she pulls out her phone. "Rogelio has been calling you," she says in a voice devoid of any emotion. After her incoherent rambling, her sudden clarity is chilling. "At least a few times now. It must be important."

I grab my phone so swiftly that I lose my balance and fall on the sofa. The app is still recording; the battery is critically low. I speed-dial Rogelio.

"Aliyah," he answers. "What the hell took you so long to call me back?"

It's such a relief to hear his voice. "Rogelio! I need you to come to Darius's place right away."

"I can't. I'm not in the city now."

"What?" The panic surges higher than before. "Why? Why aren't you at work?"

"I'm taking a long lunch."

Pulling the phone away, I check the time. It's after noon. I've lost hours of time.

"– to do," he's saying when I return the phone to my ear. "But you need to know about –"

"You need to get someone over here," I interrupt frantically. "Someone you trust. Right now."

"Aliyah, calm down." He takes on the tone of command that tells me I have his complete attention. "What have you done?"

"What?! I haven't done anything! I'm not safe. I need help."

Amy screams, and it frightens me so badly I drop my phone on the floor.

"Oh my God!" she sobs, rocking back and forth while staring at her phone. "Oh my God!"

Something about her demeanor ices my blood. The rocking. The wide mouth, as if she's silently screaming. The eyes that are too big.

I grab her phone and look at it. On the screen is a black-and-white image. A video. The screen is so small it takes a minute to process what I see. It's the living room. Darius's living room. He's standing. Kissing Amy passionately. Her arms are wrapped around him; one hand cups the back of his neck and the other cups his buttock.

"Ugh." I almost look away, and then they move, revealing a dark spot on the bright sofa. Peering closely at the screen, I realize it's Amy sprawled on the cushions, unmoving, and it's another woman who's with Darius. Amy's limbs are unnaturally placed. Not like she fell asleep, but like she was thrown there. "What is this?"

The two entwined figures separate. It's definitely Darius; I'd know him anywhere. The woman, though . . . The way he was holding her. Too intimate.

Too familiar. She laughs, and I recognize her as she steps back. I know those distinctive clothes and the figure inside them. What the hell is her name again . . . ?

Clarice. That's it. She works for Amy.

I struggle to understand, but my horrified surprise bleeds into anger. My son *is* cheating on his wife. And the way Amy lies there as if she's been tossed like trash deepens the sickness still clinging to my throat and curdling in my stomach.

There's a noise competing with the ringing in my ears, and it becomes so insistent it gains my attention. Rogelio. Rogelio is shouting.

Picking my cell up from the floor, I lift it to my ear, still holding Amy's phone and watching my son begin to undress his mistress. I don't want to see, but I have to know absolutely. When? When did my middle son become some sick blend of Paul and Alex? I can't bear it. I feel nauseous all over again.

"Stop shouting," I tell Rogelio with no inflection because I feel dead inside. The one thing I'd believed I did right was my children, but this . . . this is warped . . . obscene.

"What happened?" he yells. "What's going on?"

"I don't know." I shake my head. "I don't know."

"You said you're not safe. Is Darius there? Did he hurt Amy?"

"How did you know?" My arm drops to my side so I no longer have to watch. I've seen enough.

"Know what? Aliyah, you need to start making sense, or I'm calling the police."

"No, don't!" Just the thought makes me so anxious I fear I may pass out again. "No cops."

"Is Darius there?"

"No. Not yet."

"If you don't feel safe, you need to get out of there," he says urgently. "Now. Before he gets home. Take Amy with you."

"Why?"

"Are you walking out the door?" he snaps.

"No. Rogelio, what's going on?"

"Grab your shit and Amy. Start walking."

"What the hell is going on?" I scream.

He curses in Spanish. "Darius has been juggling the money at Baharan, moving funds between accounts. Most of the transactions use your electronic signature. He's also talked with the contractor in Seattle about that land you bought. It's not buildable due to zoning and environmental restrictions. They've known that all along. He plans to go to the board and tell them."

"No. No, that can't be right. Darius wouldn't –"

"You want to argue with me about it, fine. Just get the fuck out of there first. You've gotta trust your instincts, Aliyah. Always."

I glance at Amy, who looks catatonic, tears flowing in an endless stream from unblinking eyes. The woman I see now is too familiar. I was her once.

I have to protect her.

I don't understand what's been done, but I know what I saw, and I cannot – will not – defend a man who's culpable. Not even one I gave birth to.

My phone screen goes black as the battery dies. Grabbing my purse, I reach for Amy's arm. "We're leaving."

28

LILY

Long Island Sound shimmers with the light of the bright afternoon sun. The breeze is warm; the blue sky is cloudless. Seagulls circle above, their raucous cries a familiar and beloved sound. Closing my eyes, I tilt my face and focus on every sensation: the smell of salt in the air, the rustling of the beach grass, and the warmth penetrating my skin and loosening my tense muscles.

"Hey." Your voice is low and intimate, a gentle intrusion into my moment of reflection. I felt your approach before you spoke, the subtle change in energy I feel whenever we're close to each other.

"Hey," I say back, opening my eyes and turning my head to watch you come toward me. You're wearing navy dress slacks, and your pale blue dress shirt is open at the collar and rolled up at the sleeves. The color suits the tan you've gained in the past few days. You're breathtakingly handsome, even with the grim set of your mouth and jaw. "Taking a break?"

You've been busy in your office since breakfast. I know you're thinking of walking away from Baharan, but you love the work. You come alive when you focus on your job and grow even more energized when you address something particularly challenging.

"Something I've been waiting on has finally come in." You've got a piece of paper in your hand, and you walk to me barefoot.

Joining me at the patio table on the veranda, you put the paper in front of me. I glance at it, curious, and read. Curiosity turns to dismay when I see that you are the patient named on the lab report, but I keep my face impassive. I look at you and say nothing.

"This connects to Erika Ferrari," you say, your dark eyes somber. "The woman you ran into when you were shopping with Witte."

"Yes, I remember." I set my hand flat over the lab report, keeping it on the teak tabletop as the breeze attempts to blow the paper away.

"Before I explain, thank you for being patient and giving me time to get those results. I wanted to be certain before I told you. We've all heard the stories about vasectomies that reverse on their own."

Something inside me breaks to have you confirm the reason for your zero sperm count. It would have been terrible enough if nature had chosen to sterilize you. But you sterilized yourself at some point during your widowhood.

A tear slides down my cheek, and I brush it away, but another follows.

You reach over and set your hand atop mine. "It's physically impossible for me to impregnate anyone," you expound needlessly. "Erika's child is absolutely not mine."

I would never have married again or built a family. I remember you telling me that and how deeply it hurt to hear it because I want joy for you above anything else.

"I'm not grasping for excuses here," you continue. "I could have abstained, but sometimes I didn't. I've told you why . . . what I was thinking and feeling when I chose to sleep with other women."

I nod because I'm unable to speak. I remember your words all too well.

The longing for you was crippling. Some days, I couldn't stop myself from looking for you, searching for you, in every woman I saw.

Your grip on my hand tightens. "So, with that said, Laska entered Amy's life and hired her company around the time I met her. And Witte has learned that Erika is a waitress at one of Laska's bars. Another woman was a physical trainer at his gym. Again, I'm not making excuses for my actions. Still, I can't help but think the Laska connections aren't random."

I'm vibrating with emotion, overwhelmed by competing feelings: relief that my mother must still be alive, joy, love, worry, fear, anger. "There's nothing random in anything Val or my mother does."

"I don't understand. What would he get out of setting me up with women?" You search my face, and I see the torment in your eyes. "*Why* would he do that?"

"Could be anything," I say, suddenly exhausted. "They don't understand what love is. To them, you and I couldn't really be choosing each other above everyone else. Surely, I'm just your type and I could be replaced. Maybe a woman pregnant with your child would be more attractive than I am."

"God." You push away from the table in an explosion of frustration and stalk away, only to pace back to me. "It fucks with my head! I can't wrap my mind around it."

"That's because you're sane." In contrast, I understand my mother very well. I think like she does. "Erika may be in trouble. Coerced in some way. Have you talked to her?"

"Not yet. You were my priority, *Setareh*. Always." You pivot toward me again when your pacing reaches the edge of the slate tiles. "You worry about everyone."

"Not everyone," I correct. "Only my mother's pawns and victims."

"God, *Setareh*. When will you accept that you're not responsible for what she does?"

"Someone has to be responsible, Kane. She can't go around unchecked!" I wipe at the tears that, now started, won't stop streaming. "Val could think of something like this – putting women who look like me in your path – but my mother is the one who would actually do it because she'd find it very entertaining."

"Entertaining to watch me make the wrong choice over and over again?" you growl, and your hands are clenched so tightly your knuckles are white. "I've never been worthy of you, but it stings, it really fucking stings, to prove that to other people."

"There was no way to win her approval, Kane, so don't beat yourself up." I crush the lab report in my fist.

You stop moving. Extending your hand, you take the wadded-up paper from me and lob it with pinpoint accuracy into the trash can on the side of the house.

"I don't want you upset about the vasectomy. It's reversible," you assure me, your big body thrumming with frenetic energy. "When – *if* – you decide you're ready, Araceli, we can make a family together."

Standing, I refuse to imagine that dream. "I can't even hope for that as long as my mother's alive."

You grow very still. "You told me you killed her."

"I thought I had, but Erika's pregnancy makes me think twice about that. Based on how far along she appears to be, Erika must have met you shortly before you found me again. There are many things Val would keep in motion for my mother, like watching me and hunting you, but finding women who resemble me and pushing them toward you? No way. Not his style. Amy also came along after my mother was supposedly dead. And Erika approaching you after Val died? No. It's my mother. It has to be."

"Maybe it's as simple as Erika wanting money."

I look at you wryly. "Is that what you think?"

You hold my gaze. "I don't know her well enough to say. I didn't even know her name until Witte told me afterward. I'm not proud of that. It's just how it was."

For a long moment, only the sound of the water surging rhythmically against the shore fills the silence between us.

"I've felt my mother nearby, Kane. I can't explain it, but I have." My arms cross. "I've even seen her. For weeks now, I've tried to convince myself that guilt and grief were fucking with my mind, but I knew. Somehow, I knew she was out there still."

I survived the storm with the help of my crew. My mother could've done the same with Val's help, especially if I missed inflicting a mortal wound. She wore red that day and was soaked with rain. *La Tempête* was tossed by violent waves. It's possible she escaped unscathed or with only minor injury during the time I was unconscious.

"Is that what's been going on with you the past few weeks?" You come to me and pull me into your arms. Your scent envelops and soothes me. "You should've talked to me. I've been so worried."

"I'm sorry." I hug you tightly. "My mother is a rabid animal and there's no way to fix her. She needed to be eliminated. I can't ask for sympathy for being the one to do it. Especially when I wouldn't want anyone else to."

"*Setareh* . . ." You sigh heavily. "How many times and in how many ways do I have to tell you that I accept all that you are and everything you've done?"

"There are limits, Kane!"

"Not to my love." Your embrace tightens. "We're imperfect people. I've made mistakes, and I'll make more. We're both morally gray, but we're better people together. I try harder for you. You call me on my bullshit and make me fix it."

You pull back and catch my gaze. "And you, Araceli – you need someone who doesn't want or need you to change and understands that you'll do what's necessary and suffer for it. I will always love you unconditionally. You've got to accept that. It's way past time."

Lifting onto my tiptoes, I press my lips to your jaw, but you shift and take my mouth, kissing me with passionate savagery. My lips are bruised when you pull away, but so are yours.

"I'm going to call Erika," you tell me gruffly. "I'm going to figure out what's going on. When we know more, we'll determine our next moves. Then we'll work together. Don't try arguing about it. You want to keep me safe, and I want you safe. Got it?"

I nod as if I agree.

Your eyes narrow in warning. "I know you're thinking you'll just handle it yourself, but that's not going to cut it. Your mother might be the reason you were hit by that car, so I've got a right to be involved. You try going it alone, I'm going to have a big problem with that."

"I understand," I say, so you'll do what you must.

You head back into the house through the open patio doors. I wait until you turn the corner to your home office, then I follow you inside to the living room. After waiting a few minutes to ensure you're occupied, I pull a book off the shelf and retrieve the burner phone and portable charger hidden inside a concealed space. I text Rogelio.

> We have to talk.

I'm about to close the book again when the screen lights up.

> I'm on your street. Be ready to leave.

That gives me a start. We don't meet when you're home. One day, I'll introduce you to my family and tell you everything I did while we were apart. But today is not that day. Especially when I have new concerns about my mother.

I text back what he already knows.

> Kane is home.

I wait, but Rogelio doesn't reply. I return the book to the shelf and turn around, unsure how to manage leaving. You brought me here because you fear for my safety in the city. Going out is something you've specifically avoided.

A snapping of fingers turns my head to the veranda. Rogelio stands there and gestures for me to come. He's wearing what I think of as his Baharan uniform but has discarded his suit jacket somewhere.

Hurrying over, I tell him in a whisper, "I can't leave."

"I just sent Black a very long report, *querida*," he tells me sternly. "It's going to take him a while to get through it, and then he's going to be on the phone for a long time. He probably won't even know you've left. And after I show you what I came here for, you may decide not to return."

I frown at him and feel unsettled.

"Let's go. Now," he growls, grabbing my hand and pulling me out the door.

"Wait!" I run back to the coffee table and scratch out a note.

Went for a walk.

I add a hasty reassurance:

Back soon.

I remember how you reacted the last time I walked down the beach. I can't do that to you again.

We leave, scurrying around the side of the house to reach the street, where Rogelio's metallic black cherry Dodge Charger waits. The engine is still running.

"What's going on?" I ask as he pulls away from the curb. "Where are you taking me?

"I don't even know where to start." His gaze is on the road, but his profile is tense. "I thought I'd covered all the bases, but I've missed things I shouldn't have."

"You don't miss things."

"I did this time. Alex Gallagher called Aliyah at work recently because he knows the calls are recorded, and he wanted to use the system to start building a false narrative of what happened between them."

I ponder the calculation, the maliciousness. "The guy's a real piece of work."

"Yeah." Rogelio's hands flex on the steering wheel. "I had to put him on the backburner after the detectives visited you so I could focus on the hit-and-run driver, but I went back to Gallagher last night. I duplicated the recordings and reviewed the transcript. Turns out Aliyah took a call just before, from the contractor in Seattle. Usually, she takes those calls on her cell and talks to Vishal Singh. This time, she heard from his brother, Ram Singh."

My head falls to the headrest. "She's getting more brazen. We'll have to intervene if she's pushing forward with that."

"She's not. But the brother's name rang a bell. I was sure I remembered it from somewhere. I ran searches through the transcripts, but the name was repeatedly spelled wrong by the transcription program, so I had to hit the correct misspelling to find it." He glances at me. "Darius has been talking to Ram Singh regularly, and he's not as wily as Aliyah. He received and made the calls through his office number."

"Well, we knew he was working on the project with Aliyah." I note where we're going. "We're not leaving town, are we?"

"No," he answers brusquely. "The thing is, he's not working *with* Aliyah but against her. He's sabotaged the whole thing from the beginning and set it up to look like she was shady with the company's money to buy the land in Seattle, which is worthless for the intended purpose. He bought it cheap, using a shell company, then sold it to Aliyah for way beyond its value. The Singhs worked with him to hide the permitting issues from her."

I stare at his profile. "Holy shit. Is that the information you sent Kane?"

"Yeah, I've warned Aliyah, too, but it's too late. She can't clean it up now." He punches the steering wheel with his fist. "Darius was ready to go to the board with it. He's meeting with a few of them, including Landon, in the morning. I had to try and prevent that. And I have to hope your man will protect his mother."

I want to question his concern for a woman set on undermining my husband's authority, but I lose my train of thought when we turn into the marina and park. "Why are we here?"

"You'll see. It's something else I missed." He hops out of the car and has already rounded the trunk to my side as I push open the door. Extending his hand, he helps me up from the low-slung car. He pauses, squeezing my hand. "I'm sorry. I've failed you."

"Rogelio, if another person I love says that to me, I'm going to lose it. And if you don't stop talking in riddles, I'm going to hit you, and I've got a great left hook."

"Don't I know it. But this time, I'd deserve it." With my hand still in his, he takes me to the gate leading down to the docks. Punching a code into the keypad, he unlocks it.

"How'd you get that?"

He shoots me a bold glance. "I haven't completely lost my mojo."

We head down the ramp, and then he tugs me to the right. We walk, and then I see her. My steps halt abruptly.

She looks exactly as I remember her. As beautiful and impressive as ever.

"My God," I breathe. "How is she here? How did you find her?"

"How did I miss something as substantial as *La Tempête* is what you should be asking," he says ruefully. "Dealing with misspelled names got me thinking. When we searched Laska's cloud for his contacts, we investigated every name because you said your mother might use an alias. In the process, we compiled a list. I ran through the names again, and one jumped out: Tear eye, spelled '*T-i-e-r space e-y-e.*' Only mentioned once. *Isn't Tier eye clever?* was the text. Possibly a nickname for one of Laska's thugs, right? Like a teardrop prison tattoo. That was the thought at the time."

I put the letters together with the way they sound, and my heart begins to pound. "Are you saying it was an autocorrection of Tierney? As in Paul Tierney, Kane's dad? Is he alive?!"

"We didn't find anything about Paul, but I wondered if Kane Black might use his birth name sometimes. And that led me to your boat."

I glance back at *La Tempête.* "How?"

"The person renting that slip is Kane Tierney."

My thoughts scatter, replaced by a rapid resurgence of memories.

Time rewinds until I wake up on my boat again, drenched by the rain and storm-tossed seas. Rogelio bends over me, shaking me, shouting at me. My head throbs from thumping into the deck when I fell, and my stomach heaves along with the sea.

"Where is she?" I cry. "Where is she?!"

But my mother is gone. I shot her straight through the heart, and she'd crumpled like a doll whose stuffing had disintegrated. I felt the pain of that bullet wound in my own chest and was horrified by what I'd done. I let go of the lines and stumbled toward her, but the swells threw *La Tempête* high, and I slipped headlong. When the hull crashed into the water, I slammed into the deck and lost consciousness.

My head was pounding when I came to, and I struggled to see through blurred vision. There was no body. And no other boat in sight except for the one piloted by Salma to rescue me.

We towed *La Tempête* down the Eastern Seaboard. We changed her name, repainted her and replaced some of her fittings. She was sold, and my crew and I started our hunt for Laska.

"It can't be the same boat." My head is shaking back and forth as I try to process the implications. How could you know, my love? *What* do you know? How *long* have you known?

"Don't you recognize her?"

I spin so fast at the sound of your voice that I stumble into Rogelio. "Kane."

Your face is hard, your gaze harder. You're intimidating; the force of your rage is like a firestorm. It's so hot I sweat.

"Thank you for corroborating your involvement, Rogelio," you say with anger singeing your voice. "It seemed obvious after my wife accessed the safe, but confirmation is always nice. So, it's you and Lacy. Who else?"

I'm so startled by all you know that I can't immediately find the words.

Rogelio stands beside me, his hand gripping my biceps. He can't seem to find words, either.

"Take your hand off my wife," you order with dangerous calm, "and return to the office. I want my brother's passcodes, keycards and access to the Crossfire building revoked. Shut off his remote access and work number. I've already locked him out of the bank accounts. Search his office, box up his personal items and drop them off with building security downstairs."

"I know what to do," he tells you grimly.

"Then go do it." You step aside and gesture for him to leave. "Call me when it's done."

He looks at me, but I can't take my eyes off you.

"I'll be fine," I tell him. My worry is for you and what you're having to do to your brother. Yes, you two have been estranged for a long time, but I know you. The forgiveness and generous heart you give to me is part of you and extends to everyone in your life you care about.

Rogelio leaves. It's not long before I hear the gate close. I should've heard it open when you arrived, but you can move stealthily despite your size.

"You shouldn't be mad at him," I tell you.

You close the distance between us. "He's been with you the years I suffered without you, hasn't he? I can hate him for that."

"He's saved my skin a few times. You can be grateful for that."

Your gaze is shadowed but you give a slight nod as your anger diffuses. "Would you like to be reunited with her? You loved *La Tempête* so much when she was yours."

"Isn't she still mine through you?"

Your mouth lifts in a wry half-smile as you slide your arm around my waist and walk beside me. The sun still shines, although it's moved further west. The seagulls still scream to the heavens. The breeze still runs through my hair like a lover's fingers. Yet the whole day has turned on its head as if I've stepped through a looking glass and entered a parallel reality that mirrors the one I woke up in.

"How did you find her?" I ask.

You don't answer for a moment, and I wonder if you won't. Can I blame you for holding your secrets when I've had so many of my own?

"The body recovered by the Coast Guard," you tell me flatly. "It was missing your scorpion tattoo."

The lack of inflection in your voice is like a roar of agony, and I feel it in the marrow of my bones.

It's scant information, but my mind expands from it to complete the picture. The tiny scorpion on my wrist is you, my passionate Scorpio, and it was the telltale sign that betrayed my obsession with you. I tried to hide it, as I tried to hide my attraction, and my mother wouldn't have known about it. She wouldn't have known any corpse passing as me would need to bear it. But you knew, my love, and thought to search for it.

My eyes sting as tears well. How is it possible to feel ever more pain?

"I would never do that to you," I vow hoarsely. "I would never deliberately put you through the horror of identifying my body for any reason. Ever."

"I know." You tug me closer and kiss the top of my head.

"I had no idea there was a body until Aliyah mentioned it to me. I wouldn't have let you live with that if I'd known."

"I knew it wasn't you and that you would never destroy me that way, but anything else was possible." Your fingers at my hip tighten their grip on me. "Had you been kidnapped? I waited for a ransom demand. Had you been abducted? I didn't know about your mother or Laska then. And I couldn't be sure you didn't just want to leave. After Ryan and everything else . . . I knew I was holding onto you by my fingernails. But the body . . . it was a piece of the puzzle that didn't fit anywhere."

"I'm sorry," I tell you, although it's profoundly inadequate.

We reach the boat, and I see how beautifully she's been maintained. She's also been restored to how I kept her. She even has her name again. Her mast juts proudly, piercing the sky.

Holding my hand, you support me as I step onto the gangway. I kick off my sandals before boarding and carry them. The sea breeze blows my dress around my legs and chills my bare arms. It's not cold, not at all, but I'm freezing. It feels like I could breathe frost into the summer air.

Securing the companionway is a smoked glass hatch etched with a phoenix matching the one on my back. I look to the spot on the weathered teak deck where I last saw my mother lying in a puddle of crimson silk, and then I look away because she's almost certainly alive. Who else would Val have texted about how clever "Tier eye" was?

Val knew all along that Kane had recovered *La Tempête*. Val wanted me to find her, but why? What did he expect would happen when I did?

The boat rocks gently as you join me. "I searched online for boats like yours. I wanted to see how they were built and if it could have survived that squall and you with it. I had to do something, or I'd have gone insane. I hired Rampart to search your past and look for you now. And a picture of this boat, completely unrecognizable, came up in my search. Her new owner was selling her."

I face you. The wind tousles your hair as it does mine, blowing it across your brow. The collar of your shirt flaps gently, teasing me with flashes of the tanned skin of your throat. I ache with love and longing. "But you knew it was her. How?"

"You left scratches in the stateroom bulkhead when I made love to you. They're lacquered over now, but the gouges are still visible. I saw them in the listing photos."

Surprise holds me tightly for a moment, and then I laugh. "You can't have remembered that! Or seen it in a photo."

Your hands go to your lean hips. "As if I could forget it. Or any other time I've had you."

My smile is so wide it hurts. "I left them there on purpose when I found them. I gave specific orders not to fill them. I didn't want to erase that memory and I wanted to leave my mark on her. My God . . . the odds are astronomical."

"Didn't you once say the universe wants us to be together?"

"I did, yes. And I suppose she's proven that." I turn around, taking in everything. The restoration is so precise it seems almost like the refit was a dream. "Why didn't you tell me?"

"Why didn't you tell me about Lacy or Rogelio?" you rejoin. "Why haven't you told me what you were doing during the years we were apart?"

Exhaling in a rush, I feel stripped bare. "I was afraid. It's so much, Kane. Maybe too much. And no one ever knows what that line is until it's crossed."

You shake your head. "There is no line, Araceli. No division at all between us. And no more secrets. No more lies. Tell me now if there's something else I don't know."

I've never seen you so earnest, so open. Almost pleading, yet entirely in command of yourself. And of me.

"There are others who work with me," I confess. "Some are around the world. Others are here. I want you to meet them, to know them."

"Of course. Anything else?"

My heart is racing. I must tell you everything now. "About Val . . ."

"I already know," you interject softly.

At some point I stopped being a step ahead of you. You've caught up to me, maybe even managed to get ahead of me. But we're together now.

"I'm glad you told me, *Setareh*." There's a tenderness in your dark eyes that makes my soul sing. "Come here."

I consider asking how you found me so quickly, but it doesn't matter. Every time we've been lost, we've found each other. How that happens doesn't matter.

29

WITTE

I WAS TRAINED TO RESIST SLEEPING FOR DAYS AT A TIME IF DANGEROUS situations warranted it. It's a skill I hadn't used in so long it seemed like a lifetime ago.

Last night, I'd feigned sleep all evening, listening instead to the steady breathing of the woman who's like a fire in my blood. Her smell, the sound of her voice and the feel of her body all seem to have been designed to affect me ferociously. From the moment we first bumped into each other at the Green Market, I was captivated and intrigued. Her face is unforgettable. Once you've seen it, you will never forget it. Whether in person or a photograph.

I thought of that stunning face all night, as I have many a night. I thought of it until a thin band of the dawn's light framed the blackout curtains, and Danica's steady breathing altered into the less regular rhythm of wakefulness. I thought of it still as she rolled over to me in the bed we shared.

The brush of her silken skin stirred my blood along with her huskily voiced, "Nicky, darling."

The feel of her curves pressed to my side made me instantly hard. She pressed a kiss to my throat, and her hand slid down to my cock. While she stroked me into full hardness, she whispered things in my ear that were so raunchy and lustful I could scarcely resist rolling her over and taking her roughly. But I resisted because we've been together for years now and I knew what she wanted.

She was like a wraith when she rose above me, straddling my hips. Scarcely discernible from the room's shadows, her silvery hair and luminous eyes were the only points of reference, as if I were entangled with someone who didn't truly exist. As always, her beauty stole my breath. Her smile was infectious. Then she slid the silken grip of her pussy over my aching dick and began to ride.

She took her pleasure with no holds barred, unashamedly vocal when she orgasmed, and so greedy for more. I fisted the sheets and gritted my teeth, holding back my climax so she could come repeatedly. Only when she gasped, "Nicky! I can't . . ." did I sit up and catch her, twisting to take the top and thrusting heavily between her lithe thighs until my mind was lost to the pleasure of it.

Now, as I read the report Mr Black forwarded me, it's a relief to push Danica from my mind. I've known Darius Armand felt no love for his elder brother, but I wasn't aware that faithlessness extended to their mother.

Moving outside to the balcony, I sit at the patio table and feel a slight shiver from the soft bite of the early morning chill. It won't last long. Soon it will be oppressively hot.

I call my employer.

"Witte," he answers.

"I'm sorry," I tell him by way of greeting, and my tone conveys my deep sincerity.

He sighs heavily. "Thank you. I am, too."

"Treachery of this magnitude within a family is almost beyond comprehension."

"I keep trying to find a reasonable explanation. It's like I can't accept that he would act this maliciously."

There's a weighted pause before he speaks further.

"You wouldn't know it now, but Darius and I used to be very close. Because it was just him and me for a little bit and our age gap was smaller, our bond was different than the ones I had with Ramin and Rosana. I adored him. And he gave that love back to me when no one else did." His shaky exhale reveals his anguish. "I don't know how it came to this. And I don't understand how he could do this to our mother. What he's set her up for is criminal."

"What does your mother say?"

"We've only spoken in short bursts. She's getting Amy settled at a friend's and says handling one thing at a time is all she can manage now. We're meeting at the penthouse at ten."

My brows lift. "Your brother and his wife are separating?"

"Yes, there's apparently a story there, too. Considering what we've learned so far, I'm not sure I want to hear it."

"You'll have to take charge of the family, Kane," I say sternly. "Your mother will need time to process the betrayal. Amy will need support if she intends to divorce. And even Ramin will likely need guidance."

Mr Black sighs again, and I hear the weariness in it. "I know. And I'll make the time and find a way, but the timing couldn't be worse. My wife thinks her mother is alive. She says everything that's been happening points to that. And she's definitely been working with Rogelio. I'll explain how that was confirmed when you and I are back in the penthouse. I have some things I haven't told you."

"That's become apparent. But then, we all have our secrets, don't we? And we anticipated Rogelio's involvement, so that's not a surprise."

"It's infuriating!" He growls softly. "All these years that I've been dead without her, she's had people all around me. At home, at work. Thinking about it drives me crazy."

I think of when I hired Lacy years ago. And all the times I've worked with Rogelio on security for the penthouse, our personal electronics, and installing the safe in the sitting room.

"She's terrified of her mother, but, Witte . . . the way she thinks of her. It's like her mother has become larger than life in her mind. The fear is . . . Well, it's unnatural. It's become confused with awe and a twisted kind of love. Even respect."

"A child's love for their mother is a unique bond. You understand how complicated it can be."

And I also appreciate the tenacity of that bond. I'd watched for years with helpless fury as my daughter acted as the adult in her relationship with her mother and never complained. To this day, she speaks of her mum with the same reverence I've often heard in Lily's voice when she describes her mother.

"Yes, I know," my employer says grimly. "And I don't doubt that Stephanie's dangerous. I'm not saying my wife is being irrational in her fear. I know what kind of man Laska was and that Stephanie is believed to be as horrific a human being as he was. I'm just worried that even if she's dead, my wife's fanatical fixation on her mother will continue to be a problem."

I hear the drumming of his fingertips on a hard surface.

"We have to find Stephanie if she's out there," he continues. "I won't have the life I want if my wife can't sleep at night."

Movement inside the condo draws my gaze to Danica. She's returned from visiting the bakery on the bottom floor with a paper bag in one hand and a drink carrier with two cups.

Don't donuts and lattes sound delicious? she'd asked as I lay panting and boneless after a wrenching orgasm.

"Witte?"

"Yes, I'm here." My hand reaches up and rubs over my aching heart. "We'll find her. And amidst all this unpleasantness, it's reassuring to have dispelled any doubts about Mrs Black working with Laska or her mother to harm you. With Rogelio and Lacy so close, if that was her intention, it could have been accomplished long ago."

He's silent for a long moment. "Is that what you thought?" he asks quietly.

"It was a possibility," I say. "With what we knew, it was the simplest solution. To leave the money with you until they needed it, or it was safe to claim it. It makes as much sense for them to work together as it does for them to work in competition."

"I thought you liked my wife."

"I do. A great deal, actually. And I believe she loves you deeply. But it's my job to be objective."

His soft laugh holds little humour. "I'll be leaving shortly."

"I'll be waiting at the penthouse."

The call ends, and I heave a sigh, attempting to alleviate the strain that's knotted my shoulders. I type out a text but don't yet send it.

Standing, I twist from side to side, cracking my back. I don't anticipate needing to get physical, but one never knows when emotions are high. There are still so many questions, but I have the answer I need: Lily Black – Araceli – isn't a threat to her husband. It's time for me to deal with the other hazards.

I open the sliding door and step into the cool interior of Danica's apartment. It's a small space: one bedroom, one bath. With smaller furniture, she could place a compact dining table in the corner but chose an oversized sectional instead. We've made love countless times on that sofa. And throughout the apartment.

Entering the bedroom, I hear the shower running. I turn to the wardrobe. There are two, hers and mine, separated by a space of wall on which the television hangs. Hers is closest, and I step into it, flicking on the light switch.

The confined space smells strongly of her, and I take a deep breath. She's highly organized, with her clothes sorted by garment type, colour, and length. On each hanger is a unique cataloguing system comprised of a card hung from each hanger. There are two versions: one bears an image of the sun and the other an image of the moon, denoting day or evening wear. On the front, her handwriting lists which of her other garments pairs best. On the back, she's written which accessories are optimally suited.

I've seen that system used by only one other person – her daughter, Mrs Black.

My mother used this system in her closet, Lily told me once. It only confirmed what I already knew.

I've never forgotten what it felt like, five years ago, to turn around at the Green Market to address the person who'd bumped into me and see nearly the same face I saw every day in the life-sized photo of Mrs Black that hangs in my employer's bedroom. For a long moment, I couldn't speak, my mind scrambling to understand if it was indeed Mrs Black and, if so, how she could have aged into salt-and-pepper hair so swiftly.

"I'm so sorry," Danica had said, flashing a smile that struck a chord deep inside me. "I'm so clumsy."

We'd started chatting, then walking together. We had lunch. Within hours of meeting, I was invited to her condo and then to her bed. She was charming, cultured, and keenly intelligent. A delightful companion. A lusty lover. We hadn't yet learned of Mrs Black's many aliases. And while I often stared at Lily Black's image and found the resemblance between the two women remarkable, it wasn't until a few months into our relationship, when Danica attempted to access my tablet while I was in the shower, that I understood all was not as it seemed. The security software installed by Rogelio tracked numerous future attempts to access my devices. But figuring out her connection to Lily was what kept me playing along.

The rushing water in the shower is abruptly silenced, and I flip off the light.

Exiting the wardrobe, I sit on the edge of the mattress. The bed is fully dishevelled, reminding me of how deeply ensnared I am by a notoriously deadly woman.

"All done with work?" she asks, stepping into view. Her hair is wrapped in a turban, and a towel is tucked between her breasts. Barefaced, she looks younger than she must be and less like her daughter. It's cosmetics that enhance their striking resemblance.

"No, I'll have to leave in a little while."

She heads to her wardrobe and speaks over her shoulder. "Is your boss coming back to the city, or will I see you later?"

I don't answer her question but ask one of my own. "Will you miss me?"

I will certainly miss her. And I've stopped berating myself for that.

When I leave, I'll send the text to my contact in the NYPD. He'll know where to find Stephanie Laska. If she loves her daughter as much as Lily believes, she won't betray the connection between them and will take the fall for Laska's death without argument. It's a big *if*. In another time, I'd handle Danica myself, but I've crossed the line of neutrality where she's concerned.

"I would," she says brightly, appearing in the doorway completely naked except for the clinging skeins of her wet hair. "But you're not going anywhere."

I hardly have time to register her hand lifting and the weapon it holds before my body contorts in excruciating pain. I slam into the mattress, my back arching in a violent cramp before I thrash uncontrollably. The coppery taste of blood fills my mouth.

The electrifying pain stops as abruptly as it began, but I can't move. I can't do anything at all, can hardly process a thought when she shoves me over and zip-ties my wrists together. My ankles are bound, too, and both are linked, leaving me hog-tied.

When I come to my senses, gasping for air, I find Danica sitting beside me, still naked.

She reaches out and brushes the hair off my forehead. "How long have you known?"

It's a struggle to relax my jaw enough to lie. "Years."

Her brows lift, and then she laughs. "Was it exciting to know? Did it turn you on when we fucked?"

I don't answer her. I don't recognize her. The warm, affectionate, passionate woman I know now radiates a deep cold.

She smiles and circles the taser barbs in my chest with a caressing fingertip. "Like you, I can be very patient. But it's also exciting to finally be able to end this."

"End what?"

"This whole debacle with Kane Tierney Armand Black. The man has almost as many names as I do. He's been a thorn in my side for ages, and I can't wait to pull it out, crush it, and burn it to ashes."

She talks in a singsong, cheerful rhythm which only makes what she says more terrifying.

"He's out of town," I tell her. "And well guarded."

"Oh, Witte. You're delightful." She runs her fingers over my jaw with a tenderness I'm familiar with and now find extremely disturbing. "I have a very sensitive microphone hidden on the patio table. So, I know he'll be at the penthouse at ten o'clock. Which is just enough time for me to get ready."

"You'll never make it up there," I bite out.

"Watch me." Her grin is like that of a child. "I was really hoping my daughter would come to her senses and get the money back on her own, but she's got Stockholm Syndrome or something. After he's dead, I'll need to deprogramme her."

I study her from my position on the bed, unable to discern if I'm still paralysed or simply in shock and lacking the will to move. She looks and smells the same as the woman I fell in love with, but she's energized in a way I haven't seen before, nearly vibrating with feverish excitement.

"And when I get back," she goes on, "you're going to help me drain their bank accounts and liquidate assets."

"You should get on with killing me," I tell her coldly, "because you'll never get what you want."

She lies down on the bed so we're side by side, facing each other. "Everyone says that at first. They imagine all the tortures they've read about or watched in movies and think they can bear it or die before they break. But I know how to reach that breaking point without touching a single hair on your head."

I stare at her defiantly, my brows raised in challenge. My fingers are starting to go numb, and my left shoulder throbs from bearing the brunt of my weight while stretched behind my back.

She taps the tip of my nose with a crimson nail. "Catherine."

The sound of my daughter's name is like another jolt of the taser. Horror floods me.

"Ah." Danica giggles. "See how easy that was? She's been dating a very handsome young man for over a year now. She thinks he works in finance, but Christian works for me. You give me what I want, and maybe she won't end up sold to the highest bidder. She is *really* lovely. She'd fetch a pretty penny on the black market."

I stare into those jade-coloured eyes and see a mad light behind the translucent green. I don't know how she's hidden it this long. It alters her entire face as if when she exited her wardrobe, she returned as a totally different person.

Placing a hand over my heart, she gives me a sympathetic look. "You know how it feels to have a daughter. How scary it is to think of all the dangers they face because men are animals. Admit it, Nicky darling. You wouldn't want Kane Black fucking Catherine, either."

My skin crawls.

She sits up and leaves the bed. "I have to get ready. Ten o'clock will be here before we know it."

I turn my head to look at her. "I can get you the money without you having to kill him. We could do it now."

Danica thrusts her fingers into her damp hair and shakes out the roots. "Where's the fun in that?"

30

AMY

"I CAN'T EVEN PROCESS WHAT YOU'RE TELLING ME," SUZANNE SAYS, sitting beside me on the couch. She sets down both cups of coffee she's brought in from the kitchen. "It's . . . it's just really fucking unbelievable. I mean, I know the guy. I've seen how Darius is with you."

I stroke my hand over Ollie's head. He has his chin and front paws resting on my thigh. "I was up all night, going over and over it. Reading the letters we used to write each other. Looking at our wedding photos. A few weeks ago, Darius was over the moon that I might be pregnant. And now he's poisoning me?! What the fuck? It doesn't make sense. It doesn't make any fucking sense."

She sets her hand over mine. "Thank God you have him on video. You'd never know he was capable of something like that. At least you have proof."

"Right? Aliyah and I watched hours of recordings last night. He's been doctoring my drinks, food . . . even my shampoo and face wash. For years! And he talks to himself while he's doing it. Like rambling. Incoherently. He's insane, right?" I look at her. "He's got to be insane. Like a split personality or something."

"I don't know, honey." Her face is so kind and concerned. "I write fiction and couldn't make this up."

I have to look away from her sympathy. I'm a breath away from sobbing every second. "I don't know what to do. And Clarice . . . she's been with me since before I even met Darius. They're going to investigate her and see if we have grounds to fire her because fucking my husband apparently isn't enough. Can you believe it?"

"No," she says flatly. "I still can't see it."

"I think she's been tampering with my food, too. I thought it was Aliyah's fault that I was feeling sick at work, but Clarice brought the food back to me when she went out to lunch. And my company's been whittled down to the bone. Clarice said it was Aliyah, but Aliyah says she never messed with it, and Clarice had control."

"You've got to be able to fire her. No way she keeps her job after this." Suzanne shakes her head.

"Let's fucking hope we find proof of something with her, too."

"Not that there's a plus side to this craziness, but Aliyah seemed much nicer than I expected."

Sighing, I lean back into the cushions and close my tired eyes. "I can't tell if she's just trying to butter me up, so I don't file charges against her son and cause a scandal or if she really cares about what's been happening to me."

"Are you thinking about calling the police? I would if I were you."

"I mean, I can't say I haven't thought about it." I lift my arm as Ollie shifts to cuddle closer, then rest it on his back.

"He's worried about you, too," she points out gently.

"He's a good boy, aren't you, Oliver? Stick with this guy," I tell her wearily. "He's loyal."

He heaves a long-suffering sigh.

"Well?" Suzanne prods. "Are you going to have Darius arrested? You have the evidence."

"Honestly, I'm just trying not to scream because I'm not sure I'll be able to stop if I get started."

"Oh . . . I'm sorry. I don't mean to push you."

"You're not. It's just that we can't rule out that Darius was poisoning himself, too. Never, in any of the times he was recorded spiking my stuff, did he wear gloves."

"Girl, do not try and sell me on him being a victim."

"I'm not making excuses for him." Opening my eyes, I stare at the ceiling. "But his behavior . . . It's just not right. Not sane. And I know how I've felt since this started – at least since I think it started – and I can't be held responsible for what I did."

I try not to hate myself for what happened with Ramin, my fixation on Lily, the way I stalked women Kane slept with . . . too many things.

She scoffs. "That doesn't absolve him from thinking of drugging you in the first place!"

"Of course not. But it makes the whole thing even more convoluted."

"I say let the authorities sort it out."

I nod because she's not wrong, but I don't know how to explain that it feels like I'm suffocating in my skin. Maybe it's the relentlessly cheerful yellow walls that are oddly jarring today.

Aliyah's overwhelmingly neutral condo had been soothing, maybe because it was like mine. Or maybe because my life feels like it's been leached of all color. Or perhaps it's because she acted like a mom for once.

After taking us to a lab for testing, she took me back to her place and made soup from scratch, which I could acknowledge was delicious even though I wasn't at all hungry. She ensured I had a shower and everything I needed, even a pair of her pajamas. She tucked me into her guestroom bed and sat beside me, telling me I would be safe and financially taken care of. Just before I drifted off, I heard her murmur that she couldn't fix the past, but she'd make sure I was in a strong position moving forward.

It's still possible I'm crazy because I believed her.

Suzanne's phone rings, and she stretches over to the end table to grab it. "Hello?"

One of her eyebrows wings up, and she gets a sharp, dangerous look. She takes the phone away from her ear and glances at me. "Darius is downstairs. Can I tell the doorman to call the police?"

I stare at her for a long minute, totally confused by my emotions. I don't know what I want or what I want to happen.

And then realization strikes.

"Let him up," I tell her. "Or I'll go down to him if you prefer that."

"What? Are you nuts?! The guy's been trying to kill you!"

"I know that!" I snap. "I want to know *why*. I need to know. I'll lose my mind spinning my wheels, imagining a thousand different scenarios. I have to look him in the eye and hear him tell me why."

Suzanne glares at me and shakes her head. "What if he attacks you? He's all muscle. The two of us together can't fight him off."

"Ollie won't let anything happen to you, but it won't get to that. I've got pepper spray in my bag."

"Pepper spray for a would-be murderer. Great."

I stand gingerly to avoid displacing Ollie. "I'm going down there. Have the doorman tell him to wait."

"No. Fuck. Okay." She lifts the phone to her ear again. "Go ahead and send him up."

Dropping her hand to her lap, Suzanne sits there with her foot tapping restlessly. "I'm going to video this when he gets up here. Maybe he'll think twice about acting crazy."

Walking over to her tiny foyer, I glance at myself in the mirror by the door. I look like complete shit. My hair is messy, my eyes are red and rimmed in dark circles, my face is pale. For a moment, I debate whether I want him to see me like this. Will it give him satisfaction to see what he's done to me? And then I realize I don't care what he gets out of it.

I'm still staring at the shell of myself when the doorbell rings. Taking a deep breath, I thumb open the deadbolt, then pull the door wide.

I gasp. "Oh my God. Darius."

As bad as I look, he looks worse. He's wearing the same suit he wore to work yesterday, but now it's wrinkled so badly it bulges oddly all over. His usually lustrous dark hair is dull and disordered. He's got a day-old beard, and his blue eyes are wild.

"Amy!" He lunges toward me as if to hug me.

Thrusting my arm out, I barely hold him back. "Don't fucking touch me! I'm serious, Darius. Get the fuck back!"

Ollie barks, and Darius stops pressing forward and backs away, but his jaw is clenched. "Why weren't you home last night?"

I gape at him for a long minute. Has he not talked to anyone in the family yet? "I know what you've been doing to me. I put hidden cameras around the condo."

He frowns at me like he can't understand. "Cameras?"

"I know you've been poisoning me!"

He blinks rapidly. "I would never poison you," he says firmly. "I love you."

"You're a goddamned fucking liar!" I scream in his face. "You've been lying and gaslighting me this whole time! And cheating! You're a fucking cheater. With Clarice? Fucking gross, Darius. You disgust me!"

Ollie begins growling.

Recoiling from my rage, Darius takes another step back. His chin lifts, and he tugs on the hem of his jacket as if that might restore his appearance. "I wasn't poisoning you. You weren't going to die. Just be a little sick."

"Oh, that's okay, then." My hands clench tightly against the urge to punch him. "Why did you want me sick?"

His throat works on a hard swallow. "You fucked my brothers, Amy."

My eyes widen, and it feels like I've taken a blow. I register the pained look on his face, and it resonates inside me. It's a shock that I can feel guilty. And even more shocking to realize I still care about him. That I haven't turned it off yet. "You're fucking certifiable! I slept with Kane before I even knew you existed."

"I wanted one thing that was mine!" His face is mottled with fury. "Just *one*."

"I was, Darius. When we said our vows to each other, I meant every word. Ramin . . . Ramin was a huge mistake," I admit hoarsely. "Things between you and me were too perfect. You were so wonderful . . . Everything seemed too good to be true, and I didn't trust it. I couldn't believe in it. So, I tried to sabotage it. Therapy helped me to figure that out. There's no excuse for what I did, but Darius . . ."

My breath catches on a sob. "That mistake made me realize how much I loved you. It made us stronger because I knew I didn't want to lose what we had. But turns out, it was too good to be true after all."

"Ramin couldn't stop rubbing in that he'd had you!" he whines. "He would remind me he'd fucked you every chance he got. I could never get away from it. Every day, I'd see his smug face and think about him on top of you. I couldn't stand it!"

"Then hit him! Duke it out. Do whatever it is that brothers do to get over shit. Go to counseling or something. You don't fucking *poison your wife!*"

"It wasn't poison," he repeats as if that makes his actions okay.

"Whatever you're rationalizing in your head just reinforces how batshit crazy you are." I back away.

"Stop!" he barks, and I see something drift across his face like the shadow of a fast-moving cloud.

Shivering violently, I pull Aliyah's cream cashmere cardigan tighter around me and feel Suzanne hovering at my back.

My husband visibly composes himself. "I was keeping my promise to you. I told you I'd get my mother out of the way at Baharan, and I am. We're so close to having everything you wanted."

"What I wanted was you and my company, that's *it*! And then you started drugging me, and everything got all screwed up in my head. I didn't know which way was up or down. I was doing . . ." I find I can't elaborate. ". . . things. And I don't even know half of what I was doing! I have false memories, and I'm missing actual memories."

My crossed arms tighten. "Do you understand? Whatever we've talked about since you started drugging me is worthless. It doesn't mean anything."

"That's not true! We had plans. Get my mom out of Baharan. Use that to show Kane's incompetence. Then you and I take over."

"I don't want a pharmaceutical company! I don't know the first thing about chemistry or biology or anything else, and I don't want to know. I like dealing with people, not pills. Do you not know me at all?"

Shoving his hands in his pockets, Darius begins to rock on his feet. He starts vibrating with energy, like something is restrained tightly inside him, fighting to get out. "Of course I know you! I love you."

"Stop saying that. It's a total fucking lie." I take another step back.

"Don't you dare walk away from me!" he growls, his gaze narrowing in a wholly intimidating way. "I've lost everything for you! They've locked me out of Baharan. I can't log in to the systems. I can't get past security at the Crossfire. I've been completely shut out."

Surprise floods me. I don't know what I expected Aliyah to do, but cutting Darius off so swiftly wasn't a thought I'd had.

But then it settles in, and I nod grimly. "Now you know what I mean about your mother. She's a scary bitch when she wants to be."

"We need to come up with a plan. We need to get cleaned up and talk to my family because Kane's in on this, too. It was probably his idea to fire me, and Mom is just going along to save her neck."

"I'm not going anywhere with you, you fucking lunatic!" Jumping back, I slam the door shut and twist the deadbolt.

He crashes into the door so hard I swear it rattles from the pressure. I hear

Suzanne's frightened gasp and am equally as terrified. Ollie leaps from the couch so swiftly the coffee cups rattle and tip over, spilling creamed coffee. He launches himself at the door with all his strength, barking ferociously.

"Amy! Goddamnit. Amy! Open the door!"

"Go away, Darius!"

He begins pounding with his fists. "You're my wife! You're coming home with me! Get the fuck out of there!"

"Jesus!" Suzanne grabs me and pulls me back, still aiming her phone's camera at the door. "Oliver! Come here!"

But Ollie won't stop because my husband is like a madman, ramming into the door, screaming and ranting. We stumble back into the living room.

Suzanne fumbles with her phone. "I'm calling the cops!"

"No, don't!" I yell, knocking it out of her hands.

"Are you crazy, too?!" she screeches. "He's going to break down the door and kill us!"

"Just . . . Hang on!" I grab my phone out of my purse and power it on. "Get Ollie in the bedroom!"

Suzanne hesitates, and I feel like I'm going to explode into a million pieces, the pressure is so great. "Now!" I order, even as I hear one of the neighbors – a man – start yelling at Darius. Then I hear the crash of bodies in the hallway.

"Jesus." My hands shake violently as I search for the correct number. There. Got it. I tap the screen repeatedly. Ringing. Thank God . . . Tears splatter onto the glass as the ringing suddenly stops.

"Black."

"Oh my God, Kane! He's here. He's here, and he's crazy!" I struggle to breathe through my sobs. "Like fully out of his mind!"

Ollie continues to bark nonstop through the wall, scratching frantically at the bedroom door.

"Slow down." Kane's voice is clipped and hard. "Are you talking about Darius?"

"Who the fuck else?!? He's fighting with the neighbor now." I choke in another breath. "Like punching each other. In the hallway."

"At your friend's place?"

"Yes. Yes, Suzanne. He's insane! He acts like what he's done is okay. Oh God!"

The pounding resumes on the door, followed by hard thuds, like Darius is throwing his weight against it. I begin to fear it won't hold. "Do you hear him?! He's a fucking animal out there. I-I don't know what he d-did to the neighbor."

I can't stop crying. My sobbing is so loud it's nearly enough to drown out the rampage in the hall.

"Amy!" Kane yells. "Put me on speaker!"

Fumbling with my phone, I try to find the speaker button. "Can you hear him? Oh God! He's going to break in!"

"Darius!" Kane snaps. "Darius, can you hear me?"

Realizing what he wants, I hit the volume button repeatedly and run over to the door. "Darius! Darius, calm down!"

The frenzied attack against the door stops abruptly. "You need to come out of there," my husband says, panting.

"Darius," Kane calls out. "You need to get away from there."

"Kane," he growls back. "What are you doing with my wife?"

"He's on the phone, asshat!" I yell.

"Amy, calm down," Kane orders. "Darius, I want to help you. I'm prepared to help you, but you've got to leave Amy alone now and go to the penthouse. Leave now, before you get arrested."

"What the fuck do you care?"

"You're my brother. Of course I care."

"Then why'd you shut me out of Baharan?" he shrieks.

"We can talk all about that when you get to the penthouse. Amy's not going anywhere, right, Amy?"

It takes me a minute to understand what's going on. Ollie has blessedly stopped barking, although he continues to scratch at the bedroom door. "No . . ." I clear my throat. "I'll be right here. You've got to . . . to fix this, Darius. You have to fix this first. Go fix it."

There's silence for what feels like forever, then, "Why don't you go home?" Darius says in a voice so normal-sounding it's eerie. "I'll meet you there when I'm done with Kane. We can go into the office together."

"Oh . . . Okay. That's a good idea."

Kane's voice comes through the speaker, more conciliatory and cautious. "I'm on my way now, brother. I'll meet you there."

It's deathly quiet on the other side of the door. Too quiet. And then I hear the ding of the elevator. I look through the peephole and see only empty space. I take the phone off speaker and whisper, "I think he's gone."

"Check with the doorman to be sure he's left, then order a car. You and your friend go to a hotel."

"She has a dog," I say lamely as if he hadn't heard that, my breath catching with every shuddering breath.

"Go to a pet-friendly hotel. You can do this, Amy. You're holding up great. You were smart to call me." Kane's voice is deep and soothing. "I'm going to take care of this, and the family will take care of you. I promise you that."

I inhale sharply, trying to get enough air. "That's what your mom said."

The bedroom door opens, and Ollie rushes to check the front door, sniffing around the cracks. Suzanne steps into view, crying as hard as I am.

"You're family, Amy," Kane tells me. "I know it hasn't always felt that way, but we *will* protect you."

"I'm not staying with him." Panic sours my stomach. "You can't ask me to do that."

"That's not even a thought."

"Okay." I try to gather myself. I've waded through shit before. I can certainly do it again and come out the other side. "I'll make sure he's left, and then we'll go."

31

ALIYAH

I STAND IN MY OFFICE, UNABLE TO SIT BECAUSE I'M TOO AGITATED. Rogelio is at my desk, walking me through his investigation into Darius's misdeeds step by step. I believe Rogelio, but I need to understand every move that was made so that I can defend myself.

I never expected an attack from one of my children. It was a blessing to have Amy to look after last night. When I'm alone, I overthink. Cry too much. How did everything go so terribly wrong? What have I ever done to Darius that would turn him against me this way?

My cellphone screen lights up, and I pick up my phone from the desk. Seeing the caller's name and photo, I feel relief. "Kane," I answer, "I'm going through the report with Rogelio now."

"We've got bigger problems," he says grimly. "Darius needs to be committed for observation. He's having some kind of breakdown."

"Committed?" My stomach knots. "No, we're not doing that. Can you imagine if word got –"

"It's too late to worry about appearances!" he snaps, and I recoil from his intensity. "He's a danger to everyone right now. He's already gotten into a fight, and Amy tells me it's bad. Suzanne called an ambulance. We'll have to convince the man not to press charges."

"Oh, Kane." I brace myself with a hand on my desk, trying to slow my rapid breathing. "How did it come to this?"

"We're going to figure that out. He's meeting me at the penthouse. You need to find out if we can have him committed. I don't know what the steps are for something like that. Do we need a lawyer? A judge? You'll have to see if—"

"I know what needs to be done." I sigh heavily. "I looked into the process on Amy's behalf, when I thought she was the one who needed her head examined." It distresses me to realize how wrong I was about my son and his wife. "Amy's the one who'll need to file the application. We'll have to line up two doctors who'll sign off on it. It would be easiest to convince Darius to go of his own volition."

"Honestly, he sounded delusional. I'd be surprised if he went willingly."

My eyes squeeze shut against the painful truth. "Where's Witte? Can't he manage Amy's part of it while we're dealing with Darius?"

"He's not with me, and I can't reach him, so it's up to you. Try Dr. Goldstein. He'll salivate over something like this, and he's got the clout to get someone else to agree."

"Goldstein . . . ?" My wildly racing thoughts take a second to remember who Kane's talking about. Joseph Goldstein. The psychiatrist who ran the tests on Lily when she first returned. Pompous. Egotistical. Eager for more recognition and prestige. "Yes, you're right. He'll do it."

Opening my eyes, I find Rogelio watching me intently. "I'll make some calls and get to the penthouse as soon as possible."

"See you soon." The line beeps briefly as the call ends.

"Something's happened," I tell Rogelio. "I don't know the details, but . . . I need to arrange for Darius to get psychiatric care. He's . . . he's . . ."

He nods. "Has he threatened someone?"

I press my palm to my forehead. "How do you always know? He got in a fight."

"Who was there?" he asks in a clipped voice. "I need to talk to someone who witnessed what happened."

"Yes, of course." I dial Amy's number and put my phone on speaker.

"Aliyah! Oh my God. Darius has gone totally crazy! Suzanne and I are moving to a hotel."

"Amy, this is Rogelio. Tell me what you saw."

I listen with mounting horror as Amy and Suzanne speak over each other in a tangle of rapid-fire words.

"Okay. Okay," Rogelio says. "Is there a security camera in the hallway?"

"I don't know," Suzanne answers.

"You have to find out. If there's a recording of what happened – get it. And I'm going to need –"

"I recorded it!" Suzanne interjects. "On my phone. I thought he'd behave if he were being filmed, but he didn't even look at me."

"Great. That's great. Send it to Aliyah. I still want you to obtain footage of the hallway if it exists. And we'll need you both to write statements. And get the name of your neighbor. If you know which hospital he was taken to, even better."

"All right. We'll find out."

"Good. Stay safe, stay together," he tells them, in that deeply reassuring tone of his, "but you've got to be quick on this. The sooner we get Darius settled, the safer you both will be."

"Settled?" Amy asks. "What does that mean?"

I answer her. "It means he needs to be someplace where he's not a threat to you, him, or anyone else. Only a person who lives with him can apply to put him under observation. We'll get the paperwork to you as soon as we can." My voice softens. "Amy . . . I'm begging you. I know you've been through a terrible ordeal, but please. Help me get my son somewhere safe."

"Oh . . . I see." She clears her throat. "Okay."

"We're not circumventing the law here," Rogelio adds. "When you're ready, you'll decide what you want to do, but you called Black, not the police, so I'm guessing this is more like what you wanted to happen."

I frown at him for his presumption.

"No, Aliyah's right," she says. "He needs help right now. And I need to get my head straight before making big decisions."

"Good. Call Aliyah back as soon as you know more. And keep an eye on your texts and emails."

"Thank you, Amy." My voice trembles with sincerity. "Thank you very much."

"You're welcome."

Killing the call, I glare at Rogelio. "Sending Darius to jail is *not* on the table."

"Not your call where Amy is concerned," he says flatly. "Or the neighbor. Now, call Dr. Goldstein."

I sit to do so, feeling light-headed. The conversation with Joseph Goldstein drains me further. Suzanne's video comes through during the call, and I forward it to the doctor. We watch it together, and I struggle to keep my voice even. It destroys me to see my son so . . . unhinged. I hardly recognize him, and it's heartrending to see how much he needed my help while I was oblivious, too focused on Baharan. And myself.

Ending the call, I feel defeated. Standing is an effort, my entire body feels weighted, but I manage. I always, somehow, find a way to manage.

"Hey." Rogelio grabs me by the arm and pulls me close, wrapping me into a tight embrace.

It's too much.

I start crying, then sobbing, leaning heavily into him. He holds me close, swaying gently. He's smart enough not to say anything and kind enough to be patient. I learned long ago that the well of tears is infinite, but still, it feels like forever before I run temporarily dry. My sobs fade into hiccups, then finally to stuttered breathing.

I pull away, wiping at my face. "I'm exhausted." I sigh heavily. "But I have to go. I can't let Kane deal with this alone."

"Want me to go with you?" he asks quietly.

"Yes, but no." I manage a smile when he huffs out a laugh. "We need to get everything together for Goldstein. If you can find the neighbor, that would be a great help. We need to reach out to him, cover his expenses at the very least and avert a lawsuit if we can. There has to be a way to negotiate a settlement with him."

"I'll find him."

I nod, knowing he can. "I'll call Ramin on the way and see what we can do that isn't illegal. I'll have to tell him what's happening. How do I do that?"

"You're a tough broad. You can do anything."

I look at him and appreciate all he's become to me in the past few weeks. "Why couldn't you be twenty years older?"

He winks. "You flatter me."

I wave that off as he heads toward the door to leave. "Cocky bastard."

It takes a few minutes for me to wash up and reapply my makeup. While I do so, I strengthen my resolve. I've made mistakes to get where I am, but I can fix them. My fractured family has been a perpetual distraction and concern. It's time to put it back together, to heal the cracks that weaken us, so we can do the work of building our empire. Maybe the future won't look the way I've always hoped for and envisioned – I'll just have to accept that.

If I've learned anything in the past day, it's that a plan doesn't have to come together exactly the way I wanted as long as the desired result is achieved.

When I exit my bathroom into my office, I take a moment to look around. So many elements of the decor were carefully selected for optimal effect. I need to look strong, successful, powerful, in command . . .

If only I'd paid as close attention to the welfare of my adult children.

32

ALIYAH

Despite the early morning traffic, the drive to the penthouse isn't long. The ride in the elevator seems longer. When I exit into the entry vestibule, I see the two guards, who nod at me in greeting, but Witte doesn't appear at the door as he always has. It sets the wrong tone immediately. Something is wrong. Very wrong. The silence is profound, and the eeriness intensifies when I step into the living room.

The penthouse, always thrumming with rich dark energy, feels like a tomb. While the sun shines brightly just outside the windows, the interior is shadowed and cool. I feel a chill and shiver.

Placing my handbag on the console table by the doors, I step deeper inside and wonder if I could be the first to arrive. It doesn't seem possible, considering it's already past ten o'clock. I walk down the hallway to Kane's office, but he's not there. The master suite is also empty, with fresh flowers in vases, which perversely deepens the sense of abandonment. I circle until I finally hear voices as I approach the library. I pause within hearing distance.

"– taken everything! And you want me to be *calm* about that?" Darius's voice is strange. The cadence is off, and it's hoarse.

"I can't help you fix this if all you do is hurl accusations and yell," Kane shoots back. "You have to tell me how we got here if I'm going to figure a way out."

"How *we* got here?" Darius laughs, and again, the sound is strange. "Remember when you took off without a fucking word, never came back and left us with two parents who couldn't give a shit about anything but themselves?"

My whole body jolts as I'm startled by both his words and the vitriol with which he says them.

"Darius, for fuck's sake, that was years ago! That has zero to do with your trouble now!"

"Be real, brother. Standing in the shadow of someone who wants nothing to do with you means figuring out shit on your own. That's all I've done! My trouble – if you want to call it that – comes from trying to protect my wife from a pack of vultures!"

"Protect her by poisoning her? That makes perfect sense."

"It wasn't poison!" His denial carries a disturbing note of hysteria.

Taking a deep breath, I start forward.

"I don't know why you think otherwise, but you were everything to me," Kane says roughly. "My father had left. Your father hated me. Our mother was . . . Hell, I don't know what she was. She changed after my dad took off. I wish you'd known her before. I had no one but you. *You* were my family. You have to know I loved you – still love you."

"Am I supposed to feel sorry for you? Because your dad left you behind? Boo hoo," Darius mocks. "What do you think it was like for me when you left? You were the only father figure I had! And if you think Mom was fucked up after your dad ditched her, you should've seen her after you were gone. She checked out – and man, it couldn't be clearer to the rest of us that you were the child she loved."

"You know that's not true, Darius. And I'm sorry about leaving. I really am. If I could've taken you with me, I would have. I did my best, and when Baharan became more than a pipe dream, I brought you into it."

"You needed robots who'd do what you wanted and have no control. We're not actually a part of anything. Look what's happened! I started exerting a little influence, and you threw me out immediately. You'll do anything for Baharan, but not for me."

"God . . . you couldn't be more wrong." Kane's words are clipped and fast now, his temper building. I'm amazed he's held it in check this long. If Darius had any sense, he'd know what he meant to his brother from that effort. "I'm stepping back from Baharan and getting out."

I cover my mouth with my hand to mute my gasp.

Darius laughs. "Hilarious. And totally un-fucking-believable."

"I'm dead serious. Lily has other interests, and I want to focus on her. I planned on offering you and Ramin the option of buying some of my shares. Mom would have control, but you would've had a say."

"Would have. Easy to offer and deny something in hindsight. You talk a good game, Kane, but you forget I've seen you in action at work and with women. All lies and bullshit."

"No. It isn't," I intercede, entering the room to find my two eldest children squared off from each other on either side of the fireplace, both standing. Darius bristles and seems wholly unaware of the tears streaming down his face. Kane looks relaxed, but his stance is one of preparation.

They've never come to blows but look ready to.

Darius is completely disheveled. If I didn't know better, I'd think it'd been weeks since I last saw him. Kane is his polar opposite – fit, tanned, glowing with health and vitality.

And all the thrumming energy that usually permeates the penthouse? It's concentrated here, as a crackling tensity that reminds me of a breaking storm.

"Kane adored you." I stop just behind Darius and off to the side, forcing him to adjust his stance away from his brother. "I asked him to leave the house."

Darius turns toward me, scowling. "Rewriting history now? Don't bother."

"It's the truth. Your father was awful to him. I couldn't bear it anymore, and I couldn't leave." I lift both hands to ward off any argument to the contrary. "I could not leave," I reiterate. "So, Kane had to go."

"He didn't have to fall off the face of the earth, though, did he?" Darius says snidely.

"He tried to keep in touch, but your father didn't like it, and I couldn't listen to the three of you ask about him every day. It was horribly painful for me not to have him home, and it was like salt in the wound every time you mentioned him. So, I told you what you needed to hear to end it."

Kane stares at me with those dark eyes – so like my own. I squirm under that steady gaze, wishing I could've been the mother he needed. That I could be worthy of the man he's grown up to be. I contributed so little to his rearing. I tried so hard, but I failed him.

"You just going to let her take the blame?" Darius asks his brother.

"Blame is pointless," Kane answers with a long sigh. "What's done is done. We need to figure out what to do now to keep you out of jail."

"Jail?" Darius looks back and forth between the two of us. "I'm not going to jail. You're insane even to suggest it."

"You attacked a stranger!" I remind him.

"He was trying to interfere while I talked to my wife."

"I've seen the video, Darius!" I glance at Kane, wondering how we're going to convince his brother to see reason. "You scared the hell out of Amy and her friend."

"Suzanne needs to stop interfering, too. I can make Amy understand if I could just talk to her."

"Understand what, exactly?" I ask incredulously. "Poisoning her? No one is going to understand that."

"It wasn't poison!" he screams, and the sound is like a banshee's shriek, high-pitched and somehow inhuman. It's a visible effort for him to regain a modicum of control. "I needed her to understand that I'm the only one who will be there for her when she's sick and exhausted, and her hair is falling out. Kane won't want her then. Ramin won't."

Frowning, I struggle to understand. "What does Kane or Ramin have to do with this?"

"They both fucked my wife!"

Astonished, I glance back and forth between my two boys. "I can't believe Ramin would –"

"You never believe me!" he yells. "I've never been right or capable. Not in your eyes."

"So, explain why I'd put you in such a high position at Baharan?" Kane rejoins.

Darius bares his teeth in a quick, vicious grin. "I can't even get past the lobby. Explain that."

"You were sabotaging me!" I accuse. "Methodically, over months."

"You mistreat my wife," he says flatly. "She doesn't like it. I don't like it."

I gape. "So, you set me up for criminal malfeasance for that?"

He gestures at Kane with a toss of his wrist. "You were sabotaging him. Don't act innocent."

"Nothing I planned was going to harm Kane! It was simply meant to demonstrate that I'm forward-thinking and aggressive about expansion. Women have to prove those things, Darius."

"You buying that?" he asks Kane casually.

"Amy is a sister to me," Kane argues. "Nothing more. And I know Ramin feels the same way. He would never cross that line."

"He did. He fucked her, too," Darius bites out. "Oh, come on! Don't look so shocked. You two can't tell me you haven't noticed how often he rubs it in."

Applause behind me makes me jump. I turn quickly, as does Darius.

Lily walks in, immaculate as ever in a sleeveless red floral maxi dress. Her glossy black hair is once again styled in a sleek bob, and her crimson lips are curved in a wide, delighted grin. Despite the indoor gloom, she wears sunglasses and looks like she should be lunching in Greenwich, not intruding on a serious matter.

"Very entertaining," she says, her voice as strange as Darius's, low and husky instead of helium-high. "I wish I'd brought popcorn."

"Pull up a seat," Darius offers, returning her grin. "It's going to get better."

"Indeed."

I turn my back to her. Her sense of humor is misplaced. "This is family business, *Lily*. Take yourself somewhere else."

A shift in Kane's energy draws my attention to him, and I prepare myself for a fight. He always comes to her defense.

But then I see . . . His gaze is narrowed on his wife in a way that reminds me briefly of how Darius looked at Amy in the video. It's chilling, and I'm abruptly uneasy.

My eldest child stands completely still. His handsome face is like stone, and ice frosts his words when he speaks. "That's not Lily."

33

LILY

HOLDING MY PHONE TO MY EAR, I LISTEN TO IT RING AND TRY NOT TO worry about you, my love. The turmoil in your family has hit you hard. Your concern is extreme and surprising. Certainly, I know your capacity for love, but you've hidden how deeply you love your family. Did it make you feel too vulnerable to share it? Or were you perhaps hiding those emotions from yourself? Your family has wounded you deeply over the years.

"Do you want to come with me?" you'd asked before leaving me behind at the beach house, although mentally you were already miles away.

"If you want me there, I'll go. If I'd only be a distraction, I'm fine with staying here. Whatever you need."

With a sigh, you cupped my face in your hands. "I know you're capable, but Darius isn't in his right mind now. I don't want you anywhere near him."

I understood what you were saying. You didn't want to hold me back, you know I'm not defenseless, but you didn't want me to go. "I'll wait here for you."

So, you're facing your brother now and I'm trying not to imagine the worst. It's hard because that's what I do best. I've never been one to look on the bright side because those who do are perpetually caught unprepared when things go wrong. I have to account for every eventuality to stay alive and keep my crew alive.

"The caller you're attempting to reach is unavailable. Please leave a message after the –"

Damn it. I kill the call and chew on my lower lip. The sense of disquiet that's been building inside me all morning is now a wailing alarm. I stand, unable to sit on the couch when I'm so agitated. Heeding my instincts, I call Rogelio.

"*Querida*, to what do I owe the pleasure?" His words belie the stress in his voice.

I don't waste his time. "Do you have a second to trace Witte's phone?"

"Is he still not reachable?"

"No. I've called a dozen times, at least. Maybe he's busy at the penthouse with Kane and Darius. If so, I'll be relieved. I just want to know Kane's not dealing with his brother alone."

"Hold on."

I wait.

"He's not at the penthouse," he tells me absently. "Looks like he's on the Upper East Side."

"Crap." I heave out a frustrated breath and begin pacing the length of the living room. Sunlight pours in through the open patio doors and a warm sea breeze flutters my dress. "Why isn't he answering? I don't like Kane being alone with someone who's already been violent today."

"I can run over to the penthouse if that'll make you feel better. I've found the neighbor and Ramin is handling that situation, so I'm free."

"Would you, please? I'll feel much better if you're there." Maybe Witte's tangled up with his girlfriend. I can't blame him for that. As far as he knows, he's not needed.

"I'm on my way."

"Thanks, Rogelio."

Tossing my phone on the sofa, I run my hands through my hair. I should've gone with you. Now that we're together with no secrets or lies between us, our relationship feels newly fragile. Not that you and I aren't more solid than ever before, but I'm wholly yours in a way I couldn't be previously. That weakens me.

My phone vibrates, and I glance at it, seeing Lacy's pretty face on the screen. It's liberating not to hide my crew from you anymore, sneaking peeks at hidden phones and arranging covert meetings. One day, we'll have my family over for dinner. We'll order in and Witte will join us at the table. He's family, too.

Where the hell is he?

"Hi," I answer in greeting. "Are you heading to the penthouse today?"

When we stay at the beach house, the penthouse staff enjoys short every-other-day shifts.

"I'm not scheduled to. Why? You need something?"

I quickly fill her in.

"Oh, wow." She whistles. "That's a curveball. How's Amy?"

"I've only texted with her because I'm sure she's got a lot to deal with now, but she says she's fine and safe. She's worried, of course. So am I."

"Yeah, don't stress, though. Witte's dangerous and he watches out for your man."

"That would be reassuring if Witte were actually at the penthouse."

"Huh? Why isn't Witte there?" she asks with a note of suspicion. "He's always around when Kane needs him."

"I don't know. I can't reach him."

"Okay, that's totally bizarre. Witte answers his phone at all hours. I've even caught him when I'm pretty sure he was mid-fucking. You know, all breathless and gruff. That guy lives to work, I'm telling you."

"And I'm telling you, he's not answering his phone." Reaching up, I rub the knots in the back of my neck. After a night with you in which we hardly slept and made love repeatedly, I should be loose as a ragdoll. But with every minute that passes, I grow more uneasy.

"I'll try him when we hang up," she offers. "Maybe he's got his phone set up to only notify him of known numbers. He's not going to have your burner programmed. By the way, get a real phone now. Please."

"Kane tried to call him, too, but yes, please try. Tell him to get to the penthouse if he answers. And let me know either way, okay?"

"Sure. But listen, that's not why I called you." Her tenor abruptly changes and I'm instantly alert. "I was taking a cab up to a nail appointment – my gal moved shop a couple of months back and no one else has her mad skills – and I saw a woman on the street who looked just like you but with long silver hair. I was thinking that can't be Stephanie, not with that hair. But wow, her face."

I'm frozen where I stand, scarcely breathing. The alarm bell ringing inside me is abruptly deafening. "How good a look did you get at her?"

"I was stopped at a light, so pretty good. She was leaving a donut place with some coffees and a bag. But the hair is off, right? I feel like your mom would keep looking as young as possible."

I will myself to calm down, to think clearly. "You said you were going up, taking a cab up. Where were you?"

"Madison and 88th."

My breath leaves me in a rush. Upper East Side. "You said coffees, as in multiple, right?"

"Yeah, she had two, in one of those cardboard carriers. Why? You think it's her?"

"I don't know. I agree with you about the gray hair but then, she's also a woman who believes she's the perfect version of herself every day. And coincidences . . . I don't trust them." I spin abruptly, racing toward the stairs. "Can you get to the penthouse?"

"I'm already on my way. Should I call the others?"

"I'm calling Rogelio. Wait to call Tovah and Salma."

"Okay. Bye."

I'm speed-dialing Rogelio on speaker as I shimmy out of my dress.

"I'm stuck in traffic," he answers, "but I'm on my way to the penthouse."

"I need a precise location for Witte's phone. What's the address? Text it to me."

"Okay. Why?"

"Just a hunch." I pull on a sleeveless black unitard, which will afford me maximum ease of movement.

"Your hunches usually mean someone's dead or about to die," he says tightly. "I'll meet you there."

"No!" I tug the spaghetti straps into place and grab some socks. The odds that Lacy actually did spot my mother are long, but I'm not risking any member of my crew by sending them to investigate. "Get to Kane. And text me that address. I'll call you when I'm on the road."

Hanging up, I shove my feet into running shoes and grab my bag. I head outside in a dead run and cross the street, banging on the guesthouse door. "I need car keys," I tell the bodyguard who answers.

He's the tall, big one. Linebacker-sized. He sizes me up in a glance and grabs the keys from the entry console. "I'll drive."

"Fine." I know better than to argue with Rogelio's guys, especially if he's given them an order, which he probably had. Damn it.

We're on Interstate 95 in minutes and the man – Casey – drives like a professional. Still, it takes just over an hour to reach the city. And the news I receive on the way causes a low-grade panic.

"Taking the stairs," Rogelio tells me when I answer his call. He's breathing hard. "Power outage. Elevators are dead."

"*All* of them?"

"Fucking all of them."

"You're climbing ninety-six floors?" I ask, aghast.

"You don't have to remind me how many floors there are!" he gripes. "Lacy told me . . . about the woman. Don't do anything . . . stupid!"

"When have I ever?" I tease, but my stomach churns. I don't like the timing of the elevator system failure. Am I headed to the wrong place? Should I have gone to the penthouse and sent my crew to investigate Witte's whereabouts?

"I'm hanging up," he gasps. "Gotta save my breath."

The line dies. I call Lacy. "Are you at the penthouse?"

"I was. Rogelio sent me to you. I'm about fifteen minutes out."

"Fuck. Don't come into the lobby until I tell you."

"He told me you'd say that," she says wryly.

"Bye." I end the call.

Casey pulls over, briefly double parking. "We're here. I'll park and meet you –"

I'm already out of the car and on the sidewalk.

Pushing through the front door, I skid to a halt in front of the doorman. "Hi." I read his badge. "Tony. Nice to meet you! Do you have the key my mom left with you?"

He blinks in surprise. "Excuse me?"

"Sorry." I push my hair out of my face and grin. "My mom, you know. Looks like me but with long gray hair."

"You're Danica's kid?"

I take a step back, in absolute shock. Mute for a moment. Fighting back tears. To know for certain after all this time wondering . . . hoping . . . dreading . . .

"Hey, are you okay?" Tony asks.

Danica. Okay. I wipe my cheeks dry. "Yes, I'm sorry. Allergies. Someone bring a cat through here recently?"

"Not that I recall, but it is allergy season." He gives me a thorough once-over and I appreciate the additional benefits of skintight clothing.

"You have no idea what it took to find this place!" I exclaim. "Anyway, she told me she might be sleeping in and have her phone silenced, but she'd leave me a key."

"She didn't leave one." He taps some keys on his keyboard and looks at the screen. "What's your name?"

Danica . . . Danica . . . "Danielle!" I say cheerfully. "She's Big Danny, I'm Little Danny. To the family, anyway."

"She didn't put you on the visitor list, either."

"She must've forgotten." My thoughts scramble. I should've mapped this out before arriving, but I'm worried about you and it's damn near all I can think about. "Witte's here, right? Mom probably got distracted. I can call him and see if he'll come down and get me. But if they're both asleep . . ." I let that trail off.

"Yep, Witte's here." If he notes the way I become suddenly alert, he doesn't indicate it. "Why haven't I met you before?" He's not suspicious, just curious.

"I volunteer with Habitat for Humanity in South America. I'm just home for a visit."

"Huh. That's pretty cool."

"It can be." I smile again and set my phone on the counter so he can see Witte's name appear on the screen. It rings several times before the generic voicemail message kicks in. After all, a man who always answers his phone has no need to record a personal message.

"See?" Disappointment colors my voice. "They're probably sleeping or whatever. That's why she wanted me to have a key."

He gives me a sympathetic look.

I sigh heavily. "I was going to crash on her couch. Twenty hours, three layovers, lost luggage. I'm beat."

"Let me try calling her," he offers as Casey walks in.

"You know what," I improvise, stepping back, "help this guy out and I'll try calling Witte again."

Casey's eyebrows lift above his sunglasses, but he doesn't hesitate to step in,

"Thanks. Hi, Tony. Do you know who owns that gray sedan out there? I think it sideswiped my car last night."

Tony follows Casey outside and the second they're out of view, I lean over the counter to read the computer screen. Danica White. 10G.

The juxtaposition with Kane's surname ices my blood. My mother's sense of humor is often morbid. I dart to the elevator and push the call button, feeling lucky that the doors open immediately to a waiting car. I get in and start up to the tenth floor, digging in my bag for my lock-picking kit. One day, my love, we'll need to go through my handbag together. You'll learn a lot about me when you see what I consider an everyday essential item.

But when I get to 10G, I find a numeric lock. I don't hesitate. I type in my date of birth and the lock whirrs as the bolt disengages. How did I guess? Because I know my mother very, very well.

I'm both elated and deathly afraid when I step into the condo.

My mother's scent, so beloved and familiar, hits me like a sledgehammer. I stand for a moment, just breathing it in, absorbing all the familiar feelings the scent evokes.

She's not here. I sense that right away. Something in me comes alive when she's nearby. A child's love maybe. A child's hope. I scope the place out in a single glance and dismiss it as being nothing like her. The white carpet and pale furniture may fit Danica, but not my mother.

I search for Witte's phone and the man himself, who would answer it if he could. What made her leave, and did she take him with her? The likelihood of her spotting Lacy in the back of a cab is slim. Does she know I found the boat, which Val had urged me to do? Is she watching you that closely? Watching *me* that closely?

Walking into the bedroom, I freeze. For a heartbeat, I'm horrified. The body hog-tied on the bed faces away from me and is unmoving. Dressed only in black dress slacks with bared feet, the expanse of exposed skin seems terrifyingly vulnerable. Then that familiar – and beloved – leonine mane of white moves as Witte looks over his powerful shoulder at me, his piercing blue eyes staring at me from above a ball gag.

"Witte! Jesus . . ." I'm digging in my bag as I go to him, pulling out my pocketknife.

I unbuckle the gag first. "Are you hurt?"

He flexes his jaw. "My pride, maybe. I'm otherwise fine."

But I see that's not quite true after I slice through the zip ties and spot the taser barbs protruding from his muscular chest. I splay the fingers of my right hand around the first barb, applying pressure. Then, I yank it free from his flesh with my left hand in a quick, firm motion. He doesn't even flinch and is utterly silent. I repeat the process with the second barb, and when I step back, he rolls onto his stomach, flat and nearly motionless.

He groans, the sound muffled by the comforter, and I realize his arms and legs must be numb from lack of blood flow.

Turning his head, he looks at me. "She's gone after Kane. She knows he's at the penthouse."

My breath leaves me in a rush as if I've taken a blow. Fear claws its way into the pit of my stomach. "The elevators aren't working."

I want to hope for coincidence, to think for just a moment that happenstance will prevent her from getting to you.

But I don't believe in coincidence.

"She disguised herself as you," he says gruffly.

A low moan escapes me. My phone buzzes and I pull it out of the pocket on my thigh. "Lacy. Are you here?"

"Downstairs with a big guy who works for Rogelio."

"Grab a bag of donuts and tell the doorman you're delivering to 10G. I'll have Witte call down and approve it."

"Got it."

I hang up as Witte flops over onto his back. Blood trickles from the small holes in his pectoral and abdomen, staining the neatly groomed crisp white hair on his chest. "You'd be dead if she didn't want something," I tell him bluntly. "What is it?"

"The money you stole from her."

"And how does she think she'll get that from you?"

"She's threatened my daughter."

I wince. "Where's Catherine?"

"London."

"Okay. We'll get someone on her."

His brows lift. "I can do so as well. As soon as I can move my bloody arms!"

Picking his phone up off the nightstand, I use his thumb to unlock it and call downstairs. I hold the phone to his ear as he tells Tony to expect a food delivery. When he's questioned about me, he steps in as neatly as Casey did.

Calling Rogelio, I tell him about my mother.

"I'm thirty-three flights from the top," he tells me, panting hard. "My guys aren't answering my calls."

My eyes close against the sheer terror that washes over me. We both know why they're not answering.

And you, my love. You have no security, no Witte. Only a brother who's not right in his mind and a mother who's no match for mine.

34

ALIYAH

THAT'S NOT LILY.

I'm completely baffled by Kane's pronouncement for a moment. Darius, too, scowls in confusion.

"Who the hell is it then?" I ask crossly, wondering if I've reached a stress point bordering madness. There cannot be multiple Lilys.

But then . . . there is evidence that suggests there may be.

She slides the sunglasses atop her head. "Don't you remember me, Aliyah?"

I scowl. Hers isn't a face one forgets. I would certainly remember if I'd met a woman who looked so much like Lily.

Curious, I take a more thorough look. The woman who's joined us is more voluptuous than Lily. And the face . . . it's eerily similar but not identical.

She glances briefly at the photo of Lily's tattoo hanging over the fireplace, then smiles at Kane. "You look so much like your father. Brings back memories."

"How do you know my husband?" I glare at her. I'm feeling too many things at once, but within that chaos is sharp, keen jealousy.

"Guess," she answers blithely, and a hunger for violence surges within me.

"Where is he now?" Kane demands.

She taps her chin with a long crimson fingernail and purses her lips as if

243

pondering the question. Then, she shrugs. "Hart Island. Possibly. They all kind of blend together after a while."

Her blithely tossed words rip open an old wound that's never healed. To love someone who's missing is a special hell. Never knowing what happened to them, never shedding the faint hope that they're alive somewhere. So much of my anger and bitterness has been centered around Paul choosing a new life without me in it. To think of him buried unmourned in a potter's field, lost among the unclaimed, the insane and imprisoned, the victims of terrible diseases . . . My sorrow is wrenching.

I note the way Kane tenses visibly, and my aggravation increases. What she's said is cruel and as badly as it hurts me, it will damage my son much more. "What are you talking about?"

"Paul didn't know his own mind. Couldn't go through with an exit plan he helped to design. I'd say your resemblance to him is more than skin-deep, Kane. Wishy-washy and faithless."

"Don't talk about Paul or Kane that way!" I'm unable to bear the vicious tension building by the second. The room feels airless, making it hard to breathe.

"Aliyah." She clucks her tongue in disapproval. "Women like you giving men a free pass is why they're all animals. I can't believe you still defend Paul after what he did to you. Although I have to say, the way you handled Alex Gallagher was well done."

I feel the blood drain from my face. "Who are you?" My voice is no more than a choked whisper.

She looks at me with those bright green eyes. Like a snake, they're devoid of mercy. While her voice teases and taunts, those eyes remain emotionless and keenly focused. Her gaze is paralyzing, as if I'm being circled by a cobra preparing to strike.

"Our lives have somehow intersected for years," she tells me. "And the lives of the weak, pathetic men around you. I should've killed you along with Paul and spared the world any more of your offspring."

"Fuck you, bitch!" Darius yells, stepping toward her menacingly. "Who the fuck do you think –"

She moves so swiftly I can't track the movement. *Pap. Pap.* Pain explodes in my ears, slams into my chest. I scream and watch Darius spin and fall to the floor as if he's taken a punch from an invisible fist. That same force knocks me back into a chair, spilling me into the seat. I can't catch my breath. My chest is on fire. Clawing at the agonizing burning, I realize with shock that I've been shot in the left shoulder.

"Uh uh," she admonishes, ducking behind my chair when Kane lunges toward her, pressing the gun barrel against my temple. I cry out and recoil from the heat, but she only shoves it at me harder. "She doesn't have to die, Kane. Just you."

Darius writhes on the floor in the fetal position, sobbing and screaming.

"Get on with it, then," Kane growls, moving to his brother and crouching beside him. Reaching up and back, he grabs the collar of his T-shirt at his nape and yanks it off, pressing the bunched cotton to his brother's torso. "Why wait?"

"No!" I try to stand, but she grabs me by my injured shoulder and wrenches me back. I cry out; the pain is searing.

"You know," she starts in a conversational tone, "That's almost exactly what Nicky said to me earlier. Oh, I'm sorry – Witte. Witte said something very similar. But then he made you who you are, didn't he, Kane? Molded you like a rough piece of clay into someone who imagines himself worthy of my daughter."

"I've never thought that," he says sharply. "What have you done with Witte?"

I didn't think it possible to be more afraid, but if this woman can take down the formidable majordomo, none of us has a chance of surviving.

"Whatever I've felt like doing to him," she purrs, "and he loved every second of it."

Kane stands, and his body seems to expand as his muscles thicken with rage. "Why isn't killing me enough? Why go after my family? My friends? They've got nothing to do with any of this."

I can't see her face anymore, but her voice takes on a razor-sharp edge. "My daughter has waged a vendetta that's cost me a dozen valuable men. You owe me a few bodies, I'd say."

"Do you hate her, too?"

"She's my child. I grew her inside me and nursed her at my breasts. All of my love is for her. And because of you, she's turned her back on everything she's ever loved and everyone who loved her. I want to know why."

"You know why," Kane retorts. "But it's beyond you to understand."

Realizing we're dealing with Lily's mother feels like a heart attack must. My chest squeezes tight until spots dot my vision. That my son so quickly accepted that his wife's dead mother is evidently not dead raises my alarm further. Yet I can hardly think of the ramifications, my attention focused on Darius, whose agonized cries weaken by the second. To sit captive while my son dies before my eyes is torture unlike any other.

"Don't whine, Kane," she chides. "You only make it harder for me to see your appeal, even bare-chested. Convince me you were worth all the carnage you instigated."

He kneels beside Darius again but speaks to her. "You nearly killed her when she was hit by that car."

"An unfortunate lapse in judgment by a man who's now dead. Now, get up," she orders him, stepping away from me. "You're going to open the safe."

I feel a spurt of hope. More time. Moving from one room to another. There may be an opportunity there for Kane to gain the upper hand.

He glares at her over his shoulder. Then his gaze moves beyond her, and his jaw hardens further. I've seen my son intimidate others deftly, but I have never seen him look murderous.

I attempt to go to Darius, but a hand on my shoulder stays me. I look at who's behind me and see one of Kane's maids. What's her name again?

Lily's mother hands her the gun.

"You surprise me, Bea," my son says as he stands with lithe grace. Shirtless, the power of his body is undeniable. Lily's mother wouldn't stand a chance if he could get his hands on her.

"She has my brother," Bea explains quietly.

Unseen walls close in on all of us. With every word spoken, Lily's mother becomes more monstrous. I begin to lose what little hope I had. Death seems inevitable. But I'm not ready. I haven't said everything I need to or done all I could. To die, having failed all my children, would be the darkest hell.

"You could have told me," Kane tells the girl. "I would've helped you."

"Too late now," Lily's mom dismisses. "Get moving."

"I'm not opening the safe." My son's tone is far too casual.

Impossibly, my pulse races faster. The calmer Kane gets, the more dangerous he is. His temper is fearsome, but there's safety in that release. It's when he grows quiet that the threat becomes real.

"I can kill you," she suggests indifferently, "and cut off your thumb to open it."

"Be my guest."

"Stop it!" I wrench away and onto my feet, stumbling over to Darius and falling to my knees beside him. He's drenched with sweat and clutches his stomach, but blood seeps through the black cotton of Kane's shirt. I yank off the silk scarf draped around my shoulders and press it over his hands. "Give her what she wants, Kane!"

"What she wants is to kill me. Maybe she wants the money, too, but she could've taken it anytime if so. Araceli learned the tricks of the trade from you, didn't she, Stephanie? Or is she better than you?"

"She's always been better than me. Flawless." The pride in her voice only makes her actions more perverse. "She never made a single mistake until you, and it's a mistake she can't seem to stop making. She'll learn the lesson one day, but I'm not letting her waste her youth on you."

"It won't end with my death, just like it didn't end with hers."

Bending over, I press my lips to Darius's forehead, murmuring to him that I'm here, that I love him, that he'll live. He thrashes, lost to his suffering, and a storm begins to brew inside me.

Stephanie scoffs at Kane. "You didn't believe she was dead long enough."

"If I'd lived the rest of my life as a widower, it wouldn't have changed anything." His tone is too relaxed. Nonchalant. "I would still love her, and she would still be my wife."

Is he goading her with his fearlessness? Or is he as hopeless as I am and better prepared to die? For years he suffered living without Lily. Maybe he made his peace then.

Where is Lily? Could she stop this insanity?

Her mother laughs. "But knowing she was alive didn't stop you from sleeping around, did it? Your vows were meaningless in the end, weren't they?"

Kane's jaw clenches. "Knowing she was alive and not with me – *choosing* not to be with me – whatever the reason . . . Yeah, I was angry and hurt. I wanted her to hurt. Enough that she'd come back. Not something I'm proud of. And I'll live with the shame always."

"Or you could die with it. It's a pity you had a vasectomy. You've no idea what it took to knock Erika up, then synchronize her meeting with you. It would've been entertaining to watch that play out for however long it took you to discover the baby isn't yours. See how predictable you are?"

"She's safe now," he bites out.

"I think 'worthless' is the word you're looking for," she suggests in a sunny tone so horrifying we all are stunned by it.

The momentary silence is broken by a loud click that makes me jump. I recognize the sound. Recoiling behind an armchair, I peek and find Bea pointing the gun at Stephanie. The trigger clicks again. And again.

Stephanie looks exasperated. "Did you seriously think I'd hand you a loaded weapon, you stupid girl?"

And then she moves with uncanny swiftness. Bea gasps, and her hand falls to her side. The gun thuds onto the rug. The hilt of a knife protrudes from her heart.

The maid stares at us all with wide-eyed, unblinking horror. Then her knees buckle, and she crumples to the floor.

Opening my mouth, I let loose a scream from the depths of my soul, and once it's freed, I can't stop it.

Swishing her long skirt to the side, Stephanie exposes an empty sheath strapped to her thigh and quickly bends to retrieve her knife. Kane moves, lunging toward her, and she pivots to defend herself, charging at him with the blood-streaked dagger.

My scream pours into the air, a violent spewing of fury and hysteria. Kane has rage and size, but Lily's mother has skill and speed.

She doesn't throw the blade, instead slashing across his chest with a slender arm and nimbly ducking his swinging fist. She spins around and behind him in a whirl of crimson skirts. Her arm lifts, the knife aimed at his neck.

"*No!*" Darius manages somehow to explode past me, hurtling into Stephanie so she's tackled away from Kane. She hits the floor with incredible violence. A sickening noise fractures my scream abruptly, like a switch. The sound of something hard colliding with something harder.

Darius rolls onto his side, groaning.

Stephanie lies on her back, her stunningly beautiful face framed by a rapidly spreading pool of blood on the marble hearth.

35

LILY

"THEY'RE UP AND RUNNING AGAIN," THE STAFF AT THE LOBBY DESK tells me. "We're very sorry about the inconvenience."

I run to the elevator. Casey is right behind me. Lacy stayed with Witte to coordinate a protection detail for Catherine and serve as backup.

"If my mother gets by me, she'll come back here for you," I told Witte gravely before I left. "You'll have to end this."

He was sitting up by then, his wounds cleaned and bandaged. His blue eyes took on a flat, lifeless chill. "I know what to do."

Catching him by surprise, I leaned down and hugged him tightly, trying to convey my many regrets without words.

He hugged me back, his hand tangling in my hair.

"Don't make Catherine's boyfriend suspicious," I told them when I headed for the door. "We don't want Christian in the wind. He could be useful."

I remember the look on Witte's face before the door shut behind me. He sees me now as I genuinely am, yet he doesn't judge me harshly. Eventually, he and I will have much to discuss if we make it through the day.

But I can't think about that now. As the elevator climbs the tower to the penthouse, I pull out my phone and call Rogelio. "The elevators are working."

"I heard 'em kick back on. Catching one now." He's got his voice back, and it's grim. "They couldn't get that shit fixed before I climbed sixty flights?"

"You're a champ. See you in a minute." I hang up and tap my feet, desperate to act. Standing still is a slow death.

I'm poised to rush out when the elevator doors open, but horror awaits.

"Jesus," Casey mutters.

We each go to one of the two downed guards and check for a pulse, but the quantity of blood and the positions of their bodies warned us not to hope before we made the effort. It's a blow to find them and to know how hard their deaths will hit Rogelio. He'll be here soon, and I regret that my mother has caused him yet more pain.

Standing, I move around the bodies and open the door, entering the penthouse. Abruptly, my agitation and patience drain away, like stepping into the eye of a hurricane, leaving me focused and alert. I immediately feel an all-too-familiar pull. Is it you, my love? Is it her? Perhaps it's both of you, together for the first and last time.

My footfalls are silent as I go to the kitchen for a knife I won't use. I can't. I know that already. I can posture and bluff, and she'll see right through me, but maybe I can buy time for you to escape. It's the tiniest of hopes, but it's all I've got.

The penthouse is too quiet. Even when Witte is out, and I'm home alone reading, the penthouse is never silent. The wind caresses the tower forcefully, making it sway. It creaks and moans plaintively, a lover begging for mercy from a passion too great to bear. To hear nothing feels unnatural. Even shouting or a scuffle would be welcome signs of life.

From the kitchen, I circle. Passing Witte's room, the guestrooms, my office. I turn the corner and approach the library.

That's when I hear sobbing.

Breaking into a run, I'm light on my feet to make no sound. I turn the corner into the room at full speed and slow my momentum with a sweeping slide, my gaze raking the room from one side to the other.

Darius is on the floor. Aliyah kneels beside him, sobbing, applying pressure to a towel folded over what must be an abdominal wound. I look for you, blood roaring through my ears.

"Kane!"

Aliyah jolts, startled by my cry.

And there you are, standing quickly from where an armchair hid you. You hold your phone to your ear but extend your other arm toward me. I rush to you, dizzy with relief, until I see the long gash along your torso that's bled so profusely your jeans are soaked with blood.

"You're hurt!"

I'm okay, you mouth as I take your outstretched hand. You give my fingers a hard, reassuring squeeze. "She's here now," you say into the phone.

Then you tilt your head toward the fireplace, your expression painfully somber.

I see the swath of red material spread across the rug.

"Momma!" I drop beside her, the knife clattering on the marble hearth as I take her hand. She's nearly as cold as the guards she left in the vestibule, deathly pale beneath sun-kissed skin, and for a heartbeat, I think she's gone. A threat no more.

But then she blinks slowly, and her eyes slide over to look at me.

It's surreal to see her looking so beautiful, lying as if she's napping, while the grotesque, congealing pool of blood beneath her head tells the truth. She lays unmoving, her chest barely rising and falling.

"Araceli," she whispers. A violent tremor ripples through her.

"I'm here, Momma." Bending, I kiss her forehead, then press my cheek to hers. "I love you."

"My precious girl." Her words float soft as mist to my ear.

I straighten, searching her face. She's serene, her features soft. The mad light in her luminous eyes is gone. I see my mother again. I begin to sob, struggling to hide my pain and grief from her.

Gripping the limp hand that once brushed and styled my hair, I push the strands of her wig back from her face, arranging it neatly once again.

"I know you'll be good," she tells me so quietly it's mostly just the movement of her lips. "Soon, you'll . . . kill him."

I recoil from her, horrified by her final thought.

Her lips curve in a tender smile, and her eyes stay fixed on me as the life leaves them. A violent spasm shudders through her body. Then she's gone.

My fingers tremble as I close her eyes. Then I bow my head and sob.

I feel you crouch beside me. "*Setareh . . .*"

Dropping her hand, I turn into your embrace.

"I'm sorry," you tell me, nuzzling my hair.

"She wouldn't have stopped. Not ever. This was the only way it could end."

"Darius was protecting me from her." There's a tremor in your voice. "He's seriously wounded, and he still fought for me. I don't know if he'll make it."

Pulling back, I look over at Darius with gratitude and remorse. I meet your gaze. "Have you called for help?"

"Witte has a private ambulance on the way."

I cup your cheek in my hand. "You have to take him down in the elevator to the garage. The paramedics can't come up here. The guards are dead in the vestibule. Rogelio is here, and one of his men, they can help carry Darius."

You take a deep breath as you absorb what I've told you, then you nod.

"You need to go with him, Kane," I insist urgently. "Both of you require immediate emergency care."

"And what will you do?"

"Clean up. My mother can't be found here. You know that. Darius has committed a litany of sins, but her death isn't one of them. And her connection to me can never be known."

You press your forehead to mine, our breaths mingling. Your hand is at my nape, holding me tightly. I'm exhausted by my profound relief and the weight of mourning.

"Wait for me," you murmur. "I want to be with you."

As always, I know what you're thinking. You don't want me to lay my mother to rest alone.

"*Querida.*"

Grim-faced and hollow-eyed, Rogelio enters the library and takes in the scene in a single glance. He squats beside Aliyah, checking Darius's pulse. Then he puts his hand on Aliyah's shoulder and whispers to her. She nods, her body quaking. She seems to take strength from him, though, her posture straightening.

"An ambulance is on the way," I tell him.

Standing, he nods. "We've got work to do."

But he walks over to my mother first and takes a long, hard look. "I don't know how you came from her," he says tightly, fury threading through every word. Then he turns away and pulls out his phone.

"We don't have much time." I stand and you rise, too, gingerly, wincing with the effort.

An explosion of activity shatters the horrified stillness. I leave the room to gather more towels and a comforter to act as a gurney for Darius. When I return to the library, I find Witte and Lacy have arrived.

Lacy kneels beside Bea's body, her coworker of many years. "I wish she would've confided in me. I thought we were close. I had no idea."

Witte is on one knee beside my mother, his face impassive. But he's taken her hand as I did, and quarters have been placed over her eyes.

"Do you know what you'll do with her?" he asks without looking up.

"Yes."

He nods, takes another moment, then rises agilely to his feet. His gaze goes to the items in my hands, fully aware of what purpose they're meant to serve. "I'll see to this."

36

LILY

THE SUN SHINES BRIGHTLY IN THE CLOUDLESS SKY, AND THE OCEAN breeze is soft. The day could not be more different from the one so long ago when the sea raged at me for my choices, and I prepared to kill the woman who'd given me life.

The waves rock *La Tempête* gently beneath my feet. We set sail hours ago and now we're miles out in the Atlantic. There is nothing but cold, dark water as far as my eye can see. I've missed the ocean and my boat. I've missed my mother, and now I will always miss her. There will never be a cessation of that longing. Still, I grieve for a woman who existed only in my mind – the mother I wanted, not the mother I had. A woman whose true name and history I may never know but who will never be forgotten because she scarred every life she passed through.

The coordinates of that fateful moment long ago when I lifted the gun and the waves tossed me high in retaliation are lost to that storm. I cannot take my mother back to that exact place and close that circle, and perhaps that's best. That's a point on the map marked by betrayal and turmoil. Today I can give her the peace she never knew in life. I can say goodbye with love instead of fear and pain.

Closing my eyes, I tilt my face to the warmth, standing fully in the light. It seems ages have passed since the bloodshed in the penthouse, but it was only yesterday. Only hours have passed.

I feel you come up behind me, your arms wrap around me, and I lean into you – my anchor and support.

You don't say anything. You don't rush me. You helped me carefully sew my mother's body in sailcloth and weighted her down with a chain. When I'm ready, you cradle her in your arms before releasing her to her watery grave. She disappears within a heartbeat, pulled down to the peaceful depths where she can help other things grow and contribute to the cycle of life in a way she couldn't while living.

I toss lilies into the water and say goodbye. To her. To the past, that was its own burial at sea, weighing me down in darkness where there was no love or light, where you and I could never be together. I say goodbye with the salty tears of the ocean, then I turn *La Tempête* about, and we silently sail home.

EPILOGUE

ALIYAH

I STUDY MY REFLECTION AS I CAREFULLY APPLY THE DEEP CRIMSON "Blood Lily" shade of lipstick and rub my lips together. I'd debated wearing a nude gloss, thinking that would soften my appearance and sex appeal, which some might say would better suit the circumstances.

But I decide not to diminish myself that way or in any way. I've been liberated from my past and have secured my future. I won't hide in shame anymore.

"Ready?" Ramin asks, filling the doorway behind me. He looks quietly confident and breathtakingly handsome in a tailored navy suit with a striped tie that enhances the rich blue of his eyes.

"Yes," I answer, turning to face my youngest boy.

He's changed so much in the past year. Becoming a shareholder in Baharan has given him new purpose and has helped him recover from his unfortunate and misguided love for Amy.

Kane was right when he said Ramin needed to step out from under his shadow, although I miss my eldest boy daily. I call him often, seeking both his advice and the beloved sound of his voice, but I still grieve the death of my dream to build a family empire. Kane and his wife are hardly ever in the country anymore. Still, he serves as a retained consultant for Baharan, and Ryan Landon has been a steadying presence on the board.

Ramin comes to me and smooths the lapels of my cream suit jacket. "I'm really proud of you," he tells me, and I wonder if he knows how deeply that sentiment affects me.

"*Me, too, Mom.*"

Rosana's voice lures me to look past Ramin's shoulder to find her. She waits just outside the bathroom threshold, in my office. She's lovely in a skirted business suit of teal.

And behind her, Kane waits with a slight smile.

"Kane!" I exclaim, delighted that he would appear today of all days. I squeeze Rosana's hand as I pass her, but I hug Kane with all my strength. It's been a few months since I last saw my eldest child. "I'm so glad you're here."

"I wouldn't miss this," he says, returning my embrace.

When I pull back to look at him, I note that all three of them have dressed to coordinate. A matching set, almost. A united front.

My heart hurts for a moment. I miss Darius. I visit him as often as possible, and he seems to progress steadily. Still, his doctors tell me he has a long way to go. I'm encouraged by the statistics: half of those diagnosed with schizophrenia achieve long-term improvement. I remain hopeful that Darius will be one of the luckier ones.

I cup Kane's cheek in my hand. He looks good. I still struggle with Araceli's past and resent that Kane has left his life to travel the world with her, but I cannot deny that she makes him tremendously happy.

My phone rings, and I cross my office to pick it up from my desk. Rogelio's face lights up the screen and my mood.

"Well, hello, you," I greet him. I miss him, too.

"Just wanted to tell you to break a leg."

"You remembered." And it touches me that he did. It's terribly unfair that he would decide to move on from Baharan just before Kane left. I could've used some moral support then, but he's become a dear friend despite his absence. Because of Rogelio, I can move forward with my life without fear.

"You betcha. You're going to be great. I'll be tuning in."

"Thank you." The emotion conveyed by the tremor in my voice tells him that my gratitude is for more than his support. I will never forget when he sent me a link to a cloud file that finally set me free from the trauma of my past. He'd somehow gotten his hands on the videos Alex took of our . . . meetings. Along with videos of his other victims. And evidence of fiscal malfeasance during his tenure at Baharan.

"Anytime, babe. You know where I am."

"No, I don't," I counter wryly.

"You know how to reach me, which is pretty much the same thing."

We say our goodbyes, and I sigh. To have the worst of my past known not only by my children but others I care about is still hard to accept at times. I'm working on giving myself grace.

Justice is even harder to achieve. Time is not on my side, and I can no longer seek a reckoning legally, but I hired an attorney anyway and turned everything over to her. Bellamy Daniels is well known as a champion of women's rights, and a single call from her to Alex scared him so thoroughly he moved out of the state of New York.

Now, she and I have joined forces to change the laws limiting how long a woman has to seek justice for sexual assault. We're announcing our initiatives in front of the Crossfire building – I check my watch – now.

Turning, I face my children. "It's time."

AMY

I step into the restaurant's cool interior and take off my sunglasses. The hostess greets me with a smile and inquires if I have a reservation.

"I do, yes. Amy Searle, party of two. I'm meeting my sister here."

"She's already been seated. Follow me."

Digging out my glasses case from my bag, I look ahead, searching for Lily. She stands and waves, giving me a big smile. She wears a black crochet mini dress and yards of gold chains.

"Hi. Am I late?" I ask, hugging her. She smells as she always does – amazing. "It's good to see you! You look fantastic, as always."

"Aw, thank you. I got here early, hoping to request a table with a view of the television." She gestures toward the bar, and I see the local news is on.

259

"That's right," I pull out my chair and sit, fluffing out the skirt of my gray silk shirtdress. "Aliyah's press conference is today."

Settled, I study her. Her hair is glossy and thick, tumbling over her shoulder in a new, longer style. There's a bit of color to her ordinarily pale skin and she appears to be a healthy weight. It's reassuring to know she's doing well.

"I love what you've done with your hair," she tells me.

I reach up and touch it, squishing the short, thick curls. "Thanks. It's fun. I felt like a change."

Her eyes are kind. "A lot of changes for you in the past year. How are you holding up?"

"You know, not too fucking bad." I laugh and place my napkin in my lap. "The divorce is finally finalized – say that five times fast – and it was easy enough to dissolve the merger agreement and separate Social Creamery from Baharan."

"You must be relieved that it's over. Your divorce took longer than I thought it would," she admits.

"There was the prenup, you know. Aliyah agreed to dissolve it, but she had to get power of attorney first, and that required waiting for Darius's doctors to agree that he was rational enough to grant consent." I shrug and try not to show how sad it is for me to say that aloud. My therapist told me I'm experiencing grief, mourning the man I married who no longer exists.

Lily's sympathetic smile tells me I didn't quite succeed. "I'm glad you could work it out with Aliyah."

"Me, too. I don't want to say she was generous because that's not the right word. This is Aliyah we're talking about, after all. She's a born businesswoman."

"I'm hoping the word you're looking for is *fair*?" she suggests.

I nod. "Yes. That's exactly it. It was fair. And Baharan is still my biggest client, although I'm doing some pretty nice things for LanCorp now. I've made good headway on rebuilding my company. But enough about me. What have you been up to? We have to do a better job of staying in touch."

"You're right. The time zone difference has been the biggest problem, I think."

The server stops and takes our drink order. We both order iced tea.

"How long are you in the city this time?" I ask.

"Overnight."

"Really? You just got in."

She shrugs. "I know. We're in the middle of something in Barcelona, but Kane wanted to be here for his mother. He also visited with Darius this morning."

"That's good. Really good – on both counts." I mean it. I don't wish bad things for my ex. "It was tough listening to Aliyah's story. She's really brave for sharing it, and I'm glad we've become close enough that she wanted to share it with me. Sometimes, memories resurface from when I was being drugged, and I won't ever share them with anyone."

Leaning forward, Lily assures me, "When you find the right person, you'll tell him everything. And he'll love you more."

I swallow past a sudden lump in my throat because I thought I had already found that person. "You know, one of the things that surfaced includes you."

"Really? I hope it's a good memory." Her smile lights up the room.

"It's not a memory at all. Or maybe part of it was, and I made up the rest. I thought we met for drinks once, after work. You told me about the exit clause in my agreement with Baharan. You also suggested we work together to create a kind of package for some of your startup investments, where I'd help them brand and launch their social media presence."

"I wish we'd had that talk. That's a great idea."

"Something to think about, maybe. We were enjoying martinis. Obviously, before I quit drinking. I realized it never actually happened because you don't ever drink." I play with my silverware. "Maybe some of the other stuff I remember never happened, either."

I fucking hope so anyway.

Lily lifts her glass in a toast, and I clink mine against hers. "Here's to accepting the past and embracing the future."

I take a sip. "I'm thinking my future might be in sunny California."

"What's waiting for you in California?" she queries.

"A fresh start. New faces, new places. Content creator collectives. Nothing we don't have here but different. Expanding to a second office on the other coast might just be another good change."

"We'll really have to watch that time zone difference then." She takes my hand and squeezes my fingers. "We'll make it work. And I'd love an excuse to go out there and visit."

We smile at each other, and then I glance at the television. "There's Aliyah."

Lily and I read the closed captions together.

ARACELI

I slide my sunglasses onto the bridge of my nose as Amy and I exit the restaurant.

You wait at the curb, looking breathtakingly sexy as you lean against the Range Rover with your ankles and arms crossed. Languid, yet still dangerous. The strength of your body is evident under the precision tailoring of your suit.

"Hello, handsome," I greet you. Heads turn as pedestrians pass you, but you're locked in on me, as always, your heated gaze felt even from behind the mirrored sunglasses that shield your eyes from the late afternoon sun.

You unfold leisurely, your big body moving with powerful elegance. "Hello, wife. Amy."

I tilt my head up to accept your kiss. "The press conference was a triumph."

"Mom was great." You pull back only inches from me and smile. "I'm proud of her."

You gift me with an extra kiss on the tip of my nose, then pivot to Amy. "Hey, stranger. How have you been?"

Amy steps into your open arms, and you two hug briefly. "Oh, you know. Still being strange."

"We wouldn't want you any other way," he rejoins. "Mom wants everyone over for dinner tonight at her place to celebrate. She said she expects you there – no excuses, unless you have a hot date."

Rolling her eyes, Amy laughs. "I've sworn off men for a while. Which means I'm free for dinner."

"It'll be good to catch up. Text her and let her know you can make it. She said to be there at seven."

She nods and grins. "Glad we've learned how to get together and have fun, or I'd be downloading Tinder fast."

You laugh as your arm slides around my waist and tucks me close to your side. "And we'd be catching an earlier flight, trust me. You want a lift somewhere?"

"Nah," she declines. "Thanks. My office is a couple of blocks up, and I could stand to burn off ten of the million calories I just ate."

I step to her with open arms and hug her goodbye. "I'll see you in a few hours."

She takes off down the street, a lovely figure in stormy gray with short, bouncy curls of deep chocolate.

Then I turn to you. "Do you have plans between now and dinner?"

You open the passenger door for me and offer your hand. "We could run through the Barcelona job again."

"We could," I agree, sliding into the seat. "You can never overprepare for a takedown."

The week after we buried my mother at sea, we combed through Danica's condo and found a utility bill in the kitchen's junk drawer with a different address and name. That's where we found the apartment where my mother actually lived. There I discovered framed photos of me, from infancy to shockingly recent. I found her clothes and jewelry, the personal items that reflected her true identity. That was the good stuff, things I will keep and treasure always.

We also found a notebook in code that I knew how to break, which revealed Val's entire network and gave us new targets. We found a photo of my mom when she was young, holding hands with a guy. Both looked to be in their early twenties. The image was notable because it was the only photo of her with a man.

With all the other information we gathered from her belongings, we hope to track him down. Is he a brother? A friend? My father? Is he the one who warped my mother's mind? I know such a man exists from what my mother intimated over the years. Was she sane before that? I don't know. Some women eventually come out stronger after a brutal assault, like Aliyah. And others will forever be broken, like my mother.

You shut my door and round the hood to the driver's side. When you join me, I sigh, happy as ever just to be near you.

"It's eight o'clock in Spain," you point out. "We could call the crew and catch up."

"Yes, we could do that, too."

Rogelio, Salma, Tovah and Lacy are busy with the Spanish crew, laying the groundwork. I've resigned myself to the fact that they're committed to dismantling Val's organization.

And so are you. Or, I should say, you're committed to me and to protecting others from conscienceless individuals like my mother. Coming face to face with her opened your eyes to the depravity that exists in the underworld and impacts the lives of innocent people every day.

I worried about involving you, changing you. I've always wanted to keep that part of my life separate, but you wouldn't allow it. *We work together*, you insisted. And I've watched you grow into our new life together, straight and strong as a giant oak tree, thriving. I still keep you away from the wet work, but the organization, coordination, facilitation . . . Not to mention more than once, your charm and charisma have smoothed the way. You've become an invaluable member of the crew. We're partners in every way, sharing everything, two halves of a whole.

You glance at me as you push the ignition button, and the powerful engine roars to life. "You don't sound like you want to do either."

I turn my head to look at you, pulling down my sunglasses so you can see my eyes. "I'd rather do you."

You arch a brow and give me a slow, sexy smile.

WITTE

"How do three weeks fly by so fast when you're doing nothing?" Catherine asks as we stroll down a beach with aqua waters and pink sand.

We were meant to holiday here last year but ended up staying at her flat while I nursed her through near-inconsolable grief.

I take a deep breath of the salty sea air and smile. "I'm going to take that as a compliment. I must not have bored you too much."

Laughing, she turns her head towards me, and her lovely strawberry blond hair blows across her face. She is a stunningly gorgeous young woman, an amalgam of the best of her mother and me. She has my eyes, and I regret that they're shadowed with sadness. She's kept up a brave front during our holiday, but I know the murder of her beloved boyfriend, Christian, remains a trial for her.

She mourns a man who wasn't real: an attentive financier with a great sense of humour. He loved animals of all kinds. She thinks they would have married eventually, and he would've fathered her children.

In reality, he was a thug whose good looks and charm were most often used to lure women into unsafe situations where they could be kidnapped and sold into the sex trade. He had a lengthy charge sheet and was wanted by Interpol. My daughter is the only person on earth who cares that he's no longer breathing, and I carry the guilt of causing her that pain.

I'm also in the unique position of knowing precisely how she feels. While I knew to be suspicious of the woman I'd grown to love, I had no inkling of how vast her subterfuge was. Danica wasn't simply a woman hiding a secret agenda; she was hiding an entire personality. Our last hour together revealed a person I did not know in any way.

So, like my daughter – and Mrs Black to an extent – I mourn a fictional persona.

"Dad, you are many things," Catherine says, reaching for my hand, "but never boring."

"I'm gratified to hear that."

"You live the most exciting life of anyone I know. I used to think it must be awful being stuck in New York all the time. Now, you're everywhere."

Releasing my hand, she turns and walks backward in front of me. "It's romantic how Kane just threw off the shackles of the daily grind" – she spins, her hair streaming like a banner – "and now travels the world with his wife, making up for lost time."

My smile widens. Flashes of the saucy, joyous girl I know have appeared more frequently with every day that's passed. "Yes, they're very much in love."

And very dangerous as a pairing.

I've seen teams work seamlessly after years together, developing a rhythm that facilitated their work. Mr and Mrs Black, separated far longer than they were ever together, now reunited, have an affinity the like of which I've never seen. Recently, in a moment of crisis, I saw them glance at one another across a crowded hotel lobby in Cairo and silently communicate a spontaneous revision of the initial, backup, *and* failsafe plans instantly. They then moved as a unit and averted disaster.

So far, only a handful of individuals – all of whom we trust – know that Stephanie Laska is dead. Since the knowledge she had a child is unknown to most, Araceli has found opportunities to exploit their likeness to gain extraordinary access. It's whispered that Stephanie Laska is on a mission to eliminate the lieutenants of her late husband's organization who aren't loyal to her. For now, it's a helpful misdirection.

"Where are you off to next?" Catherine queries.

"Barcelona."

"On my list!" she exclaims, referring to the places where she wants us to holiday. "You'll know all the best things to see and do when we go."

"I'm sure you already have some idea of what you'd like to do there."

"Of course!" She runs over to a swing hanging from a gnarled tree that looks like it's perpetually blowing in a strong breeze.

We've made this walk every morning, and she's swung for a few minutes every time. I sit on the sand and watch her, committing the sight to memory. She's a woman grown now, but I still see my little girl at times like these.

As if she reads my thoughts, she asks, "Do you think they'll have kids eventually? Or just keep roaming?"

Her long legs stretch towards the horizon as she swings forward.

I wrap my arms around my bent knees and picture the Greenwich beach house filled with children's laughter. I long for that and know they've discussed it. "Yes, they'll settle down when the time is right."

"Will they get a nanny? Or are you adding diaper duty to your job description?"

"Such concerns are far off yet, but I can confidently say that any child in the household will be my pleasure to look after. I won't have a nanny coming along and stealing my joy."

She laughs. "Okay. You polish your baby skills for when it's my turn to be a mum."

The tightness in my chest from her lingering melancholy begins to ease. The resilience of the human spirit is miraculous. I've only to look at Amy Searle, Aliyah Armand, and Kane and Araceli Black to see that proven.

Catherine flies off the swing with its forward momentum and lands on her feet in the sand. "I'm starved," she announces. "Let's get breakfast and hit the pool."

I stand, and she links her arm with mine. I'm content – with my past, today, and all that the future promises to bring.

Read on for a little more of
KANE

KANE

I WAS OUT OF THE CAR BEFORE THE RIDESHARE DRIVER CAME TO A complete stop, running toward your house in Greenwich, where we first met. Panic twisted my gut into knots, making me sick and shaky. The hour-and-a-half drive had been torture, the time spent calling everyone who knew you, trying to find you.

No one had seen you in weeks. Your social media accounts had been deleted. You'd released your condo; a place I assumed you owned but which turned out to be sublet.

I hadn't believed it when your doorman told me you no longer lived there. I'd pushed past him and raced up the stairs, pounding on the door because you blocked my calls and texts. When it opened and the new tenant answered with a towel slung around his waist, I almost decked him but caught myself when I saw the decor behind him was nothing like yours. I even checked the number on the door, thinking I'd exited on the wrong floor.

For all intents and purposes, you'd simply vanished without a trace. Driving out to the beach house in Connecticut was my last hope.

Under the narrow-eyed gaze of the quarter-round second-story windows, I leaped up and over your porch stairs, jamming my finger into the doorbell. My foot tapped restlessly as I waited, panic building into a sense of overwhelming urgency.

i

You were twisting me into knots. You were such a mindfuck I no longer felt sane. Instead, I was in the throes of a mindless addiction, wracked by cravings for you that I was afraid could never be assuaged, no matter how many times I had you. And I *would* have you – because, in the most fundamental ways, you were mine the instant we set eyes on each other.

I tried to turn the knob, but it was locked. "*Lily!* Lily, if you're home, open the door!"

It had been hours since Ryan told me he was going to propose to Angela and that you were a distant memory. I texted him after, wanting him to put it in writing for both of our sakes. I'd been waiting for him to get over you, recovered from your breakup and happily with someone else. It was the only way you and I could move forward without any more regrets. But now that he was finally settled, I couldn't find you.

That was not a random circumstance. I knew you, *Setareh*. In ways you didn't want to acknowledge, but that was no less true because of your denial. You were still running from me, from the undeniable attraction and affinity between us. The strength of it – the potential permanence – frightened you more than it frightened me. I knew that much, even if I didn't know what sparked your fear.

You weren't getting away, though. Wherever you went, I'd find you. But the longer it took, the angrier I'd get. You'd been fighting the feelings that took root between us the moment we met, but it was time to face them. To face *me*.

I pounded on the door, shouting your name. Over and over. The answering silence mocked me. You had no right or reason to treat me this way.

I stepped back, catching my breath, not wanting to accept that you weren't there. That you would even *think* you could run from me. That you would *try*.

The longer you kept us separated, the deeper I'd slip into the blackness.

Creatures left too long in the dark turned feral.

Moving to the big bay window, I peered inside the kitchen. The cabinet doors were open, exposing empty shelves. Through the arched passthrough, I saw the furniture draped in dustcovers. Your home looked abandoned and lifeless, yet the house felt coiled and expectant.

"Fuck." I rested my forehead against the cool glass. Memories assailed me, a rushing kaleidoscope of moments spent with you within the walls that now kept me out.

Those memories entrapped me. You made me need you so desperately that I was barely human. I had no reason, no self-respect or any thought of self-preservation.

A low groan of despair rumbled out of me. My eyes stung. My breath came harsh and thick, steaming the glass. When I pulled back, the glass mirrored the desperate anguish in my twisted features. It infuriated me. I wanted to ram my fist through the window and destroy that reflection. The desire was so fierce my arm drew back.

But I would not give up, and I wouldn't destroy what you loved, even while you were trying to destroy me and what I felt for you, with actions calculated to wound deeply.

I walked to the back of the house instead, taking a moment to pull myself together before planning what move to make next. How to search for you, how to find you. I worried less about what I would do when I had you in front of me because I knew you felt the same way I did.

Truth was, you were a hard woman who was nevertheless all too easy for me to love. When you chose, your charisma could fill a room. You could be funny, witty, and warm. But at your core, you were someone who didn't like herself very much, and you tried very hard to make me not like you, either. You always had a cutting word at the ready, like a switchblade you could deploy with surgical precision. It was handy, keeping people at a certain distance, but it didn't work on me. Oh, it could piss me off to no end, but it couldn't deter me.

My steps were slow and heavy, as weighted as my shoulders. I was delaying the inevitable realization that I didn't know when I'd see you again or how I would make it happen. Perhaps you'd left something behind that would give me a clue.

How could I live with more waiting? I was already half-mad.

Then I heard the music. Louis Armstrong. His distinctive gravelly voice weaved with melancholy jazz.

I rounded the side of the house, and there you were.

Lounging in an Adirondack chair, you held a cigarette between slender fingers tipped in your signature red, and a slow stream of smoke escaped your pursed lips. You'd twisted your dark hair into a sleek bun at your nape and decorated your ears with a cascading row of small diamond-encrusted hoops.

One day, I would be the Richard Burton to your Elizabeth Taylor. I would drape you in the most precious jewels, the rarest of the rare – just like you.

The only makeup you were wearing was some sort of red lip balm, just a swipe of translucent color that let me see your mouth beneath it. You didn't need even that. You had the face of an angel without any enhancements at all.

I loved you best like this, casual and comfortable. It made it easier to picture us settled in as a couple. Of course, I'd be sitting beside you, and you'd be curled up to me. I would be touching you – twirling your glossy hair around my fingers, massaging your neck, stroking your arm.

Jesus, none of that was sexual, but I felt the slow simmer of arousal anyway. You made me ravenous just by breathing.

I bent over and put my hands on my knees, overcome by dizzying relief to have found you. At long last, nothing was standing in my way.

A teardrop fell like rain onto the stone pavers, then another. I knew the thought of losing you was tangled with my past, with always feeling less than and left behind, and the entwining was like a net suffocating me. But I also trusted my instincts. Not having you would shatter the rest of my life. I would never be the same without you, never have the same chance at happiness.

"You run all the way from the Bronx?" you asked casually, your gaze on the waves lapping delicately at the shore. Like a siren of old, you'd beckoned me to be shipwrecked against your rocky defenses. And while I was already battered by months of your formidable resistance, I could suffer more and would if that's what it took.

My heart pounded violently while you lounged just feet away as if you hadn't ripped me into tiny pieces by ghosting me.

"I would have," I said tightly. "I'd do anything to get to you. But it looks like I would've missed you if I'd wasted any time."

You took another drag of your cigarette. "I was supposed to leave this morning. Then I told myself I'd give you twenty-four hours to track me down. If the universe wanted us to be together, you'd show up. If not, you wouldn't."

I didn't believe all the spiritual, existential stuff you did. But I did believe you were a kingmaker, and I was born to be your king.

"The universe has wanted us together all along, Lily. Why stop fighting it now?"

"Because I'm a selfish person with no self-control when it comes to you."

Your head turned toward me, smoke roiling from the side of your mouth as you put out your cigarette.

You rose to your feet with feline grace and faced me. Your feet were bare, your toes bright red. You were wearing some sort of silk jumpsuit, black with gold embroidery, held up by thin straps on your shoulders.

I saw the bright hot flash of reciprocating need in your eyes, a tormenting glimpse of deep gnawing hunger, before you shuttered your gaze. Seeing that look was brutal, knowing you felt the same need and desire.

Angry about that, I was curt. "I don't have a problem with you being selfish with me or out of control." I straightened, swiping at my tears impatiently and without shame. "I love you so fucking much. No one will ever – or could ever – love you as much as I do. But you're a goddamn coward."

"I'm a lot of really nasty things, Kane. You've made a terrible mistake coming here." There was a sharp edge to your features, a look that turned a face from the heavens into a lifeless sculpture, and the bite in your tone told me there was something deeply personal in your words.

"I didn't have a choice – you were waiting for me."

You always took the hard line with me, but I saw all of you – the good and the great, the bad and the worst – and I loved every facet. You might've thought you wanted a man who only saw the best in you, but your dark side wouldn't stand for being ignoring, *Setareh*. She wanted to be loved, as well. Perhaps she was the part of you who wanted me. I was fine with that. I had a dark side, too.

Your cat's eyes study me with soulless curiosity. "So . . . what is it you want?"

"You know what I want."

Your eyes dilated, the gorgeous green retreating to a mere ring. You were otherwise frozen, instinctively still now that you recognized that the predator at that moment wasn't you. "If we spend the night together, will that be enough?"

My mouth curved in a hard smile. "It won't be enough for you."

"Ah, that swagger. Gets to me every time." You gave me a mournful half-smile that touched me in a place so deep no one else had ever reached it.

Studying you, I noted the signs of capitulation and submission. Your lust for me ensnared you. I could feel the silent demands of your body, the signals it was sending to mine. Your gaze became seductive, your body fluid and sensuous even while standing still.

Lush with desire, you studied me with focused interest. There was no suspicion nor fear. No defiance. Just watchful curiosity and the slow burn of longing.

I stepped closer. There was a breath between us – if that. If I swayed even a centimeter, we would touch.

A moment passed, then another. Your perfume slipped around me in an illusory embrace, enhanced by your body's heat. Our awareness of each other grew, the tension ratcheting higher. The attraction was a tangible thing, a deep inexorable pull. My skin tingled with it. My lungs were seared by it.

"I'm incredibly good with my hands," I murmured. "My fingers are talented and tireless. I can't wait to slide them into you, to feel how soft and wet you are, how greedy."

Your breathing quickened into soft pants. A hard shiver wracked you.

"And my mouth . . . Lily, the things I'm going to do to you with my mouth. First, I'll kiss you for a really, really long time. I'm starved for the taste of you."

I lowered my lips to yours, so close I could feel the warmth of the soft breaths that escaped you. I was shaking then, my cock hard enough to drive nails. "Then your nipples . . . I've seen them get hard for me. I can't wait to suck on them, to tease them with long slow licks. And your pussy." I groaned aloud, just thinking of it. "I'm going to spread you like a feast and tongue that sweet pussy until you're begging me to use my cock instead."

"Kane . . ."

"No one has ever or could ever make love to you like I will. They don't have the skill, the patience or the endurance I do, and they'll never put your pleasure ahead of their own the way I will. Because I'm so fucking into you. You're everything to me."

You inhaled a ragged breath.

I smiled grimly. "You've been prolonging the inevitable. You can't stop this any more than I can. Weren't you the one who called it a mad attraction? A dark obsession? You're wet and ready, and I haven't even touched you. Imagine what it'll be like when I fuck you until you can't take another orgasm without losing your mind. Only your fear is keeping you from that pleasure."

Straightening, I backed away. "I love you, Lily. I'm proving it every day. I'm tired of living without you – I can't do it anymore. Stop running scared and take me. I'm yours."

You looked at me in the way you had that completed me, that saw me not as the unfinished man I was but as the man I could be. I would only become that person for you, *because of* you. I think you must've come to accept that fact – and how much I needed you because of it – because your subsequent surrender was absolute.

Sliding your thumbs under your shoulder straps, you pulled them off. The silk whispered down to puddle at your feet, revealing the beauty of your bare body. Blood rushed past my ears like a roaring surf. My dick lengthened and swelled with lust.

The jumpsuit had been your only garment. You stood fully naked, barefooted, in full view of anyone strolling down the beach. Your sleek arms reached up and unclipped your hair. It tumbled down your back and around your shoulders in an inky cascade.

Sirens envied you, *Setareh*.

I posed your question back to you. "What do *you* want?"

"It's obvious what I want."

I reached behind to grab my collar and yanked my T-shirt over my head. I dropped it on a chair as I walked toward you.

It was impossible to shake off the panic fully. I'd wanted you for so long that it didn't seem possible that the apparently endless yearning was over. I feared the moment was an invention of a fevered mind desperate for sanity, that you were a mirage conjured by madness that would vanish as soon as I touched you.

"I intended to take you to dinner," I told you. "Charm and romance you. Seduce you. Make you mine with rose petals and candlelight."

Your throat moved on a hard swallow. "I'm already seduced."

"Let's be clear: I'm not here to get laid and then return to my regularly scheduled programming. *We* start now, *Setareh*. Today is Day One of the rest of our lives together. If you think I'm an option and not your endgame, you need to think again."

Your eyes, those translucent jade pools, were bottomless and suddenly soulful. You met me halfway. I scooped you into my arms, my body igniting with erotic heat as your skin *finally* touched mine. You were real and warm. I heard and felt your breath catch, and then your silken arms draped across my shoulders, and your lips brushed my jaw. The contact jolted me, my steps faltering. Your slim body trembled with silent laughter.

"Behave," I muttered, carrying you toward the house that now yawned open in welcome.

"I never will," you breathed, your tongue stroking across the madly throbbing vein in my throat. "I've told you that, and you won't listen, so . . ."

"Upstairs or down?"

"Are you going to fuck me or take a tour?" Your hand slid down to cover my heart, your fingertips brushing featherlight over my nipple. It felt like a livewire had touched me, the electric current searing straight to my dick.

"Lily . . ." With a growl, I set you down just inside the patio doors. I steered you to the couch, and with a hand at your nape, I urged you to fold over, my other hand cupping your inner knee and lifting your leg onto the back of the sofa – the one piece of furniture not covered in cloth.

You were an expert at needling me, challenging me in a way that goaded me to act before I was ready. I would have to work on my control and set some rules for you. We both needed discipline.

The position I put you in completely exposed you to me, your most intimate skin bare except for a triangle of closely cropped inky curls above pretty pink labia. Pinning you with my hand on your lower back, I cupped you in my palm. You were hot and slick, desperately ready.

I sucked in a deep breath at the proof of your arousal. With the pads of my fingers, I rubbed the slippery lubrication over your clit, massaging you with firm leisurely strokes. You were softer than silk, softer than anything I'd ever touched.

Your low moan and the hard shudder that wracked your slender frame were my reward.

"You're so wet, *Setareh.*" I smiled, able finally to be amused by your obstinance.

"Kane . . ." You squirmed, and I pinned you more firmly. Your nails left claw marks on the jewel-green sofa.

Your hips swiveled, seeking the pleasure. I slid my middle finger into you. You cried out, and I groaned. You were creamy and greedy, the plush walls trembling at the intrusion. I was so hard it was painful. Our bodies were primally aligned and heedless of all else. As complex as our relationship was, *this* was simple and uncomplicated.

"Damn, you're tight." My voice was thick and hoarse, my penis jerking with the need to feel that grip for itself. The torment of the day had stripped me raw and left me defenseless. I was moving with instinct when I thrust a second finger into you. "You've been waiting for me all this time, haven't you?"

"Have you?" you cried, your back arching as my fingers fucked you with smooth, quick thrusts.

I didn't answer. If thoughts of me with other women tormented you, you deserved it for what you'd put us both through. I added a third finger, my forearm taut, the veins in stark relief as I drove you higher. You were writhing then, begging.

"Don't move," I ordered, reaching into my back pocket for my wallet and digging out the condom with shaking hands. You shifted, and I swatted your gorgeous ass. "What'd I tell you?"

"You're a sadist!"

"You're one to talk. You would've been wrapped around my cock for months now if you hadn't been so fucking stubborn."

Dropping my wallet, I yanked open the button fly of my jeans while simultaneously ripping the condom wrapper open with my teeth. I rolled the latex on, my gaze locked on you. You were beautiful everywhere, the most gorgeous thing I'd ever seen. Your pale skin was flushed pink all over, the curve of your spine a sculptured work of art.

With the slim separation between us, reason returned.

We weren't doing this your way, hot and fast, all physical and brainless. I wanted more. With you, I always would.

"Not like this." I stepped back. "We're not going at it like this."

"What?!"

"You got a bed left in this place?"

"Are you *kidding* me?" You looked over your shoulder at me, then your gaze dropped to my penis. You exhaled shakily. "Of course, you're perfect everywhere."

"We're not starting like this."

"We've already started, Kane."

"Up or down?" I bit out, losing the battle to get this right. You'd straightened, and the look of you – the feverish gaze, the plump red lips, the locked stare on my raging dick – was undoing all my best intentions. I was just a man, after all, and you were the love of my life.

"Right *here*, Kane. Right *now*!"

I tugged you to face me and caught you close, taking your mouth with wet openmouthed need. The feel of your breasts, exquisitely subtle, was divine torment. With an arm banded around your hips and a fist in your hair, I held you immobile while I kissed you the way I'd been dying to and dreaming about for over a year.

Your lips were plush and warm, your taste a blend of sweetness and tobacco. Your tongue tangled with mine, dueling, while your hands gripped my hair in your fists. The smell of you, seductively warm and floral, intoxicated me. You were ardent, a dancing flame. Then you melted into me, your hands gliding and stroking over every bare inch of skin you could reach.

Joy, hot and bright, rushed through me.

Finally, *Setareh*. Finally.

I was breathless, half-crazed, my hips grinding my erection into your taut belly, and you gave as good as you got, as eager, as hungry. Bending my knees, I hooked my forearm beneath your buttocks and lifted your feet from the floor. Your long legs twined around my waist, and the wet heat of your labia aligned with my cock. I growled into your mouth, and you pulled at the roots of my hair, the strokes of your tongue growing even more frantic.

Your uninhibited response to me, your aggression, was so heady I felt drugged. I scarcely remembered where I was, why or how. There was just you, only you, and the fierce poignancy that filled my chest so completely I could barely breathe.

I took a step toward the covered dining table, and you shifted, positioning yourself over the head of my dick. I yanked my mouth away and hitched you higher. "Not yet."

"You're a fucking horrible tease," you snapped.

"You're impatient," I shot back, stumbling toward the dining table. None of this resembled the tender seduction I'd envisioned. We were wild and unchecked, skipping too many steps and falling headlong into unbridled fucking.

You fought my grip, a hellcat in my arms, distracting me with a nip of your teeth at my earlobe. You tongued my ear, and I lost strength, barely able to keep hold of you. Before I could stop you, you sheathed half my penis in your searingly tight depths, your soft cry of relief lost in the roar that powered from my lungs.

If I'd stepped in fire, I couldn't be hotter. Sweat was trickling down my neck and between my shoulder blades. Your breasts were wet with it, our torsos sliding against each other. Your body heat had increased with mine, and your fragrance poured off your skin, clouding any possibility of coherent thought.

"Oh God," you moaned.

"For fuck's sake . . ." I stumbled to the table, every step driving me deeper into your wet heat. Between the trembling of your body, your erotic whimpers of need, and my muscles locked in euphoric agony, I don't know how I didn't just fuck you upright, aside from that being the last thing I wanted.

I sat you down on the table edge, and you tightened your legs, trying to pull me further into you. Your head fell back, your dark hair pooling atop the dust cover.

You moaned, a low deep sound of pleasure and anguish. "You feel incredible."

"Lily." I kissed the slender column of your throat, my hands gripping your hips as I withdrew from the sweet torture of your snug depths, then thrust forward again, sinking deeper. Your inner walls rippled along my length, clenching and releasing rhythmically, and those waves of sensation echoed through me so that I felt you everywhere.

Lifting your head, you met my gaze with heavy-lidded eyes, then kissed me deeply, embracing me tightly. My hips swiveled in tiny circles, screwing deeper into you, trying to fulfill my need to feel you all around me. Your whimpers of pleasure flowed into me through your mouth, the sensation of your hands running up and down my back nearly too much to bear. You were as yielding to me as I'd ever dreamed, your touch conveying both need and adoration.

"You feel so good, *Setareh*." My words were thick and slurred; my entire body flooded with intoxicating gratification. "Nothing has ever felt this good."

You nuzzled your nose against my throat, inhaling deeply. Then, you slipped away from me like mist, laying back and stretching your arms over your head, taunting me with the utter perfection of your body. Bending, I dragged my tongue over a taut velvety nipple before pulling it into my mouth and suckling. You writhed, the gyrations of your hips taking more of me inside you.

"Kane . . . how much more is there?"

I licked a trail across to your other breast, circling it with my lips, worrying the tight tip with rapid flicks of my tongue. Hunched over you, I lifted your hips from the table, your legs falling open wider so I could thrust deeper. I was lost in you. I wallowed in you. Animal instinct spurred every thrust of my hips; I couldn't have stopped for any reason. It was like fucking a wet hot satin fist, the pressure sublime. The fact that it was *you* who pleasured me so intensely was almost impossible to comprehend. To have this, to have you, endlessly . . .

The groan that left me was so laden with sentiment and ecstasy it sent goosebumps across your skin. Lifting your head, you gripped my wrists and watched as I fucked you, your excitement glistening along my dick every time I withdrew. The feel of your gaze on me, knowing there was no longer any doubt you were mine and would always be, goaded my next thrust. Hard and fast, I shoved all the way into you. You bowed upward from the table, screaming my name.

Christ . . . the feel of you around the base of my cock was fantastic.

You climaxed, tightening around me then pulsing, your entire body taut and quivering. The sight of you wracked by the pleasure I gave you drove me insane. Primal satisfaction roared through my body, tightening my muscles and thickening my erection. I straightened and gripped your inner thighs, holding you wide open to the powering lunges of my hips. It wasn't the rose-petal-strewn bed I'd imagined, with soft kisses and deliberate lovemaking. It was raw and hard, raunchier than I allowed myself to fantasize because I treasured you. But it was perfect, as you were perfect.

We were perfect.

I fucked you with everything I had, my fingers digging deep, my cock digging deeper. I wasn't quiet; I couldn't be. I was too aroused to contain it, deep and desperate groans marking every hard plunge.

You gripped the table's edge with white-knuckled force, holding yourself in place as I hammered my dick into the sleek, tight creaminess of your stunningly beautiful body, angling my descent to stimulate your clit. You were taking me to the root, my sac slapping in a steady rhythm against the curve of your buttocks. The visual of you, submissive and vulnerable, took me to the edge too quickly, but I ground my teeth and held on, determined to make it last.

Then you gasped my name on the cusp of a second orgasm, your neck straining as you arched. Your eyes squeezed shut against tears that escaped anyway. You wiped at them with the backs of your fingers, revealing the scorpion tattoo on your wrist.

There was no restraint left after seeing that symbol of your obsession with me. My balls drew up tight, my body inundated by concentrated sensation. Your pussy gripped me forcefully, almost too tightly to thrust. Jaw taut as I groaned with relief, I pumped myself into you, the climax so wrenching darkness swallowed the room around us until I could see nothing but you.

ACKNOWLEDGMENTS

My deep gratitude to my editors, Maxine Hitchcock, Hilary Sares, Lauren McKenna and Clare Bowron, for helping me realize my vision, and to the entire team at Penguin UK, with a special shoutout to Tom Weldon and Louise Moore. Thanks also to my agent, Kimberly Whalen of The Whalen Agency, for her support and encouragement.

Thanks to my editors at Brilliance Audio, Sheryl Zajechowski and Liz Pearsons, and the wonderful teams at IPG, Heyne, J'ai Lu, Psichogios, Swiat Ksiazki, Harper Holland, Politikens and Kaewkarn.

I'm so grateful to have strong, exceptional women in my life. The support of my dear friends Karin Tabke, Christine Green and Tina Route was invaluable. Ladies, you make everything better.

And thanks to *you*! You've made it as far as reading my acknowledgments, so you've completed the Blacklist journey with me, and I'm so very grateful for your time and support. Sharing the characters and stories in my mind with you is a very special connection I never take for granted.

ABOUT THE AUTHOR

Sylvia Day is the #1 *New York Times*, #1 *USA Today* & #1 international bestselling author of over twenty award-winning novels, including ten *New York Times* and thirteen *USA Today* bestsellers. She is a number one bestselling author in twenty-nine countries, with translations in forty-one languages and over twenty million copies of her books in print. Visit her at sylviaday.com.